Cherish the Magic

Gioacchino Nigrelli Giampapa

Writers Club Press

San Jose New York Lincoln Shanghai

Cherish the Magic

Published by Writers Club Press
an imprint of iUniverse.com, Inc.

For information address:
iUniverse.com, Inc.
620 North 48th Street
Suite 201
Lincoln, NE 68504-3467
www.iuniverse.com

ISBN: 0-595-00687-6

Printed in the United States of America

Dedication

To the man who taught me to Cherish The Magic

and left this world far too early.

Vincent J. Giampapa

Veteran, Father, Friend

I love you Dad...and I miss you.

Epigraph

Life is a little bit tragic but mostly magic.

Live with the tragic and Cherish The Magic.

The Author

Acknowledgements

Although a work of fiction, this book is based on the little known duties of the military Working Dog program, specifically US Air Force Patrol Dog Teams. From their introduction into the Vietnam conflict until the last days of hostilities it is estimated that the combined presence of American Military Dog Teams saved over ten thousand American Servicemen's lives. No book of this nature could be written without acknowledging the unselfish acts of these courageous men and their canine partners.

My unwavering gratitude must also go to my family and friends without whose encouragement this work might never have seen the light of day. A special thanks must also go to my agent and friend, Leonard Bloom, who saw something in the original manuscript and molded it into a story worth telling.

Finally, and most importantly, eternal thanks must go to our veterans…those who served and returned, and those who paid the ultimate price. What we were, what we are, and what we will become starts and ends with their sacrifice. May life grant you all your dreams and more.

Prologue

It was worse than he ever expected...far worse. Twenty-six tons of aircraft thrown through the air as easily as a gust of wind carries a garbage can lid. He hadn't heard the explosion as much as he felt it. One second he was jinking the F-105 Thunderchief around exploding anti-aircraft shells, the next he was being thrown against his restraining straps, his sunglasses shattering against the instrument panel like Waterford crystal toppling off a credenza. He heard tearing metal, shrieking like a banshee in the night, as the wings tore from their spurs, the ear splitting whine as the Pratt & Whitney engine digested bits of wreckage, self-destructing as torn fuel lines, deprived of their electrical commands, pumped aviation fuel onto an already growing inferno.

Stuart Schalamon, Captain, United States Air Force knew he was going to die if he didn't do something fast. His shoulder straps, left loose so he could lean forward to follow the path of his bombs or scan the sky for missiles provided just enough movement for his head to bounce off each side of the canopy, spider web cracks snaking across the sides of the helmet as it slammed into the bullet resistant Plexiglas. Schalomon's gaze passed over the control stick and its radio button. There was no time. He would have to hope the rest of the fight saw him eject…if they weren't too busy trying to avoid their own SAM's and anti-aircraft fire. Pulling his hands off the canopy rails, he reached for the yellow and black ejection handle between his legs, praying to God that it was going to work.

He had a habit of locking his helmet visor in the up position, preferring to wear his sunglasses. The three hundred mile an hour slipstream that blasted into his unprotected eyes blinded him as the parachute opened, jerking him up and backwards as the ejection seat fell away. He was still wiping the streaming tears from his eyes when something whizzed by his right ear, traveling fast enough to create a deafening super-sonic crack. He blinked hard, to regain his eyesight…what he saw terrified him. The sky was alive with tracers. Green streaks of flame, rising up from the trees, searching out his parachute. He pulled on the risers, trying to change the direction. The flashes streaked past, below him, to the sides, and between his head and the flimsy silk canopy. Schalamon knew that behind each tracer were four more bullets…invisible finger-sized pieces of metal whose sole purpose was to shred flesh and splinter bone. He yanked with all his might on the left riser. The parachute dipped, pulling his body up and to the right as he swung completely around.

Swinging like an out-of-control pendulum he saw more streaks of light, red, driven from the sky and into the trees below. The first Thunderchief dove to within two hundred feet of the jungle, replaced by the second in a line of four. The high-pitched whine of the scream-ing engines obliterated the sound of the twenty-millimeter canons. Schalamon looked down. Branches and leaves were thrown into the air as the line of bullets dug through the green canopy, silencing one gun after another. He punched a gloved fist into the air. "YES! YES! KILL THE MOTHERFUCKER'S! *Yessss!!*"

The time was nearing. He was drifting away from the gun positions but the trees were coming up fast. He knew the other pilots would see where he landed and call for help. It would only be a short time until he would hear the wop-wop-wop of helicopter blades coming to pick him up. That was the way it was supposed to work and he prayed some money-conserving-minded, anti-war bureaucrat hadn't suddenly changed the procedure.

He tugged the right riser, hoping to drift closer to a clearing in the distance. He had never cherished the thought of being pulled up through the trees on a jungle penetrator. Not only did it make the rescue helicopter a sitting duck, it made anyone dangling underneath it part of the flock as well. As he neared the treetops it became obvious he wouldn't reach the clearing. He clamped his legs together.. Landing in trees was bad enough; straddling a pointed branch was worse. As his feet touched the top of the trees, he wrapped his arms around his face and tucked his chin into his chest. Branches stabbed at his legs, tearing both flight suit and flesh. Twelve feet from the ground his fall was jerked to a stop as the silk canopy tangled in the limbs. Lowering his arms, he looked around. He thought about slipping out of his parachute and simply falling to the ground, but to someone who made his living flying at twenty thousand feet, twelve feet looked awfully high. Struggling to swing his body, he finally managed to get one foot on what was left of a broken branch. In less than two minutes was standing on the ground.

Taking a quick look around, and listening for voices, he did an inventory of his survival vest. With any luck he wouldn't need anything but the radio. He could hear his fellow airmen flying overhead, they would be waiting to hear from him, but first he had to put distance between himself and the still hanging chute. The Dinks would know where he landed, and they wouldn't be far off.

The hundred yard run on a track field would have taken him twelve seconds, it took almost ten minutes through the jungle. He stopped to wipe away the rivers of sweat running down his face and pull out the survival radio. Crouching next to a thick stand of broad leafed bushes he held the radio close to his lips and whispered.

"Corvette Five to Corvette One, Corvette Five to Corvette One, do you copy?" Schalamon looked up and tried to spot the rest of his flight through the thick canopy of trees.

"Roger, Five, I copy. You all right, SS?", he used the nickname Schalamon had been given when he first arrived in country.

"Yeah, boss, scraped up a little but I'm fine. Any word on gettin' me outta' here?"

"Hang tight, SS, RESCAP and choppers are advised, be here shortly…can you advise on position? We have a visual on your chute."

Schalamon gazed at the jungle around him. Everything looked the same, no land marks, no breaks in the dense growth. Every tree, every bush, every fallen log looked the same. He looked back in the direction he had come. "Roger One, I'm, ahhh, I'm about a hundred yards north, northeast of my chute…headed for a clearing. Copy?"

"Roger that, will advise choppers on pick up point…ah, wait one, wait one."

He started moving again and hadn't covered more than fifteen yards when he stopped short at the sound of machine-gun fire followed by the booming report of an F-105.s twenty-millimeter cannon. His survival radio suddenly blared to life.

"SS, come in! Corvette one to Five, come in, come in!"

"I got ya', boss. What the hell's goin' on?"

"The place is crawling with Dinks! They're all over the clearing and some are headed toward your chute! You've got to clear the area!"

Schalamon spun his head from side to side, desperately trying to figure out which way to go. Everything still looked the same for as far as he could see, which was only about ten yards. He put the radio to his lips, then heard the voices behind him. They made no effort to be quiet, there was no need. The soldiers knew a downed pilot would be armed only with a pistol. The American helicopters hadn't arrived yet and there were no ground troops to deal with. His friends in the jets would be of little help since they wouldn't risk dropping bombs on one of their own.

Named in honor of the legendary general, Vo Nguyen Giap crouched at the base of a large tree. Shifting the AK-47 to his left hand he wiped away the rivulets of sweat from his eyes with the sleeve of his black pajama like shirt. Glancing back over his shoulder he motioned for the squad of NVA soldiers he commanded to move up abreast of him. Not yet twenty-three years old, Giap had begun fighting his country's invaders three months before his twelfth birthday when he had labored throughout the night digging a pit in the trail the French soldiers routinely traveled. His long and torturous wait in the bush beside the trail had been rewarded the next morning with the agonizing screams of a soldier impaled on dung coated bamboo spikes at the bottom of the pit. Using the sound of panic driven gunfire as his target, Giap tossed a homemade grenade on to the trail, killing three more soldiers and wounding two before he melted away into the thick underbrush. That day, his proudest day in his mind, he became a fighter in the Vietcong. Much had happened in the years past. The French had been defeated and fled his country in disgrace. He had seen many comrades die during the struggle for independence. Many, many had died…all in glory. Now it was the Americans he fought. They were more powerful than the French, there were more of them and they had better weapons. Giap shuddered as he remembered the planes, the planes that had roared over his village, the sound reaching his ears only after the planes had passed. He remembered the metal canisters falling end over end through the sky as they sought out those who could not save themselves. He saw the vivid picture in his mind as the canisters split open in the tops of the trees, raining down their deadly cargo of liquid fire. He squeezed his eyes tightly as he saw the image of his wife and daughter, charred black, their bodies still smoking as the sickly sweet stench of their burnt flesh filled his lungs. It had been almost three years since his family had been killed, along with his friends, neighbors, and Vietcong comrades. During that time he had gone to any length to kill Americans and in doing so had become a hero to his people. Revered for his courage and willingness to hunt down the enemy and destroy him, Giap had been awarded the honor of leading NVA soldiers during his personal missions of vengeance.

He watched as his men moved up through the trees. As he nodded in approval of their quick, almost silent movements he thought about the flyer they now hunted and the men that flew the planes above him. 'The Americans were strange. They came thousands of miles to fight a war, and when they had a chance to kill great numbers of the enemy, they refused to do so to spare the life of one of their comrades; yet they would sacrifice many just to save one. The Americans had no stomach for war, but yet, they refused to go home. If they wouldn't go...they would die.'

The voices got louder, and with the voices, the sounds of men crashing through the trees. Someone shouted, calling the rest over to see what he had found. Schalamon couldn't see but he knew they had found his chute and he knew it wouldn't take them long to find him. He had to move.

Whether it was a root that pushed up, and then back into the ground, forming a natural man-trap, or just a partially exposed piece of deadfall, it didn't matter, it had the same effect. As his right flight boot caught underneath it, he went sprawling headfirst into the tangled undergrowth, the weight of his body snapping twigs and branches as he crashed to the ground, the involuntary grunt of pain announcing his presence just as surely as if he'd waved a red flag. The emergency radio that had been in his right hand now lay on the ground, partially hidden by the thick brush. He pushed himself to his feet and moved as fast as the Vietnam jungle would allow, the voice from the lost radio calling to a man who was running for his life.

Schalamon thought he was about a hundred yards ahead of the NVA when he fell exhausted to his knees. The heat was unbearable and thirst forced him to pull out his canteen. He took a long hard pull to quench his initial need, then short, shallow sips. As he looked around, he took one last sip, then put it back in the survival harness. The voices were getting much closer now. He ran, and ran, and ran, trying to stay ahead of those who would kill him.

Minutes seemed like hours as he ran, walked, and crawled. He rested twice more, sucking in breath as sweat ran off him in torrents. He thought he saw movement back in the trees but he couldn't be sure. Taking the gun out of his shoulder holster, he started to move but ducked back down when he heard it. New sounds, overhead, high above the trees. Propellers. It was the sound of propellers! The A-1 Skyraiders had arrived! RESCAP had come to protect him until the choppers could pull him out. The slow flying World War Two planes could dive low and place their rockets and machine gun bullets precisely where they wanted. If only he could find a clearing, find some way of letting them know where he was, they would keep the Dinks away until the choppers arrived.

He had just started to think that he might hug his wife and daughter again when he heard them. The voices. The voices were very close now, close and excited. He spun around at the sound. They saw him, they saw him and they were coming. He knew his only chance to be rescued, his only hope of living, was the chopper. For those who found their strength, fought their wars, and ultimately, entrusted their lives with machines, there was no other way. He had to stay alive long enough for the machines to reach him, he had to slow down his pursuers. Holding the gun in both hands, he fired three rounds. The first shot hit the tree to the right of an NVA soldier. He didn't know where the second shot went, but the third found its mark squarely in the neck of the man, shattering his Adam's Apple, crashing through the windpipe, and lodging in his spinal column. The soldier's own reaction, more than the force of the bullet, flipped him on his back, the flowing blood gurgling as it was pushed out of the wound by the air that remained in his lungs. Without stopping to help, or even slowing, his fellow soldiers ran around, and over, his body to continue the pursuit.

Schalamon ran, hoping the Skyraider pilots would see him, but knowing they would not. Still gripping the gun, he pulled a smoke grenade from his survival vest. Struggling to pull the pin without losing his grip on the gun, he let the safety spoon fly and heard the pop of the ignitor. Clouds of yellow smoke billowed out around him, drifting up through the trees. He knew the canister would soon be too hot to hold but he hoped the pilots would see the smoke as he moved through the jungle. He held the canister, and held it, and continued to hold it long after it burnt the flesh from his hand, long after the nerves were so charred he could no longer feel the pain. He held it until the searing heat ate through the tendons of his fingers. The canister rolled to the ground, freed from the grip of useless burnt flesh.

Giap knew their time was short. The American rescue planes had arrived and the helicopters would not be far behind. They had wanted to capture the American flyer but would now have to settle with killing him, and with Giap himself adding to his macabre collection of patches. The pilot would not be allowed to escape. With all their military might, the Americans relied on their machines rather than their wit. If this American had been smart enough to hide in the jungle rather than run to where the helicopters could pick him up, he might have lived through the day, and maybe, with time, and luck, made it back to his American friends.

Yes, the Americans were foolish. Instead of using the jungle, letting it be their friend and protector, it terrified them. They did not have the patience or courage to wait. They refused to learn, refused to accept that the jungle was not terror and death, but salvation. They were foolish and they would lose the war for which they had no stomach for. Uncle Ho had predicted it, and it would be so. This foolish American, however, would not live long enough to see the inevitable.

Schalamon saw the trees in front of him splinter before he ever heard the burst of fire. He was terrified beyond belief. It was one thing to strafe the enemy, to drop bombs and evade SAM's or triple A. He had even resigned himself to the fact that one day, his body might be scattered over South Vietnam, but that was quick. Your plane blew up and you died with it. You never felt a thing, you never knew what happened. This was different. He didn't want to do this, he wasn't trained to do this, he didn't know how to do this.

Another burst from an AK-47. The ground kicked up behind him. The fear intensified. He didn't want to die. God, he didn't want to die, not like this. His bladder let go, the bottom half of his flight suit growing even darker than his sweat had already made it. He thought of his wife, his daughter. Would they ever believe that he could be this scared? 'The anticipation of death is worse than death itself.' He had read that somewhere, long ago, in another life.

He didn't hear the sound this time, just felt the violent jolt in his shoulder, like being hit with a baseball bat...except for the burning. A baseball bat didn't burn and this felt like he had fallen into the depths of hell. His feet went out from under him and he fell forward, skidding on his chest and face, not noticing that his top front teeth had snapped cleanly off at the gumline. He pushed himself up with his right arm. The left one hanging useless, blood spreading out over his chest. Shouting, sounds of men running through the tangle of trees, propeller-driven aircraft and helicopters quickly approaching. He could hear it all clearly and knew that it didn't matter anymore.

More bursts of automatic gunfire. He turned to face them, still on his knees. He raised the gun and fired until it clicked on an empty cylinder. Holes punched through the Vietnam jungle, more evidence of American technology that would lay useless and forgotten for all eternity. A single round hit him in the right hip, shattering it and sending splinters of bone through his intestines. The pain was blinding. Stuart Schalamon knew he was going to die.

The group of soldiers stood around their American prize. He lay there, gasping for breath, pleading to live, but praying to die. He knew of no words to describe the pain. If there was indeed a Devil, this kind of agony was his mark in trade. One soldier kicked at the wound in his hip while another dug the point of a bayonet in the hole in his shoulder. The screams pierced the jungle like an animal in the jaws of a predator. The face of a grinning soldier appeared above him. He was different, different from the others. He didn't wear the khaki tan of the NVA soldiers that surrounded him, their eyes half hidden by pith helmets. No, this man wore black, black pajamas, a now familiar sight to those Americans who followed the war from the comfort of their living rooms or dinner tables. The man in black thrust his hand in front of the dying American's face. He held something in his dirt crusted fingers. Schalamon tried to focus on it through the pain. It was a radio, his lost and forgotten survival radio. The other hand came into view, an AK-47, blocking out the rotted-tooth grin.

They all heard it. Each man, strapped in the safety of his plane, unable to block out the terror that erupted from their radios.

"*Nnnoooo! Please God, Nnnoooo!*" In time, in another world, they would forget the sounds of the shots…they would never forget the laughter that followed.

The camera pulled back from the mural of the Fort Lauderdale skyline and focused on the newscaster who sat, eyes down, reading over his script. At the floor director's cue he looked up and stared directly into the lens.

"Good evening and welcome to EyeWitness News. The Vietnam war takes its toll on Fort Lauderdale this week in a most personal way. Air

Force Captain Stuart Schalamon, an F-105 pilot was shot down and killed on Tuesday. Captain Schalamon graduated from Stranahan High School before going on to attend the University of Miami and enlisting in the Air Force in 1967. The Department of Defense reports that Captain Schalamon was part of a five plane mission to bomb anti-aircraft targets when his single seat fighter-bomber was struck by a surface to air missile. Captain Schalamon died instantly when his plane exploded in mid-air. He is survived by his parents, his wife Kathleen, and their one year old daughter, Christen. Captain Schalamon would have turned twenty-eight on April first."

The camera pulled back for a wider view as the anchorman's face brightened. "The start of spring break brings welcome relief to hotels and businesses along..."

CHAPTER 1

SUNDAY
MAY 11, 1969
FORT LAUDERDALE, FLORIDA

The Fountain Of Youth. Ponce de Leon had looked for it, and four hundred years later, millions found it. It wasn't the fabled spring that promised perpetual youth, or even the Promised Land that overflowed with milk and honey, but it was close…and they called it Fort Lauderdale.

With its clear, fresh air that carried the slightest fragrance of the Jasmine tree, to the aquamarine waters of the Gulfstream warmed Atlantic, Fort Lauderdale was a dream come true. The annual host to hundreds of thousands of college students on spring break, Fort Lauderdale was the place to be…and the place never to leave. From Ponce de Leon's first step into its hostile, mosquito and snake infested unknown, it had been transformed into a virtual Garden Of Eden, and no one would have willingly gone back to that most primitive of times. No one, save one…

"ARE YOU OUT OF YOUR MIND! WHAT THE HELL ARE YOU LOOKIN' TO DO, GET KILLED?"

"Shut up will ya, everyone is starin' at us," the traffic on the sidewalk seemed to freeze in motion as heads turned at the sudden outburst, "and, no, I'm not tryin' to get killed. I said the Air Force. Not the Army or the Marines, the Air Force. Nobody gets killed in the Air Force."

"Oh really? What about that guy we saw on the news a couple of months ago? The one from Lauderdale. He's dead and he was in the Air Force."

"He was a pilot."

"Yeah, so? He was still in the Air Force and he's still DEAD."

"Damnit Chuck, use your head. He flew a jet and gettin' shot down is one of the risks they take. Besides, pilots are the only ones that see any combat in the Air Force, everyone else is on a base miles away from any fighting. The most that happens is a mortar shell hitting a runway."

Chuck Malool had known Gianni, (Gee-Ah-Nee, put it all together and say it fast was how Gianni explained it), all his life. They had grown up together, gone to school together and to say that they were best friends was a gross understatement. If there was any way to be brothers without being related, Gianni and Chuck were it. Even though Chuck was of Arabic decent, they looked enough alike to frequently be mistaken for actual brothers, at least until Gianni cheerfully pointed out the lack of Italian blood that flowed through his friends veins plus the huge, and obviously non-Italian nose that adorned the front of his face. Dark swarthy complexions, enhanced by a lifetime in the Florida sun gave unexpected sparkle to their youthful brown eyes and although Chuck's brown hair was a shade lighter than Gianni's, one had to look close to see the difference. At six-two and a hundred and eighty pounds Gianni was several inches taller and a good twenty pounds heavier than Chuck, but that just added to the confusion by making him look like the big brother. That minor inconsistency didn't bother Chuck in the least, since it came in very handy when someone from a rival school decided it was time to uphold the school's honor at his expense. Gianni not only made a great surrogate brother, but a hell of a bodyguard as well. Slow to anger, and even slower to fight, he would rush to the aid of a friend in danger but walk away from taunts and insults that were hurled his way.

The only exception that Chuck could remember was the time the quarterback from Stranahan High and a couple of his buddies squared off with them in the parking lot between the intercoastal waterway and the Lums restaurant on the beach. Gianni had stepped in front of the quarterback when he tried to pick a fight with Chuck, and was doing his best to talk their way out of trouble when the 'bad ass' from Stranahan made the biggest mistake of his young life. He called Gianni a 'fucking WOP'. No one knew who called the police, but by the time it was over, they were at the Fort Lauderdale Police Department waiting to be picked up by their parents. Chuck would never forget what Gianni's father had said when told what happened. "Some things are worth fighting for." That was it. No scolding, no grounding, no temper tantrum. Just, "some things are worth fighting for". Yes, there were differences, but they were as alike as two teenage boys could be. Or so Chuck thought, until now.

"MORTAR SHELL! What the hell do you know about mortar shells? You probably can't even spell it! Jesus Christ, I can't believe this! Fucking mortar shells! Will you listen to yourself, will you just stop and listen. This is crazy Gianni, this is really crazy." Chuck slumped back in the bucket seat and stared up at the sky while he nervously ran his left thumbnail across the indented calluses on his finger tips.

Gianni tapped his fingers against the steering wheel to the beat of Mustang Sally on the radio as he gunned the engine waiting for the light to change. If you had to get stuck at a red light, the corner of A1A and Las Olas Boulevard was the place to do it. On the passenger side of the car was the Elbo Room restaurant and bar. Smaller than imagined, it had been made bigger than life by Connie Francis in the movie "Where

The Boys Are". Leaning against its front wall were always an assortment of bikini clad women who took delight in knowing that they would be the main attraction in some teenage boy's sexual fantasy later that night. Running north along A1A was a line of businesses offering over-priced Cokes, overpriced suntan lotion, overpriced liquor, overpriced souvenirs and every other overpriced item a tourist could want. Locals knew better than to venture into these money traps except for the most dire of emergencies. Tourists were another matter altogether.

On the other side was the beach. Stretching from Birch State Park, south, to the Yankee Clipper, it was an endless sea of bodies in search of sun, fun, and of course, the opposite sex. Shadowed only by the circling of screeching seagulls or the occasional dive-bombing of a pelican in search of an elusive meal, the beach was crowded with people soaking up the rays or frolicking in the warm waters of the Atlantic. The rows of Royal Palm trees that lined the sand gave the beach a picturesque paradise look. Underneath the palms, stretching the length of the beach were the ever present rental cabanas. Constructed of molding blue and white canvas, they offered protection from the main thing tourists went to Fort Lauderdale for; The Sun. Decked out in their newly bought leather sandals, black calf length socks, Bermuda shorts with contrasting flowered shirts and the mandatory palm frond hat, these middle aged risk takers whiled away the day in the shade of a cabana sipping frozen daiquiris and reading the Wall Street Journal, or the newest romance novel that would set off hot flashes when the word 'intercourse' jumped from the page.

Just feet closer to the water's edge, the world seemed to grow younger, and more energetic. Lying on beach towels were 'the beautiful people'. If not by facial features than certainly by physical form. Bikinis designed to comply with the law while disregarding any pretext of modesty grudgingly clung to bodies that would not only stop traffic but cause men to totally abandon their cars just for the chance to stand in the shadow of such creatures. Tanned to a golden brown, their skin glistening with droplets of baby oil and smelling of Coppertone or Hawaiian Tropic, the women made Fort Lauderdale what it was; The place to be. Male eyes, hidden by reflective sunglasses sitting atop Sun-Kote covered noses would search for hours, praying for a glimpse of a milk white breast as it's owner, lifted up to brush away a phantom grain of sand, *forgetting* that she had unsnapped the bikini top to avoid a tan line. Over the din of radios or wannabe Bob Dylan's with their twenty dollar, out of tune, guitars was the occasional scream of a woman as a bored breast watcher tried to speed up the process by dumping a cup of ice water on her back. The screams were always followed by the giggles of a willing victim or the sound of an open hand against the attackers face. Either way it was never more than a brief interlude in the quest to attain the perfect tan, or find the perfect mate.

Even paradise has its pitfalls. What they wouldn't see if they bothered to look, something that the Chamber of Commerce would never print in their brochures, were the sharks, cruising up and down the beach, dorsal fins never breaking the surface, even though they were a mere tail thrust away from a veritable smorgasbord. As with the locals, even the sharks seemed to know that the tourists were necessary for the Fort Lauderdale economy.

Without turning or even thinking about it, Gianni and Chuck knew what they would see. It was the same mixture of locals and tourists it had always been and there was no reason to believe it would ever change. As long as there was sun, sand, and ocean, there would be locals, tourists, and sharks.

As Mustang Sally faded away, the first strains of "When I Grow Up To Be A Man" filled the air. Gianni turned up the volume, the irony of the song totally lost to him as the sound blasted out of the convertible. He gunned the engine harder, slipped the clutch and inched The Car even closer to the one in front. The Car. That's what everyone called it. A 1964 Chevrolet Malibu SS, it bore little resemblance to its designer's original intent. With a 409 dual quad engine, Hurst four speed shifter, racing slicks and custom paint job, it was one of the most "bitchin'" cars in Fort Lauderdale. Bitchin' and fast. Just the way Gianni wanted it.Except for working at the Winchester Skeet and Trap club, it was his only passion in life.

As the light turned green the driver of the car in front, intimidated by the throaty rumble of The Car behind him, popped the clutch, and stalled.

"Learn to drive asshole." Gianni said it more to himself than to be heard.

Chuck shook his head in disbelief then reached over and turned off the radio.

"Hey…"

"Just leave it off will ya, I'm tryin' to talk."

"There's nothin' to talk about Chuck, it's no big deal." The car in front was almost through the intersection when Gianni slammed the shifter back into second and pulled around him. The satisfaction of hearing the chirp of the tires as they found purchase on the pavement was tempered with the thought of trying to explain a traffic ticket to his father. Fighting to uphold the family name or defend the heritage might be overlooked…but a ticket…no way. He might as well cut the top off The Car and make a planter out of it.

Chuck braced himself with one hand against the dashboard as they accelerated through the intersection, then reached over his shoulder to steady the flat top Gibson guitar that was sliding off the rear seat. He grumbled something about feeling like a monkey fucking a football while he looked to the right, checking the parking lot of the Forum for police cars. He had been trained well.

"It IS a big deal Gianni, and we ARE gonna talk about it." He started to pull out a Marlboro then thought about Gianni's stupid rule of not smoking in The Car. Not smoking in a convertible…made about as much sense as the conversation they were having. "And what about these mortar shells? Where the hell did you hear that? Who've you been talking to?"

"The recruiter." Gianni backed off the gas as a police car passed in the opposite direction.

"What? What recruiter?" Chuck turned around in the bucket seat and stared at his friend.

"The Air Force recruiter. I went to see him Friday right after school. Remember, Hank gave me the afternoon off for my birthday so I went to see him then, before my party." Two days prior, May 9th, had been Gianni's eighteenth birthday. His parents had thrown him a surprise party that wasn't much of a surprise. He knew his parents wouldn't let a day like that go by without making a big deal of it.

He reached over to turn on the radio but pulled back when Chuck slapped at his hand. "Ah ha, a recruiter. You go talk to some recruiter who lies through his teeth and you think it's no big deal."

"Who said he lied?"

"Are you crazy! He gets paid to lie. There's a fuckin' war going on. How many people do you think would enlist if they went waltzin' in there and some jerkoff said, 'Hey, no problem, sign right here, then we'll ship your ass off to Vietnam where we'll let some people shoot at ya 'til one of 'em gets lucky enough to blow you away, then we'll ship your ass home in a box. Oh, by the way, can I put you down for the US Savings Bond program?'" The veins in his neck throbbed as he shouted. "It doesn't work that way, Gianni. They'll tell you anything you want to hear just to get you to sign up. They need bodies, they got a quota to fill. If they don't do their job, somebody ships their ass off to Vietnam. Besides, if it's so safe over there, how come this asshole is over here?" Chuck was almost screaming, saliva flying out of his mouth. It had never occurred to him that he would be having this conversation with Gianni. The whole idea of enlisting was crazy. It was more than crazy, it was fucking nuts.

"May I remind you that you'll be eighteen in nine days."

"Yeah, so?", Chuck shrugged, "get me something nice for my birthday."

Gianni put on his blinker to turn left into the beach parking lot. "Graduation is less than a month away and neither one of us has applied to a college yet. Even if we had, we probably wouldn't have been accepted anyway. This may come as a big shock to you but we're not exactly rocket scientists." There was a small gap in the traffic but big enough for The Car to power through. "You know that when you turn eighteen, you have to register, and if you're not in college, you stand a good chance of gettin' drafted." Gianni was having fun now. In a matter of moments he had gone from being yelled at to being on the offensive. Or so he thought.

"I didn't overlook anything. You know as well as I do that Broward Community starts a new semester three weeks after we graduate and all we have to do is enroll and we'll be exempt from the draft. I already planned on it. As a matter of fact, we both planned on it, at least until you came up with this bullshit idea. Damnit, Gianni, by the time we finish two years of school, this stupid war will be over and we can get on with the rest of our lives." The tone of Chuck's voice sounded as if he were pleading with his friend. "You don't have to enlist, Gianni. You don't have to go."

Gianni stopped The Car in the middle of the parking lot, turned his head slightly, and without looking Chuck directly in the eyes said, "Yes, I do."

They made their way down to the jetty that marked the edge of the private beach for the Yankee Clipper Hotel. In theory, the jetty helped keep the beach from eroding back into the ocean. In practice, the huge boulders just provided a hard slippery surface for tourists to fall on.

"Okay, now tell me what's really going on." Chuck plopped down next to Gianni, nestled the Gibson across his lap, and after lighting a Marlboro and sticking the flip-top box in the sand started to absent-mindedly strum the tune of an Elmore James song. The sweet, melodic sounds of the blues always helped him calm down when he felt like things were getting too serious, which for Chuck wasn't very often. Smoke curled up from the cigarette and drifted toward Gianni as Chuck's fingers effortlessly flew over the frets. Never once looking at his hand on the neck of the guitar, or even consciously thinking about what he was playing, he started at the sand in front of him and thought about what his best friend had just told him.

"How can you smoke that thing?" Gianni's eyes started to sting as the breeze blew the smoke directly into his face and he wished he had remembered to take his Ray Ban's off the console of The Car. They might not have kept the smoke out of his eyes but they would have cut down the glare reflecting off the water. They had been a birthday present from his parents and now he hoped someone didn't reach in the open convertible and swipe them.

Chuck turned to his left, emphasizing the cord progression as he answered. "Don't try to change the subject. What's going on?"

"I told you. I enlisted."

Chuck sucked in a lung full of smoke, tilted his head back and blew the foul cloud at the clear sky. "You couldn't have enlisted. Graduation is still almost a month away and even YOU aren't stupid enough to miss that." He changed the tune to one by Muddy Waters.

Gianni really didn't want to talk about it any more but knew Chuck wasn't about to let it die. "I signed up under the delayed enlistment program. They give you up to six months to finish school, stuff like that. I won't miss graduation." As Chuck continued to play they sat staring out over the bluegreen waters, watching small pleasure boats throw up white foamy salt spray as they plowed through the two foot waves. Farther out, a line of ships waited their turn to be guided to a berth in Port Everglades. Gianni had always liked looking at the huge ships, thinking about where they had been, and where they would go. He was wondering if the aircraft carrier laying at anchor would be going to Vietnam when his quiet daydreaming was broken by Chuck's voice.

"Why? Why do you want to go?"

Gianni knew that question was coming, knew other people were going to ask it too, especially his parents. "I don't know. I mean, I'm not sure why. It's just something I gotta' do." He turned back and looked out over the waves breaking against the shore and thought for a moment. How could he explain it? If Chuck didn't already understand, how would he ever? He escaped in the sound of the music as he tried to find the words to the question he had no real answer for. He knew that it wasn't just some idea he had come up with because he was bored with going to school or because it might be something exciting to do. He knew it was more than that, but he didn't know what. Maybe he had been born with it, a need that some people had that others didn't. Maybe it was the way he had been raised or maybe it was just as simple as knowing that somebody had to go, and if it wasn't him, then who? He didn't have the answer, he just knew it was something he had to do. As the smoke drifted by and stung his eyes it brought him back to the moment. "I guess it's like you and your music. You know, the way you can't put down that stupid guitar…always playing, making up new songs and stuff." He turned back and looked directly at his friend. "Why do you do that?"

As much as The Car, and the gun club were passions for Gianni, playing the guitar and singing were passions for Chuck. He had been born with the God given talent to hear the music. Not just play it, but hear it, in his mind, in his heart, and if there was such a thing, his soul. To Chuck it didn't matter whether it was rock, blues, show tunes or classical. It was all music and that's what he had been born to love. That's what he had been born to do. For the last two years he had worked at Melody Music giving guitar and music lessons and if the truth had been known, he would have done it for free…even paid them to do it. It put him around guitars, around music, and to use his father's favorite expression, he was 'as happy as a clam at high tide'.

He took a long pull on the Marlboro and let the smoke seep out with a loud sigh. "It's not the same Gianni. There's a big difference between going to war and playing the guitar."

"NO! No, there's not. Not with you. You don't just play Chuck...you *have to* play! You don't have a choice. I don't know what it is, what makes you do it...but...it's like something you have to do. Like you don't have any choice." He ran his right hand through the sand and picked up a broken piece of seashell. I guess...you know...I wonder why that pilot...the one who went to Stranahan High...the one that got killed...why did he go? He had it made. He had already graduated from college...he was too old to get drafted. I don't know...I...it just seems like, if he thought he had to go, then...shit, I don't know, it's something I gotta do. I gotta see what it's like. You have to play your music...I have to see a war."

"Gianni, it's not the same."

"No, it's the same Chuck. I can't explain it, but it's the same."

Chuck took another drag on the cigarette. "What're your folks gonna say?" .

"I don't know. I guess they'll be pissed but they'll get over it, especially my father...he went to war...almost four years...never talks about it but my mom's told me a little bit of what he went through in Africa and Italy. She's never said much about it.." He stretched out his legs and kicked at a discarded pop-top with the big toe of his right foot, trying to bury it under the sand. The one thing the beach didn't need was the trail of some tourist's blood marking the path of his or her stupidity. "Ya know, maybe that's it, maybe that's why I have to go...because he went. Didn't bitch about it, didn't try to get out of it, just went...did what he was supposed to do." With the pop-top hidden under three inches of sand he turned back to Chuck, his far away gaze seemingly staring right through him. "Shit, I don't know, maybe that's it, maybe it isn't. All I know is I gotta go and one way or another they'll get over it."

Rubbing the lit ember out on the sand, Chuck flicked the butt at the waterline and watched as the next wave pulled it out into deeper water. "I don't know Gianni, I don't think parents ever get over seeing their kids go to war."

The City of Plantation was an island of land surrounded on three sides by the much larger, and more recognized, Fort Lauderdale. Although proudly proclaiming its sovereignty with sculptured brick and stucco greetings of "Welcome To Plantation—A Better Place To Live", it was always referred to by those who didn't live there as just 'Lauderdale'. Less than forty square miles, Plantation was a quiet bedroom community with wide, palm tree lined residential streets that were seemingly designed with baseball and flag-football games in mind. For those who didn't want to drive into the larger and traffic jammed Fort Lauderdale, the city had its own small shopping center. Quaintly named "The Village", the L-shaped rows of rustic red brick buildings with gleaming white tile verandahs provided a shaded walkway to window shop out of the broiling Florida sun. In the span of two hours one could get freshly coiffed at LaPoint's Barber Shop, pick-up the dry cleaning at Sunshine Cleaners, shop for that night's bar-b-cue at The Village Grocer, buy a six pack of cold ones or a bottle of squashed grapes at Leisure Times Liquors and still have time left over to pop into The Handy Man's Den hardware store to grab a gallon of pesticide for that pesky Chinch bug problem on the front lawn. For those so inclined, The Village was also the perfect meeting place to trade gossip or embellish the otherwise mundane academic feats of offspring. Despite its trappings of modern day convenience, and unknown to the occasional tourist or newly transplanted Yankee, The Village sat less than three miles east of one of the most inhospitable areas known to man: the Everglades. With an average water depth of eighteen inches, choked with razor sharp sawgrass and thick mangrove stands, the massive swamp bristled with alligators, poisonous snakes, blood sucking leeches and mosquitoes; always the mosquitoes. Fighting a never ending war against the spiked nosed invaders the locals found solace in informing complaining tourists or visiting relatives that there wasn't a single mosquito in Florida…they were all married and had large families. Three miles from The Village, five miles from Gianni's home, one could, if one were brave enough, or crazy enough, step back in time and challenge the land that Ponce De Leon had failed to conquer.

The twelve year old center fielder's ears perked up at the boom, boom, boom of the base guitar and hard drum beat. The growing volume meant that a car was coming. He turned his head, trying to identify the music as he looked for the unseen car. The now blaring chorus of "I've got the rocking' pneumonia and boogie woogie blues" meant that it wasn't his parents driving the car. They wouldn't be caught dead listening to what they called Devil music. For just a moment he wished they could be cool like the "Little Old Lady From Pasadena" in the Jan and Dean song. Looking back at his infield and the batter standing over the welcome mat that had been magically turned into home plate he yelled the warning.

"Car comin', car comin'! Grab second." The center fielder shuffled over to the grass swale on the side of the street, staring at The Car that had come into view as the shortstop kicked away the trash can lid disguised as second base. The throaty rumble of the engine mingled with the music as Gianni downshifted to second, slowing for the ball players as they took their time clearing the road. The Car elicited its usual wide eyed stares of appreciation and pleadings.

"Hey, COOL car."

"I'm gonna have one like that some day!"

"Punch it! Punch it!"

"Peel out man! Peel out!"

The thought of laying rubber and leaving the group of kids standing in clouds of blue smoke brought a grin to Gianni's face but he simply pushed in the clutch and revved the engine as he coasted by. The rumble of power brought a cheer of approval from those who would some day show off in the same way.

He glanced in the rearview mirror and watched as the young boys pushed their makeshift bases back out into the middle of the street and resumed their game. Gianni knew they would repeat the process over and over again as cars made their way down the street. He also knew the ballplayers would quit only when their mothers stuck their heads out of front doors or yelled through screened windows that it was time to get washed up for dinner. He knew it because he had grown up the same way. Playing ball in the street, riding his bike around the neighborhood, peddling faster and faster, imagining that the baseball card held in the spokes with a wooden clothes pin was, in reality, the engine roar of The Car that he would some day own. It was a good neighborhood...no, it was a great neighborhood, a great place for a kid to grow up, a place to cultivate memories, to learn...and to someday leave. That day had come, he was sure his parents knew that the day would come, after all, they expected he would go away to college, he was also sure they weren't expecting what he was going to tell them.

He pulled into the circle drive of the corner house and parked behind his father's Impala. As he got out, his father appeared from around the corner of the house on his Sears riding mower. Growing up, it had always been Gianni's job to cut the grass whenever needed, which, during the summer meant, at least twice a week. The previous summer his father had come home with a large box tied to the trunk of the Impala. It contained the riding mower. They spent the better part of two hours putting it together and were utterly amazed when it actually started on the first pull. Before Gianni had a chance to make a move, his father jumped on the machine, and with a huge smile on his face, Gianni's grass cutting career had come to a sudden end. In the year that the mower had been part of the family, Gianni had never, not once, been on it.

Dressed in his usual khaki shorts, V-neck-T-shirt and sneakers, Gianni's father steered the mower toward The Car.

"Hi, son, you're home early." The sound of the mower died away as he hit the kill switch.

"Hey, dad. Yeah, there wasn't much goin' on so we decided to call it a day. Want me to finish up for ya?"

"No, don't worry about it. If I go in too early, your mother will just find something else for me to do." Gianni knew how much his father enjoyed working on the yard and hadn't really expected him to accept the offer. He restarted the engine and drove off to attack a not-yet-manicured section of the yard. Gianni wondered how he was going to make the announcement of his enlistment. His father would be worried but he would understand. After all, he had spent more than three years fighting in North Africa and Europe during World War II.

Vincent James Giancarlo, Gianni's father, was called Vince by most people but Jimmy by his wife. Although he and Gianni were instantly recognizable as father and son, there was not an abundance of physical similarities. At five feet ten, Vincent was a good four inches shorter than Gianni and during the latter part of his fifty-three years had developed what he described as a "fully-paid-for" spare tire. The most striking things about Vincent were his hair and classic Italian looks. Blessed with a full, thick head of salt and pepper hair (the salty portion quickly overtaking the pepper), and a natural wave that rarely needed the touch of a comb, he could walk through a hurricane and never have a hair out of place. His standard response to the numerous complimentary remarks was a simple, "Thank you, God loves Italians". Apparently God loved this Italian a lot. A cross between the easy going manner of Perry Como and the rugged chiseled look of Tony Bennett, he was a man that people enjoyed being around. Deeply tanned from years in the Florida sun, with prominent laugh lines and just a hint of crows feet he was easily mistaken for being ten years younger than his actual age. While others tried to look younger, or older, depending on where they were in their lives, he was content with the way things were. He was a man who was truly happy with his lot in life and if anyone doubted it they simply had to gaze into his eyes. Unremarkably brown in color, they had the mischievous glint of knowing a secret that only a chosen few would ever be privy. They were eyes of compassion and understanding, and the knowledge that although life was a little bit tragic, it was mostly magic. He had heard someone say that the man who died with the most toys would be the winner. Vincent sincerely believed that a man with a loving family and caring friends was already a winner.

While most teenage boys had their own ideas of heroes and idols, be they athletes, rock stars, presidents, or whatever, Gianni knew exactly who his hero was: His father.

His mother was watering the plants that adorned the house. Bernadette "Ann" Giancarlo loved plants, especially indoor plants. As much as cutting the grass was both therapy and relaxation for Vincent, Ann found her plants equally refreshing.

"Hi, mom."

Bernadette turned from a rack of potted African Violets as Gianni closed the front door. "Oh, hi, honey. You're home early."

"Nothin' much goin' on at the beach so we left early."

Bernadette held a towel under the spout of the watering can and moved to the next plant. "You dad's out cutting the grass, why don't you go out and give him a hand."

"I just saw him. I'm lucky to get to live in the same house with that lawnmower much less get to ride on it."

"Your father does have the ability to form relationships with the strangest things."

"I don't think I'd say that to too many people, Mom."

Bernadette still had a snicker on her face when she looked at Gianni. "Why not?"

"He married you…"

Vincent switched on the television as they sat down for dinner a few minutes after six. Gianni intended to tell his parents of his enlistment and started to speak as they passed around the three-bean salad but the commercial faded away and Walter Cronkite appeared.

Vincent held up his hand and turned to look at the television. "Wait a minute son, hold that thought, I want to here the news.

"…and in news from Vietnam, thirty-one American servicemen were killed and one hundred and seventy-two wounded in what the Defense Department termed 'light action'. The enemy reportedly suffered significant casualties…"

Gianni held the thought.

CHAPTER 2

Although torrential downpours were not uncommon, it was uncommon for them to last all day. This was one of those days. As Gianni turned onto the gravel road, the wipers of The Car desperately trying to clear away the sheets of rain, he could barely make out what had become his home away from home...the Winchester Gun Club. Unlike the pricey resorts along Hotel Row with their lifeguard-patrolled beaches gently sloping into the Atlantic, or their olympic size swimming pools surrounded by fish-white skinned tourists with New York accents, the gun club was crude and rustic. Less than two miles west of the hustle and bustle of State Road 7, the gun club sat on thirty acres of wilderness. Reclaimed from a decades old gravel pit operation, the resulting lake, sitting in front of the eight skeet and trap ranges was a constant murky, gray soup, dotted with flocks of black feathered coots and the occasional bloodied corpse of a white egret...the unsuspecting victim of the many alligators that called the lake home. Although the eighty yards of weeds between the lake and the ranges were regularly cut down with a tractor pulled brush hog, it was done so only to keep the wrist thick water moccasins from crawling up to the shooters. Unfortunately for the range masters who had to constantly reload the trap machines with clay birds, the cutting didn't discourage the snakes from slithering into the cinder block constructed bunkers to avoid the fierce Florida heat. Entry into these pillbox like trap houses was always preceded by judicious probing of a long stick, and if needed, plenty of foot speed. Most of the club's land had been left in its natural state, which was nothing more than a gravel parking lot surrounded by scrub brush dotted with wild fruit and palm trees; all of which would have provided welcome shade if not for the swarms of insects that had long ago laid claim to them as their domain. The saving grace of the club was the club house itself. Totally out of place in this less than hospitable surrounding, it had been constructed in a hunting lodge style. Through its huge wood plank door set into natural rock walls, one entered the imagined world of Louis L'Amour, or at the very least, Sergeant Preston of the Yukon. Rough-hewn half log walls set off the massive moss rock fireplace that took up the center third of the south wall. Obligatory head mounts of moose, elk, and caribou hung above the mantle looking down on those that never considered the fact that moose, elk, or caribou didn't live in Florida, but to the shooters, it didn't matter. It was where men went to feel the recoil, smell the gunpowder, smoke their pipes or cigars, drink coffee, and swap lies over a friendly game of gin rummy. It was a place where men went to be with men and where, if a woman was so brazen as to violate the male sanctum, was politely, if less than enthusiastically, tolerated.

He could see that the lot was deserted except for Hank's car. Hank Parrish was the resident manager, club pro, and Gianni's boss. He was the main reason the club was so successful, and, with the exception of days like this, accounted for the busy skeet and trap ranges. Physically, Hank was not impressive or intimidating. At slightly over five-six, he had to jump up and down on a scale to hit a hundred forty pounds. Having not yet reached his forty-fifth birthday, Hank was a world class skeet and trap shooter. He was by far the best shooter Gianni had ever seen. His effortless, graceful swing, his concentration, and his deadly accuracy were all things Gianni worked at imitating and one day hoped to duplicate.

Two walls of the clubhouse were lined with hundreds of trophies, ribbons, and plaques Hank had won in tournaments around the world. In addition to the trophies, there were framed pictures of Hank shooting both in civilian attire and in his Army uniform. In the center of west wall, hanging just below crossed Civil War swords, was a picture of a much younger and remarkably enough, thinner Hank Parrish, standing at attention as a one-star general pinned something over his left uniform breast pocket. Next to the picture, in a mahogany case, hung the object of the picture: The Silver Star. As proud as Hank was of his military career, always signing his name with his official military title, Hank W. Parrish, Major, US Army, Ret., he had never once spoken of the Silver Star or how he won it.

It had been almost two years since Gianni and Chuck had first driven to the gun club just to see what went on there. One of the range masters had talked Gianni into taking a few free shots at the fast moving skeet and trap birds, and that was all it took. After two more visits to the club it was evident that this young man had an uncanny knack for shooting. Hank watched from the clubhouse and took it upon himself to give him a few pointers. Within three months, Gianni was one of the best shooters at the club. After he'd entered and won a combined skeet and trap tournament, Hank offered him a job as a range master and instructor. Shooting became Gianni's passion, a passion that grew stronger as his shooting continued to get better.

Gianni parked next to the Porche and high-stepped it through the four-inch puddles to the rear door of the clubhouse. As he entered, Hank looked up from the Model 1200 pump shotgun that he was cleaning.

"Gianni, what the hell you doing here?"

"I work here, remember?" He stood by the door shaking the rain out of his hair as his water soaked sneakers made circular puddles on the floor.

"Damn, son, it's rainin' like a cow pissin' on a flat rock. You didn't have to bother comin' in." Hank could be as articulate and proper as the next man but around friends he lapsed into his down-home Georgia drawl, and he considered Gianni a friend.

"I thought if it stopped raining, you might get busy, and I didn't want to leave you short-handed."

"Well, you're the only one that thought of it. No one else showed up. Didn't even bother to call. Lord knows how people raise their kids now-a-days. No consideration, no respect, don't think of nobody but themselves." Gianni knew that in his own way, Hank was telling him that he appreciated his being there.

"No big deal, Hank. If it does get busy, the two of us can handle it." Gianni walked behind the counter and got a Yoo Hoo out of the fridge. "Any shooters at all today?"

"Not a soul. Been rainin' like this since I opened. Figured it's a good time to clean the guns." Hank finished tightening the barrel nut and was lightly spraying the gun with WD-40.

"Here, Hank, let me have it, I'll put it back for you." Taking the gun, Gianni looked in the open chamber for a shell. He didn't do it consciously, just from force of habit. Hank had trained him well. From inside the armory, Gianni yelled back at Hank. "Which one do you want now?" When he didn't hear an answer, he yelled again. "Hey, Hank, which one do you want next?"

Hank appeared in the doorway wiping his hands on a white rag. "Quit yellin', will ya. I ain't deaf." That was Hank's favorite lie. He had lost half his hearing from exposure to years of gunfire but too vain to admit it, he refused to wear a hearing aid. Gianni knew that even if the other range masters had tried to call in, Hank probably wouldn't have heard the phone. "That was the last of 'em. I told ya, I haven't had so much as a phone call today."

Gianni was impressed. There were over fifty rental shotguns in the armory, not counting the privately-owned guns that belonged to the range masters, plus Hank's own collection. Without looking, Gianni knew that Hank would have cleaned every one of them, Gianni's Model 12 skeet and trap guns included. It wasn't that Hank was a fanatic about guns, he just looked at them in a practical light. If you owned animals, you fed them; if you had children, you raised them; if you had guns, you cleaned them. Simple.

"Hank, you didn't have to do all these alone. I would have helped you."

"I know you would've, Gianni." Of all the range masters Hank had working for him, Gianni was the only one who really liked being around guns. Sure, the others liked to shoot but they looked at cleaning them as just so much work. Gianni, on the other hand, was more like Hank. He enjoyed the time it took to get the guns into pristine condition. Hank had taught him; 'take care of your guns, know how they work and how to keep 'em working. When it's time to make a shot, whether it's a clay bird or something that's breathing, concentrate on the shot and nothing but the shot. You already know the gun is gonna do what it's supposed to do'.

Hank never referred to the guns at the club as weapons. Never. Gianni had once referred to one of the shotguns as a weapon and Hank had been quick to correct him. 'We don't have weapons here, Gianni. We shoot at clay birds, not people. These guns are sporting equipment, same as a golf club or a baseball bat. If I handed you one of those, would you call it a weapon? No. But if you used a baseball bat to beat the hell out of someone, it would be a weapon. These guns are no different. Unless you use them against someone, they're guns, that's all'.

Gianni hadn't known why Hank made such a big deal over whether he called them guns or weapons but it seemed important to him so Gianni nodded okay and forgot about it. During the next two years,

Gianni himself gave the same speech to shooters on frequent occasions. Guns were used for sport. Weapons were used to kill people. Sometimes it was necessary, sometimes it wasn't, but it was never, never, a sport.

"Gianni, why don't you head on home. It's still rainin' like hell and no one's gonna' be comin' by the rest of the day. Hell, they'd need waders just to get out to the ranges. Go ahead, take off."

Gianni headed for the door but hesitated as he reached for the handle. "Hank, can I ask your opinion about something?

He looked up from the workbench and saw a confused, almost troubled look on Gianni's face. "You got a problem?"

"Yeah, sort of."

"You get a girl in trouble?" Hank almost laughed out loud at the thought. Wouldn't it be nice to be so young your biggest worry was where your next piece of ass was coming from and then wondering if you knocked her up? Wouldn't it be nice to have your whole life in front of you instead of memories of things you wished you hadn't seen and still couldn't forget?

"No, it's nothing like that. I have to tell my folks something and I don't know how to do it."

"Well, it can't be that big a deal. Just tell 'em."

"I enlisted."

Hank didn't say a word, just closed the case of the gunsmithing screwdrivers he was wiping down and placed them on the shelf.

"Hank, did you hear me? I said I enlisted." Gianni was starting to get worried. Hank looked like he was a million miles away, like his body was there but his mind wasn't. Had he known what Hank was seeing at that moment, what he was re-living, what he had tried so hard to forget, it might have changed the rest of his life.

"I heard ya, son. Do me a favor, will ya? Get me a cup of coffee."

While Gianni got the coffee, Hank sat down on the leather couch in the middle of the room. Gianni handed him a heavy ceramic mug with the red and blue emblem of a US Army tank division embossed on its side. Hank motioned for Gianni to sit in the chair across from him. He leaned forward and put the mug on the table without ever tasting the steaming black liquid. "Why?"

"Why does everyone ask that?"

"Because it's a good question and it's something you need to have an answer for." Hank had lost his good-old-boy accent.

"I don't know why. It's just something I have to do."

Hank leaned back and pulled at his lower lip. He looked past Gianni, over his left shoulder, at the framed medal on the wall. "Out of everyone here, I knew you'd be the one." His voice was flat, like a victim testifying about a grisly crime that he wanted to forget.

"The one what?"

"The one who thought he had a responsibility to fight for his country. That's what you're going to tell me, isn't it?"

"Well, I guess that's part of it. I mean, there is a war going on and somebody has to go."

"But that's not all of it, is it."

Gianni squirmed in his seat, attempting to get comfortable.

"Look, Gianni, I know what's going through your mind. I felt the same way when I was your age, but believe me, it's not like you think it is. You're eighteen, you think you're immortal, you think something's only going to happen to the other guy." Hank was talking quicker now, like he had to get it all out before Gianni stopped listing. "Well, that's bullshit, it doesn't happen that way. There are no good guys or bad guys, there's no right or wrong, and sure as hell, there's no fucking glory."

Hank got up and paced the room, his mind traveling back nineteen years to a frozen wasteland in Korea. "It's just a bunch of people tryin' like hell to stay alive while another bunch are dying all around 'em." He turned and looked directly at his young friend. "They don't just die, Gianni, not like in the movies. They die in horrible ways, ways you can't even imagine. They die screaming, crying for their mamas, begging God for the pain to go away, or reaching for their guts layin' on the ground next to 'em." His mind betrayed him. The horror, the sickening vivid memories of a time he had tried so hard to shut out, came back in frightening reality.

Gianni was reeling. He hadn't expected this. He figured Hank would have been pleased, even proud. After all, he had enlisted, gone to war, even won the Silver Star. "Hank, let me explain, it's not what you think."

Hank turned to the medal on the wall. "That's where you're wrong, Gianni. It's exactly what I think. It's exactly like I know."

"But you were in the Army, in combat. I enlisted in the Air Force. Only their pilots get into combat and a tour of duty in Vietnam is only a year long. Hell, there's a chance that I won't even go there. I might spend my whole time right here in the states, or in Germany, or Iceland, or…or anywhere."

"No, Gianni, you won't. I know you. I know the way your dad raised you. You'll do what you think is right, and what you think is right is going to fight. I don't know how, hell, I don't guess you do either, but you'll find some way to get over there." Hank was shaking as he turned and stared directly into Gianni's eyes. In a cloud of disbelief, Gianni saw a single, shimmering tear roll down Hank's cheek. In that instant Hank turned and walked back toward the armory. "Stay right there, I'll be back in a second."

Gianni heard the big locks being removed from their hasps and the door open. A minute later Hank reappeared with Gianni's trap gun and eight boxes of shells. "What's going on, how come you've got my gun?"

"Gianni, is there anything I could say to talk you out of this?"

Gianni nervously glanced around the room, then looked back at Hank. "No, sir…I don't think so."

"I don't think so either, so the only thing I can do is help you. Until now I taught you how to handle a gun, and you've learned real well. Now I'm going to teach you how to handle a weapon, and you're going to learn even better, a whole lot better."

"Now?"

"Now, right this minute."

"But you said yourself it's raining like a cow pissing on a flat rock."

Hank looked at the Model 12 and gingerly handed it to Gianni. "War doesn't wait for good weather."

SATURDAY
JUNE 14 1969

Graduation was a week away. School had let out and the anticipation of walking across the stage of War Memorial Auditorium was quickly growing with the knowledge that it would be a milestone event in the lives of six hundred young adults. Gianni and Chuck had passed their finals and would graduate with their much-sought-after B average. Chuck had applied to and been accepted at Broward Community College.

For the last three weeks, Gianni had spent every free moment at the club. Hank would meet him with the Model 12 and they would head off to the most isolated skeet and trap range. It made no difference to Hank how busy the club was or how many shooters were waiting for a round to be pulled. He had a "RANGE CLOSED" sign that he set up against the fence as Gianni started shooting each day. Rather than skeet or trap, Hank had developed a totally alien form of shooting. There were no set positions that Gianni shot from. He didn't call for a bird, they came at random from either of the skeet houses, or the trap house or from all three at the same time. Gianni had taken out the magazine plug that limited the gun to three shells. He was now loading four shells in the magazine and one in the chamber. Hank had never allowed anyone to load more than two shells in a gun at anytime, up until now.

As the days passed, Gianni fired thousands of rounds. Four, five, six hours a day he shot, listened to Hank's instructions, shot, cringed as Hank yelled when he lost his concentration, and shot some more. When his shoulder became so black and blue he couldn't touch it, Hank had him shoot left handed. Under Hank's unrelenting tutelage, he learned to use his ears as well as his eyes to determine the order of shot. With his back facing downrange, he learned to identify his first shot before he turned and actually saw the flying birds. Standing and waiting for birds was strictly forbidden. Walking, running, bending down to pick the gun off the ground while the birds were in the air; rolling over and over with the Model 12 between him and the ground and making the shots from the prone position, became the norm. Hank's imagination was limited only by the facilities at hand. The scratches on the barrel and receiver, and the gouges out of the wood stock, were of no concern. Guns were supposed to look pretty but Gianni wasn't learning how to handle a gun, he was learning how to handle a weapon, and he was learning well.

Sweat poured off Gianni. Hank wouldn't allow him to wear shooting gloves and the palms of his hands were raw and pitted from pushing off the ground. The barrel of the Model 12 was blister-raising hot from the combination of the setting Florida sun and the constant, rapid fire. Gianni had just knocked down two trap birds and two high house skeet birds thrown as fast as the machine could recycle itself. Four birds shot at, four kills, one live round in the chamber. Hank had emphasized over and over again, 'Know your status, keep track of how many rounds you've fired. If you don't have an immediate target, use the time to reload'.

The report of the last round was still fresh in the air as Gianni pushed four new shells into the magazine and listened for a new set of targets. He sidestepped across the range, keeping the shotgun at the ready, knowing that Hank would wait for the most inopportune moment, such as when he was wiping sweat out of his eyes or brushing away the swarms of mosquitoes.

"Okay, Gianni, make your gun safe and let's take a break." Hank started toward the middle of the range. Unloading the gun and balancing it in the crook of his arm, Gianni took out his soft foam earplugs and waited for Hank.

"Not bad, not bad at all. Your moves are fluid, your concentration is good, and if I had a nickel for every one of your misses, I couldn't buy a pack of cigarettes."

"You don't smoke."

"Good thing. You don't miss."

Gianni grinned slightly. "After awhile it gets pretty easy."

"We don't want it to be easy, we want it to be natural. Assess, determine, react, all within the span of the same thought. What's the rest of it?"

Gianni let out a small sigh. How many times did Hank think he needed to go over the same basic stuff? "Identify the target with the most immediate danger potential, stay with the target until it's neutralized or until it's no longer an immediate threat then move to the next targets in their order of danger potential. If no other targets are identified, move your position if possible and again look for targets or threats, starting with the closest terrain and moving outward."

Gianni had repeated it so many times he could, and on more than one occasion did, say it in his sleep. Even though he was starting to get bored with it and even found it a little over dramatic, his shooting showed that it had produced the desired effect.

Hank nodded his head with approval. "Good, lets call it a night."

"Are we done already? It's still early."

"Gianni, there's only so much you can learn out here, and there's only so much I can teach you. Hell, as it is, you'd clean my clock if I went up against you in skeet or trap."

"That'll be the day."

"Well, that day has arrived. Ever hear the saying, 'teach someone everything they know but don't teach 'em everything you know?'"

"No, but I'm not old enough to know about those ancient proverbs." Even as dog tired as he was, Gianni managed to crack a smile.

"Don't be a wise-ass. Anyway, I've taught you everything you know as well as everything I know. I can't take you any further, at least not with what we have to work with. There's not a shooter here that can do what you're doing. Not even close."

"I could still use some more work, I'm still a little…"

"Whoa, whoa! I didn't say we were done for good. We'll still train but for now you need a couple days rest more than you need to shoot. Let's call it quits for tonight so we can both get some rest. Go be a teenager for awhile."

Gianni just grinned and nodded his head. "Okay, I am kind'a sore."

Just before they reached the clubhouse door, Hank stole a sideways glance at Gianni. "Don't you think it's about time?"

"Time for what?" Gianni knew what was coming.

"Your graduation is next Saturday. Don't you think it's time you told your parents what you're going to do?"

Gianni looked at the cars pulling out of the parking lot, trying to delay his answer. Ever since the night Walter Cronkite had ruined his plans to tell his parents, he had avoided bringing up the subject. His father once told him that the only problem that goes away if you ignore it was your teeth. Gianni was starting to understand what he meant. "You want to tell 'em for me?"

"I'd rather take a knife to a gunfight."

"Me too."

"Gianni, it's time. You owe it to them."

"I know, but they're going to kill me."

Hank touched him lightly on the arm. "You just identified the major problem."

"What's that?"

"Their fear that someone might ACTUALLY kill you."

SUNDAY
JUNE 15, 1969
FORT LAUDERDALE

As he opened the door, he heard his mother singing one of her well worn Italian songs while Glenn Miller was doing his rendition of "In The Mood" on the stereo. The two definitely didn't go together. She was straining the rigatoni, preparing to cover it with the meatballs and sauce simmering on the stove. A big bowl of salad sat on the counter with a loaf of Italian bread and a dish of freshly grated Parmesan cheese.

She did a quick double-take as she caught a glimpse of him walk into the kitchen. "Hi, honey. You're almost late."

"Almost doesn't count except for horseshoes and hand grenades. Where's dad?" Gianni broke off a piece of the Italian bread and dipped it into the pan of sauce.

"Be careful, don't drip. He's washing up, he just finished cutting the lawn."

"Good thing he doesn't spend as much time with you as he does with that lawn. You guys would have twenty kids instead of just one."

"Yes, well, just be glad he started paying this much attention to the lawn after you were born. Besides…" Bernadette held her next comment as Vincent appeared from around the corner, pulling on his trademark V-neck T-shirt.

"My ears are burning, somebody must be talking about me."

"Hi, dad. I was just telling mom that it's a…"

"Never mind what you were just telling me." Bernadette cut him off before he could go any further.

Vincent shrugged his shoulders and tore off his own piece of bread. "How was the beach?"

"We watched 'em dock a submarine at the port. It was pretty bitchin'".

"Watch your language, young man."

"Yes, ma'am."

"Yeah, I guess it would be pretty bitchin' to see that." Vincent grinned and looked at his wife.

"Jimmy! You're supposed to set a good example." She did the best she could to keep from laughing.

"I'd rather set an example of how to dip into that rigatoni. I'm starved, when do we eat?"

"Right now. Both of you help me take everything to the table."

Vincent put the bowl of rigatoni on the table, then turned on the television for the six o'clock news. Walter Cronkite was just coming on as he sat down. As they started to eat, Bernadette stared at her husband, then nodded toward Gianni.

"Whaaaat!?"

"Well...ask him."

"What's the matter, you speak a foreign language or something? You ask him, otherwise he'll tell us when he's ready." Vincent started chewing a mouthful of the sauce covered pasta. "Mmmmmm, this is good." As he swallowed, he washed it down with a sip of Dago Red.

"Jimmy, you're the father, it's your job. Besides, graduation is only a week away, we don't have much time."

Gianni was taking a swig from his bottle of Coke. He had never developed a taste for the Dago Red, even though it was tradition. "What's going on? What do you want to ask me?" He had a bad feeling. He didn't know if he was about to have the wind taken out of his sails and have his announcement overridden by something else, or worse. Had Chuck or Hank said something to them and was he about to be confronted? Another of Hank's lessons came back to him. 'If possible, always choose the place and time to fight. If you must fight on their terms, remember, a good offense is usually the best defense. Take the fight to them.' Gianni wondered if those same rules applied when you were dealing with your parents.

"Gianni, I wanted…we wanted", Vince glanced quickly at his wife, "your mother and me…we wanted to ask you something about your graduation."

Here it comes. Defense, defense, offense, offense, take the offensive, take control of the situation. Identify the threat, neutralize it. It was as if Hank was sitting at the table with them, whispering in his ear.

"Yeah, there's something I wanted to talk to you guys about, too. It kind'a involves graduation." Gianni had stopped eating and was picking at one of his meatballs with the tip of his fork. "You know how Chuck enrolled at Broward Community and how you just assumed that I'd go there, too?"

"Gianni, look, if you don't want to go there, that's all right. You can pick somewhere else. Have you given any thought to where you might want to go?" His mother was hoping, as she asked the question, that he wouldn't pick anywhere too expensive. Things were tight enough as it was.

"Yeah, I have. The Air Force."

Vince choked on a piece of bread, reddish crumbs shooting across the table.

"Jimmy, take it easy." She handed him a napkin and waited until he stopped coughing. "You all right now?"

He wiped his mouth, cleared his throat, and took a sip of wine. "Gianni, it's nice that you want to go to the Air Force Academy but you have to be appointed, and accepted, and I don't think your grades allow for either of those. Besides, how come the Air Force Academy? You never mentioned anything about wanting to fly."

"Not the Air Force Academy, dad. The Air Force. Just the Air Force. I enlisted." He cringed as he said it and sat back in his chair, not knowing what to expect.

"Oh, no. No, no, no, no. Are you crazy? There's a war on. What has gotten into you, young man? You can't enlist. You're not old enough, we won't give our permission, you haven't even graduated high school yet!"

Bernadette had dropped her fork on the tablecloth, splattering sauce over the white fabric. She pushed her plate away and faced her husband. "Jimmy, this is crazy! Tell him, tell him that we won't give our permission, tell him that he can't do this! Oh, my God, oh, God, no, no, we won't allow it." She turned and looked directly at Gianni. "You're just a boy! You can't go waltzing off to war like its a summer camp. It's that gun club, that's what it is. It's that gun club and that Hank Parrish putting crazy ideas in your head. Well, you can forget all this foolishness. You're going to Broward Community or some other college, but you are not going into the Goddamn Air Force!"

The only time Gianni had ever heard his mother swear was when she was very, very mad, or very, very upset. She was swearing now. This wasn't a good sign.

Vincent slammed his hand down on the table harder than he intended. "Ann, be quite for a minute! Lets hear what Gianni has to say." He reached over, and taking his wife's hand in his, gently squeezed it.

"But, Jimmy!!"

"No, it's Gianni's turn. All right, son, what's going on?"

"Nothing's going on, dad. I enlisted, that's all."

"That's all!? That's all!? Let me tell…"

"Shut up, Ann. Damnit, shut up! Let the boy speak." Vince never spoke to his wife like that, at least not in front of Gianni. "Are you saying that you want to enlist instead of going to college?" Vince had pushed his plate away, too, and was looking straight at Gianni as he held his wife's hand even tighter.

"Not exactly. I'll still go to college, just after I get out instead of now. And I don't want to enlist, I already have." Not to be left out, Gianni pushed his plate toward the middle of the table too.

"What do you mean you've already enlisted? You haven't even graduated yet."

"They have a program that lets you enlist and then delay going in for up to six months. I signed up on my birthday, after school."

"And you waited until now to tell us?"

"I didn't know how to tell you. I figured you'd be upset."

Vincent ran his left hand through his hair, finding pause to take in what he was hearing. "Well, it's not the kind of thing any parent wants to hear."

"I know, but it's not that big a deal. I'm going in the Air Force. They don't go anywhere near the fighting and I might not even get stationed overseas. The recruiter said that chances are I'll never leave the states."

A slight grin spread across his father's face. "Son, if you believe what a recruiter says, you're not ready to leave the house, much less enlist."

"Dad, all I'm saying is that it's not that different from going away to school. I'll learn a trade, see some of the country, maybe the world, and get paid for it at the same time."

"Gianni, ordinarily I'd agree with you, but…"

"I knew that was coming." Gianni tried to lighten things up a bit but it didn't work.

"There's a war going on son. You don't know where you'll end up. They might send you right into the middle of it." Vince knew he was trying to reason with someone who wouldn't have his mind changed.

His chance. Offense, offense, take the offense. "You went."

"I went where?"

"To war. World War Two. You went. Mom told me all about the things you did, the places you saw, how you came back at the end of the war and went to work at the post office. How come it was good enough for you and its not good enough for me?" Defense, defense, take the offense.

"You mother told you the things I told her. She heard about the people, the places, the funny little things that always seem to happen no matter what's going on around you. She didn't hear about the war, Gianni, nothing more than what was in the papers or what was on the radio. There are some things that people just don't need to know about. Besides, I didn't go because I wanted to. I went because the whole world was at war. We all went, we had to. It was different. It was…" He turned to his right, staring at his wife but not really seeing her. His eyes had a hypnotic glaze of someone who was there, but somewhere else at the same time.

"Why?"

The voice floated toward him, searching him out from a place he didn't want to be. Hank was not the only one with memories of horror. "What?" His eyes focused back on his wife for a brief moment before turning back to Gianni. "Why what?"

"Why was it different? If I had been born when you were, I would have been there. If I was twenty years older than I am now, I would have been around for Korea. Well, what makes this different?" Gianni wasn't sure if this was taking the offensive but it was the best he could come up with.

"Why are we talking about this? Just tell him he can't go!" Bernadette was looking at her husband with tears in her eyes. She hadn't raised a son to go off and fight in some Goddamn war that no one wanted in the first place.

"Ann, please! Why don't you go and watch the news for awhile." It was a command more than a request. Gianni had never heard his father yell at his mother before and he had never seen his mother drink more than half a glass of wine. Now she filled her glass to the brim with the deep dark Dago Red and walked over to the recliner in front of the television. It sure was a night for firsts.

Vincent pushed his plate further toward the middle of the table, rested his arms where the plate had been and paused while he stared at his clenched hands. After an uneasy moment of silence he looked up at his son.

"Gianni, this war is different. You know it, I know it, everyone knows it. There's nothing in it for us…nothing that will benefit our country…nothing that will benefit anyone. There's no reason for you to go…no reason to risk your life. Its just not the same, Gianni. It's not the same." Vincent knew the war wasn't the same, but he knew that something about it was. The killing. The killing and the dying.

Gianni looked over his father's shoulder, through the sliding glass doors and past the screened in patio, into the back yard. He saw himself lying under the orange trees, reading a paperback or drinking a Coke while Chuck sat next to him Indian style, his guitar snug in his lap as his fingers flew across the frets. He saw the times they threw a football while his father lit the bar-b-que for a weekend cookout. He saw all the pleasant times he's had while at the same time remembering the face he'd seen on TV of the dead pilot from Stranahan. He sucked in a deep breath, letting it out as his gaze slipped by his father's and came to rest on the three plates in the middle of the table.

"There are people that need help dad. Good or bad, they need help…and somebody has to be willing to go. I, ah…I guess…I don't know…it's like…other guys are volunteering, and if they go, I should too. I guess…I guess some things are worth fighting for. Know what I mean?"

Vincent knew. He knew that there were things worth fighting for, even if others might not understand, and he knew that he was as proud of a son as any father could be. "There's nothing I can say that will make you change your mind, is there." As proud as he was, he realized that by raising his son with his values…doing what was right…he might have led him down the path to destruction.

"Someone else asked me that."

"Who?"

"Hank. It's just something I gotta do, dad. I want to go."

"I know. It's ironic, I guess. I told my father the same thing when I went. It was something I had to do." His lower lip quivered and he was barely able to control his voice." Son, look, there's nothing in this world that I wouldn't do for you and your mother. I wish I could give you more…make more money so you could have anything you wanted, go to a good school…"

"Dad, there's nothing I want…I mean…I have everything I want, everything I need…you've always made sure of that." He glanced over at his mother sitting in front of the TV. "I know you never planned on always working for the Post Office. Mom told me, a long time ago. She told me how you went to college at night under the G.I. Bill…how you always wanted to be a lawyer. She told me that you had to drop out when I was born and how you drove a cab as a second job to help pay the bills…" He couldn't remember the last time he had cried in front of his father and he fought to keep from doing it now. "I, I guess it's like…I don't know…you went to war, you gave up part of your life to go to war and then you gave up another part because of me. I, ah, ah, I guess maybe it's time for me to give up something. I guess it sounds kind'a crazy…but I don't know how else to explain it."

Vince looked away for a moment while he wiped the tears from his face. "No, no son, it doesn't sound crazy. It doesn't sound crazy at all." He reached across the table and took Gianni's hands in his own. "Son, if they let you stay here, stay; if you have to go over there, be careful. It would kill your mother if anything happened to you. It would kill me, too."

Up until that moment, Gianni had thought his decision to enlist only affected him. Now he knew different. He started to speak when his mother's scream jerked them both back to reality.

"Oh, my God!" Five feet beyond her, the TV screen showed a row of poncho-wrapped dead American soldiers waiting to be loaded into helicopters. GI's with rifles aimed off into the jungle watched nervously as the bodies were quickly and unceremoniously tossed into the waiting aircraft. The sound of gunfire could be heard behind Walter Cronkite's voice. "The Department of Defense announced today that sixty-three US ground troops were killed in heavy action. More than two hundred were wounded, along with the downing of three Air Force fighter planes supporting the ground action. Spokesmen report that the crews were not rescued and are listed as missing in action."

CHAPTER 3

SUNDAY
JULY 6,1969
LACKLAND AIR FORCE BASE, TEXAS

The blue Air Force bus picked them up at the airport and drove them
to the base. It was just after midnight when it passed through the base's
main gate and stopped in front of a large green building. The driver, a
buck sergeant dressed in green fatigues, shut off the engine, glanced
over his right shoulder and flashed a big 'shit-eating' grin as he pulled
open the door and stepped off the bus. A man dressed in a khaki uniform, the top of his left breast pocket adorned with rows of ribbons and
a dark brown Smoky Bear hat sitting at a rakish angle stepped aboard
and turned to look at his new charges. He placed both fists on his hips
as a sinister grin spread across his lips. His voice reverberated with the
power of a force-five gale.

"All right, recruits, listen up! I am Air Force Technical Sergeant
Paine." He stood silent for a moment to let his presence sink in. "You
heard me right. PAINE! And that's just what I'll inflict on you if you
fuck up. I will be your drill instructor during your stay at our little summer camp, a camp, that I assure you, you will never forget."

The grin spread wider as the recruits shifted uncomfortably in their seats. "The rules here are simple. You will do as I say, when I say it, without question or hesitation. If I say 'SHIT', you will squat and shit until I say stop. If I say 'RUN', you will run until you drop or I tell you to stop. If any of you don't like these rules and think you are Billy Bad Ass and want to try a piece of me, then please step forward. I GUAR-ANTEE you will witness firsthand the fine medical facilities that are housed on this base."

Paine stood silent again, waiting for what he knew would not happen. "I thought not. Now, if any of you are having second thoughts about your decision to enlist, it's TOO FUCKIN' LATE." That answered Gianni's question. "You are members of the United States Air Force and life as you once knew it is now no more than a memory and I would suggest that you forget it as fast as your feeble little minds will allow. This crap about having rights and being an individual is for those pussy civilians who don't have the balls to fight for their country. You are now part of a team, the Air Force team, and for those who can't spell, there is no 'I' in team."

He took another moment to look at the recruits and make sure his message was getting across. "Now that we understand each other, and I trust we do, we will begin turning you little scumbags into something your former parents can be proud of. At my command you will gather your gear and quickly dismount this vehicle. You will make your way, single file, through the door of that building and into Hell's Kitchen. You will place your gear on the floor in an orderly fashion, take a tray, and move through the mess line where you will be served an evening meal. You will take that tray to the dining hall where you will seat yourselves, four to a table, and you will consume that meal. You will remain at your table until told to do otherwise. You will, I repeat, YOU WILL accomplish all of the aforementioned without talking or in any other manner communicating with each other. Now, if there are no questions", Paine was met with stares of silence, "we will proceed. Recruits, DISMOUNT!"

Each recruit scrambled to grab his overnight bag, waiting his turn to move to the door. His Smoky Bear hat bobbing up and down, the Sergeant gently mouthed encouragement, "Move it, move it, MOVE IT! Come on, motherfuckers, get the lead out! Go, go, GO. The fuckin' war will be over 'fore you assholes get in the building. What are you looking at, shithead!? Get in there, now, now, NOW!"

WEDNESDAY
JULY 23, 1969
TAN SON NHUT AIR FORCE BASE
SOUTH VIETNAM

Tan Son Nhut Air Force Base, located on the fringe of Saigon, the capital of South Vietnam, was built out of the necessity to serve its master, War, specifically the air war. As headquarters to the 7th Air Force, it was the center of air operations for all bases in Vietnam as well as home to the Military Assistance Command, Vietnam, which ran the war from the American perspective. To the American public, however, this was of little importance since the war was brought to them in living, and dying, color through the miracle of television. Tan Son Nhut was just another foreign name in a foreign country.

The casual observer would not mistake the base for anything other than what it was: A fully operational, highly capable center for destruction. Standing on the tarmac, surrounded by hundreds of aircraft with the support material necessary to keep a war in action, one could only marvel at the lengths man went to, to kill his fellow man.

Because of its strategic importance, as well as the vast array of high ranking officers continually stationed there, base security was both tight, and effective. The main responsibility for that security fell upon the men of the Air Forces' 821st Combat Security Police Squadron, augmented by the Army's 716th Military Police Battalion. Although their combat readiness and capabilities had been tested in repelling the Tet Offensive in '68 and occasional enemy incursions, their job was boring. The combination of effective security and enemy reluctance to intervene made for good wartime duty.

But for the fact they would rather have been back in 'the World', most of the base personnel were content, especially Scott Yerremian. In less than four months he'd rotate home to be discharged. He wasn't sure if he was going to work with his father at his Atlantic gas station or try for a job with one of the airlines as an engine mechanic…but he sure wasn't going to re-enlist. Four years was enough. He'd paid his dues. He was a short-timer and he let everyone know by telling them his standing joke. "Right now you can call me Sarge, but in four months you can call me long distance". That type of humor left little doubt as to why there were few, if any, military stand-up comedians.

The hanger was a beehive of activity. Eleven F-4E Phantom jet fighters were parked between the yellow lines painted on the concrete floor that marked the plane's parking space and allotted work area. Engine stands cradling huge GE J79 powerplants stood behind the aircraft, waiting their turn to replace worn out or combat damaged ones. Bright yellow ladders and maintenance stands surrounded cockpits, wings, and vertical stabilizers allowing mechanics to get to every nook and cranny of the pointy nosed machines. Gray Air Force issue tool boxes, mounted on low four-wheel dollies with greasy rope handles dotted the floor, never far from the working hands of their owners. In spite of the inherently dirty work that progressed twenty-four hours a day, the entire hanger was remarkably clean. Oil and hydraulic fluid spills and drips were wiped up immediately, no matter how minor. Push brooms were scattered throughout the hanger and two or three of them were always in use. It was not uncommon to see a mechanic walking across the hanger floor suddenly stop to pick up an almost invisible piece of debris.

Unlike the neighborhood service station whose floor might be covered with litter and its walls plastered with 'Playmate' of the month centerfolds, Air Force hanger walls were decorated with one, no-nonsense, to-the-point directive: "THINK FOD!". To the uninitiated, "FOD" might have stood for "Fuck Our Draftboard", but for those whose job it was to keep a plane from falling out of the sky, it stood for "Foreign Object Damage". The Achilles Heel of jet engines was their habit of swallowing objects that didn't belong there. Not blessed with the ability to throw up something it didn't like, the engines had a tendency to suck up whatever was lying around, swirl it around so it would do as much damage as physically possible, then shoot it out its red hot ass. As much as taxpayers, and the Air Force, disliked paying for a new engine, or a whole new plane, the pilots got even more irritated when their flying machines suddenly turned into the aeronautical equivalent of a brick.

The near hundred degree temperature inside the hanger was bad enough, but within the confines of the port-side air intake the temperature was at least fifteen degrees hotter. Scott Yerremian looked forward to finishing up so he could crawl out of the coffin-like space and enjoy the benefits of the slight breeze flowing through the open hanger doors. Two or three cold Cokes would also help until he could kick back with a six-pack of something stronger.

He had been inside the engine intake for just short of two hours changing out the constant speed generator. As with a car generator, a jet csg supplied electrical power to the rest of the machine and, just like a car generator, from time to time it had to be replaced. You couldn't just raise the hood, however, and simply fix the problem. The easiest way to do anything on an F-4 Phantom was still difficult and time consuming. Strict procedures had to be followed every step of the way and be done right the first time. Whether you were zipping along at thirty thousand feet or hugging the earth at tree top level, you couldn't just pull over to the side of the road and call the auto club if something broke.

Yerremian knew this and took pride in the fact that his work had never resulted in a scrubbed mission or in-flight emergency. Unlike many of the other mechanics who would turn their work over to someone else when they got too tired or their shift ended, Yerremian always finished his own work. Always. He felt the pilots were paid to deliver ordinance to a target and he was paid to deliver working planes to get them there. Getting back was another matter. During the eight months he had been in Vietnam, eleven of the Phantoms he worked on failed to return. Luckily, some of the crews did. Some, but not all.

Many of the mechanics couldn't stand the oppressive heat inside the intakes and climbed out every twenty minutes or so for a break. Yerremian found it easier to take a canteen of water with him and take a sip every few minutes. The tepid water enabled him to keep working but always tasted like stinking sweat, hydraulic fluid, and JP-4 jet fuel.

Chief Master Sergeant LaBrode was the squadron's First Sergeant, traditionally referred to as "First Shirt". C/Msgt LaBrode had been in the Air Force for over twenty-three years and loved his job. Having been divorced for the last sixteen years, he was on his third tour in Vietnam and really had no desire to go back to 'the World'. Having been born and raised in New Orleans, he wasn't bothered by the Vietnam heat and over time had learned to love the food. LaBrode was also enough of a realist to know that as a black man with rank, he commanded, and was willingly given, a lot more respect than he probably would have gotten as a faceless civilian. LaBrode did indeed love his job, except for times like these.

Yerremian had just attached the safety wire to the first of the four hexagon bolts that secured the csg cowling when he heard his name being called. "Yerremian, hey Yerremian, crawl outta' there, I need to talk to you." LaBrode stood at the bottom of the maintenance stand.

Yerremian looked up for a moment at the sound of his name but shrugged it off. "I'll be out in a couple minutes, I'm just about done." He had been sitting cross-legged almost the whole time and knew that once he got out, he would experience the pins and needles of limbs that had long ago fallen asleep.

"This can't wait, I need to talk to you now." LaBrode could feel the eyes of others boring into him. The appearance of the First Shirt in the work area did not usually mean good news.

Yerremian leaned over on his left side to peer out the intake. He was about to tell whoever was calling him to fuck off when he recognized LaBrode. "Oh, hey, First Shirt. Can you hang on for a second? I just have to safety wire this pig."

"Don't worry about that, Scott, it'll wait. I need to talk to you."

The First Shirt never called him Scott, and what was so fucking important that it couldn't wait for a couple of minutes? Yerremian moved his canteen out onto the maintenance stand and crawled out after it. "What's up?"

Knowing that everyone reacted differently to tragic news, LaBrode backed up a couple of steps as Yerremian descended the stairs. "Scott, look, there's no easy way for me to tell you this. We just got word from the Red Cross. Your mother was involved in a traffic accident, a serious accident. She was killed."

Yerremian stood stock still, the meaning of the words taking time to sink in. The energy in his body seemed to drain out of him as his expression changed to a look of pleading and denial. "No, no, Shirt, no, ah, there's…there's some mistake! I mean…I, ah, I just got a letter from her…she's…she's making plans for my…she told me…no…oh, God, no!!! The young sergeant started to shake, his hands trembling so violently he had to grab the maintenance stand to hold himself up. The lump in his throat made it almost impossible to swallow and, as his lip began to quiver, the tears started to roll down his cheeks.

"Shirt...please, please...it's a mistake...please tell me it's a mistake, please!! She can't be dead...she can't be dead! Goddamnit, I just got a letter...I just got a fuckin' letter!!" He was screaming in desperation, not knowing what to do, not wanting to believe. "She can't be dead!" Racked with sobs he started to fall forward. LaBrode stepped up and as tender as any father could have done, held him tightly.

"Oh God, GOD! Why, why, why does she have to be dead!? Why my mom...WHY!! The anguish was more than he had ever dreamt possible. As the tears flowed, he rocked back and forth in the arms of the big First Sergeant, the image of his mother blazing in his mind.

A very large, noisy hanger can become a very small, quite place when a friend's life is suddenly shattered. The other mechanics stopped what they were doing and started to move closer, not knowing how, but wanting to help their hurting friend. Someone turned off a radio that was playing the Vietnam GI's theme song, "We Gotta Get Outta This Place". As LaBrode noticed Yerremian's fellow troops moving closer he slowly raised his right hand to waist level and waved them away. There was a time for condolences, but this was not that time.

Both the tears and the sobs slowly started to subside as he fought for control. He held the big sergeant tighter as a wave of fear flowed through him. "What about my dad? Is my dad all right, was he hurt?" He was hesitant to ask the question, afraid of what the answer might be.

"Your dad's fine, Scott Your mother was the only one in the car."

He slowly pulled back from LaBrode, wringing his hands so tightly they turned white from lack of blood. "Oh, God, what's my dad gonna' do? He's all alone." He looked up into the eyes of his First Sergeant as if asking him to make everything all right.

"Scott, look, you're a short timer, you've got more than half your tour done. Personnel is cutting your orders right now, you're getting emergency leave. You go back to 'the World' on the Freedom Flight tomorrow morning. Go home and do what has to be done, then apply for a hardship discharge...you'll get it. Your dad needs you more than the Air Force…or this fucked up war. Get on that plane and don't look back. Your dad's not alone, he's got you, and you both need each other."

Yerremian wiped the tears from his eyes with his still greasy hands, leaving dark streaks down his cheeks.

"Come on, I'll walk you over to base communications, we'll put in a call to your father. I'm sure he's waiting to hear from you."

Yerremian started to walk with the First Sergeant, then hesitated and looked back over his shoulder at the Phantom. "Ah…Shirt, do you think…could meet you over there in a few minutes?"

LaBrode looked at Yerremian, then at the tool box sitting on the maintenance stand. "Don't worry about that stuff, I'll have someone get it for you."

"No, it's not that, Shirt. I need to finish the job."

"Scott, don't worry about it, I'll get someone else to do it."

Yerremian continued to stare at the Phantom, its' battle-colored camouflage paint scheme urging him home and calling him back at the same time. Both he and the plane knew that there was business to be finished. One final task before he started the rest of his life. "I want to do it, Shirt, really. I have to…I need to."

"You sure?"

He never took his eyes off the plane, knowing that it would be the last time he ever worked on a jet engine. "Yeah, I'm sure.

LaBrode started to say something then thought better of it. "Okay son…you do what you need to do, I'll meet you at communications." He turned and walked across the hanger floor.

An F-4 Phantom is fitted with two engines that produce almost eighteen thousand pounds of thrust each, which even at idle creates enough vibration to loosen screws and bolts throughout the entire airframe. Manufactures and designers had long ago solved this potentially deadly problem by developing safety wires. Screws and bolts had holes in them through which a loop of wire was attached, braided around itself, and then through the next, and so on, to produce a strong counterclockwise tension. This simple, yet lifesaving procedure kept the bolts from backing themselves out and was one that Scott Yerremian had done hundreds of times.

He settled himself in his Indian style cross-legged position and picked up his safety wire pliers. The csg cowling had only four hex bolts and even though they were in an awkward position, it would take only three or four minutes to complete the job. The bottom two bolts went the quickest since they were the easiest to get to. As he ran the wire to the third bolt, he had to strain to see it. Thoughts of his mother filled his mind, and with that, tears filled his eyes. Finally he got the wire through the third bolt and pulled the pliers to create the braid. He pulled, not hard enough to break the wire, but harder than the specs called for, and hard enough to cause an invisible stress tear on the back of the braid. Less than two minutes later the last bolt was secured and the braided wire anchored off. Scott Yerremian had completed his last Air Force job.

THURSDAY
JULY 24, 1969
TAN SON NHUT AIR FORCE BASE
F-4 PHANTOM MISSION

At 7:28 a.m. it was already hot enough to cause waves of heat to rise from the concrete runway. Off to the left, the flight line was alive with activity. Helicopters lined up at the underground refueling tanks before they flew back to their parking slots and stood down from their night-time missions. Blue "Follow Me" trucks, with their blinking yellow arrows, led C-130 cargo planes to their unloading areas while mechanics worked on other aircraft and ground crews loaded ordinance on those planes that were scheduled for combat missions. To the right, far out of sight, past the edge of the perimeter, Air Force Security Police patrolled in pickups, jeeps, and on foot, guarding those who toiled to keep the war in motion.

Less than two hours earlier, the sharp observer might have noticed K-9 teams being driven back to the base after their night of duty. At Ton Son Nhut, daylight security was pretty mundane, almost pleasant, except for the constant heat, persistent insects, torrential downpours, and the ever present danger of relieving yourself next to, or stepping on, a poisonous snake. Nighttime security was a different matter entirely. Motorized patrols were limited since the lighted vehicles made clear and fruitful targets for VC snipers, as well as causing a distraction for the main security element: The Air Force dog teams.

Normal security troops patrolling a perimeter at night were at a disadvantage because their sight and hearing were often tricked by swaying trees that looked like advancing enemy troops, or enemy troops that looked no more dangerous than elephant grass blowing in the breeze. Patrol Dog handlers were no less susceptible to these tricks of the mind or the bone chilling fear that accompanied them, but their one advantage were their partners: Their dogs.

The dogs saw the same swaying trees, even heard them when the handler couldn't, but unless the sight and sound had the scent of humans, it was not a threat and not worth more than their briefest attention. A snapping twig was just that, unless a sandal wrapped foot caused it to snap. The dogs alerted to different sights, sounds, and smells in different ways and a handler quickly learned to read the "alert" signs of his partner. The presence of enemy troops might have been rare but the call of nature always seemed to beckon while on duty, and it was comforting to know that while the utter blackness of the jungle night surrounded you as you squatted in the bushes, your dog would sit patiently and watch for snakes or other inquisitive creatures.

Four F-4's sat at the end of the runway, their engines belching black kerosene-smelling smoke. Lieutenant Colonel David Runyon scanned his instrument panel looking for telltale red lights, low oil pressure warnings, or any other sign of impending mishap. Satisfied that everything was in order, he keyed the intercom to his backseat Weapons System Officer (WIZZO). "Hey, Tep, you all tucked in and ready to go play?"

Captain Frank Tepley had completed his cockpit check and was gazing out the left side of his canopy. "Huh? Oh, yeah, I'm all set back here." Three months shy of his twenty-seventh birthday and one month into his tour in Vietnam, Frank Tepley was a man who was less than happy. Born and raised on the outskirts of Boston, in the small town of Medford, he had accomplished more than his parents, or he, had ever dreamed. Earning a full scholarship out of high school, he attended Tufts University where he not only excelled academically but rose through the ranks in the ROTC program. Enlistment in the Air Force seemed only natural and although disappointed that his dream of becoming a pilot had been sidetracked when he was overlooked for flight training and instead assigned to Weapons Systems Operator school, he had resigned himself that flying back seat was better than flying no seat. Marrying his college sweetheart the day after graduation had been a fitting finale to years of studying and sacrifice. Now, just a little more than a year later, he sat in the back of an F-4, waiting to fly over the very thing that made him less than happy: the jungle. It wasn't so much the thought of being shot down, you really couldn't do anything about that, and it wasn't the thought of people trying to kill him, after all, that happened to the other guy. No, it was the Vietnam jungle, and the things in it that terrified him. Boston had nothing like it, Massachusetts had nothing like it and the instructors at Jungle Survival School in Pensacola Florida had said that as much as they tried to make it realistic, they had nothing like it. That terrified Tepley even more. The leathery skinned, eat anything that swam, crawled, flew or slithered, afraid of nothing instructors, had dropped him, and the rest of the class, in a swamp filled with alligators, lizards, leeches, spiders and snakes and tried their damnedest to teach them how to survive long enough for the rescue choppers to get to them. Although the course was designed to build confidence in the flyers, it often had the opposite effect. It taught the scared men that they had more to worry about than enemy soldiers with guns or frightened villagers with pitchforks and sharpened bamboo poles. It taught them that an agonizing death lurked in the closeness of the jungle…waiting…waiting for the one mistake that would allow it to claim its next victim. For some, the fear was of the unmerciful heat that sapped energy like water rung out of a sponge and the accompanied thirst that screamed for the relief of death. For others, it was the bugs. Swarms of flying and crawling flesh eaters that drove men into insanity while they were slowly eaten alive. They had dropped them out there, each armed with an olive drab, plastic bottle of oily insect repellent and advised to use it sparingly. Once it was gone, they were told, they would be at the mercy of the chiggers, gnats, the flies, and of course, the mosquitoes. Each man found his own fear and quickly, but silently, learned if he could overcome it. Tepley was no exception, and he knew that it was his greatest, unconquerable fear. It was the snakes. He hated the snakes. The very thought of them sent a shudder of revulsion through his body and the actual sight of one brought out the irrational phobia that he hadn't known existed. After all they had been put through, all they had seen in that northern Florida swamp, the instructors said that the jungle in Vietnam was worse. Tepley didn't see how that could be.

"Stay with me, Tep, we've got work to do."

"I know, boss. I guess I was just daydreamin' for a second."

"Yeah, I know. I see it, too." They were referring to the TWA 707 passenger jet, the Freedom Flight, parked on the tarmac just in front of the tower. They had no way of knowing that Scott Yerremian, the mechanic who had worked on their plane the day before, was just boarding, on his way home to bury his mother.

"Boy, those are some lucky motherfuckers." Tepley was thinking about his wife and how much he wanted to be back home with her.

"Hey, things could be worse." Runyon grinned inside his oxygen mask.

"Things could be worse? We're eight thousand miles from home, living with a bunch of horny guys, dropping bombs on helpless trees, shooting at people that we never see and who haven't done a fuckin' thing to us if you don't count the SAM's, triple A, and machine gun fire, and you tell me things could be worse? What's worse? They gonna' start making us pay for the gas to fly these things?" No, Captain Frank Tepley wasn't thrilled with being in Vietnam.

"Hey, we could be slugging through the jungle like the Army grunts." Runyon chuckled in his oxygen mask as he continued to stare at the Freedom Flight, recalling his own two flights on it.

Lieutenant Colonel David Creedmore Runyon, United States Air Force. He liked the sound of it, always had, except for the rank of course. He had every expectation of pinning the silver eagles of a "Full Colonel" on his collar some day, shedding the career stigma of "Light Colonel" for the more prestigious military nickname of "Full Bird". It wasn't that he was power hungry, far from it, he was just pragmatic. At thirty -eight, he knew his days as an F-4 driver were numbered. Flying the most advanced fighter jet in the world was a young man's game, especially when that flying was through surface to air missiles and anti-aircraft fire or searching the skies for a Russian Mig to tango with. The day would come when the good natured cat calls of "old man" would take on a more serious tone and eagles on his collar would give him a far better chance of a Squadron Commander slot. That at least would keep him around his beloved F-4's, and with any luck, a few hours flying time every month. It was the flying that he loved, truly loved, and until he had gotten on that Freedom Flight for the first time he had never realized how much he loved it. He had no sooner nestled into the window seat of the plane, surrounded by laughing, cheering, and back slapping drunk soldiers and airmen on their way home after a year in hell that he realized he didn't share their boisterous elation. Oh, he had nodded his thanks when the stewardess handed him a plastic glass of cheap champagne and even held it aloft to acknowledge the toast of "Next stop...The World." He was just as anxious, no, desperate, to see his wife, parents, and friends as any man on the plane, but something was missing. All the pieces of what should have been a great day didn't fit and it wasn't until the plane started to taxi out to the runway that he realized what it was. He had stared at them out the window, their silhouettes waving lazily through the mirage of heat rising from the tarmac, partially obscured by the clouds of black smoke belching from the plane's engines. Men scurried in, around, and over them, loading bombs, rockets, fixing battle damage, and ensuring that the giant green and brown monsters were ready for their next mission. It was then he knew, sitting there in the luxury of the Freedom Flight with good looking, sexy stewardesses pampering a cabin full of thankful, horney men, it was then he knew what was missing...what he would miss. The F-4's...the combat...the thrill of not knowing if the sun would rise for you tomorrow...the wave of relief when death had been cheated one more time. He knew that he'd miss it, he knew he wasn't ready to live without it...and he knew that he'd have to tell his wife that he was coming back. The first time was hard, she didn't understand, no wife really ever would. The second time was easier, at least she made it easier on him, but only after he promised that his third tour would really be the last. Now, as he sat there in the trembling beast that was his F-4, surrounded by the flight he commanded, he wondered if it really would be.

"Tan Son Nhut tower to Buick Flight One."

"Buick Flight One, go." Runyon turned his head slightly as he answered the controller in the tower.

"Buick Flight One, cleared to roll on active. Turn on heading 350, cleared to angels two zero, contact Tiger at target on 123.6. Good hunting."

"Ah, roger tower, rolling now." Runyon turned to look at the F-4 sitting to his right. He keyed the microphone on the control stick in his right hand. "Buick Flight, copy?"

He was answered by three microphone clicks in his helmet. For men who liked to live life on the edge, fighter jocks tended to be very closed mouthed when it came to the radio, preferring instead to communicate with head nods, hand gestures, or simple microphone clicks.

Runyon made another quick scan of his instruments and keyed his mike one more time. "Two, go to burners." Red hot flame replaced the black smoke as raw JP-4 shot into the tailpipes and the two loaded planes slowly started to creep along, struggling at first, then quickly gaining speed. Just past the halfway marker of the runway they rotated up and raised their landing gear. Before they had even cleared the end of the runway, the last two planes of the flight started their takeoff roll. Less than three miles from the base, all four planes were flying in a tight formation.

They settled in for the relatively short trip of less than two hundred miles. The target was a battery of SAM launchers and anti-aircraft guns that had been harassing flights on their way to other missions. No one really knew if the missiles and guns were still in place, but when you were spending the taxpayer's money to carry bombs and napalm, you felt obligated to use them.

Buick One and Two were loaded with MK-82 five hundred pound bombs, Buick Three and Four with canisters of napalm. If nothing else, they would give the jungle a reason to regenerate itself. Dropping bombs was easy, the problem pilots faced was identifying the exact location to deliver those bombs. They needed the target marked before they could make their run and the job was often left to the slow flying and vulnerable OV-10 Broncos. It was their job to fly low and slow over the intended target and mark it with smoke rockets. Much to the chagrin of its pilots, its slow speed earned the Bronco the reputation of being the only combat aircraft susceptible to bird strikes from any direction. Any lack of common sense Bronco pilots might have suffered from was more than made up for by an ample set of balls.

"Buick Flight, this is Tiger."

Runyon scanned the horizon as he hit the microphone button. "Go Tiger."

"I'm twenty miles out and prepared for marking." The Bronco pilot took great pride in his call sign of Tiger, even if the combat capabilities of his plane were closer to that of a lamb.

"Ah, roger that, Tiger." Runyon reached forward and switched the intercom to the locked on position. "You all set back there, Tep?"

Tepley made a quick check of the cockpit and tightened his restraining straps. "Do I have a choice?"

"Not really."

"Well, then, lets get this over with. I gotta' take a shit."

"Didn't your mother ever teach you to go before you left home?"

"My mother never took me on a bombing run."

Any other time Runyon would have laughed out loud or thought of a snappy comeback. Now there was work to be done. He keyed the mike. "Okay, Buick Flight, master arm on, now." Each pilot moved the switches that would allow the bombs and napalm to fall away at just the right moment.

"Buick Flight, this is Tiger. Commencing run now."

Buick Three's Wizzo was the first to spot the slow-moving plane just above the tree tops. Its location was made even more evident by the lines of green tracers rising up through the trees in an effort to knock it out of the sky. The four aircraft adjusted their headings slightly and waited for the telltale marking smoke.

Tepley pressed his helmet against the canopy, staring at the trees, trying to spot the smoke. "One has purple smoke. Purple smoke, confirm."

"Two confirms purple smoke, purple smoke."

The Bronco pilot nodded to himself as he pressed his microphone button. "Purple smoke confirmed. Heavier than expected triple A and small arms fire. Clearing the area now, heads up and good luck."

"Buick, roger Tiger, enjoy the show. Out." Runyon tightened his straps one last time and took another quick look around. "All right, everyone, heads up now. One and Two will drop on the smoke and clear to the left. Three and Four, watch for secondaries, then follow us in and clear to the right." He released the microphone button and spoke to his Wizzo. "Tep, how's it look?"

Tepley was staring intently at his threat warning display, looking for signs that they were being painted by radar-controlled SAM's or anti-aircraft guns. "Clear green, no threats, but with as much shit as they threw at Tiger, ya' gotta' figure they got some SAM's down there!"

Runyon dropped the nose of the bomb-laden aircraft and headed down to the target with Two following his every move. As they approached the drifting smoke from the marker rockets, Runyon lined up the patch of jungle with his sighting pipper.

"Holy shit! Watch it...watch it!" Two's Wizzo was frantically twisting his head from side to side trying to identify all of the triple A locations. Green tracers and bursts of black smoke from exploding shells filled the sky.

The pilot of Three keyed the mike, his voice betraying his concern. "One, you guys are in major shit! Don't hang around there!"

As the target area loomed bigger and centered in the pipper, Runyon triggered the bomb release and pickled all twenty of the five hundred pound bombs. Two's bombs followed a fraction of a second later. No longer burdened by the ten thousand pounds of dead weight, both planes shot forward even before their pilots slammed the throttles into afterburner in an attempt to escape the wall of anti-aircraft fire and gain the safety of altitude.

Unable to see the results of the bomb run behind him, Runyon keyed his mike. The strain of five positive G's from the rapid climb distorted his voice into grunting sounds. "Three...arrgh...what'd...arrgh...we...get?"

He could hear the scream of Three's engines as the voice broke into his helmet. "The whole fuckin' place is going up! Big time secondaries!"

"Can...you...arrgh...make...your...arrgh...run?"

"Roger that, but we gotta' go in high. Too much shit in the air."

Runyon eased off the throttles as he gained altitude and sighed as the strain of the G's melted away. "Ah, yeah, that's a roger. Do it and lets get the hell outta' here."

One and Two were just breaking through four thousand feet when Tepley gave the alarm. "We're being painted! I knew it, I knew it! They had way too much shit down there not to have SAM's. Lock on, lock on! They've got us locked!"

Runyon hit the mike without waiting. "Three! Four! Drop and break! SAM's, SAM's!"

Three and Four didn't need to be warned, their Wizzos' had picked up the threat warning the same time Tepley had.

Runyon swung his head from side to side trying to pick up any sign of the missiles. "Tep, Tep, you got 'em?"

"Negative, negative...wait! Okay, okay, two SAM's at three o'clock. There they are! Get ready...ready...wait...wait...BREAK LEFT, BREAK LEFT, NOW NOW!"

Runyon kicked in full rudder and threw the stick to the left, the force of the turn pressing them back into their ejection seats, their faces contorted under their oxygen masks. With white hot flames streaking from their tails, the two telephone pole size missiles automatically corrected their direction and gained on the two fleeing fighters.

"Two...arrgh...separate...arrgh...separate!" Runyon kicked hard right trying to confuse the determined missiles while the pilot of Two inverted and dove for the deck. The force of the maneuvers caused the G-suits of the four men to tighten around their limbs and stomach, directing blood to their brains to keep them from blacking out. The missile following Two was unable to match the high speed maneuver and automatically detonated where it thought its target should be. Two's pilot pulled the aircraft back into a steep climb. It didn't do any good to evade a SAM just to get tagged by ground fire.

"Where's One? You got 'em?"

"Two's Wizzo was watching his flight leader's plane through the top of his canopy. "Yeah, yeah, one o'clock high! SAM's still on 'em!"

The pilot looked up and to his right. "One, it's on your six and closing! Go over the top! Go over the top!"

Runyon rolled the plane inverted and shoved the stick forward to its full stop pushing the nose of the aircraft straight at the ground, then kicked it into a hard left turn. Like its partner, the missile lost its radar lock and automatically detonated.

"We've got green all around, all green. We're okay, didn't feel any impacts." Tepley raised his gaze from the instrument panel looked out his canopy checking the wings for holes. Seeing none, he watched as the pilots of Three and Four pulled their planes above the range of the anti-aircraft fire.

Runyon let out the breath he'd been holding in a loud sigh. "Boy, ain't this fun."

"Yeah, right. Now I really gotta' shit."

"I'd a thought our little ride would'a taken care of that problem." Runyon chuckled to himself as he scanned the sky for signs of more missiles and the rest of his flight.

"I think I'll wait, if it's all the same to you. In the meantime, you just go ahead and do your pilot stuff. I'm gonna' take me a little nap." Tepley was a firm believer that if the pilots were going to get all the credit, they might as well do most of the work. "Wake me when the war's over."

"Okay, Buick Flight, lets form up and head for home. One has the lead." Runyon smiled to himself and relaxed for the routine flight back to Tan Son Nhut. They had gone through a few tight moments but overall it was turning out to be a beautiful day.

Runyon and Tepley's plane had suffered no visible battle damage. There was no way to know just when the stress tear in the braided safety wire broke, nor did it matter, since once it broke, it allowed the rest of the wire to slip through the hole in the bolt head and the bolt itself to vibrate out. The effect of it being sucked through the spinning engine turbines was about to change Runyon's opinion of how the day was going.

Tepley jerked himself awake. "What the fuck was that!? Are we hit? Are we takin' hits!?" He scanned his panel as Runyon fought to control the violently bucking aircraft. "Red lights! Port engine, port engine, shut it down!"

Runyon pulled back the throttle on the port engine cutting off the fuel in an attempt to shut it down. Even without fuel, the constant air flow caused the turbine blades to spin and disintegrate as the hex bolt was sucked through. Centrifugal force threw metal fragments, now as dangerous as any anti-aircraft shell, against the thin aluminum skin of the engine housing. With a force far greater than the airframe could withstand, the burning hot fragments sliced into the fuselage fuel tank and on through to the starboard engine.

Fighting the arm wrenching left-handed pull from the loss of the port engine, Runyon now felt a more sudden deceleration as the starboard engine began to destroy itself.

"What the fuck is goin' on, Tep!? What'a we got?"

"Oh, shit! Fire light, fire light! Right side!"

"Tighten up! We're gettin' outta' here!" Runyon mashed down on the radio transmit button. "MAYDAY, MAYDAY, MAYDAY! Two, we're punchin' out!" Thick black smoke and flames were now streaking from both engines.

"One, we got ya' covered! Get out, get out!"

Runyon lowered his helmet visor and with both hands pulled down on the yellow and black ejection handles above his head.

"Chutes, chutes! Anyone see chutes? Where the fuck are they?" Major Benjamin Brotzman, Two's pilot, had spent several frantic moments trying to evade the scattering cloud of debris from the exploding fighter and was now pulling his aircraft around in an attempt to locate his flight leader.

"Four has two good chutes. Your three o'clock low."

Brotzman hit the transmit button as he spotted the two parachutes. "Tiger, this is Buick Flight Two, Buick Flight Two. Mayday, Mayday, Mayday!"

"Buick Flight, copy your Mayday, go."

"Buick One is down, repeat, Buick One is down."

"Roger, Buick Two. Advise on crew."

"Two good chutes, two good chutes."

"Roger. Stand by, Buick." The radio was silent for several moments while Tiger arranged for a rescue attempt. "Buick, Red Crown is in contact with choppers, RESCAP alerted. Do you have a visual on crew?"

"Negative at this time, they landed in the trees. Will advise." Brotzman attempted to raise his flight leader. "Buick One, this is Buick Two. Do you copy?"

Runyon and Tepley were lying prone in a thick stand of bushes about a hundred yards from their still dangling, and very obvious parachutes. Runyon heard the voice, and while clutching his Air Force issue .38, pulled the emergency radio out of his survival vest. "Ben, what's the deal? It ain't no fun down here."

"Red Crown is diverting some choppers, two Cobra's and a slick. RESCAP is getting up but if we're lucky, the choppers will get to you first...wait one...Red Crown is advising Tiger that the slick doesn't have a jungle penetrator, they need an open LZ."

"Goddamnit! What do they think we're doing out here, making bomb runs over the fucking White House! This is a jungle, not a Goddamn parking lot!"

Brotzman swiveled his head around, looking for a place big enough for a helicopter to land. "Looks like you guys are gonna have to take a little hike. Copy?"

Runyon swore under his breath, then looked at Tepley and shrugged his shoulders. "Ah, yeah, roger. How far?"

"There's a clearing about two klicks, maybe a little less. From where you went in, head southwest, stay in the trees at the edge of the clearing and wait for the choppers to get on station. Can you make it?"

"Yeah, we'll make it. We're moving now. Out." Runyon slipped the radio back in his survival vest and turned the volume down. Tepley kept his radio turned off to save the batteries, just in case. "You ready, Tep?"

Tepley's eyes were constantly moving back and forth, feverishly looking for movement, both human and reptile. "Ya think we went down far enough away from those Gooks?"

"I don't think we're gonna' hang around to find out." Runyon shot a line with his compass and led off through the thick brush.

"Buick One, Buick One, come in. Over."

"One here, go." The two men were trying to suck in breaths. Their flight suits were soggy from the torrents of sweat running off their bodies. Both had chosen to forego the protection of their hot Nomex flight gloves in favor of exposing their skin to whatever breeze they might find. It hadn't taken long to realize that there was no breeze, and an even shorter time for the branches, leaves, and thorns to cover their hands with razor thin cuts and scratches.

"One, the Cobras are three minutes out. What's your position?"

"Shit, Ben, we can't see a fuckin' thing through these trees. I think we're on the right line but I can't be sure. Over."

"All right. What about popping smoke so we can get a visual on you? Over."

"Negative Two, negative. No tellin' who's down here with us. Have the Cobras stand off and we'll keep goin' a little longer. Copy?"

"Ah, roger that. Out."

Runyon checked the compass again and headed off in the same direction, rechecking each time they had to divert around a stand of deadfall or a particularly heavy area of brush. Less than twenty minutes later they were on the edge of the clearing.

"Buick Two, Buick Two, come in, over."

"Two, go."

"Ben, we're at the edge of the clearing! Is the slick on station yet?" The excitement in Runyon's voice was unmistakable.

"Roger, boss, they're waitin' for ya. Pop smoke, pop smoke, now"

Tepley already had a smoke grenade from his survival vest in his hand and was pulling the pin. As it made its arc through the air, there was a soft popping noise followed by a growing cloud of smoke.

"Buick One, this is Two. Chopper has visual on yellow smoke, repeat, yellow smoke. Confirm. Over."

"Buick Two, this is One. Confirming yellow smoke, that's us!"

Even though neither Runyon nor Tepley had ever had to be rescued before, they were well aware of the VC killing or capturing downed flyers and as rescue choppers neared the area, throwing out a smoke grenade and shooting down the chopper when it tried to land. Helicopter pilots had learned the hard way to spot the smoke, call out the color and wait for the downed pilot to confirm it. It couldn't always be done that way, but when it wasn't, it often resulted in dead airmen as well as a destroyed helicopter and crew.

The slick came in at tree top level, flared, and set down with its chin bubble almost directly on top of the smoking grenade. Runyon and Tepley burst from the trees and ran for the open door. The M-60 machine gunners swung their guns from side to side searching the tree line for movement or muzzle flashes. Runyon slowed as he reached the chopper to let his Wizzo go first. Without slowing, Tepley threw himself through the door, landing in a heap at the feet of the far gunner. Not waiting to be invited, Runyon flopped down on the floor belly first.

As he helped pull Runyon the rest of the way in, the door gunner shouted at the pilot. "They're in! GO, GO, GO!!" Without hesitation, the helicopter slowly moved forward, then up, and away from the thankfully cold LZ.

Once they had joined up with the two Cobra escorts, the door gunners turned their attention to the rescued airmen. As one of the gunners passed them a canteen of water, he wrinkled his nose, looked around, then leaned over and sniffed the floor of the helicopter.

"What the hell is that smell? Jesus Christ, it smells like someone shit his pants."

Runyon just smiled as he shrugged his shoulders. Tepley ignored the question entirely and took a swig from the canteen. He couldn't have cared less.

CHAPTER 4

FRIDAY
AUGUST 29, 1969
COMBAT SECURITY POLICE TRAINING
SQUADRON FIRING RANGE
LACKLAND AIR FORCE BASE, TEXAS

Like thirty obedient little children, they lay prone on the ground, side by side, with the muzzles of their M-16's pointed downrange at the dark green silhouette targets. Clad in heavy, long-sleeved fatigues with the top button fastened and the collar turned up to guard against hot shell casings making an unexpected, and unwelcomed journey down their backs, the Security Police trainees sweltered in the hot Texas sun.

They had just finished firing their first twenty rounds and were waiting to check their targets. Even though one hundred yards is a relatively short distance for a rifle, it can be more than a match for the inexperienced, and the four instructors had not been surprised to see bullets impacting the dirt a scant ten feet in front of some of the shooters. If winning the war depended on the marksmanship of the average soldier, or airman, the United States was in deep shit. As the range master looked over the line of shooters and convinced himself that it was as safe as could be expected, he gave the order to "check 'em and weep". The range master was not overly optimistic.

As the trainees approached the targets, their shooting skills, or lack thereof, quickly became apparent. Hoots of laughter, frowns of disgust, and in some cases, utter disbelief, were more common than not. Technical Sergeant Jerry Vannoy walked up to target number seven. "Whose target is this?"

"Mine, Sergeant."

Vannoy turned toward the voice and found himself staring at an airman who couldn't have tipped the scales at more than a hundred and ten pounds. Vannoy glanced at the name tag over the airman's fatigue shirt pocket. "This is your target, Airman Paulie?"

"Yes, Sergeant."

"Where are the holes?"

"Pardon me, sir, er, Sergeant?"

"The holes, Paulie, where are the holes? There are supposed to be holes in the target after you shoot at it. That's why we go through the expense of putting bullets in the weapon. You did load your weapon with bullets, didn't you, Airman Paulie?"

"Yes, Sergeant."

"Well, when you pulled the trigger, did it make a big noise with smoke and fire coming out the front or did you just point it down here and yell BANG?"

Paulie flinched at the word "bang" while the other trainees listened, relishing in his discomfort. "No, Sergeant, my weapon was loaded and I fired all twenty bullets."

"What did you fire them at, Paulie?"

"My target, Sergeant, that one right there." He half-heartedly raised his arm and pointed at his target.

"Well, why aren't there any holes in it? If you shot at it, there should be some holes. Ideally twenty of them, but at least one. Just one crummy hole. Don't you think so, Airman Paulie?"

"Yes, Sergeant."

"You know what I hope, Airman? I hope you fuck better than you shoot, 'cause if you don't, we might as well start training you to be a Chaplain right now."

The instructors walked up and down the line giving advice and recommendations. Technical Sergeant Brad Freson was on sixteen when he happened to glance over at the next target. "Who's on seventeen?"

"I am, Sergeant." Gianni had long ago looked at his target, figured out his sight adjustment, and made the corrections in his head.

"Not a bad group, Airman..." Freson stole a glance at the name tag, "...Giancarlo."

"Thank you, Sergeant. I think I can do a lot better once I get used to the gun...ah, weapon." Unlike Hank, the military never used the word gun, they were always weapons. Always. The taxpayers paid good money to teach their young men how to kill, and killing was never a sport. "The stock is a little short for me. I'll get used to it, though."

Freson was impressed with the group. Although it was a little low, it was in the middle of the target and all twenty holes could have been covered with a playing card.

"What about your sights?"

"I'm about two inches low. I'll adjust the for that. Windage seems pretty good so I'll leave it alone."

Freson had to admit that the group was pretty tight, especially for someone firing an unfamiliar rifle, but it might also be beginner's luck. He'd wait and see how he did the rest of the day. "All right, paste over the holes."

As they headed back to the firing line, Freson maneuvered his way over to Vannoy. "Hey, Jerry, watch the guy on seventeen during this next round."

"I gotta' baby-sit the dipstick on seven. That kid Paulie. He couldn't hit the ground with a bowling ball."

"Well, if ya' get a chance, take a gander over to seventeen. See what ya' think."

"Why, he any good?"

"We'll know by the end of the day."

As the day got hotter, the shooting got worse for the most part. Gianni managed to cut the size of his groups by a third, finishing his twenty shot strings in less than half the time of the other trainees. Each time they went downrange to check the targets, Freson and Vannoy made a point of checking his first. On their fourth trip back to the line, Freson made his way over to Gianni. "Where'd you learn to shoot, troop?"

"A friend taught me."

Freson stopped walking and motioned Gianni to stay with him. "You don't learn to shoot a rifle like that by going out with a friend. This takes practice, lots of it."

"Well, I guess I've done some shooting before, but not with a rifle, except for the one day in basic."

Vannoy walked up behind them and looked at Freson. "The kid shot a pretty good group that time."

"Yeah, I know." Freson looked at Gianni, then back at Vannoy. "Says he never fired a rifle before."

"Bullshit. He's a ringer. Probably grew up in the boonies shootin' squirrels or coons for dinner."

Freson shrugged slightly. "Giancarlo, you said you've done some shooting before. Just what kind of shooting would that be?"

"Shotgun."

The sergeants stole a quick glance at each other, slight grins spreading over their faces. "Bird hunting, tossing beer cans in the air, knocking over gas stations? Come on, troop, getting answers outta' you is like pullin' teeth."

Gianni was getting embarrassed. "Skeet and trap shooting at the Winchester Gun Club in Fort Lauderdale. I, ah, I guess I've got a knack for it. You know, it comes pretty easy. I, ah, I was an instructor and a range master." He nodded to the row of targets behind them. "It was a lot more fun than shooting these M-16's. This is pretty boring."

Freson nodded his head. "Yeah? Well, next week you guys will start learning to fire on full automatic. Gets to be a lot more fun then." As Gianni walked back to the firing line the two sergeants hung back. Freson, smiling like the cat that swallowed the canary nudged Vannoy.

"Did ya hear that? Instructor and range master."

Vannoy managed his own ear to ear grin. "You thinkin' what I'm thinkin'?"

"Way-a-heada-ya boy...way-a-heada ya."

Gianni had finished cleaning his rifle and was sitting on the bench next to the water cooler when Freson and Vannoy walked up. Freson lit a Salem and offered one to Gianni.

"No, thanks, Sergeant, I don't smoke."

Freson put the pack back in his pocket. "Giancarlo, you guys have the weekend off and Sergeant Vannoy and I were wondering if you had any plans for tomorrow?"

"No, not really. I'll probably just hang around the barracks, write a couple of letters, do my laundry. Why, do you want me to pull some kind of extra duty?" Gianni knew his weekend was about to be shot to hell.

"Extra duty? No, no, nothing like that. Actually we were interested in seeing you shoot a little skeet and trap. We shoot every weekend and were wondering if you'd like to come along tomorrow and shoot a couple rounds?"

"I, ah, I appreciate the invitation but, I, ah, I really can't afford it."

"Don't worry about that, Uncle Sam will pick up the tab. You know where the base skeet and trap ranges are?"

"No."

"All right, look. One of the base buses stops near your barracks every half hour. Catch it tomorrow morning and tell the driver you need to go to the ranges. We'll meet you there around eleven."

"Well, I guess so, but I don't have anything to shoot."

"Don't worry, Uncle Sam will supply that, too."

They were interrupted by the sound of the range master's voice. "Hey troop, you gonna bullshit all day or ya gonna get on this truck and ride back to the base with the rest of these no shootin' dipshits?!" ·

Freson nodded to Gianni that he was dismissed and watched as the young airman ran toward the two and a half ton truck. He was just about to pull himself over the tailgate when Freson yelled after him.

"Hey, Giancarlo! What's your first name?"

Gianni looked over his shoulder and yelled back. "Gianni."

"Johnny?"

"No, Gianni. Gee-Ah-Nee, put it altogether and say it fast, GIANNI.

SATURDAY
AUGUST 30, 1969
SKEET AND TRAP RANGES
LACKLAND AIR FORCE BASE, TEXAS

Gianni was impressed with the four combination skeet and trap ranges. Apparently, once you achieved a little rank in the Air Force, life wasn't really all that bad. They even had a club house that wasn't totally unlike the one at home. He was watching four men in civilian clothes shoot a round of trap when he heard his name being called.

"Giancarlo, hey, Giancarlo, over here."

Freson and Vannoy were seated at a round wooden table with a third man. "Glad you made it. We'd like you to meet someone. This is Chief Master Sergeant Reynolds. This is Airman Giancarlo, Gianni, the Airman we were telling you about."

Gianni extended his hand toward the Chief Master Sergeant. "Morning, Sergeant."

"Hello Gianni, have a seat." The three men waited while Gianni pulled a chair over to the table. "I'm told you used to shoot some skeet and trap before you enlisted."

"Yes sir…I mean Sergeant. I worked at a gun club, you know, after school and on some weekends."

"Just call me Sarge, it's all right. How long you been shooting?"

"Oh, I guess it's been a little over two years."

Reynolds looked at Freson and Vannoy. The stare didn't go unnoticed by Gianni as they both settled a little lower in their chairs, thinking that maybe they had opened their mouths to Reynolds a little too soon. Gianni sensed the sudden coolness in his three companions.

"Is there a problem, Sarge? Did I say something wrong?"

"No, Gianni, no problem. It's just that Sergeants Freson and Vannoy figured you'd been shooting for a lot longer than that. Especially after what they saw you do on the M-16 range yesterday."

"No, sir, I never shot before a couple of years ago. I guess it just sort of comes naturally, plus I had a really good teacher."

"Is that the friend you told Sergeant Freson about?"

"Yes, sir, Hank Parrish."

The three sat bolt upright at the mention of the name. Reynolds moved his bottle of Lone Star beer aside and leaned forward. "Is this Hank a small wiry guy, retired Army, couldn't hear a bomb blast if it went off next to him?"

Gianni chuckled at the description of Hank. "That's Hank all right, except he refuses to admit that he has a hearing problem."

"Yeah, I know." Reynolds smiled and sat back in his chair, reaching for his beer and taking a long swig. Freson and Vannoy grinned. All of a sudden things were looking a lot brighter. "I'll be a motherfucker. Hank Parrish taught you to shoot."

"Do you know Hank?"

Reynolds held the beer bottle in his lap and started picking at the soggy label with his thumb nail. "Hell, yes, I know Hank. Shot against him many times in inter-service matches. Never beat the little bastard, not once. Never seen that kind of concentration in a shooter, never. Hell, you could set fire to his pants and he'd wait 'til he made the shot before he pissed himself to put it out." Reynolds chuckled at his own joke. "Lets see what Hank taught you. Freson, how about you and Vannoy going inside and grabbing us some equipment and we'll see if Gianni here can do more than blow some holes in the sky.

They had planned on shooting three rounds of both skeet and trap but before they had gotten half way through, the catcalls started flying over the fence. "Way to go kid. Take it to 'em, it's about time we had some new blood around here! Hey, Reynolds, I got twenty bucks that says the kid cleans your clock!"

As Freson and Vannoy started picking up the empty shell casings, the crowd drifted away. Reynolds waited for a minute or so, then dragged Gianni off after hearing comments on how Gianni had humiliated the three sergeants. "That was some very nice shooting out there, Gianni. Hank did a good job teaching you but he forgot one thing."

Gianni had no idea what Hank had forgot to teach him. "What's that Sergeant?"

"Never outshoot someone who outranks you, especially someone who outranks you by a shitload. Like me!" Reynolds' face burst into a broad grin.

"You're right, he never taught me that. He just said to shoot your best everytime. Anything less is just making noise and wasting ammo." Gianni hoped the grin on Reynolds face meant he wasn't serious.

Reynolds' gaze wandered off, remembering all the times Hank had beat him. He was shaking his head in amazement as he looked back at Gianni. "Jesus Christ, now that little bastard is beating me by proxy! You get lucky today, kid, or can you shoot like that all the time?"

"I don't really know. Like I said, it all comes really natural, I've never had to struggle at it. I guess I can do it all the time. Actually, I'm trying to get better."

Reynolds grinned at the thought of the young airman getting better than he already was. "Come on, kid, lets go get a drink."

They sat at the same table. Vannoy had gone into the clubhouse and returned with four Lone Star beers. The three sergeants took long pulls as Gianni rubbed the sweating bottle over his forehead.

Freson glanced over at Reynolds. "Sarge, we haven't started pistol training yet but if Gianni turns out to be as good with a .38 as he is with a rifle, well, shit, someone from the Combat Team is gonna' snatch him up big time."

Reynolds nodded his head in agreement while lost in thought. "Yeah, you may be right. Listen, Gianni, if anyone from the Combat Team approaches you, well, just tell 'em to fuck off and come see me. Don't even talk to 'em, they're nothin' but a bunch of assholes. Always tryin' to snatch up my people."

Gianni looked at him with a confused expression on his face. "I don't understand, Sergeant. What's the Combat Team and why would they want to talk to me?"

The three sergeants looked at each other and smiled. This might be easier than they expected. "Doesn't matter, kid, I'm not gonna let the problem come up. I've already made a decision."

"Decision? Decision about what?"

"You, kid. I've made the decision. I'm the one who decides who shoots and who doesn't shoot, and you definitely are going to shoot. Welcome to the Air Force Skeet and Trap Competition Team."

Freson and Vannoy looked at each other and smiled. They had been vindicated.

"Sarge, I don't understand. I haven't even finished Security Police school yet. Hell, I just got out of basic, I don't even know where I'm gonna be stationed."

"I do. Right here! Good 'ol Lackland Air Force Base. Don't sweat it, kid, it's my job to handle these things. The day you graduate from SP school, you'll have orders assigning you to the Combat Security Police Training Squadron as a firearms instructor, same as Freson and Vannoy. You'll also be assigned as a member of the Air Force Skeet and Trap Competition Team. Son, you just pulled off what every other swinging dick in the Air Force is trying to do. Keep his ass out of Vietnam."

Gianni stared at Reynolds for a moment before he was able to get any words out. "Sarge, I appreciate it, I appreciate what all of you are trying to do, but I want to go."

Freson and Vannoy looked at each other in disbelief.

"My ears must still be ringing. I don't think I heard you right." Now it was Reynolds turn to stare in disbelief.

"I said I want to go. I asked to be an SP just so I'd be sure I went to Vietnam. Our DI in basic told us. When I asked him who had the best chance of seeing combat besides pilots, he told me the SP's."

Freson pushed his chair back and stood up. "This kid's outta' his fuckin' mind." He turned to get another round of beers from the clubhouse.

"Sarge, I don't want to sound ungrateful, I really appreciate what you're trying to do, but I want to see what it's like over there. I know I might end up walking around some planes for eight hours a day, or standing at one of the base gates checking ID's, but at least I'll be able to say I was there. The only thing I'm worried about is that they may not send me. You know, I might get stationed somewhere beside Vietnam."

Reynolds and Vannoy spent the next several minutes trying to talk him into staying at Lackland and shooting on the team but Gianni was determined. Deep down Reynolds admired the young airmen, especially when other kids his age were heading for Canada by the bus load. Still, he hated to lose such a rare talent.

Freson returned and passed out the beers. "Kid still want to go to the land of rice paddies and water buffalo?"

"Damnedest thing I've ever heard. Must'a fallen on his head when he was a baby. He's actually worried that they might not sent him there." Vannoy snatched up the beer and took a long swig.

"Dogs." Freson attacked his own beer without saying another word.

"What?" Reynolds turned at the comment.

"Dogs. Sign up for Patrol Dog Handler."

"What the fuck do dogs have to do with this?" Reynolds wasn't getting the impression that Freson was helping the cause.

"Well, shit, Sarge, the kid wants to go. I don't think it's the smartest decision anyone ever made but you gotta give him credit. Seems to me you were in Korea and 'Nam, two tours if memory serves me right. If he wants to go, I think it's better if we help 'im rather than fuck with 'im."

Reynolds reconciled himself to the fact that one of the best shooters he had seen in years was slipping through his fingers. "Goddamnit, kid, you would have made us all look like heroes around here. All right, Freson, what's this shit about being a dog catcher?"

"Not dog catcher, Sarge, dog handler. Patrol Dog Handler. It's classified as a critical career field in Southeast Asia. You handle a dog, you go across the pond. Doesn't guarantee the 'Nam, might end up in Thailand, might not even go there right away, but it sure as shit increases your chances of a one year vacation to The Republic of..."

MONDAY
OCTOBER 6,1969
PATROL DOG HANDLER SCHOOL
LACKLAND AIR FORCE BASE, TEXAS

Master Sergeant Dennis King stood at the front of the classroom waiting for his eleven new students to pick a desk and settle down. King wore his fatigue pants in the traditional bloused fashion of an Air Force dog handler.

"Gentlemen, please, lets settle down so we can get started." The class turned forward at the sound of his voice. "Fine, thank you. First of all I'd like to welcome you to the Air Force Patrol Dog Handlers School. My name is Master Sergeant King, Dennis King, and I, along with Technical Sergeants Barton and Matas will be your instructors." Sergeants Barton and Matas were leaning against the blackboard at the front of the classroom and nodded at the mention of their names.

"I'm sure you all have questions about what you have gotten into and I'd like to begin by addressing some of the basic misconceptions you probably have. Lots of students come here with the idea that Dog Handlers are not required to salute officers. Let me clarify that for you. Air Force dog handlers DO salute officers but NOT when they are with their canine partners. This is not because you're special, although you'll feel that way once you are assigned a dog, but because the quick movement of rendering a hand salute is sometimes taken as a defensive action by your dog. In an attempt to protect you, he will attack the person you are saluting. I don't have to tell you that allowing your dog to rip off the balls of some unsuspecting officer is not necessarily the best path to career advancement." Quiet chuckles and a few under-the-breath comments filtered through the room.

"Next on the agenda of dispelling rumors. Many of you have probably heard that if you volunteered for dogs, there would be a good chance of being sent to Southeast Asia. You may also have heard that both the North Vietnamese and the Viet Cong have a bounty on the dogs and their handlers. Gentlemen, you were taught in Basic never to listen to rumors and to go to the source for the facts. Well, I'm the source and I'm here to tell you…the rumors you heard are true." There was no laughter this time as the students stole sideward glances at each other. "The North Vietnamese Army and the Viet Cong have indeed posted a bounty on dog handlers and dogs, and because of that, there is a shortage. And because of that shortage, you will be sent to Southeast

Asia." The only noise in the room was the sound of fidgeting by the men in their seats. "Welcome to the war, gentlemen."

King reached behind the podium at the front of the room and lifted a large color poster of a German Shepherd.

"Because you will be going to a war zone, you are going to want to have every advantage at survival possible. The cold hard fact is you will most likely see some hostile action. That is the bad news. The good news is, you're not in the Army or the Marines so you won't be slogging around in the bush looking for NVA regulars or VC. In comparison, you will have dick duty. For the most part, you will patrol along a base perimeter, your primary duty being to provide an early warning against enemy infiltration. That is a military term that simply means you detect the little motherfuckers before they sneak on the base and blow up our airplanes. If it sounds dangerous, it is. If it sounds deadly, it doesn't have to be. IF, you do your job, and IF, you learn what we're going to teach you."

"Sergeants Barton, Matas, and I have all pulled tours in Vietnam and we have all done what I just described. As you can see, we came back with all our limbs. The fact is, we had a distinct advantage over the regular SP's, the Army grunts, the Marines, and, most of all, the enemy. This advantage, gentlemen, is that we all had a four-legged partner, a Patrol Dog. That may not mean much to you right now, but I guarantee that by the end of your training, you will agree that you'd rather crawl naked over a mile of broken glass than go into a hostile area without your dog."

The old wooden desks creaked and groaned as eleven bodies straightened up and leaned forward, intent on hearing every word. The fear of going to Vietnam slowly replaced with the hope that it just might turn out to be all right after all.

"In the weeks to come, you're going to see posted signs reading: 'Danger—Military Working Dogs—Keep Out'. Those signs say it all, people. Take it to heart. These are working dogs. Trained living, breathing, pieces of military equipment. They are not pets. Forget about the little pooch you had at home or the bird dog that you thought was the greatest thing since pussy. You have never had dogs like these. You have never been around dogs like these. And you have never seen dogs like these."

"If you learn what we teach you, if you pay attention to your dog and learn to understand what he is trying to tell you, you will stay alive. If you don't...well, you will then be nothing more than a target...and that, gentlemen, is not the way to play the game. You're going to learn that your greatest weapon is your dog. Not your rifle, not your pistol, not your grenades: Your dog. He will tell you when the trees you see are actually VC, or the shapes in the swaying grass are nothing more than water buffalo. If you watch him carefully, he will tell you the place you chose to shit is not the best choice since a snake has already decided to sleep there or that the matted patch of ground you were going to step on is a booby trap. Learn to trust your dog and rely on his abilities. They're better than yours."

King nodded at the poster. "This is what you'll learn to work with, what you'll learn to trust your life with," he tapped on the nose of the dog, "and this is what makes your dog such a potent weapon. As much as we rely on our eyes to tell us what's happening, the dog relies on his sense of smell. If we're standing in the same room, we can smell a pot of coffee being brewed or an apple pie in the oven. That, gentlemen, is a spit in the ocean compared to what a dog can smell."

He tapped the nose harder. "His sense of smell is at least a hundred times better than yours. That means he will tell you a VC sapper is moving through the trees when he is still three hundred yards away, assuming you have paid attention to your training. When you are on patrol, watch your dog, not the bush. He will tell you if Charlie left a booby trapped grenade next to the trail or dug a pit filled with pungi sticks just so you could become the next pig on a spit. Trust your dog. He'll use his nose to show you that grenade or pungi pit."

"It's your job to detect people, and things, that will cause damage to Air Force assets. After you have found them, get out of the way. Let people who are trained for that kind of situation take over. You're more valuable doing what you've been trained to do as a dog handler than you are popping off rounds in the bush or trying to disarm a booby trap. Just remember, a human can't do anything without leaving his scent behind, and your dog will tell you about it, if you listen."

He looked back at the poster and moved his hand to one of the ears. "Hearing. At least twenty to thirty times better than yours. Learn to watch your dog's ears. They will point directly at the source of the noise. Whispers in the night, snapping twigs, heavy breathing, he'll hear it and he'll tell you, if you listen to him. Don't doubt what he tells you. Don't try to outguess him. You will be wrong every time. And that will get you killed."

King dropped the poster to the desk, then stood and walked to one side of the room, eleven pairs of eyes following him. "There's one thing we're better at than a dog: Seeing and identifying stationary objects. Most experts believe dogs see only in black and white or, at best, in different shades. This makes it very difficult for a dog to see and identify anything at a distance that is not moving. The upside of this deficiency is that he can detect the slightest movement at great distances. It's estimated that his ability to detect movement is at least ten times greater than ours."

"What that means, gentlemen, is if you have not used the wind to your partner's advantage and there is a great deal of noise in the area, caused by, oh, I don't know, gunfire maybe, your dog may still save your ass by alerting on Charlie moving through the tree branches or elephant grass."

"Tech. Sergeant Barton, would you move front and center, please." Barton pushed off the blackboard and moved to the front of the room. "The one thing we haven't discussed is your dog's ability to bite. A dog on the attack is impressive but if Charlie is so close you have to turn your dog on him, you are probably in deep shit. Avoid those situations at all costs. Have sense enough to get the fuck out of there, but if you can't, it's nice to know that your dog can hold his own."

"Sergeant Barton, if you would, please." Barton reached down to his right boot and pulled up the pant leg. The fish white scarring and obvious surgical repair had the expected queasy effect on all the students. "What you see on Sergeant Barton's leg is the result of a split second's contact with a Military Working Dog. During one of our classes, Sergeant Barton was acting as the aggressor during attack training. Rather than bite the leather arm sleeve, the dog ducked underneath, grabbed Sergeant Barton by the right calf and was able to give one jerk before his handler called him out. Sergeant Barton was lucky, the hospital was able to repair the muscle and sew it back in place. The one hundred and thirteen stitches and four months of rehabilitation will make a good story for his grandchildren. Remember, gentlemen, these dogs are not pets. If need be, they will fuck somebody up big time. And if you don't pay attention, they will fuck you up."

SATURDAY
NOVEMBER 15, 1969
FORT LAUDERDALE, FLORIDA

Vincent Giancarlo had just finished cutting along the side of the house when he noticed the Post Office station wagon pull away. A smile spread across his face as he realized that with the usual bills and junk mail, maybe, just maybe, there might be a letter from Gianni.

Bernadette turned to her husband as he walked into the kitchen with a big grin on his face. "A letter from Gianni?"

"No, a puppy. Of course it's a letter from Gianni."

He pulled his arm back as she tried to snatch the letter out of his hand. "Jimmy! It's my turn to read it. You read the last one."

"I beg to differ. I believe it was you who kept the last letter a secret until we were done with dinner, then served it with dessert. I also believe it was I who ate both desserts while you read the letter.

"That's right, you did. Pig."

"Call me all the names you want, you still don't get to read this one. And not only that, we don't open it until I'm done with the grass and we're ready for dinner." Before she could say a thing, he turned and walked to the front door. Taking the letter with him.

As Bernadette dished out the food and slid a plate in front of him, Vince poured two glasses of Dago Red. Opening the letter, he held it just far enough away so the writing wasn't blurred.

Hi, Guys,

Hope you both are fine. Everything is pretty much the same. Can't believe how hot it is during the days and how cold it gets at night. I don't see how people can live out here. Rumples is great! Never knew a dog like this could be so much fun. We're pretty much finished with the obedience part of the training. It's really neat what a dog will do with either voice commands or hand signals. When we got our dogs, they were, as Sgt. King put it, "untrained, undisciplined mutts". Now you can really see the difference. When we stop walking or running, they crowd up as close as they can to your left leg and look up, waiting to be petted. Even when we do off-leash training and they're maybe fifteen or twenty yards away, all you have to do is pat your leg and say "heel" and, boy, you should see them come running back to you. It's really neat, especially when they get right in front of you, then almost turn in midair so they end up sitting right by your left leg. I think Rumples does it better than the rest of them. We've been watching some of the other classes do attack training and I can't wait to start that. We've already started training on how to find someone out in the trees and bushes. They call it quartering the area. You find the downwind leg of your area and patrol back and forth. When your dog smells someone out there, he alerts. That means his ears go up and he stares at the spot. Every dog has a different alert and the instructors say you have to learn how to read your dog. Anyway, you just can't believe how far away the dogs can tell when someone is hiding in the boonies. Rumples hasn't let anyone get closer than a couple hundred yards of me. He probably smells them a lot farther away but I just don't know how to read his alert yet. Oh yeah, I almost forgot. We had a little tragedy. One of the dogs got killed. We were training out in the boonies and they figure that he stuck his head in some bushes and got bit in the face by a rattlesnake without his handler knowing about it. They say it's pretty common since the dogs are always sniffing things in the brush. Anyway, the dog got bit and before his handler realized it, his head and neck started swelling up real bad and the choke chain started to cut off his air. When his handler saw what was happening, he started yelling and screaming for the instructors. Sgt. Barton ran over and cut the chain off with a pair of wire cutters. They got the dog back to a pickup truck and they raced him back to the base, but he died before they got there. Boy, his handler was a real basket case. Cried like a baby. Guess I would, too, if something like that happened to Rumples. Going to have to get used to leaving him, though. They told us that we don't keep the dogs we train with. We get a different dog whenever we go to a new base. Well, that's about it for now, I'll write again in a week or so. I got some really neat shots of Rumples on the obstacle course and some of him wearing my fatigue hat and sunglasses.

I love and miss you both. Gianni.

Vince folded the letter and put it back in the envelope. "Sounds like he's having fun, really getting attached to that dog."

"It's too bad about that other dog dying. That must have been horrible." Bernadette picked at her salad. "Jimmy, do you think he'll be safe with all those snakes crawling around. He says they're out in the woods all the time. It could be dangerous."

"For Christ's sake, Ann, he grew up in South Florida. You can't swing a dead cat around here without hitting a water moccasin. He'll be fine, give him a little credit, will ya."

"I just worry. Do you think he's getting enough to eat? He never mentions anything about the food."

"He's in the Air Force, not prison. Of course he's getting enough to eat."

The Ford commercial was just ending and Walter Cronkite's face replaced the shiny new Mustang convertible.

"To recap our top stories. Earlier today the country witnessed the largest demonstration in US history. An estimated two hundred and fifty thousand anti-war demonstrators marched down Pennsylvania Avenue and held a rally at the Washington Monument. Police were forced to break up the demonstration by firing tear gas after the crowd started throwing rocks and bottles and burning the American Flag. Over one hundred arrests were reported. Turning to news from Vietnam, the Defense Department reports during the last week thirty-nine Americans were killed in action and one hundred and thirteen were wounded. Four pilots and crew members are listed as missing in action after being shot down. The Secretary of Defense attributes these low casualty figures as a sign South Vietnamese forces are displaying a willingness to bear greater military responsibility."

CHAPTER 5

MONDAY
FEBRUARY 2, 1970
TAN SON NHUT AIR FORCE BASE
SOUTH VIETNAM

As Gianni rode in the passenger seat of the Security Police pickup truck he constantly switched his gaze from one new sight to another. He was amazed at the size of Tan Son Nhut and at the mixture of civilian and military aircraft lining the flight line. The base easily dwarfed Homestead five times over and if it hadn't been for the stacks of bombs, rockets, and napalm littering the tarmac, it could have been mistaken for a base back in 'the World'. Except for the Air Force Security Police and the Army Military Police, nobody carried guns. There seemed to be no real fear of getting killed, or even hurt. It was not what Gianni expected a war zone to be like. Sure, the VC assassinated someone in Saigon every once in a while, or blew something up, but shit, that kinda' stuff happened in Miami all the time. Maybe the John Wayne movies were all a figment of some writer's imagination. A wave of disappointment washed over him when he realized that going to war wasn't as exciting as he had thought.

Staff Sergeant Jerry Maiberger had been at Tan son Nhut for almost seven months and was the permanent CQ (Charge of Quarters) at the kennels. He had picked Gianni up at the barracks and was taking him to the kennels for his first meeting with his new dog.

They were parked on the side of the runway waiting for two C-130's to land before they could cross over. Maiberger shook his head in utter disbelief as he lit a cigarette.

"All right, let me get this straight. You were pissed off because you were the only one in your dog class that didn't get orders for Southeast Asia and got sent to Homestead instead, right?"

"Yeah." Gianni was watching the first of the C-130's touch down on the runway, black puffs of smoke streaking from its landing gear as the pilot stood on the brakes.

"Okay, okay. So you get stationed at Homestead which is…how far did you say from your home?"

"About sixty miles."

"Yeah, right, you get stationed sixty miles from your home…oh, fuck, this is unbelievable…sixty miles from your home and they tell you that you have to fill out some security clearance papers so you can be assigned to the Presidential Security Detail. I got it so far?"

"Yeah, that's about it."

"And this assignment to protect the President, it guarantees you'll be at Homestead for your whole enlistment, right?"

"Right, the whole four years, or at least as long as Nixon is still President and he keeps the winter White House in Miami." The second C-130 lined up on the runway and prepared to touch down.

Maiberger took a long pull on the cigarette and blew the smoke at a bug clinging to the headliner of the pickup. "And in your infinite wisdom, you told them that you wanted to come to Vietnam and that you wouldn't fill out the papers."

"You pretty much got it."

"You're a fuckin' idiot."

"So I've been told."

Maiberger introduced Gianni to the Kennel Master and some of the handlers then took him on a tour of the kennels. Like the base itself, the kennels also dwarfed the one at Homestead. There were almost thirty dogs with the teams rotating duty between perimeter security and law enforcement patrols on base at night. The duty roster had been developed in an effort to keep up morale and to keep the handlers from getting so bored with the same duty that they overlooked a potentially dangerous situation.

Maiberger pointed out the obstacle course and the dip tank which was used to ward off the hordes of bugs and parasites that always seemed to find their way into a dog's coat. They stopped at the equipment room.

"You got a web belt and helmet and all the other garbage you're supposed to be issued?"

"Yeah, I got it all a few days ago while I was 'in processing. Ammo pouches, poncho, flashlight, all that stuff."

"What about weapons, you get them issued yet?"

"Qualified with 'em two days ago. They issued me a thirty-eight and a rifle. Oh, yeah, I wanted to ask you about that. They gave me a CAR-15 instead of an M-16, said that's what dog handlers got."

"Yeah, they give us the CARs 'cause they're shorter and have a collapsible stock, easier to handle when you're holding on to a leash." Maiberger unlocked the door and stepped inside. The room was packed with leashes, muzzles, tracking harnesses, attack sleeves, and grooming brushes, more than enough equipment for a hundred dogs.

"Damn, you gonna' open a pet shop after the war? How come there's so much stuff?"

"Man, you gotta learn to play the game while you're over here. If you wait 'til you need something, it takes forever and a day to get it. You should hear some of the stories the grunts comin' outta the bush tell. Can't get mags for their rifles, no grenades, no rain gear, no flak vests, all kinda' shit. It's really fucked. Everyone tells you there's a shortage of equipment but you can go into Saigon and buy anything you want on the black market. We supply these ARVN assholes with anything they need and instead of fightin' for their own country, they sell it back to us so we can do their fightin' for 'em. This place is bullshit."

Maiberger filled an empty box with equipment and handed it to Gianni. "You ain't gonna use half this shit but the Sarge says it has to be issued. Keep the muzzle handy 'cause the Vet is real particular about the dogs being muzzled when he checks 'em over. Oh, and check your dog real good before you put him up everyday."

"Check 'em for what?"

"Ticks. The Sarge makes it a habit of checkin' all the dogs for ticks. First time he finds one he just yells and screams a lot. Second time he'll have you paintin' this place with a tooth brush. Don't sleep on post, keep your dog groomed, and he'll pretty much leave you alone. All right, time to go meet your dog."

Gianni followed Maiberger down the long row of chainlink enclosed dog runs. The barking and growling of the first dog let the rest know there was a stranger present and soon every dog in the kennel was voicing his displeasure at the intrusion. Maiberger stopped in front of run number twenty eight. Wired to the top of the gate was a small aluminum plate. Stenciled in black lettering was the name "SHADRACK".

"Well, here ya' go, this is Shadrack. Shadrack, meet Gianni, your new boss."

The dog was not overly impressed with this new figure of authority. Holding his head high, he barked and snarled while spinning round and round, his tail hitting the cinder block walls with each half turn. Not much on manners, he allowed saliva to spew in all directions with gobs of it landing on Maiberger's fatigue pants. For the most part, he looked pretty much like a German shepherd was supposed to look. Black saddle markings over a silver body with a broad chest, good-sized paws and a long, powerful snout filled with glistening white teeth. The similarity stopped at the top of his head.

"You gotta' be shittin' me! That's not a dog, it's a fuckin' mule!"

"What are you talkin' about? Of course it's a dog. We got the paperwork to prove it." Maiberger had known this was coming.

"Jesus Christ, look at his ears! He's all ears! He'd have to duck to go under an overpass!" The dog had been blessed, or cursed, with a set of ears that would have come in handy if a magician wanted to pull him out of a hat. Unfortunately, there were no magicians in sight and his overly large appendages were fodder for countless jokes and snide remarks.

"Hey, come on, Gianni, lighten up. You'll hurt his feelings. Besides, think of all the potential benefits."

"What benefits?"

"Well, let's see. You could string a hammock between his ears, or you could hang your socks over 'em to dry, and if your arms get tired out on post, they'll probably make a great rifle rack."

"That's real fuckin' funny." Gianni couldn't believe what he was seeing. The ears looked more like snorkels. "Hell, he could walk across the ocean floor at Port Everglades and still hear someone fart in Boca Raton. Man, this can't be my dog! Let me have a different one."

"Sorry, everything else is assigned. Here, let me have your leash and muzzle." With a voice that would have made the Lackland instructors proud, Maiberger gave the dog a 'sound verbal command'. "NO, OUT." The dog immediately stopped spinning and barking and stood looking at Maiberger with his head tilted in the universal canine manner as if to say, "Okay, now what?".

"SIT." The dog quickly sat down and waited for his praise. "Good boy, Shadrack, that's a good boy." Maiberger turned and grinned at Gianni. "See, his ears work, he heard me."

"Big deal. He'd a heard ya' if you had written him a letter. Man, how the hell am I supposed to send pictures of him back to my folks? They're gonna' think I ran away and joined the circus."

"Tell 'em you're on a secret mission and the Air Force is trying to develop walking radar. After they get one look at him, they'll probably believe it."

"Come on, just get the damn dog outta' there, this is embarrassing enough as it is. By the way, what happened to his last handler? He shoot himself in the foot just so he wouldn't have to be seen walking around with Dumbo there?"

"Naw, nothing so dramatic. He slipped during attack training, feet went out from under him, one of the other dogs grabbed him by the face."

The image of being bitten in the face by one of the dogs sent a shiver up Gianni's spine. "Oh shit…how is he?"

"Tore off both his lips and part of his cheek. They sent him back to 'the World'."

"Hell of a way to go home."

"Shit, he's better looking now than he was before." Maiberger turned back to the waiting dog. "Hey, Shadrack, how ya' doing, boy, huh, how ya' doing? Yeah, that's a good boy. Wanna' go out and play, huh, wanna' go play?" The dog's tail was now in high gear and swished back and forth over the concrete floor. Maiberger slipped the choke chain on and took off the leather collar. The dog crouched as Maiberger slid the muzzle over his snout. Muzzles usually meant a trip to the vet, which was not a dog's most favorite pastime. Maiberger reached down and scratched the dog's left shoulder. "Don't worry, we're not going to that nasty ol' vet today. We're gonna' go out and play. Let's see if you can tear the shit outta' your new handler, huh? Yeah, that's a good boy, let's see if you can tear his balls off on his first day, yeah? That's a good boy."

"Maiberger, you been around here way too long."

"You got that right." With a gentle slap on his left leg and a softly spoken "heel", Maiberger led the dog out of the run.

TUESDAY
FEBRUARY 17, 1970
FT. LAUDERDALE, FLORIDA

The letter was on the dining room table when Vince arrived home from work. He picked up the envelope and walked into the kitchen where his wife was just putting the finishing touches on dinner. Holding the letter up to the ceiling light, he examined it carefully.

"What on earth are you doing?"

"Just checking."

"Checking what?" She picked up the roast to put it on the table.

"Well, we haven't gotten a letter from Gianni since he left and I figured you couldn't wait to see what he had to say. I was checking to see if you steamed it open."

"Very funny. Now sit down so we can read it, and leave that damn TV off."

As Vince slit open the top of the envelope, five pictures fell out on the table. "Whoa, look at these. What the hell is he standing next to? Looks like a small mule or a huge rabbit."

"Here, let me see, come on, let me see." Vince handed her the pictures with a smile. "Oh, my God, look at that poor dog. What's wrong with his ears? They're huge! Oh, Jimmy, he's so funny looking. Why would they keep a dog that looks like that? Don't you think Gianni looks a little skinny? Do you think he's lost weight? I hope he's eating."

"Ann, he's only been there a couple of weeks. How much weight could he have lost. He looks fine. Too bad I can't say the same about the dog. Boy, is that one homely mutt." Vince continued to look at the pictures for a moment longer. "Well, we know one thing for sure. They don't have him patrolling too close to the runways...the dog's ears would interfere with low flying aircraft."

"Just read the letter." Ann continued to look at the pictures and shake her head in disbelief.

FRIDAY
FEBRUARY 20, 1970
THIRTY MILES EAST OF TAY NIHN
SOUTH VIETNAM

1st Lieutenant Will Evans huddled over the map. Beads of sweat rolled off his chin and landed with a soft plop, only to roll off the plastic covering and fall to the jungle floor. Sergeant Geoffrey Huebner crouched next to him, chewing on the corner of his mustache as he compared the map to their surroundings. He already knew what his lieutenant's next words would be. Having taken over the squad as a spit and polish 'know it all', the jungle, and the war, had taught him to trust his men and to rely on their instincts.

"What'da ya' think, Geoff?"

"You gotta' figure he knew pretty much where he went down. Tay Ninh is twenty-five, thirty miles west of here. We got An Loc north, another thirty, thirty-five miles. He sure as hell wouldn't have gone that way unless he wanted to spend the rest of the war as a guest of the Gooks. He had to head this way, try to make it to Bien Hoa, meet up with some friendlies."

Will Evans, born Wilbert Theodore Evans was twenty-six years old and the son of a retired Army physician. Holding the rank of full colonel for the last fifteen years of his career, the senior Evans was able to raise his son in the surroundings of higher echelon military and medical notables. There had never been any question in his parent's minds that young master Evans would grow up to follow in his father's footsteps. It didn't occur to them that they had never bothered to ask and it had been more than a mild shock when he announced that instead of enrolling in medical school, he would attend Virginia Military Institute. Although not overly demanding, either physically or academically, the schooling had been less than pleasurable. Constantly taunted by other students, and on occasion, instructors, because of his slight build, pallid complexion, and inability to grow more than the faintest of 'peach fuzz' facial hair, the young Evans became obsessed with dispelling any question of his masculinity. Graduating third in a class of over two hundred had convinced everyone but young master Evans.

Three months into his second tour in Vietnam, he often wondered if that was why he had volunteered to lead the Search and Rescue team; if it was his way to prove himself a man. As slow as the metamorphosis was in his mind, his body showed none of the lingering doubt. What the institute had failed to do, the jungle had. Constant exposure to the tropical sun had turned his once pasty soft white skin deep bronze. Humping a sixty pound pack, rifle, and belts of ammo through dense jungle in the searing heat had left him with broad, muscled shoulders that narrowed down to a slim waist. Scarred from pushing through thorn infested bush, he no longer had the boyish look of his school years, he looked like what his spirit hoped to become; a combat soldier.

Evans raised his compass and compared the direction to the map. "His plane went in here and they saw a good chute just south of it, here. I figure we're about five, maybe six clicks south, southeast of the chute sighting."

"Yeah, looks about right but that's what worries me. He's been out here what…four days? Should'a been able to make six klicks in that time and we haven't seen a sign of him."

"Big jungle, Geoff. We could'a walked within ten feet of 'im and never known it."

"Yeah, the Gooks could be ten feet away and we'd never know that either." Huebner was not a big believer in their ability to go into the bush and find downed fliers. Blindly walking around the jungle looking for some trace of a lost airman was not the most efficient, and certainly not the safest method. The only problem was no one could come up with a better plan. If there was the slightest chance a downed pilot was alive, they had to try. It was like looking for a needle in a haystack…a deadly haystack. Usually pilots were picked up right away by the choppers or they didn't make it out at all. The squad had been formed to change that. This was their seventh Search & Rescue Mission and so far it wasn't going any better than the previous ones.

Three times they had found nothing, absolutely nothing. No chute, no body, no equipment, nothing. It was like the pilot had never bailed out, or they weren't searching the right area. On one mission they had found a body with a broken neck. He had probably been killed after he landed in the trees and slipped out of his chute harness, risking the long jump to the ground. The risk hadn't paid off.

On another mission the F-4 crew had made it to the ground safely and had talked to the cover aircraft for over twenty minutes. They were still alive when the choppers arrived. Alive enough to see the choppers repeatedly try to land and repeatedly be driven off by the intense ground fire. They were still alive when two more Cobra gunships arrived to replace the two that had run out of ammo. Their rockets, grenades, and mini-gun fire had no more effect on the determined enemy than the first two. Sometime between the time two more gunships arrived on station, the two pilots died. What Huebner and the squad found was that the pilots had died fighting for their lives. They had holed up in a small depression next to the clearing where the choppers had tried to land. The area around the bodies was scarred with bullet holes and grenade fragments. Broken tree limbs, shredded leaves, and gouged out patches of earth were testament to the ferocity of the fight. In the end, the might of the American war machine was no match for the fear of hurting one of its own. In spite of all the rockets, bombs, and grenades that were hurled down in an effort to kill, maim, or just distract, none of them landed closer than 100 yards to the stranded airmen. Close enough to keep many of the enemy at bay, but not nearly close enough to keep away the ones that mattered.

The fourth mission had been the worst. The pilot had activated his emergency locator beacon and was just waiting for the cavalry to ride to the rescue. The mission was simple. Go in, find the pilot, let him thank them profusely, secure an LZ, get on the choppers, and haul ass. There was only one glitch. They couldn't find the downed airman. The OV-10 Bronco pilot confirmed that they were within yards of where the beacon was located but no grateful pilot came running out to meet them. Something was wrong, they could feel it, and they had to figure out what it was before it killed them. The answer came in the form of a booming explosion and nerve shattering screams.

"Booby trap, booby trap! Who's down, Goddamnit, who's down?"

Monie answered. "It's Crowley, Crowley's hit!"

By the time Evans had made it over to Crowley, the medic was already there. Crowley's high pitched screams pierced the air even more than the explosion, and if anyone was near, they were sure to be on their way. "How is he, Doc?"

Schoonhoven looked up and shook his head. "He's not good Lieutenant, looks like he tripped a grenade. Took shrapnel in the kneecap, blew most of it away…has a compound fracture of the right ankle, fragments along the radius of the right leg and a stretching laceration along the posterior region of the left thigh." Schoonhoven's blood soaked hand dripped as he pointed to the wounded man's legs and chest. "At least two pieces punctured his right lung resulting in diminished lung function and he's aspirating blood."

Evans let out a loud sigh as he drug his bush hat over his face and looked up at the thick jungle growth. "In English Doc!, give it to me in English!"

"We gotta' get him outta' here ASAP or he ain't gonna make it."

Huebner's mind still raced with thoughts of that mission. If the OV-10 hadn't been on station, or the pick-up chopper had been a little farther away, they would have had to fight their way out. They weren't equipped for prolonged contact and it had only been luck that had gotten them to the chopper seconds ahead of the NVA. It had been the first time the NVA had turned the tables on them and set up an ambush.

They had either killed or captured the pilot and used his emergency locator beacon as a lure. The scattered booby traps would have decimated a lesser experienced squad of men. Fear and experience had kept Evans and his men alive. Luck had gotten them on the chopper with their wounded comrade. Their luck couldn't last forever.

"I'm thinking we stay on this line 'til we get to the chute sighting."

Huebner took a deep drag on his cigarette and let it out with an audible sigh, "What then?"

"Shit, Geoff, how the fuck do I know. See if we can pick up some sign of his trail, find a body, walk into an ambush, follow the yellow brick road, I don't know. You got any better ideas?"

"When I think of one, I'll let you know."

"Yeah. Well, 'til then we're stuck with what we got. Let's get to it."

Huebner field-stripped his cigarette and stood up to move over to the squad. Evan's watched as he walked away, his mind slipping back to the time he had first been introduced to his squad sergeant. Huebner's slow, casual nod of the head and a, "Howdy LT", instead of the crisp regulation salute and the expected, "Good morning Lieutenant, it is a pleasure to meet you", had, in Evans' mind, been the height of military discourtesy. The silver bar on his collar, the bar that he had worked so hard to earn, deserved, no, demanded more respect than the slovenly dressed soldier standing before him displayed. With a scarred and gouged M-16 loosely held in his left hand, Huebner had been decked out in sun bleached, sweat stained faded fatigues, the material worn so thin in places that Evans could actually see through it. Tattered combat boots, the leather on the toes worn and scuffed to the point that they bore little or no semblance to the spit shined brogan's that were the order of the day in the Institute, were covered with dirt, mud, and anything else the jungle floor had to offer. As Huebner had stood there, waiting for the lieutenant to bestow his philosophy of the war, something all new lieutenants thought they were required to do, he shifted the rifle to his right hand then leaned it up against the tent wall.

Evans first saw that the tip of the ring finger on the left hand was missing and that the knuckles of both hands were calloused and scarred. At thirty-eight, Huebner had been in the Army nineteen years and had been busted down in rank no less than six times. To Evans the scars and missing finger-tip underscored the casual comments in the man's personnel file that he had a penchant for bar-brawls…but always 'only' to uphold the honor of the Army.

Evans remembered that first meeting. He remembered the cigarette dangling out of the corner of the sergeant's mouth, smoke curling up, leaving a yellowish tint to the jet black, non-regulation walrus mustache. He remembered staring up at the man who towered over him, and seeing the eyes, the eyes that he would never forget. They had bored into Evans like a tracer piercing the jungle night, and like the tracer, searching for a target, Huebner seemed to search for something inside Evans. Something Evans feared he didn't posses. At first impression the man was a disgrace. Lacking in any military bearing or protocol, he was the complete antithesis of what Evans thought a soldier should be. It hadn't taken long to find out he was wrong.

The swarm of insects buzzing around his face brought Evans back to reality as he ran a sweaty arm across his eyes. A slight grin spread across his face as he thought about Huebner. The man might be a rogue, but as Evans had come to realize, he was just what he needed and what a professional soldier should be.

"All right, listen up." Huebner crouched and motioned the squad closer to him. "We're five, maybe six klicks out, keep your eyes open." He waited as each squad member slipped his arms through his rucksack and stood up. With each of them carrying over sixty pounds of equipment, a five minute rest was as welcome as a cold beer, and more important. "Smith, take the point; Monie, back door."

Lazirus Jonas Smith a twenty-year-old black man from Mobile, Alabama, hated the Army, and only sometimes tolerated whites, but had developed a fierce loyalty to the rest of the squad. Up until he had been assigned to search and rescue, contact with the VC or NVA had been fairly regular, and no matter how he had been treated by the 'honkies' back in 'the World', out in the bush he was just another ground pounder. The color of his skin didn't mean 'shit'. If he was out of water, one of the white boys was as quick to hand him his canteen as his closest friend, Delmar Robinson, the only other black man in the squad.

In total contrast to Smith's jet black skin and 130-pound frame, Robinson was light-complected and tipped the scales at over 220, of which maybe half a pound was fat. His size had always been an advantage back in 'the World' since few were dumb enough to 'fuck' with him. Being in the bush, however, was another matter. Not only did his bulk make it harder on him in the heat, it also meant he had to lug around the heavy M-60 machine gun. The rest of the squad carried two extra belts of the M-60 ammo criss-crossed over their shoulders, but not to be outdone, Robinson carried a third belt around his waist to, as he put it, "cover your skinny white asses when the shit really gets deep." No one would ever say that Robinson wasn't as fearless as he was big.

Smith moved out, his eyes constantly darting back and forth along the ground and up and down the trees. Walking point was not only the most dangerous position, it was also the most tiring. When they were forced to walk down a trail, which they avoided like the plague, it was the point man's responsibility to look for booby traps as well as signs of ambush. When they made their own trail through the heavy jungle vegetation, he had to hack, or push his way through. More than once the point man had looked down to see the body of a snake cut cleanly in half, the two pieces wriggling in their separate death dances. The sight of the dying reptile was overshadowed by the thought of what would have happened if the swinging machete had missed its unseen mark. All in all, walking point was a walk in the park...a very deadly park.

They reached the area where the pilot had bailed out two hours before sunset. After his first and only radio transmission, nothing more had been heard from the downed pilot. The chances of his being alive or not captured were slim, but as long as there was a chance…

The squad crouched just inside the tree line at the clearing where the chopper had tried to pick up the pilot. The jungle was shredded from rocket impacts and thousands of 7.62 machine-gun bullets. Evans strained to see through the thick growth on the far side of the clearing. A whole NVA battalion could be in there and they'd never know it until the shooting started.

"Geoff, have Robinson set up his gun here, that'll give us some cover if we have to come back in a hurry."

"Ya' know, this is as good a place to bed down as any. How 'bout we drop packs here and just carry water and ammo?"

"Good idea. Tell Boardman to try and raise the Bronco while we check out the other side." He glanced up through the canopy of trees. "Let's do it, we don't have much light left."

Evans led the remainder of the squad around the clearing, staying well inside the tree line. With everyone huddled inside the thick growth Huebner made his way to the edge of the tree line and signaled to Robinson. Wordlessly the squad moved out in the direction of the chute. Each man alternated his attention between the ground, his front, each side, and up in the trees. The evidence of a fierce firefight was unmistakable. Bushes, small trees, and ground cover had been trampled flat by men crashing through the jungle. Empty shell casings littered the ground. Shreds of clothing, most of it blood stained, some still wrapped around pieces of flesh, lay scattered about. Monie stopped and looked down at a boot, five inches of leg protruding from its top. Three feet away a colony of ants worked on what was left of the top part of a skull. Close-cropped black hair still clung to the gray, curved bone. Monie moved on. Dead Gooks didn't bother him anymore; it was the live ones he was worried about.

Smith saw it first. It hung from the trees, gently fluttering back and forth. He froze and looked back over his shoulder. Craig Tuckett,

Crowley's replacement, saw Smith standing five yards away with his finger to his lips. Smith pointed to the hanging chute, raised his right fist above his head and moved it in a circle. Tuckett acknowledged with a nod of his head and moved off to get the rest of the squad.

The squad crouched in the trees, nervously alternating their gaze from the chute to the surrounding jungle. Evans whispered, "What'da ya' think, Geoff?"

"They either beat feet before they could get it down or they left it on purpose and this place is fucking alive with booby traps."

"Only one way to find out."

"Yeah, thanks." Huebner turned around and looked at Smith. "Lazirus, how 'bout you and me takin' a walk through the tulips?"

"Just what I always dreamed of, gettin' my ass blown to hell with some white boy. Lordy, Lordy, how did I ever get so lucky."

Evans made his way to the hanging chute where Huebner and Smith were standing. Huebner's eyes constantly searched the area as he spoke.

"Doesn't look like they even tried to pull it down. No sign of any traps, no spent brass near the chute, and no blood trail. I think they were way too busy dealin' with the choppers and Spads to worry about it. Question is, did they snatch the pilot or is he wandering around out here somewhere?"

"Well, nothing we can do about it now," Evans tilted his head and looked at the fading light filtering through the tree tops, "gonna' be dark in a little while. Let's leave it hanging in case someone comes snooping around tonight, we'll try to pick up some kind of trail in the morning."

Evans sat down next to Boardman, his back propped up against his rucksack, the rest of the squad silently setting up the night's defensive perimeter. "You contact the Bronco?"

"Roger that, LT. "

"Any news on the pilot?"

"Naw, that's what he wanted to know from us. Told 'im we were in the area but we hadn't found anything."

Evans unscrewed the cap of his canteen, reached into the pocket of his jungle fatigues, pulled out a plastic bottle of salt tablets and popped three into his mouth, chasing them with a swig of water. As he slipped the canteen back into its canvas pouch he strained to look across the clearing. "Big time fight back there. Pieces of bodies and shell casings everywhere."

"Booby traps?"

"Didn't find a one. Found the chute, though, still hanging from a tree. Doesn't look like it was touched"

"Maybe the guy's got a chance."

"Yeah, if the Gooks don't already have 'im."

They started their search as rivulets of light started to stab through the trees. It was slow, tedious and nerve-racking. Even though Huebner and Smith had checked the area around the chute the night before, it had to be checked again. You didn't have to be in-country long to know that the night belonged to the Gooks. Just because they hadn't heard anything didn't mean no one had been there.

They checked below the chute itself, then pulled it down and carefully, looking for any message the pilot might have left. Direction he was planning to head, map coordinates, some kind of code word, anything. The only thing they found was a small indentation in the ground where the pilot had jumped the five or six feet after he slipped out of the harness. As the sunlight got stronger, the distinct sole markings of his flight boots glared back at them.

Evans and Huebner crouched over the boot prints as the rest of the squad stared out into the trees. This was no time to be taken by surprise. "If he made his radio call before he got out of his chute, we know he lived long enough to get down."

"Yeah, and if he made it after he was down, ya gotta' figure he didn't just stand around here shootin' the shit. He had to go off in the bush, which means he had to leave some kind of trail."

Huebner looked in the direction the boot prints pointed. "Here, look, part of a heel mark. Here's another one. Shit this guy was bookin', look at the stride."

Evans pushed himself up and followed Huebner. "These Air Force guys may not be the smartest people in the world but they probably know enough not to stop and smell the roses when the gardeners are trying to kill 'em.

"LT, take a look at this." Huebner was standing behind a thick stand of bushes, pointing at something that was invisible to Evans who was only five feet away. The glove was lying on the ground at the base of the bushes.

Evans checked the area before he bent down and picked it up. "Flight glove."

"He probably made his call from here. Took the glove off for some reason, maybe to use the radio, then either left it here on purpose or forgot it if he had to leave in a hurry. See the boot marks? He was crouched down and twistin' around a lot, probably watchin' to see what Charlie was doing. There's a couple more prints, headin' out that way."

They followed the boot prints through the bush and found two pieces of torn flight suit clinging to the branches. The trail abruptly vanished when the patches of bare earth turned into a sea of dead and rotting leaves.

"Fuck, now which way?"

Huebner crouched down, resting his weight on the stock of his M-16 and wiping his face with his bush hat. He was dying for a cigarette, but now was not the time. "Well, ya' gotta' figure he was still moving pretty fast and probably not worrying about making noise. The choppers had to be makin' a hell of a racket givin' him cover. He probably picked a line and went for it, just tryin' to put distance between him and the Gooks."

"Yeah, but if he kept going on this line, he would have run right into the area they hit with napalm."

"If he stays here, he gets shot or captured. If he keeps going, *maybe* he gets zapped by our guys. The *maybe* is a better bet. I say he kept goin' straight."

"Okay, let's give it a shot." Evans didn't like the idea of crossing the leaf covered ground, God only knew what could be hidden under there. No one really thought it would never happen to them, but Crowley had probably thought the same thing. The rest of the squad lagged just behind them and to both sides.

Ten minutes had gone by and they were starting to think they had guessed wrong when Evans tapped Huebner on the arm and pointed off to the right. Lying next to a fallen log was the limp and decomposing body of an NVA soldier, the blackened hole in his left cheek small testament to the fist sized piece of skull blown out of the back of his head. Huebner prodded the body with the muzzle of his rifle, shaking off the swarm of flesh eating insects.

"Looks like our boy's work. Small caliber entry, powder burns on the face...probably ran right into 'im then shot 'im close up."

Evans swatted at the bugs clinging to his face. "This guy's got an angel siting on his shoulder."

"Yeah...or the Devil is fuckin' with 'im"

They searched 'til just before dark when Robinson, stopping to take a leak, spotted an empty water bottle wedged between the branches of a bush.

"What the fuck is the matter with them? Don't they teach 'em to hang on to these things? What's he gonna' do if he finds water? Pray for rubber pockets? Stupid motherfuckers." Evans was furious. "The guy's been doin' so good at staying alive, up 'til now."

Huebner looked at the bottle. "Maybe he left it here on purpose, hoping someone would find it."

"Bullshit. If he was tryin' to leave a trail, how come this is the first thing we've found? And if he wanted to leave this for someone to find, how come it was stuck in the fuckin' bushes?"

Huebner couldn't help but smile. Evans wasn't mad at the pilot, the jet jockey didn't know any better. He was pissed at the way they were trying to find him. Stumbling around in the bush looking for pieces of ripped flight suits and empty water bottles was not a surefire formula for success.

The sun had been up for almost three hours when Evans signaled for a break. Huebner dragged his bush hat across the back of his neck and sat down next to him. He looked at the map the Lieutenant was studying and fixed their position. "Maybe this guy's not as dumb as we thought. He's headed right for the stream."

"He's gotta' be thirstier than hell by now. We're carrying five times what he had and we're just about out."

"He probably figures he outran the Gooks and now he's just tryin' to stay alive 'til he runs into some friendlies." Huebner looked up and glanced around at the squad. Even though they had all dropped their packs, they kept their weapons in their hands, constantly searching the trees. Monie and Tuckett shared a cigarette, handing it back and forth. It was always risky to smoke on patrol, the smell carried forever, but when you had to shit in the trees and wipe your ass with soggy paper, eat cold C-rations, and sleep two hours at a time, the comfort and pleasure of a cigarette was often worth the risk.

Evans traced his finger along the route they had taken. "Looks like he's got his head on straight. He'd never make the next water without stopping at this one. Let's hope he changes direction after he makes the stream though." Evans looked over at his men, then pulled out one of his own cigarettes. "Five minutes, then we hit it."

They lost the trail after about an hour and had spent the next two hours trying to pick it up again. Smith was getting nervous. So far they had been lucky, they hadn't spotted any Gooks and the Gooks hadn't spotted them, but their luck couldn't last forever.

Evans stopped the squad, shrugging under the weight of his pack as he pulled out the map. "Damnit, now what?"

"Shit, we know he was headed for the stream, it has to be marked on his survival map. I say we quit wastin' time tryin' to pick up his trail and just head right for it."

"I think you're right." Evans folded the map and put it back in his pocket. "Have Tuckett take the point. We'll push straight through."

They smelled the water long before they saw it. Tuckett raised his right hand and dropped down to one knee. Evans and Huebner made their way up to him.

"Stream is dead ahead, LT. I think maybe we ought'a do a little recon 'fore we go pushin' through. Haven't seen any sign of Charlie but no tellin' what could be sittin' up there."

Evans turned back at the squad. "All right, let's get Robinson set up here for cover. Then you and Huebner check it out."

They were back in less than fifteen minutes. Their boots and pant legs wet up to the knees. "Looks good. Water's clear, no heavy movement through it upstream." Huebner lit a cigarette, took a deep drag, then handed it to Tuckett.

"Any sign of our boy?"

"Negative, we checked about twenty yards up and down stream on both sides, didn't see a thing."

Evans pulled out his map and fixed their position. "All right, this is where we lost his trail, right about here. We figured he'd head for the stream but he might not have moved straight like we did. If he's following his map, he's gotta' know he has to head toward Bien Hoa. That means he would have to veer south after he made a water stop. Tuckett, get the guys ready, we better go find this guy before he really gets himself in trouble."

Huebner took the cigarette back and took a long last drag of it. "How ya' want to do it, LT?"

"I figure we'll hit the stream and have Monie and Smith check upstream for a couple hundred yards. If they don't find anything, we'll head downstream and see if our hunch is right."

"Sounds good to me."

It took Monie and Smith over an hour to check the two hundred yards, returning to the squad after finding no trace of the pilot.

They moved downstream, following the bank and searching for less than an hour when Tuckett held up his right hand. Evans watched him as he studied something on the ground, checked the area around it, then picked it up and hurried back to the squad.

"This was laying on the bank, just out of the water."

Evans took it out of his hand and showed it to Huebner. "It's his other flight glove. Look at this, the fingers are all torn to shit, got blood on it, too."

"Hope this is all that's wrong with 'im. You find anything else, Tuckett?"

"Yeah, lot of boot prints. Looks like he sat down at the edge of the stream, too. Guy's not real smart, takin' a break like that where Charlie could walk right up on him."

"Ya' think he crossed over?"

"Yeah, had to. No prints leadin' further down stream, just out of the trees and up to the water."

"Just his boots?"

"Just his. Looks like this guy really does have an angel sittin' on his shoulder."

Evans muttered to himself as he signaled for the rest of the squad to move out. "I don't give a shit if he sold his soul to the Devil just as long as we either find him or he makes it outta' here on his own."

After crossing the stream and following his trail through the heavy jungle vegetation for almost three hours, Tuckett suddenly stopped and dropped to the ground. The squad spread out in a defensive perimeter. Tuckett signaled for them to stay put and crawled off into the bush. Five minutes later he reappeared and made his way back to Evans and Huebner.

Out of breath and sweating like he had just run an obstacle course, he gasped out what none of them wanted to hear. "I don't believe it, I don't fuckin' believe it. He's on a fuckin' trail."

Evans wasn't sure he'd heard his point man right. "What! What'da ya' mean a 'trail'?"

"He's movin' down a trail. He's outta' the trees and takin' a fuckin' trail."

"Jesus Fucking Christ! What is this asshole thinkin' about? Why doesn't he just pop smoke and wait for Charlie to come get 'im. Goddamnit!" The only worse news Tuckett could have given him was that he had found the pilot's body. "Maybe he just crossed over and went back into the trees?"

"Don't think so, LT. Followed his boot prints for about fifty yards. Looks like he walked right down the middle of the trail and kept on goin'. Damn boot prints stand out like a neon sign."

Huebner looked at the ground and shook his head. "Fuck! If we hadn't wasted so much time when we lost his trail, we might'a caught up with 'im before he got this far." His tongue snaked out and caught the corner of the mustache. "You see any signs of the trail being used?"

"Big time, Sarge. Cart tracks, bicycle tracks, sandals and boo coo NVA boots."

"Shit. Ya' think they've got 'im?"

"Not sure but it looks like his tracks are the freshest and I don't think he's that far ahead of us, maybe only a few hours." Tuckett knocked a spider off the toe of his boot and looked back up at Evans and Huebner. "'Course I'm not a fuckin' Indian so what the hell do I know about trackin'."

"Let's hope you've watched enough Westerns to have learned something." Huebner chewed furiously on the mustache, trying to figure out what to do next.

"I do know one thing for sure, he's hurt. He's draggin' his right leg and using a pole or branch or something to support himself."

"Well, that's great. Anything else you'd like to tell us, Tuckett? Like he took all his clothes off and left them in a neat little pile 'cause he could move faster naked?" Evans was not happy. How could anybody be stupid enough to walk down the middle of a trail, especially one being used by the Gooks? Evans was even madder knowing that the squad would have to walk down the same trail. They could never match his speed by staying in the trees, bad leg or not.

Evans glanced at his watch, then up at the sky peeking through the trees. "Damnit, Geoff, what'da ya' think about moving at night?"

"We could be in deep shit if we ran into Charlie."

"What choice do we have?"

"None. Gonna' be a bitch tryin' to track him in the dark though."

"Yeah, but we gotta' figure he'll stay on the trail 'til dark, then bed down somewhere close. We're gonna' have to chance it."

Evans turned back to Tuckett. "Send Boardman up here and tell the guys we're gonna' rest up here and move out again at dark."

"Right, LT."

Evans pulled out a cigarette and lit it. "I don't like this shit, Geoff. It's bad enough walkin' down a trail, but doin' it at night, we might as well be sellin' Avon and ring their fuckin' doorbell."

Huebner looked through the trees toward the trail. "Ya' know, Will, maybe Tuckett was right. Maybe what we really need is an Indian."

"Good idea. Then we could just walk up to the Gooks, smoke a peace pipe and trade 'em some beads for our pilot." Evans rolled his eyes. "What the fuck are we gonna' do with an Indian?"

"Tracking. We need a better way to track these guys. We need someone who knows what the hell they're doing. If we hadn't lost this guy's trail so many times and wasted so much time tryin' to find it again, we might have caught up with 'im already." Huebner's legs were cramping from crouching so long and he sat down next to Evans. "We gotta' bring in someone who knows how to follow a trail, find the things we don't even know to look for."

"Some one…or some thing." Evans had a blank stare on his face.

"What'da ya' mean 'some thing'?"

"Remember when we flew into Tan Son Nhut to see Crowley before they shipped him out to Japan? Well, how do they protect the base at night?"

"Put a curfew on the Gooks, they all have to be home by ten. How the fuck do I know how they protect the base? With guns and bullets, just like we would." Huebner was starting to feel like he was being interviewed by Jack Paar.

"Come on, Geoff, think about it. They use dog teams, they pull their grunts in at night and replace them with dog teams."

"Like I said, yeah? So?"

"Well, why do they use dogs? They must do something better than people do."

"Sure, they can take a shit without wiping their ass and they can lick their balls. Look, LT, we need some *one* out here who knows how to track, not some *thing* that wants to chase cars and piss on every tree."

They waited until it was totally dark, then set off. Spreading out, they walked on each side of the trail, as close to the tree line as possible. Smith lagged a hundred yards behind while Monie walked point, stopping every three or four minutes and crouching close to the ground with a red filtered flashlight, checking for the pilot's boot marks. The pilot was either very, very stupid, or very, very tired. His prints plodded along in a straight line.

They had been on the trail for almost four hours when Smith made his way past the rest of the squad and whispered one word to Evans. "Gooks."

Evans held up his hand to stop the squad and motioned Smith to get Monie. He signaled Robinson and Schoonhoven to set up on the right side of the trail, just ahead of the rest of the squad. As everyone disappeared into the trees, Evans held up his rifle, pointed at it, and shook his head as if to say, "no firing, let 'em pass".

Each man knew his job and quietly prepared for it. Tuckett was the last man in line, closest to where the enemy soldiers would be coming from. He pulled out two extra magazines, placed them on the ground next to him, and moved his fire selector to full auto. If they were spotted, it would be his job to open up and drive the enemy up the trail into the devastating fire of Robinson's M-60.

Smith and Monie laid two grenades apiece in front of them and switched their selectors to semi-automatic. If the Dinks took cover in the trees on the other side of the trail, they would be greeted with four quick explosions and thousands of pieces of flying shrapnel. Knowing that Evans and Huebner would have moved their selectors to full auto, they ensured that everyone wouldn't be reloading at the same time.

Schoonhoven had already stripped off his two belts of M-60 ammo and laid them next to the big gun as he prepared to feed the hundred-round belt of ammo already loaded into it. Robinson peered down the gun's barrel and waited.

Boardman stripped off the radio and propped it behind the base of a tree. It wouldn't do to have a stray bullet smash through their only means of escape.

It was less than a minute later when they heard the high-pitched voices of the Vietnamese soldiers. Tuckett saw them first. Five NVA regulars walking down the trail in a group, their AK-47s slung over their shoulders, talking to each other like they were on a pleasant Sunday afternoon stroll. Confident that there were no Americans in the area, they made no effort to hide their presence or assign a point man. If they had stopped, they surely would have seen the cluster of American boot prints.

As they passed Tuckett, he raised ever so slightly and aimed his rifle at the back of the soldier closest to him. The first, and foremost rule of combat was to never give the other guy a chance. Shooting an unsuspecting enemy in the back was infinitely preferable to letting him shoot you in the face. Tuckett knew he could kill all five of the soldiers before any of them would be able to unsling their rifles. He also knew that if these soldiers had any friends in the area, they wouldn't wait for a written invitation to join the party.

It took thirty seconds for the enemy soldiers to pass the entire squad and another two minutes before anyone dared move. Without being told, Tuckett picked up his magazines and moved through the trees a hundred yards back down the trail. Satisfied that another patrol was not moving up behind the first, he made his way back to Evans.

"All clear, LT. Looks like they're alone."

Evans looked at each member of the squad. "Anyone see a radio?"

"I didn't see one."

"Looked clean, LT."

"AK's and grenades, nothing heavy, and no radio." The rest of the squad agreed.

"Okay, good." Evans turned to Huebner. "How 'bout it, Geoff?"

"They're movin' up on our guy and don't even know it. If they decide to stop, one of 'em is bound to see his boot prints. We gotta' stay close and hope our guy hears 'em and gets off the trail, if he hasn't already."

"All right, we stay on the trail. Monie, you've got the point. Keep an eye out for them leavin' the trail, we don't need to walk into an ambush."

"What about his boot prints? How am I supposed to see 'em?

"You're gonna' have to do the best you can without a light. We don't want to walk by him if he's already holed up. Any questions?" Evans glanced at each face. "All right, let's move."

Monie stayed far enough behind the NVA soldiers so his movements couldn't be seen but close enough so he could hear their constant conversation. He couldn't believe they hadn't seen the pilot's boot marks just to the right of the middle of the trail. This was one lucky son of a bitch.

They had been following the patrol for almost two hours when Monie suddenly dropped into a crouch and raised his hand. Constantly looking over his shoulder at the enemy soldiers, he made his way back to Evans. "Bad shit, LT. I think they stopped for a break. Sounds like they're right in the middle of the trail and hunkering down for chow or something."

"Goddamnit. What about the pilot?"

"His tracks still lead right down the trail but it looks like he's draggin' his leg a lot more."

Evans motioned for Huebner to move up. "Geoff, they stopped on the trail. Ya' think you and Monie can get close enough to see what's goin' on?"

"We can get close enough...the trick is gettin' there without them seein' us." Huebner and Monie dropped their packs, quietly checked their rifles, and moved off down the trail. They had gone less than a hundred yards when the darkness ahead of them was shattered by the beam of a flashlight.

The soldier holding the light rummaged through his pack, took something out then handed it to the soldier next to him who repeated the process with his own pack. As he struggled with an obviously-entangled object, he momentarily lost his grip on the flashlight and it tumbled to the ground, its beam sending eerie shadows along the trail. Huebner and Monie could hear the rest of the soldiers laugh as their clumsy friend stood up to retrieve the errant light.

As the soldier stooped to pick up the light, his eyes locked on something that shouldn't have been there. He lowered himself to both knees, picked up the light, and shined it on the ground. Huebner and Monie watched as the soldier crawled along the ground on his hands and knees, the beam of the light stabbing out ahead of him.

The laughter of his friends died down as they watched his curious actions. The soldier suddenly stood up and excitedly called to the rest of the patrol. Another soldier, the leader of the patrol, took the light and walked several yards up the trail. He stopped and shined the light ahead of him, moving it from one edge of the trail to the other. After several moments, he turned and started shouting orders. The four remaining soldiers quickly picked up their packs and weapons and moved off down the trail.

Huebner nudged Monie in the side. "Now we're fucked, they spotted his trail. Go get the LT, I'll wait here."

"They found his trail?" Evans was crouched next to Huebner, both men staring into the dark unknown.

"Yeah, big time. Took off outta' here like Uncle Ho was waitin' for 'em."

"All right, we've got no choice, gotta' take 'em before they find him." Evans looked around at the squad, then back up the trail. "Damnit, we should'a hit 'em when they passed us." He turned and looked directly at his sergeant, the darkness making his features hard to distinguish. "Think we should try to get in front of 'em by going through the trees?"

"Can't do it, we'd make too much noise tryin' to go that fast. We either catch up and hit 'em or wait 'til they find our guy and take 'em then."

"All right, if we can get close enough to take 'em out real quick, we do it, otherwise we just follow 'em…see if they find our guy." He twisted around on his heals, motioned to one of the men behind him then whispered into his ear. "Monie, you and Smith take the point, one on each side of the trail."

It took five minutes before they could hear voices again and another two before they could see the light bobbing up and down on the trail. The NVA patrol moved like a pack of hounds on a scent. The leader walked down the center of the trail, the light pointing out the boot marks. The four remaining soldiers lagged several yards behind, staying closer to the trees.

Huebner knew that trying to hit the unsuspecting patrol now would be foolish at best and disastrous at worst. With at least a hundred yards separating them and only the thin beam of the flashlight illuminating the ground in front of the leader, their chance of killing all five men was slim. At least one, probably more, would make it into the trees. The thought of a prolonged firefight, or, even worse, one of the soldiers getting away and bringing back help, was not a situation Huebner wanted to deal with. They had no choice but to follow the patrol and hope for a better opportunity.

Time seemed to drag on forever but in less than two hours Smith and Monie both dropped to one knee and signaled for the squad to stop. Even though the nighttime heat was not overly oppressive, each man was drenched in sweat and almost totally exhausted. If the anticipation of death is worse than death itself, the same is true for combat. Knowing that you might be fighting for your very life before you take your next breath is as physically and emotionally draining as any activity known to man. Every sense is elevated to its highest level. One not only feels his pounding heart, but hears it.

The taste of fear takes the form of a dry mouth as the eyes strain to identify every possible source of danger. The brain examines and identifies every smell and disregards those that are not a threat, concentrating instead on finding those that will cause its sudden cessation: The pungent smell of powder burning in a grenade fuse moments before it explodes, a generously-applied coating of gun oil, out of place among the rotting odors of the jungle, or the smell of a hidden human being whose main source of nourishment is rice and fish. Odors that would normally go unnoticed suddenly and inexplicably scream out when the game involves life and death.

Evans and Huebner knew that every man on the squad wanted nothing more than to take a sip of their tepid water. They also knew that the sound of a sloshing canteen carries far in the silent night air and without being told, each man would leave his canteen securely fastened in its canvas cover.

Smith and Monie peered through the darkness as the beam of the flashlight was directed across the trail and into the trees. They could clearly hear the excited high-pitched voices as the five men spread out along the trail and disappeared into the jungle. Monie signaled for Smith to stay along the edge of the trail and made his way back to Evans.

"Bad shit, LT, they're off the trail."

"Maybe they're takin' a break."

"Don't think so, they moved too fast, scooted right in there. Looks like our guy went off into the bush and they're following 'im."

Evans held his watch up to his face. "All right, the Bronco should be in the area in a little more than an hour. Figure he can stay on station for an hour after that. We've got two hours, maybe two and a half, to get our guy and still arrange for a morning pickup." He looked up and down the squad lining the trail. "I don't see any choice, we gotta' go in after him. If our guy hit the trees to hold up for the night he's gonna' be pretty close to the trail; if he heard the Gooks and left the trail, he's gonna' be movin' fast and loud. Either way, the shit's gonna' hit the fan." Evans stood up, bent over at the waist. "Let's do it."

Air Force Captain Anthony Russell was dreaming of home. He was sitting on the lawn, under the huge cottonwood tree, beads of condensation from the cold Budweiser can in his right hand dripping onto his bare stomach. The coolness felt wonderful. He smiled as he watched his wife push their three-year-old son in his new swing set. Captain Russell was a proud father and enjoyed every moment of it. He took a pull on the can and watched as his son laughed and reached for the sky. Anthony's wife looked up at him and said something. Why couldn't he understand what she said? Why had her voice changed? Why was it so high pitched? Anthony's wife said something else, in Vietnamese. Captain Russell woke up.

His right leg throbbed like hell. He wasn't sure but he thought he had either torn the ligaments or at the very least the cartilage in his knee. It was swollen to the point that the leg of his flight suit was stretched tight, and trying to put any weight on it was pure torture.

He turned toward the sound of the voices. 'Oh, God, not now. Not after I've come this far'. The voices were getting closer. They knew he was in there and it was just a matter of time. He reached across his chest and took the pistol out of the shoulder holster. Anthony Russell, Captain, US Air Force, had thought about this very situation countless times since he had been in Vietnam. Do you allow yourself to be captured and take the chance of being tortured to death in some POW camp, or do you fight? He would not be tortured until he unwillingly turned on his own country or fellow pilots. If he had to die, he would die like his father did in Korea: Fighting.

The voices were getting closer. He couldn't see them yet and he knew they couldn't see him. He had been sleeping with his back propped up against the trunk of a tree. He didn't know why he had done it but when he had chosen that particular tree to use as a pillow, he had subconsciously sat down on the side of the tree farthest from the trail, almost completely hidden from view.

Grimacing against the pain in his leg, he lowered himself onto his back, then rolled over onto his stomach. With his pistol in his right hand, he took out the extra twelve bullets and laid them at the base of the tree. With any luck he'd be able to reload at least once before they got him. As slim as it was, there was the chance that he might be able to get them all before they got him.

The NVA made their way through the trees. The leader had switched off the light as soon as they had left the trail and now he stumbled around blindly with the rest of his men. The American could not be far. It was obvious from his boot marks that his right leg was injured. The leader was well aware of the Americans' aversion to moving at night. They looked at the jungle as their enemy, something to be avoided. No, this American was not trying to make his way through the jungle, this American left the trail to find a place to rest, and maybe lick his wounds.

The NVA leader grinned as the thoughts ran through his mind. The American would be close, very close, and they would find him. They would find him and capture him. Yes, they would capture this foolish American and parade him down the streets of North Vietnam, dressed in the flight suit he undoubtedly still wore. Yes, this American would be a flyer, a US pilot. He foolishly walked down a well-used trail. A soldier would not do that, would never think of it. No, this American was a pilot, and he would make a great prize.

Captain Anthony Russell lay as quietly as he could. He heard branches and twigs breaking and an occasional voice. For a moment his dream of a cold beer flashed through his mind. He had never known such thirst, could not have ever imagined it. He ran his tongue across his lips. The open sores and cracks oozed blood and the salty taste brought no relief.

At first it was only a shadow, then a flicker of movement. Then another shadow, and another, then movement farther off to the right. Russell strained his eyes in the darkness. Five, he counted five. No, six, there's six of them. No, that's a tree, it's not moving. There's only five. He moved his arm and aimed at the figure farthest to the right. Russell squinted through blurred eyes and squeezed the trigger.

Evans and his men hit the ground at the sound of the two shots. Even though the jungle was immediately filled with the sound of automatic fire, it was clear that the first two shots had come from a pistol. Their guy was alive! At least he was up until a couple seconds ago. They had to move and they had to move now. The entire squad rose as one and moved forward through the trees. It was only seconds before they could see the muzzle flashes of the NVA.

Monie was the first to fire. He squeezed the trigger and quickly let it go, trying for a short burst. His first shots hit the soldier in the middle of the back, ripping through his rucksack and shattering his spine. Evans' voice pierced the sounds of the chattering weapons. "Russell, stay down! We're Americans, stay down!!"

Two of the NVA turned at the sound of his voice and were greeted by a murderous stream of fire from Robinson's M-60. The bodies, dead before they ever hit the ground, danced in seemingly slow motion as pieces of uniform, equipment, and flesh flew through the air.

One lone figure rose and ran straight for a large tree, his AK-47 spitting fire and gilded metal. Two more shots from a pistol were heard as the running soldier jerked and slowed to little more than a walk. The soldier righted himself, lifted his AK toward the tree, then was propelled forward onto his face as three of Huebner's bullets smashed into his back. Evans jerked his head back and forth, as did the rest of the squad, checking for more threats.

"How many?"

Tuckett strained to look through the darkness. "We got four, LT. There's another one off to our left. I think maybe our guy got him."

"All right, let's check 'em all. Captain Russell, Captain Russell, can you hear me?"

Even more than the sounds of his son, Anthony Russell was never happier to hear anything in his life. "Yes, yes, I hear you, I hear you! Oh, God, yes, I hear you!"

"All right, Captain, listen up. Stay where you're at, don't move. We'll check out the Gooks, then we'll come to you!"

"Okay, okay, I won't move!, I won't move!"

The squad moved forward. Each body was carefully checked, even though there was no doubt that four of them were dead. Tuckett stood over the fifth wounded soldier. "Hey, LT, we got one over here. Gut shot pretty bad, he's still alive."

Evans didn't look back to where the voice came from. "Do it."

The burst from the M-16 shattered the stillness. Audie Murphy might have tried to save the wounded soldier, but Audie Murphy fought in a different time, a different place, and a very different kind of war.

As Evans made his way over to where Russell lay, Huebner stared down at two dead bodies, silent thoughts running through his mind. "Five minutes. If we'd been five minutes later, we'd have another body laying out here. There has to be a better way. There has to be!"

CHAPTER 6

SATURDAY
MARCH 28, 1970
CAMELOT PALACE

It could hardly be considered a base by most standards. Nothing more than a flat, dusty circle of bare land big enough for the thirty or so helicopters that flew off its dirt flight line, along with refueling and maintenance facilities, ammo dump, and rows of eighteen-man canvas tents in which their inhabitants sweltered away their tour. The entire setting would have been rather serene except for the thousands of yards of coiled concertina wire, mortar pits, and sandbagged machine-gun emplacements every forty yards.

Looking out from the wire, one not versed in the strategies and vulgarities of war would see nothing more than 150 yards of flat, seemingly good, farmland. That same observer might quickly adopt a different view when told that this farmer's main crops were trip flares, claymore mines, and buried fifty-five-gallon drums of napalm. Carved out of the dense jungle by air dropped bulldozers when the base had been built, the flat, treeless moat afforded an unobstructed field of fire and was referred to only as, 'outside the wire'.

Camelot Palace, as it was called, was forty-eight miles southwest of Saigon and north of the Mekong Delta. Bulldozed, blasted, and hacked out of barely penetrable jungle, it stood alone like a life raft in shark infested waters. 'Outside the wire', 'the bush' as troops called it, was the home of the VC...all of it. In daylight, patrols ventured outside the wire to re-arm the barrels of napalm that had been sabotaged the night before or to reposition claymore mines that had been turned toward the wire. Broken twigs, laid end to end by the VC to show the way between landmines were scattered, or repositioned, in hopes of leading someone to the hereafter. The housekeeping was done each day, always at a different time and by a different route. While patrols took care of the early warning devices other patrols penetrated the bush to provide cover. Few if any believed that they would make it back across the deadly field if the 'shit ever hit the fan' but the constant presence of Cobra gunships flying overhead kept daylight contact to a minimum.

Nighttime was another matter. At night everything 'outside the wire' was meant to be kept 'outside the wire' and the soldiers of Camelot Palace did their best to keep it that way. This was their home and uninvited guests were met with less than a cordial welcome. It was also the home for Lieutenant Will Evans and his Search & Rescue Team.

They had been back at the Palace for several days and had been using the time to catch up on their sleep, hot chow, and letter writing. Captain Russell had spent two days in the base aid station before being choppered to the hospital at Tan Son Nhut, but had demanded to see the entire squad to thank them before he left. As he shook hands with each man, tears welled up in his eyes as his voice started to fail him.

Smith was the last man to walk up and take the pilot's hand. "Ya' know, Capt'n, I'd a bet big money we was out there lookin' for a white boy. I never figured to see no Brother hunkered down next to that tree."

"Would you have looked harder if you'd known it was a Brother out there?" Russell had a questioning and disturbed expression.

Smith hesitated, drew himself up straight and answered so the entire squad could hear. "If we was back in 'the World', yeah, I would have. Fuck the white boy, what he ever do for me? But we ain't in 'the World' and things is different. Out here we all tryin' to do the same thing, find some flyboy who got his ass shot down, and try to stay alive at the same time. When we be humpin' the bush, me and Robinson here, we ain't no different than the white boys, 'cept maybe we a little harder to spot at night. We all be shittin' and pissin' under the trees, we all be eatin' the same C-rats, and when there's fightin' to be done…we all fight. Naw, Capt'n, I wouldn't a looked no harder for ya' if I'da known you was a Brother. We all look hard as we can, every time."

Embarrassed at hearing the sounds of his own words, Smith pointed a thin bony finger at Russell. "You be keepin' your ass up in the air and outta the bush. We only got so much luck down here and we can't be a wastin' anymore'n it on you."

It was hot inside the headquarters tent, stifling hot. The cans of Coke Evans and Huebner sipped did little to cool them off. Stripped down to fatigue pants and T-shirts, the sweat still poured off their bodies leaving huge sweat rings under their arms and the tops of their pants wet and soggy. The fan did little more than remind them of what a cool breeze might feel like.

Major Scott Kancilla leaned back in the chair behind his desk and rubbed the cool Coke can over his forehead. His voice had the slightest hint of hopelessness to it.

"Will, we can't expect to find every pilot that goes down. You got this last one back okay and that's a shit load better than not trying."

"Sir, we just think there's a better way. Like Sergeant Huebner said, if we'd got to that pilot five minutes later, we'd have been bringing back his dog tags instead of him. We wasted at least a whole day out there finding his trail, then losing it, then trying to find it again. We need a way to pick up the trail and stay on it 'til we find the pilots, or what's left of 'em."

Kancilla pulled his feet off the desk and sat upright. "Look, Will, this is the Army, not some sheriff's posse on the trail of a train robber. We're trained to kill people and break things, remember?"

"Yes, sir, but we're also supposed to find people. I mean, we have the ability. We're just not doing it."

"Lieutenant, one of us has been spending way too much time in the sun 'cause I haven't the faintest idea what you're talking about."

Evans looked to his right at Huebner, who nodded. "We want a dog, sir."

"You want a dog?"

"Yes, sir."

"Don't you think that's something you should have asked your folks for?"

"A dog that can track people."

"Ah-ha, and just where do you figure on getting this dog?"

Evans knew his reply would go over as well as a rat in a foxhole and looked at the floor as he answered. "The Air Force."

"The Air Force!?" Kancilla sprang out of his chair, knocking over the can of Coke sitting on the desk. "What do you mean, the Air Force? You want us to be the laughing stock of the whole fuckin' Army?"

"No, sir. What we want is for those pilots to know that if they go down, we'll find 'em. Right now we don't have a very good record and we think a dog can change that."

Kancilla rubbed his face with both hands and let out a huge sigh. "The last time I had to make a decision about a dog was whether to buy one or get married. Biggest mistake I ever made…but I guess I can still buy one when I get back to 'the World'. All right, Lieutenant, let's hear it, what makes you think some Air Force mutt is gonna' help you find downed fliers?" He glanced over at Huebner who sat there chewing on his mustache like a man possessed.

"Sir, when we were over at Tan Son Nhut, we noticed the Air Force uses dog teams to protect the base at night. Well, yesterday I took the liberty of contacting their Security Police Commander and asked him a few questions. Their dog teams are trained to find somebody out in the bush without having to see 'em, but they're also trained to track people. He says as long as the dog has something with a scent on it, he can track someone for miles."

"Something with the pilot's scent on it? Where do you get that?"

"Well, sir, I think we have that figured out. If we get to an area where a pilot bailed out and we can't find any sign of him, it means the Gooks got to him and there's nothing we can do about it. But if we get there before the Gooks, we're gonna' find his chute or gloves or helmet or something. Whatever it is, it'll have the pilot's scent on it and that's all we need."

"You got this all figured out, don't you?"

"Pretty much so, sir, except for one thing."

"What's that?"

"The SP Commander says they won't order one of their dog teams to work with us. Someone will have to volunteer."

"Will, in case it never occurred to you, those guys are in the Air Force 'cause they didn't want to hump around in the bush. What makes you think you'll find one to volunteer?"

"Duty, honor, country?"

"You're dreamin'."

"How about stupidity?"

"That might work. So, where do you go from here?"

"Well, sir, with your permission, the SP Commander said if we wanted to chopper over to Tan Son Nhut, he'd set up a demonstration. Then I guess we just play it by ear."

SUNDAY
MARCH 29, 1970
TAN SON NHUT AIR FORCE BASE
SOUTH VIETNAM

The blue Rambler staff car pulled up to the kennels just after 9 a.m. Although still early in the morning, the sun blazed down through a cloudless sky, the already oppressive heat only a hint of what was yet to come. Major A.J. Guanella, Commander of the Security Police Squadron, tucked his soft cap under the front of his belt rather than put it on and restrict any cooling breeze that might unexpectedly appear. "This is it, gentlemen. Let's head inside, the Kennel Master is expecting us."

The Kennel Master, S/Msgt. Derr, appeared through the door of his office. "Good morning, Major."

Guanella turned to the sound of the voice. "Oh, Rick, there you are, good morning. These are the gentlemen I told you about." Introductions were made as they entered Derr's office. Evans briefed the kennel master on what they did in the bush and how they were trying to find a better way to do it.

Derr pushed back in his chair as he blew a cloud of cigarette smoke at a fly on the edge of the desk. "Lieutenant, what you're asking is pretty easy. These dogs can do everything you can do out in the bush, only better. They can see better, hear better, and smell better than you...and if you were ever in a position where you didn't have a weapon, they can fight better than you. The problem is, they can't work alone, they need a handler to guide 'em, and of the twenty-eight handlers here, only one has more than six months left in his tour."

Guanella leaned forward and set his cigarette in the ashtray. "Gentlemen, we know you risk your asses trying to find downed Air Force pilots and we appreciate it, God knows we do. We also know these dogs can help you, but our guys aren't trained to live, or fight in the jungle. It's not something they know how to do."

Evans started to say something but was cut off by Guanella's raised hand. "We're not saying we won't help. What we're saying is most of the handlers can smell home and the chances of one of them volunteering is probably the same as Ho Chi Min asking Nixon over for dinner."

"Then we wasted our time flying over here?" Huebner was already discouraged.

"Maybe, maybe not. We have one possibility, a new troop...what's his name again, Rick?"

"Giancarlo, Gianni Giancarlo."

"Yeah, Giancarlo. Sergeant Derr and Sergeant Maiberger both seem to think that if anyone would volunteer for this, he's the one."

Evans was suspicious. "What's the deal, Sergeant Derr? This guy a fuck-up you're just trying to get rid of?"

"No, not at all. Actually he's already the best handler we've got. Spends most of his off-duty time working with his dog or writing letters back home."

"Well, what makes you think he'd volunteer for this?"

"Would either of you give up a guaranteed four-year tour in Miami, working with the President no less, to come here?"

"You gotta' be kiddin'?" Evans glanced at Huebner, the mustache bobbing up and down.

It wasn't the first time Derr had been asked the question. "Nope."

Huebner smiled, twirled his bush hat on his finger, and let out a long sigh. "This guy's a fucking idiot!"

Maiberger had told Gianni some Army types wanted to see a short demonstration and asked him to be at the kennels at 10 a.m. Gianni got there at 9:30 and had Shadrack groomed and ready. He was standing in the grassy area throwing a ball for the dog when the five men walked over. As they approached, he commanded Shadrack to "Heel" and snapped to attention.

Guanella walked toward Gianni and stopped three or four feet away.

"Be at ease, Airman. Gianni, I'd like you to meet Lieutenant Evans and Sergeant Huebner. Gentleman, this is Gianni Giancarlo and his dog Shadrack."

Evans and Huebner slowly moved behind Derr, trying to distance themselves from the dog. Guanella smiled to himself, deciding it was time to have a little fun. "I guess now's as good a time as any to start the demonstration. Lieutenant Evans, Sergeant Huebner, would you be so kind as to move up here in front of Airman Giancarlo." Not sure what was going on, the two men slowly moved closer to Gianni.

Without moving or even looking down at the dog, Gianni whispered "watch 'em". Both men jumped back as the dog sprang up, saliva spewing from his mouth as he snapped his jaws and growled, just waiting, and hoping for the next command. After several seconds, Gianni whispered "no, out" and the dog quietly sat back down, leaning against Gianni's leg and looking up, waiting for his praise.

"Good boy, that's a good boy. Just wait a few minutes, you'll get to bite someone in a while."

Evans and Huebner couldn't believe what they'd seen and were quickly trying to compose themselves.

"You see, gentlemen, these dogs build up a very strong relationship with their handlers and will do anything to protect them. Actually you were in no danger since Gianni just gave the command for the dog to be on guard. You'll notice he was never was more than a foot or two away from Gianni's side."

"I do have one question, if you don't mind, Major." Huebner was staring at the dog, a confused look on his face.

"Sure, what is it?"

"What's wrong with his ears?"

Maiberger turned away in a coughing fit, trying to restrain his laughter. Derr almost drew blood as he bit his lip, anticipating what was about to happen.

"Sergeant, please don't talk about his ears, he's very sensitive about them." Gianni tried to stay straight faced.

"Are you kidding? How can a dog be sensitive about anything? I was just wondering why his ears are so huge. He looks like some kind of cartoon rabbit or something."

One of the ways Gianni had kept people from making fun of Shadrack's ears was to teach him to react to a certain word. He had to use a word that didn't come up often to avoid anyone being accidentally bitten, then he simply put the word at the end of a sentence and watched the fun.

As if holding a serious conversation with the dog, Gianni looked down and began to apologize. "Shad, I'm sorry you had to hear that. There are just some people who have no consideration for a dog's feelings. It seems the Sergeant here thinks you look stupid with your huge appendages."

Shadrack had been sitting quietly and had no idea what his master was talking about, until he heard the word "appendages". Trained to react to that as if he had been told to "watch 'em," he again flew into a rage which resulted in Huebner tripping over his own feet as he scurried back out of range and landed on his back.

"No, out! As you can see, Sergeant, he's very particular about his appearance. I even have to keep him away from mirrors 'cause it depresses him and puts him in a real bad mood."

Huebner had regained his feet and was brushing the grass off the back of his fatigue pants. "Anything you say, soldier, anything you say."

"I'm not a soldier. I'm an Airman."

"Whatever." Huebner would have agreed to anything.

Guanella suggested they watch Shadrack negotiate the obstacle course first. Evans and Huebner were impressed with the ease and agility the dog displayed as he effortlessly completed the course. Standing next to Derr, Huebner pointed at Gianni. "Sarge, I haven't heard your guy say more than two or three words to the dog but he always seems to know what he's supposed to do. I was just wondering if he does this stuff so much it's just routine to 'im and he wouldn't know what to do out in the bush."

"Oh, he's used to the obstacle course all right, but it's no different than doing calisthenics every morning. That got you in shape in basic and this keeps him in shape. The only difference is he loves to do this and you probably hated it. As for not having to say anything, Gianni is talking to him, only with his hands, not with his voice. These dogs are trained to respond to hand signals as well as voice commands. If you watched real close, you would have seen Gianni pat his left leg when the dog finished the course telling the dog to heel. Here, I'll have Gianni run through a few signals, that'll give you a better idea of what I mean. Hey, Gianni, show them how hand signals work, will ya."

"Sure, Sarge." Gianni moved closer to the group of men. "The dogs are trained to respond to hand signals and voice commands. As long as they can see the signal, they'll respond. I think the only exception is the command for them to attack. We either have to tell them, or, if the situation calls for it, they'll do it on their own. I can pretty much show you what he'll do, though. Just stand over there and don't make any sudden moves." Gianni reached down and whispered to the dog. "That's a good boy." Shadrack looked up as Gianni scratched the top of his head, knowing he was about to be asked to do something.

"The first thing we'll do is show you how I can leave the dog without having him follow me." With the palm of his left hand, Gianni placed it in front of the dog's face and quickly walked away. Shadrack's already tall ears gained even greater height as he watched his master walk away. As he walked, he continued to talk to Huebner. "Since your eyes aren't getting real wide. I guess I can assume he hasn't tried to follow me."

"No, he's still sitting there, but he looks like he's ready to jump out of his skin."

"That's all right, he just wants to play, but he'll sit there all day 'til I tell him to move. He might get tired and lay down, but he'll stay there."

"What would happen if he couldn't see or hear you anymore?"

"He'd get real fidgety for a while, then come looking for me." Gianni turned and faced the dog. He swung his arm behind and forward with his palm facing the ground giving the dog the command to lay down. Without explaining what he was going to do, he gave a series of quick hand signals that had Shadrack roll to his right, then to his left, run to his right, stop, lay down, sit, and crawl forward. At the end of the short demonstration, Gianni tapped his left leg and grinned as the dog ran back to him, turning his whole body in mid-air and landing in a sitting position next to his left leg.

"This is fucking unbelievable, just unbelievable. How the hell do you guys train them to do that stuff?" Evans was truly impressed. The more he saw, the more he knew he was looking at the answer to their problems. "I had no idea these dogs could do this stuff, Major."

"Well, you haven't really seen anything. This is nothing more than parlor tricks." Guanella turned to Maiberger. "Sergeant, would you do us the honors for a little attack demonstration?"

Maiberger slipped the leather sleeve over his left arm and walked about thirty feet in front of Gianni. As he turned around, Gianni whispered "watch 'em." The dog jumped up to all fours, the sound of his snapping jaws not lost on Evans and Huebner. At the words "get 'em," the dog took off, making a run straight at Maiberger. Knowing not to turn and run, Maiberger stood facing the dog and at the last moment lowered his leather covered arm directly in front of the dog's face. The dog clamped onto the sleeve as Maiberger flailed his arm, trying to shake him off. Gianni let the dog continue to bite 'til it was obvious that Maiberger was starting to tire. "No, Out." Gianni slapped his left leg as Shadrack released his grip and ran back to his master's side.

Gianni tapped his side again and the dog followed him out to the heavily-breathing Maiberger. As Gianni stopped, another tap on the leg signaled Shadrack to sit, all the while keeping an eye on the aggressor. Signaling with his left hand for the dog to stay, Gianni walked forward, then behind Maiberger, simulating a search for weapons. Maiberger suddenly swept his arm around as if to hit Gianni. Without the need for voice command or hand signal, Shadrack leapt forward and attacked Maiberger who was barely able to get the sleeve in front of the snapping jaws. Stepping away from Maiberger, Gianni shouted, "No, Out" and patted his left leg.

Giving Shadrack several seconds to calm down, Maiberger walked up to him and scratched behind his ears. "That's a good boy, Shadrack, yeah, a good boy. You did real good. A little too close for comfort but still real good."

Shadrack looked up at Gianni as if to say, 'He's touching me, can I bite him, huh, huh, can I bite him again? This time I'll tear his balls off and hang 'em in my doghouse'.

Guanella wiped the sweat off his face with a handkerchief. "Gentlemen, there's a lot more attack work we could show you but I think you get the picture. Suffice it to say that this dog will do whatever it takes to protect his handler, and since animals don't have the same conception of death as we do, he won't hesitate. I suggest we drive out beyond the wire and show you something that will really be of interest."

Evans looked down at Shadrack, then up at Gianni. "Major, if what they do out in the bush is half as good as what they did here…well, let's just say I think we've got something."

"Like I said, Lieutenant, this was nothing more than parlor tricks."

Maiberger and Gianni took one of the pickup trucks with Shadrack sitting in the middle like an anxious little child going for a Sunday ride. Derr drove the staff car and followed them out past the wire to one of their nightly posts. They gathered around S/Msgt. Derr.

"All right, your problem is finding someone out in the bush. We're gonna' show you how to do it with just one man and a dog. The first thing we'll do is show you how we check an area for bad guys. Sergeant Huebner, if we promise you won't get bit, will you help us with this?"

"I'd be honored." His voice betrayed his concern.

Derr handed Huebner his CAR-15. "Here, you better take this. You gotta' watch out for snipers, and snakes."

"Gee, doesn't this sound like fun."

Derr told Gianni to take Shadrack back to the truck and keep him from watching Huebner. Derr explained the object of the exercise would be for Huebner to disappear in the thick jungle, choosing his own direction and distance. All agreed a twenty minute head start would be more than sufficient to afford Huebner time to find a hiding place. Huebner knew that within thirty seconds of hitting the tree line he could be hidden well enough that every Security Policemen on the base could spend the rest of the day looking for him and still go home empty handed. They might know how to protect a base perimeter but they sure as hell couldn't compete with him out in the heavy bush.

"All right, Gianni, this is no big deal. Take Lieutenant Evans with you, go find Huebner, and bring his ass back here."

Gianni took off his fatigue hat and turned slowly until he determined his downwind leg. Looking on in bewilderment, Evans whispered to Derr. "What's he doing?"

"Checking the wind."

"What'da ya' mean checking the wind? There is no wind."

"As far as you are concerned there's no wind, but to a dog…" Derr let his words drift off and smiled.

"The leaves on the trees aren't even moving. How's he supposed to tell where this 'wind' is coming from?"

"That's why he took his hat off. Watch, see how he's turning real slow, when the sweat on his forehead starts to feel cool, he knows he's downwind and he'll set up the search based on that."

Gianni put his hat back on and motioned for the Lieutenant to join him. "All right, Lieutenant, this is what's gonna' happen. Since we don't know where Sergeant Huebner entered the trees and we don't know what direction he's headed, we're gonna' start quartering in this direction," pointing to his right along the tree line. "We're gonna' walk down here about a hundred yards. If Shadrack doesn't alert, we'll move to our left about ten yards, then backtrack to this point, and then another hundred yards past here. We'll do that 'til he alerts, then follow his lead into the trees."

Gianni bent down and spoke to his dog. "Ready to go to work, Shad? Ready to have some fun, huh? There's someone out there, boy, yeah, there's someone out there." Evans watched as the dog became excited, his eyes and ears scanning the trees. "Yeah, boy, we're gonna' show these Army guys what you can do. Okay, boy, let's go. Find 'Em, Find 'Em."

Gianni let the leash slip to its full length as Shadrack started out in a straight line, his head held high in the air. After about thirty yards or so, the dog stopped, tested the air several times, ignored whatever it was he had detected and continued. When they reached the point Gianni had selected as their turnaround area, the dog had still not attempted to move off into the trees.

They reversed directions, moved ten yards closer to the tree line, and started back to where they had started. It took several minutes to reach the point where Evans knew Huebner had entered the trees. As they walked past that point, he turned to Derr and Guanella who were both leaning against the truck smoking cigarettes, and smiled. The dog may be able to bite, but he sure as hell couldn't find, as Monie so often put it, a bull in a barnyard.

Just as he shifted his eyes back to Gianni, Shadrack stuck his head even higher in the air, stopped for a moment, sniffed the air loudly, turned to his right and shot off into the trees. "Yeah, that's a good boy, Shadrack. You got 'em now. Find 'em, boy, find 'em."

The dog had more than doubled his pace and strained at the leash. He went over deadfall, around trees and clumps of bushes, and straight through the smaller ones. Without even pausing to look around, the dog continued as if his nose was being reeled in on some invisible fishing line.

Evans was starting to get confused and wondered if the dog was really smelling Huebner. He had seen where the sergeant had entered the tree line and knew they were well to the left of where they should be. After four or five minutes Shadrack started straining harder at the leash, trying to pull Gianni along. Figuring the demonstration had gone on long enough but still wanting to have some fun, Gianni softly whispered "Heel" and patted his left leg. Shadrack sat down but continued to look out into the trees.

"What's the matter, why are we stopping?"

"Just takin' a little rest, Lieutenant." "Takin' a rest? What'da ya' mean, taking a rest? We've only been out here a few minutes. Huebner could be halfway across the country by now."

"He could be, but he's not."

"How do you know he's not?"

"'Cause we already found him."

"We did? I mean, you did? You saw him?"

"Nope."

"Well, how do you know where he is?"

"Shadrack sees him, or at least knows where he is. If he's not moving, the dog can't actually see 'im, but it doesn't matter, he knows where he is."

"How do you know? I mean, how do you know the dog knows where he is?"

"He told me."

Evans' hopes of finding an answer to his search and rescue problem were suddenly dashed upon the rocks. "You guys are all fuckin' crazy. Now you can talk to dogs. Come on, either let's push on and try to find Huebner or let's go back to the truck. That is, unless that stupid dog has us hopelessly lost."

Gianni had sat down with his back resting against a tree. He gave a mock grimace of pain, lifted his butt and removed a small rock. "Lieutenant, I don't mean any disrespect, but we're dealing with something you know absolutely nothing about. Yeah, a lot of people tell me I'm crazy for being over here when I don't have to, and maybe I am, but I am not crazy when I tell you that our dogs talk to us. Any handler will tell you the same thing. No, I don't sit down and have a conversation with him but Shadrack still tells me everything I need to know."

"All right, I'll bite, no pun intended. What'd he tell you?"

"He's telling you, too, Lieutenant, you just don't know how to listen to him." Without even looking at his dog, Gianni reached down, picked up a twig and started peeling the bark off with his thumbnail. "Crouch down behind Shadrack and look between his ears."

"What!"

"Look between his ears. You'll see whatever it is he's alerting on, and what you're gonna' see is Sergeant Huebner waiting for us to come crashing through the trees like a herd of elephants."

Tentatively Evans scooted over and crouched behind the dog. "I don't see shit."

"That's 'cause you're looking along the ground. See how his nose is kinda' high up in the air?"

"Yeah, so?"

"That means whatever he's alerting on is up high, probably in a tree."

"How do you know that?" Evans crouched down to look between the dog's ears again, only this time he shifted his gaze higher up.

"If Sergeant Huebner was on the ground, his scent would travel along the ground no higher than he is, and since the feet sweat more than any other part of the body, the strongest scent would be closest to the ground. Shadrack has his nose stuck high in the air and he's picking up a constant scent, so either Sergeant Huebner is in a tree or Shadrack has found a VC sniper, in which case I expect you to do some of your Army stuff and get me the hell out of here. My money is on Sergeant Huebner, though."

Evans almost missed what Gianni had said. He was busy looking at Huebner sitting high in a tree more than a hundred yards away. Huebner had broken off a bunch of branches and had almost totally concealed himself. Evans never would have seen him except for the brief flash of sunlight that reflected off the frame of Huebner's sunglasses, something he never would have been wearing if they had been out in the bush for real. "Well, I'll be dipped in shit. I don't fucking believe this. You never even saw him, did you?"

"No, sir, I didn't need too. It's my job to find people, not to fuck with 'em. Shadrack knew where he was, that's all that counts."

"Ya' know, I could'a stood over the dog and cut loose a burst on auto and blew him outta' that tree without ever having to see 'em."

"Yes, sir, I know. We train for that. The dogs don't like it if a hot shell casing hits their fur, but other than that, they pretty much stay still while you're shooting over their heads."

"I gotta' tell ya, I'm really fuckin' impressed, really, really impressed." Evans looked through Shadrack's ears again and found Huebner. "He must think we're out here wandering around looking for him hidin' under some bush." Gianni saw the smile spread across his face. "Wait 'til I tell him about this."

Guanella, Derr, and Maiberger glanced up as the three men emerged from the tree line. "Here they come now." Maiberger walked over to the truck to get a canteen of water for Shadrack. Guanella had never actually seen Gianni work before and was more than pleased with the way he was handling the situation. "Any problems so far, Gianni?"

"No, sir, Shadrack is working real good."

"Good, good. Well, gentlemen, shall we show you how to track a downed flier?"

Huebner was not overly thrilled with the prospect of hiding in the brush again. "Ya' know, sir, it occurs to me that the Lieutenant might not think I gave it my all. Maybe he should try this time?" Huebner looked up at the cloudless sky, avoiding the stare of his Lieutenant.

"That's a very good idea, Sergeant. It might do the Lieutenant good to get a different perspective. What do you think about that, Lieutenant Evans?"

"Huh? Yes, sir, whatever the Major thinks is best but maybe I can save us some time. This 'tracking' that you're talking about, is it that much different than what we just saw?"

"No, not really. Instead of using the wind to find someone, the dog follows the scent along the ground. You just have to have something with the scent on it that you want to follow." Guanella was just as anxious to get out of the heat as Evans was.

"Like a flight suit, or gloves, or a helmet?

"Yes, I'd say that would work but Sergeant Derr knows more about it than I do. Rick, how about it?"

"No problem, they'd all work. Actually just about anything that the person you want to track has touched."

"And this tracking, the dog can do that out in the bush...as good as he just did with Sergeant Huebner?"

"If he can find the scent to begin with he can stay on it until he finds who ever you're looking for...unless that person is picked up, or if heavy rains or a river washes away the scent. Other than that, yeah, he can do it."

Evans looked over at Huebner then back at Guanella and Derr. "Well, in that case, I think we can forgo another walk in the park. Why don't we get your handler and the dog back to the kennels and talk about what we've seen."

Huebner wasn't sure if he was happy to get out of the sun or disappointed that Evans wasn't going to have his turn at being dog food.

Maiberger unrolled the hose and filled Shadrack's bucket with fresh water while Gianni checked him over for ticks. Derr had led the others into his office. Evans turned to Guanella. "Major, if it's all right with you, I think we can do business."

"Rick, what do you think?"

"They ARE out there looking for Air Force pilots, Major. Seems to me we ought to have a hand in this."

Guanella turned back to Evans. "Lieutenant, be straight with me. Have you lost anybody on any of these missions?"

"One, he tripped a booby trap, took some shrapnel in the knee and chest, we choppered him out. Probably walk with a limp but it got him back to 'the World.'"

Guanella rubbed a hand over his still sweating face. "Damnit, when you first called me about this, I thought it was a great idea. Now when it comes down to asking one of these boys to leave what is basically a pretty safe place and go off into God knows what..."

There was silence for several moments as all four men were engrossed in their own thoughts. Guanella was the first to speak. "All right, these are the ground rules. Since Giancarlo has the longest time left and is probably the best handler anyway, you can ask him if he's interested. If he says no, that's it, not another word from either of you. You thank him for the demonstration and he heads back to the barracks, and Rick, you give him the night off." Derr nodded.

"If he says yes, or shows some interest, you tell him the bad shit, all the stuff that can go wrong and what can happen. Understood?"

Evans nodded at Huebner then turned back to Guanella. "Yes sir, we can work with that."

"One other thing. If he decides to go, he can get out any time, and I mean this most seriously. If he wants out for any reason, you get his ass back here soonest. That's the deal, gentlemen, and I hope I don't live to regret it."

Derr glanced at Evans, then back at Guanella. "I'll go get him."

Guanella spoke directly to him. "Airman Giancarlo, Lieutenant Evans and Sergeant Huebner would like to explain to you exactly what they do out in the bush and why they wanted to see this little demonstration. Now, please listen to them carefully, and if you have any questions, just interrupt the Lieutenant and ask. Do you understand?"

Gianni felt uncomfortable at the serious tone the day had taken. "Sir, I already know what the Lieutenant and the Sergeant do out in the bush. Sergeant Maiberger told me they are part of a Search and Rescue team to find downed flyers. I'm guessing at the rest. They're looking for a better way to find the pilots out in the bush and they've decided a dog is the best way. What I mean is, we all know they should have been using a dog right along. Now that they've seen how Shadrack can work, they want to know if someone will volunteer to go with them, and since I'm the only one sitting here, they probably want to know if I'll go." Gianni glanced around. "Am I wrong, sir?"

"No, no, you're not wrong, but I want you to understand something. No one is ordering you to do this. It's not like walking perimeter, Gianni. These guys work out in the bush, all alone, for days at a time. You could get killed out there, get blown away, step on a booby trap, lose your legs. It's the real fucking war, Gianni, and what you do here is a game compared to what they do."

Derr spoke before Guanella could continue. "Gianni, don't take this lightly, it's serious. Take some time to think about it, all the time you want. If you don't want to go, and I sure as hell wouldn't blame you, it's all right."

"Sarge, I'm not taking this lightly. Actually it scares the shit out of me. I don't know anything about the boonies and I sure as hell wouldn't know what to do if someone started shooting at me, but I do know how to work a dog and that's what these guys need. I don't want to think about it 'cause I'll probably talk myself out of it, and if the Lieutenant and the Sergeant didn't really think they needed us, they wouldn't be here. I'd like to give it a shot."

Huebner had been peeling the paper off the filter of his cigarette while he listened to Gianni. Maybe Derr had been right. Maybe this kid was too naive and really didn't know what he was getting into.

"Gianni, look, listen to your Major. You could get killed out there, you and your dog. As much as we need your help, you gotta' know what can happen."

"Sergeant Huebner, I know I could get killed. I know that a lot of other guys get killed. I see them loading coffins on the C-130's almost every day. Maybe Shadrack can keep some of our pilots out of those coffins. I think it's worth a try. I'll go."

CHAPTER 7

MONDAY
MARCH 30, 1970
CAMELOT PALACE ARMY BASE
SOUTH VIETNAM

The helicopter landed at Camelot Palace shortly after nine in the morning. As Gianni climbed out, Shadrack jumped to the ground, looked up at the helicopter, raised his leg, and relieved himself on the right side skid. Huebner looked over at the pilot who was busy shutting down the aircraft, shaking his head in disgust.

"That dog really knows how to make friends and influence people. Let's get outta' here before the gunner opens up on us."

They piled their gear onto a flat bed ammo carrier and hitched a ride to the headquarters tent. While Shadrack basked in the attention he drew as they drove through the base, Huebner wondered why he wasn't reacting to the comments hurled at him concerning his ears. It was particularly distressing that the driver escaped completely unscathed when he commented that the dog's ears would act like a wind break and seriously affect their gas mileage.

Outside the HQ tent Evans pulled Gianni aside. "All right, kid, we're gonna go in and report to Major Kancilla. Answer any questions he asks you but don't volunteer anything. He's not real gung ho on this whole idea. He thinks we need help from the Air Force like we need rubber guns. Got it?"

"Yes sir."

"Okay, into the valley of death."

Kancilla was sitting behind his desk reading reports as the three men entered. Doing a double take at Shadrack, he stood up for a better look.

"Jesus Christ, what the fuck is that?" Huebner instinctively inched away from the dog, waiting for the fireworks to start. When the dog just sat there, he figured he was still shaken from the helicopter ride. "I thought you said you were going to get a dog?"

Evans felt badly for Gianni and Shadrack. "This is a dog, Major. He's an Air Force Patrol Dog and his name is Shadrack."

"What the fuck is wrong with his ears?"

"There's nothing wrong with his ears, sir, and he gets very self-conscious if you talk about them." Gianni was starting to wonder if he had created a monster. "This is his handler, Airman Gianni Giancarlo. Gianni, this is Major Kancilla, the CO."

Kancilla nodded a curt greeting. "Pull up some chairs and let's find out what the hell is going on."

Evans related the events at Tan Son Nhut with the Major interrupting several times to ask Gianni questions. He was particularly interested in how the dog could actually find someone out in the bush and was not shy in voicing his skepticism. During the entire conversation, Shadrack laid quietly with his head between his paws.

"All right, so now you've described how he's gonna work out in the bush. How's he gonna live? As far as I know, they don't pack dog food in C-rats...even though that's how most of them taste."

"That shouldn't be a problem, Major. I'll carry his food, and other than water, that's all he really needs."

"Isn't it going to be a little inconvenient carrying a bunch of cans of dog food? Not to mention that you'll have a hell of a time trying to find a place to plug in your electric can opener." Kancilla couldn't help but chuckle at his own joke. He was a little dismayed when no one else did.

"Well, sir, it's just dry food, a lot like you'd feed your dog at home, and I figured I'd wrap whatever he'll need in some plastic, to keep it dry, and carry it that way."

Kancilla stood up and leaned over the desk to look at Shadrack. "From the size of him, he must eat like a horse. How the hell do you expect to carry that much food? In case you hadn't thought of it, there is a war going on and it might be a good idea if you left a little room to carry a couple of bullets. You can't imagine the sense of well-being they'll give you when you really need 'em."

"Yes, sir, I, ah, I...well sir, his food won't take up that much room, he only eats a canteen cupful a day."

Kancilla leaned back and lit a cigarette. "What about water, does he live on a thimble full a day or does he just bite the nearest living thing and drink it's blood?"

Gianni sensed more and more that the Major wasn't overly fond of Shadrack. "That could be a problem, sir. He can go a long time without eating, several days in fact and still be able to function at a pretty high level. Water is a different story. Although he doesn't need a lot of water at any one time, he needs a little bit pretty frequently."

"Just what do you consider pretty frequently?"

"When I need water, he needs water. The exception to that is if he overheats or comes down with heat exhaustion. Then I have to rub him down with water and let him rest in the shade."

"Just what we need, a four-legged casualty."

"He'll do fine, sir, I'll keep a close eye on him."

Kancilla blew smoke at the ceiling and turned to Evans. "Will, you really think this is gonna work?"

"Yes sir, I do. We'll make it work."

"Okay, it's your ass, I just hope that dog doesn't get a piece of it."

Kancilla stood and walked toward the door. "All right, I guess that just about does it." He nodded his head in Gianni's direction. "Get him fitted out soonest, no tellin' when we might need you guys. Gianni, welcome aboard. You, too, dog. Jesus, now I'm talking to a dog. Anyway, listen to the guys on the squad, do what they do, don't try to be a hero and you'll make out just fine. It's gonna be a different world out there, don't let it get to ya. No one was born knowin' how to work the bush, everyone had to learn. You will too."

The tent flaps were tied up in an effort to capture any breeze that might spring up. So far it had been a useless attempt.

"Hey, the LT and Sarge are back." Tuckett walked over to greet them, then spotted Gianni and Shadrack. "Jesus Christ, will ya' look at that. Hey, guys, look at this, they found a giant rat while they were gone. Damn, LT, we ain't got enough weird things crawlin' around outside without you bringin' one in the tent. I think I'm startin' to itch already." His imitation of a man trying to scratch his entire body would have been more believable if the huge muscles on his arms had been able to flex enough to reach around the equally muscular torso. At five foot-six and just slightly under a hundred and ninety pounds, Tuckett looked more like a cast iron fire plug than he did a soldier. Unlike other men who sweated off the pounds working the bush Tuckett managed to maintain his weightlifter's physique by eating everything in sight at every opportunity. His unabashed relish of digging into cans of c-rations, or loading down his meal tray in the mess tent, then returning to the line for seconds and thirds had been cause enough for another of Monie's down home sayings: That man would eat things that would drive buzzards off a gut wagon.

"All right, Tuckett, knock it off and pipe down. Come on, you guys, off your asses and get over here." Slowly the rest of the squad made their way over. Dressed in just fatigue pants or skivvies, they looked more like a chain gang than a fighting unit. "Listen up. As of today we have a new member on the squad. This is Airman Gianni Giancarlo and his dog Shadrack." Evans was almost drowned out by the hoots and hollers.

"Shadrack? What the fuck kinda' name is that? I think he looks more like a Rin Tin Tin. Come to save us from the big bad Indians, huh, doggy?"

"Naw, man, I think he looks more like Lassie. Hey, Timmy, your mommy's callin' you. Time to go home now."

Of all the comments and laughter, Smith's voice was the one that stood out as being less than good natured. "LT, what the fuck we need this cherry for? Shit, his fuckin' uniform is still brand new. Motherfucker ain't gonna' do nothing but get us zapped, 'specially with that piece of shit dog running around yappin' his head off."

Monie tried to come to Gianni's defense. "Come on Smith, give 'em a chance. Maybe they can help us. We sure as hell can't do any worse than we been doing." He snatched at a mosquito buzzing around his face before dropping to one knee, trying to get a better look at the big eared dog. Undeterred by the swiping hand and his sudden movement, the mosquito followed him, landing on the side of his head. A cat quick slap ended the insect's life, squashing black bug flesh between scalp and short cropped light brown hair. Monie glanced at the bloody mess clinging to the palm of his hand then wiped it off on his fatigue pants.

"Yeah, we alive, ain't we? How long you think we gonna' stay that way with some Air Force white boy and a fuckin' dog humpin' the bush with us. Shit, LT, I don't mind goin' out and findin' these dumb Air Force pukes, but I don't want one of 'em watchin' my back. No way man, no way, we don't need 'em, all he gonna' be is trouble."

"All right, Smith, cool it. This ain't up for debate. He's here and he stays, whether you like it or not." Evans knew he had to make it clear that the decision had been made and it was final.

Smith turned and headed back to his bunk, his voice just loud enough for everyone to hear. "This be bullshit. We don't need no Air Force cherry with us. Why don't we just surrender and be done with the whole motherfuckin' thing."

They spent the next few minutes making introductions, Evans pointing to the back of the tent and pointing to a still brooding Smith. "That's Lazirus Smith and as you can tell, he's not real happy with this whole thing." He leaned over and whispered in Gianni's ear. "Just stay out of his way for a while, he'll come around." He motioned Gianni to follow him and walked down the middle of the tent, stopping in front of an unused one on the left side. Stow you gear here and take this bunk. After you get squared away Sergeant Huebner and I will meet you over at the chow tent and go over some of the things you'll need to know. Just ask one of the guys, they'll tell you where it is."

"Okay Lieutenant, I'll be over in a few minutes." As Evans turned to walk out Gianni took a look around the tent. At first thought it wasn't what he had expected, but then he realized, he hadn't known what to expect. The barracks at Tan Son Nhut had been pretty much like the ones he had lived in at Lackland. Three stories high with air-conditioned two man rooms separated by a bathroom. The floors had been a 'daily buffed' hardwood and were always clean enough to eat off. Like the barracks, the tent had a wood floor, but it was splintering plywood and instead of a highly polished sheen it was muted gray from being tracked over by dusty, or muddy combat boots. The roof of the tent was constructed of the same material as the walls, green canvas, that had taken on the familiar grayish tint as the floor. Running the entire thirty foot length, it sloped down at such an angle that trying to walk within two feet of a wall accomplished nothing more than scraping off patches of facial skin. Designed for eighteen men, the tent had more than enough room for the six cots lined up three to a side plus all the equipment that was stored in the rear. As Gianni counted them it occurred to him that if everyone in the tent was assigned a cot then Evans and

Huebner must sleep somewhere else. Rank Had Its Privileges. He had learned that his first week in basic. Gianni dropped his green duffel bag on the cot and jumped back when it skidded a foot across the floor. Retrieving the bag, he gently moved it to the floor and pulled the cot back into place. He didn't see how it could have supported Shadrack, much less him. With pairs of crossed wooden legs at each end and one in the middle, two wooden side rails and what looked like the same material as the tent tacked over them, the whole thing couldn't have weighed more than a pound. He glanced at the wooden foot locker sitting on the floor in front of the cot. If push came to shove he figured he could always curl up and sleep on that. He had just finished stowing his gear when he took one last look around. Something caught his eye that he had missed before. Along with pictures of centerfolds, muscle cars, families, and a newspaper clipping of Tricky Dick with a rifle drawn into his hand and the words, 'Kill all the bastards and let God sort 'em out,' written above his head, was another photograph pinned to the tent wall. This one was above the cot next to him and was the only thing that seemed out of place. Gianni looked at the photograph for several seconds, wondering why someone had put it up, then called to Shadrack and walked out.

WEDNESDAY
APRIL 1, 1970
SOUTH VIETNAM

Gianni sat in the middle of the helicopter, away from the open doors. The constant turning and banking made it difficult for Shadrack to stay in one place on the slick aluminum floor and Gianni had to hold him steady between his knees. He had decided to leave the muzzle off, hoping Shadrack would think it was just another joy ride. Gianni knew it wasn't and the churning in his stomach and sour taste in his throat betrayed his fear. The talking was over, the training was over, and the chance to back out was over. This was the real thing.

Their helicopter was one of sixteen slicks transporting ground units forty miles past where they were going to be dropped off. They would fall out of formation, land just long enough to unload, then the slick would catch up to the rest of the flight. It was hoped that if anyone on the ground saw the slick head toward the deck, then take off again, they would think it had been a mechanical problem that had been quickly fixed.

Evans waved his arm to get everyone's attention, then held up his outstretched right hand and mouthed the words, "five minutes, five minutes". Each man set about checking his equipment, tightening straps, rearranging ammo bandoleers for easy access, and, much to Gianni's surprise, tying condoms over the muzzle of their rifles. Monie tapped Gianni on the shoulder, held out a Trojan and shouted into his ear. "Here, put this over the muzzle. If you trip bailing outta' here ya' don't want the barrel full'a dirt and shit."

As Gianni placed the condom on his rifle, Evans rocked forward off the bulkhead and leaned next to his ear. "You all right?"

Gianni looked at Shadrack, then back at Evans and nodded. Evans had to shout to be heard over the engine and rotor noise, "Depending on the LZ, the landing zone, the pilot will either land or hover a few feet off the ground. Either way, when we hit the door, you follow us. Don't hesitate, it's the worst place you can be. When we're on the ground, we're gonna' fan out. You stick with Monie, stay right behind him and do whatever he does. Got it?"

Gianni nodded again. Evans leaned over to Monie and said something in his ear. Monie nodded his head, looked over to Gianni, and gave him a thumbs up.

The co-pilot reached back and tapped Evans on the shoulder, holding up a gloved finger to indicate one minute. Evans pulled a magazine out of an ammo pouch and held it up in the air. "Lock and load, lock and load!"

Gianni followed everyone's lead as he checked his rifle to make sure it was on safety, inserted a magazine, and pulled the charging handle back. He watched as Robinson uncoiled a belt of M-60 ammo and made the big gun ready for action. As the helicopter started its descent, the door gunners became more alert. Swinging their M-60's back and forth, they scanned the trees for any movement. Rushing toward the ground, faster than Gianni thought was possible, the helicopter suddenly flared, its nose coming up sharply, and lost speed. The door gunners were screaming "GO! GO! GO!" before Gianni even realized they had touched down. It took only seconds for all the men to clear the doors and for the helicopter to take off again.

Gianni and Shadrack were lying in the grass, just behind Monie, without the faintest idea of what to do next. The noise of the departing helicopter was replaced with total silence. Gianni looked around and saw each man peering down the barrel of his rifle, covering his own little section of the jungle. Evans rose up in a crouch, snapped his fingers twice, and led the men out of the clearing and into the trees. Ten yards into the dense growth they stopped, the men instinctively forming a defensive perimeter.

"Boardman, call the flight, tell 'em we got a cold LZ and we're continuing with the mission."

"Roger, LT." Boardman pulled the telephone like handset off his ammo harness, cupping his right hand around the mouthpiece as he tried to raise the helicopter. The twenty-six pound radio strapped to his back under the ruck sack was a curse in the heat of the jungle but was their only lifeline when the 'shit hit the fan' or they needed a quick extraction. Being a radio-man had never been high on Boardman's things to do list. He had requested tank crew training, figuring that a bad day of riding was always better than a good day of walking. He had quickly learned that there was no such thing as a good day of walking when you had to hump the radio and a ruck. Not one to be bitter by nature, he couldn't help but hope that all the tank guys came down with incurable dysentery.

"Geoff?" Evans scanned the bush while he talked to his sergeant.

"Looks good, LT. If we had company, they'd have tried to take out the slick. I think we're in clean."

"Yeah, me, too, but I want to get away from here before we figure out exactly which way to go. Have Smith take the point and put Tuckett on the tail. Keep Gianni and the dog in the middle. We don't need him wandering off and gettin' lost on his first day. God only knows how much that dog costs and they'd probably want us to pay for it."

They made their way through the trees for almost a half hour before Evans signaled for a break. He and Huebner checked the map while the rest of the men loosened their packs and scattered out among the trees. Monie sat down next to Gianni. "Is it all right if I sit this close to the dog?"

"Oh, yeah, that's no problem, he won't bother ya."

"Actually I was wondering if I would be bothering him. The LT says were not supposed to mess around with him. Ya' know, he's out here for the mission, not just a pet."

"Ya, well, he's still just a dog and he likes to be around people as much as any other dog. He knows when it's time to work and time to fuck off. Don't worry about 'im. Go ahead and pet him if you want. He likes to have his ears scratched. Just don't say anything about the size of 'em."

"Does that bother him?"

"No, but it bothers me." Gianni grinned. "He's my buddy, aren't ya, Shad? Yeah, you're a good boy. Ya' know, before I volunteered for dog school, I never imagined working with a dog. Now I can't imagine working without one."

"I know what you mean. I grew up with animals, love being around 'em." As Monie's weathered hand rubbed the top of the dog's head

Gianni noticed the scar for the first time. Running from the edge of the left wrist bone it traveled up Monie's arm and across, ending in the fleshy crease of the elbow. With the rest of his arm tanned a deep brown from constant exposure to the sun the half inch wide jagged scar remained fish white with its pulpy looking texture rising higher than the smooth skin around it. Gianni figured it wasn't a surgical scar and whatever had happened to him, it must have hurt like hell. He was just about to ask him about it when Evans signaled them to get ready to move out.

"Look, just stay close to me and I'll show ya' what to do. You'll be fine." Monie gave the dog one last rub and pushed himself up.

Evans made his way back to Gianni and Monie. "Gianni, 'til we get in the area where the pilot went down, I want you stayin' in the middle of the squad. Once we're there, you and the dog can do your stuff. Stay near Dustin here unless he's on point, then I want you to stick to Schoonhoven. All right, let's move out."

They moved for the next four hours, stopping only for water breaks or to check their position. Gianni was dead tired and drenched in sweat. Schoonhoven moved up next to him while Monie was on point and held his hand out. "Here, take these, wash 'em down with some water."

"What are they?"

"Salt tablets. You have to keep taking them out here or you'll drop like a lead balloon."

"Thanks, Doc."

"No problem. If you start getting light headed or anything, let me know, I'll get the LT to take a break."

"I don't wanna' hold everyone up, I'll be okay."

"Don't worry about it, we all went through it. Takes a while to get used to this heat."

"Never knew any place could be so hot, can't hardly breathe."

Schoonhoven's proper manner slipped away as he flashed a big shit eatin' grin. "Yeah, ain't we fightin' for a regular fuckin' Garden of Eden."

Answering to 'Doc', Johnathan, or simply Schoonhoven but never, ever, John, the squad's medic was an enigma of gigantic proportions. A six-foot four, blond haired, blue eyed twenty-three year old graduate of Berkley with degrees in Philosophy and Liberal Arts with an English minor, all earned between war protest marches and acts of non-violent civil disobedience, Johnathan Schoonhoven was the exception to the rule of a combat soldier. Exempt from the draft because of his age and easily qualified for status of conscientious objector due to his fervent, if not vocal opinions of the war and killing, he did what no one ever expected: he enlisted. Not one to be told how to live his life he took umbrage when informed by his anti-war classmates that anyone who supported the war was a traitor not only to himself but to his country as well. If nothing else, his philosophy studies had opened his mind to the fact that a man must answer to himself, to his own beliefs and values, and in those find his own self worth, not the worth defined by others. Had he been several years younger, or more specifically, draft age, Schoonhoven would have been torn on the horns of a dilemma. On one hand his friends would have demanded that he conform to their way of thinking and continue to protest the war and on the other hand the military would have demanded that he report for induction and fight in the war. His continued enrollment at Berkley had avoided the latter, but not the former. To Schoonhoven, the philosopher, the answer was simplistic, enlist. In good conscious he was able to defy what he considered the unreasonable demands of his societal circle and simultaneously thumb his nose at the military by showing up on their doorstep uninvited. To Schoonhoven it made perfect sense, philosophically. It also made sense to volunteer to be a medic since saving lives, as opposed to taking lives, left him on solid moral ground. Everyone, he thought, even his friends, would consider him a non-combatant. Johnathan 'Doc' Schoonhoven had been quick to learn that he should have been more concerned with what the Viet Cong thought.

Evans and Huebner made their way back to Gianni and Monie. "We're just about in the area where the chute was spotted. A Bronco pilot was still able to see it in the trees yesterday, so we might get lucky and find it right away." Evans' expression turned deadly serious. The problem is, the Gooks might have left it up for an ambush, in which case we're gonna' be in deep shit. What I need to know from you, Gianni, is how the hell do we work the dog?"

"How far away are we?"

"A klick, maybe less."

Gianni looked around to see if any leaves were blowing, then stood up and checked the breeze for himself. "If I wasn't here, how would you move in there?"

"We'd keep on pushin' through, real slow, checkin' for traps and any sign of an ambush. Problem is, if ya' find an ambush, it's already too late. Why, what'da ya' got in mind?"

"Which direction should his chute be?"

"Same way we're headed, give or take a little."

"All right, we're headed directly into whatever breeze there is, which is more than enough for Shadrack to alert on if there's someone out there. What if we keep going for another five or six hundred yards, then I'll take Shadrack and quarter each side of us for a hundred, hundred and fifty yards. That'll tell us if there's anybody up there waitin'."

Evans looked up at Huebner. "Well?"

"That's what he's here for. If he says he can do it, I think we ought'a give it a try."

"All right, do we go with you when you do this or what?"

"No, LT, it'd be better if it's just me and the dog, maybe one man to keep me from gettin' into trouble since I really don't know what the fuck I'm doing. This ain't like walkin' a perimeter post."

"Dustin, what about it?"

"I'll make sure he don't get lost, LT."

"Okay, that's it, then. Let's get movin'."

Evans spread the squad out as Gianni and Monie started the search. Smith mumbled something about stopping to let a dog take a leak in the bush was bullshit and that they ought'a be doing it like they always had. A glare from Huebner was all it took to silence him.

"What am I supposed to do, what'da I need to know?"

"There's nothin' to it. Just walk behind me, off to my left side. The dog will always have his head into the wind so as we move off in this direction, he'll basically be looking to the right. When we come back this way, he'll be looking to his left. You just have to watch in the opposite direction."

"Wait a minute, you said he's gonna' be lookin' into the wind."

"Yeah."

"Gianni, there ain't no wind."

"Don't worry about it. You ready?"

"Yeah, I guess so."

"Okay, let's go. Oh, one other thing. If you hear me yell 'DOWN,' hit the dirt. It means there's a grenade or a booby trap or something."

"What's the dog gonna' be doing?"

"Diggin' a hole big enough for me and him. You're on your own." Gianni grinned and walked off through the trees.

They searched for a little over a hundred yards, then reversed direction. As they passed the squad, Monie, now more sure of himself and quickly becoming a veteran of walking behind someone who was walking behind a dog, gave a big shit-eating grin and whispered at Smith.

"Damn if this ain't more fun than shittin' down your own leg."

Smith flipped him off. Monie felt compelled to return the favor.

They had gone a little over half their intended distance when Shadrack hesitated. Walking back and forth, he checked the air and tried to pull Gianni off to his left. Gianni crouched down and peered through the trees.

"What's going on?"

"He's got something."

Monie lowered his voice to a soft whisper. "Gooks?"

"I don't think so. Scent doesn't seem to be strong enough, he'd be showing a different alert."

Monie watched the dog walk back and forth at the end of the leash, testing the air with his nose and looking back at his master. "Think he smells an animal?"

"Could be, but it would have to be pretty small, he's having trouble staying on the scent."

"A snake?" Monie immediately started checking the ground and tree limbs around him.

"No, I know it's not a snake. He'd be growling, he hates the little motherfuckers."

"What'a we do now?"

"Go back and get the LT. I'll wait here."

Monie was back with the squad within minutes. Evans moved next to Gianni. "What'a ya' got, Gianni?"

"Shadrack is pickin' up a scent. I'm not sure what it is but I think we ought to follow it in."

"Any chance we're runnin' into a trap?"

"No, LT, I don't think so. He'd tell me if it was."

"Yeah, I almost forgot, you talk to dogs. All right, Dustin, you take the point and we'll see what it is."

"Wait a minute, LT, that won't work. The dog has to go first. He'll lead us right up to whatever it is. If Dustin gets in front of him, it'll fuck him all up, he'll get confused and won't know what scent to follow."

"All right, but, Dustin, you stay close to 'em."

They made their way through the trees for almost two hundred yards before Gianni held his hand up. He motioned for Evans. "We're pretty close now, LT, the scent is a lot stronger. You want me and Dustin to go check it out?"

"No, I'll go with you." Three minutes later Evans was staring in disbelief. "I'll be a motherfucker. He found it, he actually found it!"

Gianni reached down and petted Shadrack. "Good boy Shad, that's a good boy. You earned your pay today." Gianni looked up at the parachute hanging from the tree and the white flight helmet lying on the ground just below it.

"Big fuckin' deal, so the mutt can find a parachute hangin' in a tree." Robinson was gobbling down a can of C-ration peaches while Smith was complaining about the dog. "Why don't they just ship his hairy ass over to the 82nd Airborne, he can find all the parachutes he wants."

Robinson drank the rest of the juice out of the can, then licked the heavy syrup off the plastic spoon. "Come on, Lazirus, give the dog a break. It would'a taken us all day to find that 'chute and they did it in just a few minutes. Shit, far as I'm concerned, if they can find these boys quicker than we can alone, it means the faster we get outta' the bush and back to the Palace. 'Sides, they ain't bothered you none. 'Bout the only one they really hang around is Monie, and sometimes Doc."

"Don't make no matter, Delmar, that Air Force white boy don't belong out here, he'll get us all zapped for sure."

"I don't see why you say that, Lazirus. He made sure we wasn't walkin' into no ambush, and he did find the 'chute."

"Yeah, yeah. Well, even a blind man finds a nickel now and then. You mark my words, he be nothin' but trouble. Wait 'til the shit hits the fan. He's gonna' run or he's gonna' freeze. Then he's gonna' 'spect us to save his ass. You just mark my words." Smith watched as Robinson dug a hole with the toe of his boot and dropped the empty can into it. "You be carryin' another can of them peaches?"

Gianni reached out and grabbed Huebner by the arm. "Sarge, I think it'd be better if you didn't touch the 'chute. Shadrack can get a better scent that way."

"We gotta' check it for booby traps. Your Major wouldn't like it if we got pieces of you scattered all over South Vietnam."

"That's all right, Shadrack will let me know if anyone's messed with it."

"You sure?"

"No, but I think that's the way we should do it anyway."

Evans walked over, checked his map, then looked up at the patches of sky peeking through the trees. "I figure we've got four, maybe five hours of light left. If the dog can pick up his trail now, we might be able to gain some ground on him before we hunker down for the night."

"Hunker down for the night? Why we gonna' do that?"

"Gianni, look, the jungle belongs to Charlie at night. No tellin' what we might run into. Besides, ya' can't see your hand in front of your face out here. We'd never be able to follow his trail."

"LT, you're thinkin' like a person, not like a dog. Shadrack works better at night than he does in the daytime. We don't need to see anything. If he can pick up his scent from here, he'll follow it all night long. It doesn't have to be light."

"Well, that's all fine and dandy, but it won't do us a hell of a lot of good if we walk into a Gook patrol."

Gianni felt a little embarrassed trying to tell an Army Lieutenant how to work in the bush. "Ain't gonna' happen. Shadrack would hear 'em and smell 'em long before they could hear us. He'll tell me if anyone's even close. If we move at night, we're gonna' find that pilot a hell of a lot quicker. If he's still alive."

"You sure about this?"

"Yes, sir, absolutely. Hell, back on base, even back in 'the World', nights are the only time we ever work. That's the whole idea of using a dog, they can do things at night that we can't."

Evans wasn't sure what to do. He didn't like the idea of moving at night unless they had to. "I hope you know what you're doing, Giancarlo, this could get real serious real quick." He shifted the weight of his rifle under his arm while he looked around, trying to decide what to do. "All right, Geoff, get 'em ready to move out. Don't say anything to 'em about movin' at night, we'll wait and see what happens. Gianni, do what ya' have to do to find his trail."

"Right, LT, won't take but a minute to get ready."

Gianni fitted Shadrack with the tracking harness and led him over to the helmet and parachute. "Smell it, boy, smell it. That's a good boy, smell it." Shadrack tested the helmet, then the parachute harness, then back to the helmet. Gianni waved his hand under the dog's face. "Track, boy, track, Shadrack."

The dog sniffed the ground and took off through the trees. They followed the track for almost two hours when Gianni signaled the squad to stop. He patted his leg, whispered "Heel", and the dog came to his side. Evans and Huebner moved up next to him. "What's the problem, you lose the trail?"

"No, LT, he's got a strong scent. This guy is probably moving pretty fast, workin' up a strong sweat. That leaves a real good scent."

"Well, what's wrong, then? Why'd we stop?"

"He's not a machine, LT. I gotta' give him a break every now and then, he needs some water. Won't do us any good if he drops from heat exhaustion."

"Oh, okay, no problem. How much time's he gonna' need?"

"Just a couple minutes. Let him drink a little and take a piss."

Ten minutes later Shadrack set a pace that had the squad huffing and puffing before they had covered two hundred yards. In less than an hour the dog stuck his head beneath a large stand of bushes, then emerged dragging a bluish green piece of clothing.

"Good boy, that's a good boy." Gianni held it up for Evans.

"What'd he find?"

"The pilot's G-suit. Must'a crawled in here and took it off. Probably got too hot for 'em."

Evans looked around and motioned to Boardman. "Kent, how long 'til we check in?"

"Little over an hour."

"All right, we keep movin' 'til then. Gianni, do your stuff."

Shadrack took off through the trees straining at the 360-inch leash. To cut down on the number of times the dog got tangled around bushes and tree trunks, Gianni kept almost half the leash coiled in his left hand. He had never traveled this far or for this long during training exercises and the strain of carrying his Car-15 in his right hand was beginning to tell. Concentrating on his dog, Gianni was startled when Monie grabbed him by the arm and signaled for a break. As Monie pointed toward the sky, Gianni could hear the drone of the Bronco's engine in the distance. Boardman was already on the radio trying to make contact.

"What'da ya' think, Gianni, should we keep movin' or look for a place to hold up for the night?" Evans tried to peer through the thick jungle growth as he spoke.

Gianni stroked Shadrack's back while Monie rubbed his ears. "I think we ought'a keep movin', LT."

"All right. Geoff, get the guys ready to move out. Dustin, you stay behind Gianni. Oh, Geoff, wait a minute. Have Smith take tail end and when it starts to get dark, have him bunch everyone closer together. We don't need anyone wandering off and gettin' lost."

"He's gonna' raise hell about movin' at night, LT."

"Yeah, well, ain't war a bitch. Let's move it."

Several more times he had to shorten the leash to keep it from getting tangled in the trees. The darkness made everything blend together. Several times he'd gone around a tree only to discover the dog had gone around the other side. Branches, dead limbs, and razor sharp leaves, all high enough for the dog to glide beneath, scraped across Gianni's bare face and neck. Insects, falling out of the trees or swarming to the scent, feasted on the raw and oozing flesh. Whatever he had thought about training in Texas, it had been a picnic compared to the Vietnam jungle.

Shadrack stopped suddenly and let out a low growl. Monie almost walked up Gianni's back. Whispering in Gianni's ear, he hoped the answer to his question wouldn't be 'Gooks'.

"What is it, what's the problem?"

"Snake."

Monie strained his eyes through the darkness to where the dog's head was pointing. Evans moved up beside them.

"Why'd ya stop, what's wrong?"

"Gianni says there's a snake up ahead. The dog found it."

Evans could do no better then Monie in trying to see the snake. "Now ya' know another reason we don't like to move at night. Ya' never know they're there 'til ya' step on 'em.'"

"We didn't step on this one, LT, and we know he's there. Give me something to toss, I'll see if I can scare it away."

Evans picked up a dead branch. "Here, don't make too much noise."

Gianni tossed the stick just in front of where Shadrack was standing. Even though none of the men could see anything, they all heard something crawl off to their right. Gianni gave his dog the signal to track and followed him through the trees.

The hours went by with the dog never slowing his pace and the squad stopping only for five or ten-minute breaks. The excitement of being out in the bush had started to wear off and even though he was used to working at night, Gianni was feeling the effects of fatigue. It was becoming harder and harder to keep up with the dog's fast pace as the sixty pound rucksack tore into his shoulders. Not blessed with the thick calluses the other men had developed, he had to constantly move the straps as they rubbed away skin.

Shadrack slowed down, sniffing the ground, then raising his head to check the air. After several minutes he ignored the ground completely and strained at the leash while holding his head into what he perceived as the wind. Gianni signaled the squad to stop and changed his grip on his rifle so it would be ready in case he had to use it.

Monie crouched down next to him. "Another snake?"

"Nope, a lot bigger."

"Gooks?"

"Maybe, but I don't think so." Gianni unclipped the leather leash from his web belt, hooked it on Shadrack's choke chain and took the 360-leash off the tracking harness.

Evans and Huebner moved up next to them. "What's up, Gianni?"

"We got something, LT. Shadrack's ignoring the ground track, he picked something up in the wind."

"Yeah, you and the phantom wind. What is it?"

"A person."

"Just one or more? Like maybe a VC or NVA patrol?"

"Could be, LT, but if I had to bet money on it, I'd say it's our pilot. I think Shad kept checkin' between the ground and the air 'til he was sure it was the same scent. It's a pretty strong alert. Whoever it is, he's holed up and not movin'."

"I don't want to put any pressure on ya', Gianni, but it's not money you're bettin', it's our lives." Evans dropped down to both knees to relieve the pressure on his back. He knew they had to find out who was out there. The question was how. "Can he lead us right to 'im?"

"He can take you right through 'im if you want."

"Just get us close to where he is, we'll do the rest."

Even through the darkness they could see the heavy stand of trees surrounded by thick low lying bushes.

Trying to be as quiet as possible, Gianni whispered directly into Evans' ear. "Gotta' be that stand of trees, the scent's way too strong and too narrow for it to be coming from anywhere else."

"All right, you and Monie stay here." Evans motioned for Huebner to circle around to the left while he went to the right. Without being told, Monie sighted his rifle into the center of the trees and waited. Not knowing what else to do, Gianni laid down beside him and did the same. Evans disappeared into the trees and emerged less than two minutes later followed by an Air Force Captain.

"Jesus Christ, Gianni, you did it, you sure as shit fuckin' did it!" Monie pushed himself up off the ground and held out his hand.

THURSDAY
APRIL 2, 1970
CAMELOT PALACE

The pickup and flight back to Camelot Palace had been uneventful. Dead tired after their all-day all-night ordeal, the squad stumbled back to their tent. Within seconds, they were fast asleep. Gianni didn't awaken as Shadrack got up from the floor beside his cot and wandered across the tent.

"Jesus Christ! Goddamn motherfucker, get the fuck away from me!" Every man was up and on his feet at the sounds of the screams. "Keep this motherfuckin' dog away from me 'fore I put a bullet in his head!" Smith was standing at the head of his cot as he stared down at the dog that moments before had licked his face and awakened him from a deep sleep. "You be hearin' me, Cherry? Get this motherfucker away 'fore I kill 'im!" Smith had backed up to the canvas wall of the tent and was visibly shaking.

"Shadrack, heel. Come on, heel." The dog turned to his master and trotted over across the floor. "That's a good boy." Gianni scratched the dog's head and looked back over to Smith. "I'm sorry, Lazirus, I guess he just got bored and went looking around."

"If'n he gets bored again, he gonna' get dead! Keep him the fuck away from me, ya' hear? I don't want nothin' ta do with him, or you."

"Come on, man, I said I was sorry. He didn't do anything, he won't hurt ya.'"

"Laz, lighten up, Bro, he's just a dog. Hell, you've fucked worse-lookin' women than him." Robinson knew any more sleep was hopeless and was pulling on his fatigue pants. "Come on, man, it ain't no big deal."

"I don't give a shit. I ain't wantin' him around me, here or in the bush. Keep him the fuck away!"

"All right, all right. Look, I'll say it again, I'm sorry, I'll make sure he never gets near you again."

Smith pulled on his pants and slipped into his boots. "Come on, Delmar, lets get some chow. This place is startin' to smell like dog shit." Robinson shrugged at Gianni, then followed Smith out of the tent.

"I didn't need this, Shadrack, I really didn't need this. You better straighten up or they're gonna' have us guardin' the shitter for the rest of the war." Gianni leaned back on his cot and stared at the canvas ceiling.

"Don't let it bother you, Gianni. It ain't no big deal. He'll cool off, just some after-mission jitters. We all get 'em." Monie picked up a half smoked cigarette off the dirt covered floor under his cot and re-lit it.

"What'da ya' mean?"

"You know, after ya' get back, ya' start thinking about all the things that could'a gone wrong, how ya' might'a got zapped or how ya' might'a tripped a booby trap. All the shit that could'a happened but didn't, but still might the next time. Everybody goes through it, it's normal."

Gianni pushed himself up to one elbow and looked over at Monie. He thought about what Dustin was saying. 'All the things that could happen'. Things that you never had to think about back in 'the World'. 'The World'. He wondered why no one called it the 'states', or home, just 'the World'. Where were they now? Another planet, a dream, a nightmare, hell? Gianni hadn't seen enough to know that they were anywhere but 'the World'. He looked down at Shadrack, sniffing a bug between the two cots. As the dog nudged the frantic insect with his nose Gianni started to think about home. About his parents, Chuck, and Hank, and cruising the beach in The Car. The more he thought about it the harder it was to see it.

He looked at Dustin who had laid back on his cot blowing smoke rings at the canvas ceiling. "Hey, Dustin."

He blew another smoke ring, aiming for a hovering mosquito, then exhaled the rest of the smoke. "Yeah?"

"Where you from?"

"What?" Mosquito hunting took full concentration.

"Where you from, where'd you grow up."

Tired of the game, he snatched at the blood sucker with his left hand, missing it by a country mile. "Fuck! Huh…oh, Colorado." He took another drag and blew it at the bug.

"Colorado, no shit.

"No shit."

"Where about's, Denver?"

"Nope, Burning Mattress." The bug landed on his leg and he slapped at it, a cloud of dust puffing up from his fatigue pants.

Gianni's face scrunched as he tried to remember if he'd ever heard of the city before. "Burning Mattress, where the hell is that?"

Dustin had to fight to keep from laughing. "Just above Hot Springs."

Gianni thought for a moment. "I thought Hot Springs was in Arkansas."

"Fuckin' Flatlander…it's a joke asshole. Hot Springs, Burning Mattress, get it? He stared at Gianni in amazement. "Haven't you ever been to a rodeo?

"No.

"Jesus Christ Giancarlo, if brains were leather you couldn't saddle a bug." He dropped the cigarette in the butt can next to the cot then rolled over to face Gianni. "Think about it. Hot springs, put a mattress above it, it catches fire…burning mattress."

Gianni's expression brightened for a moment, then turned deadpan. "Hey, yeah, I get it now. It ain't all that funny."

"What can I expect from a guy who spends his days lookin' up a dog's ass. You need to get out more Gianni."

"Maybe your jokes need to be better."

"Fuck you, everyone else likes 'em."

"Well, I'm part of 'everyone' and I didn't like it."

"Like I said, fuck you."

Gianni dropped his arm off the cot and rubbed the top of the dog's head. Having gotten bored with playing with the bug he had decided to go to sleep and see what kind of adventures his doggy dreams would bring him. Gianni slid his hand down the side of the dog's head, bunching up the loose fur below his ear. Shadrack let out a long sigh at his master's touch. "You really from Colorado, or was that part of the hilarious joke?"

"No, it wasn't part of the joke, I'm really from Colorado…and it was hilarious." He reached down to the wooden floor, shook another cigarette from the pack and lit it with the Zippo. " I live about thirty miles west of Denver, in the mountains, little place called Conifer.

"The mountains, cool."

"Yeah, in the summer it's cool and in the winter it's cold. Beats the shit outta this place though. Come to think of it, drivin' a nail through your foot beats this place. Heat, bugs, and Gooks, oh boy, I've died and gone to heaven."

Gianni grinned. "Except for the Gooks…and maybe being hotter, this isn't much different than South Florida."

"You can keep it, I'd rather have the snow. If you get cold you can always put on more clothes…if you're hot the most you can do is get naked, then you're naked and still hot. Ya-hoo, ain't that a treat." He went back to blowing smoke rings at the mosquito, slightly annoyed that it had been joined by several friends. The bugs joined forces and attacked his bare left foot. He shook them off and turned to Gianni, a quite, serious look on his face. "Ya know what's weird Gianni? When I first got over here I thought the thing I was gonna miss most were women. Ya know, goin' dancin', seein' a movie, knockin' off a half bottle of Jack and gettin' laid." He felt the sudden urge to explain away the last statement. "Hey, I miss gettin laid, don't get me wrong…but it's not what I miss the most. I thought it would be, but it's not. I miss ridin' out in the pastures in the early morning, movin' through the herd, watchin' the calves feedin' and smellin' the grass. I miss sittin' on a horse an feelin' 'im shake off the flies while I watched the elk bedded down in the trees or a hawk circlin', looking for a rabbit." For the moment, Dustin was back where every swinging dick in Camelot Palace wanted to be; 'The World'. He took another drag on the cigarette and blew the smoke with a loud sigh. "Christ, I'd give up a blow job right now just to step in horse shit or smell a wet saddle blanket."

Gianni smiled at Dustin's wish list. "You sound like a homesick cowboy."

"You got it Gianni…that's what I am." He snatched at another mosquito.God, I miss that shit! I'd give my big nut to get out of here."

The sound of chuckling filtered over from Gianni. "You're big nut huh?"

"Yeah." Dustin made a big show of grabbing his crotch then rooting around like he was looking for something. "Found 'em…no doubt which is which. The big one's about the size of a rice grain, the other one is a little bitty motherfucker."

Gianni grinned as propped himself up higher on the cot and watched the artillery barrage of smoke. It made him think of Chuck. "You got any brothers or sisters?"

"Naw, just me and the folks…my Mom and Dad. I guess they figured that with breeding stock like me anything else would just spoil the herd." He rolled his head and flashed Gianni a huge shit eattin' grin. "One good bull does a lot of fuckin'."

It was another one of the western expressions that Dustin was fond of irritating everyone with, including Gianni. He didn't understand half of them. "What's all this stuff about pastures and horses and stuff, you live on some kinda' ranch or something?"

"Do cows shit green." Another one.

"Huh?"

"Flatlander. Yeah, I live on a ranch. Born and bred."

"Really? I was just kiddin'. How big is it?"

"Little over a thousand acres."

"A thousand acres!" Gianni had trouble comprehending anyone growing up on a thousand acres of land. "You own it…I mean, you know, is it yours or do you just work there, or…?"

"Its' my folk's, but I guess it'll end up being mine, it's where I grew up. It's sure as hell where I'd be right now if I hadn't got drafted, and no, I don't work there. I'm a bullfighter."

"What'da ya' mean, a bullfighter? With a cape and a sword…stuff like that?"

"No, asshole, a rodeo bullfighter…a rodeo clown. Ya' know, clown faces and baggy clothes." He pointed above his cot at the picture Gianni had seen the first day. Gianni looked up at the picture and studied it carefully. It took a moment but he finally realized that it really was a picture of Dustin. He was heavier than his now rail thin hundred and fifty or so pounds but the broad brimmed cowboy hat added several inches to his five-foot eight frame. The bushy light brown mustache in the picture changed his appearance enough that Gianni had trouble believing that the soldier lying in the cot next to him was the same man as the cowboy in the picture. The scar on the left arm dispelled all doubt. It was the same scar he had noticed on Dustin's arm in the bush. Gianni stared at the picture a moment longer. A slight grin spread across his face as he dropped his gaze back down to Dustin.

"Looks like you ran away from home and joined the circus…either that or your mother dresses you funny."

Dustin flipped him off. "The orange wig and baggy clothes and painted clown face are for the spectators, ya know, to keep 'em entertained between bull rides. That's where the jokes you don't seem to appreciate come in." He glanced over his head at the picture. "That part of it is all fun and games, what we're really there for is to keep the bulls away from the riders." He tossed a casual arm at the photo. "My folks took that at the last rodeo I worked before I left for boot camp."

The shot was of Dustin in his costume, standing in front of a wooden fence with what looked like seven or eight huge bulls behind it. Gianni stared at the picture. If Dustin said he was a bullfighter he'd believe him...but he sure looked like a clown.

"We keep the bull away from the bullrider when he gets thrown or goes the eight seconds." Gianni pushed himself up farther on his cot as he listened. "See, bulls aren't like horses, they'll go after the rider once he's on the ground and try to hook 'em, get 'em with their horns. We get between the bull and the rider and distract 'em 'til the rider can get away."

"You ever, you know...you ever get hit by the bulls, get rammed...whatever the hell you called it."

"It's called gettin' hooked, and yeah, we get hooked all the time. Mostly it's no big a deal, ya just get thrown around some or get flipped over the fence, usually nothin' more than some cuts or a couple of broken bones." He held his left arm in the air, momentarily lost in the memory of the blinding pain that now lay dormant as a scarred badge of honor. "That's how I got this. Like I said, no big deal really...but every once in a while it gets hairy. Bullfighter got killed couple years back up in Cheyenne when a rider got hung up." Dustin's eyes seemed to glaze over as he recounted the event. "Guy was gettin' thrown around pretty bad. Snapped his wrist while it was still in the bull rope and from what I hear he was takin' a horn to the side of the head everytime the bull spun. That's bad shit when a rider gets hung up, sixteen, seventeen hundred pounds of mad bull will fuck you up in a New York second...ya gotta do something to help 'im. Anyway, the bullfighter went over the top of bull, got the guy's hand turned over and pulled 'im loose. I guess that's when he stepped in it. The bull tried to go after the rider while he was layin' on the ground and the guy jumped between the two of 'em, tryin' to draw 'im away...got hooked in the chest...fuckin' horn went right through 'im. He died in the dirt."

"Jesus, what a terrible way to die."

Dustin looked up, blinking away the fog. "No Giancarlo, no, it's a great way to die. He cowboy'd up, he did what he was out there to do, save the rider, and he died doin' what he loved...ya' can't ask for more than that."

Gianni looked back up at the picture of the man who made a living jumping in front of bulls. 'Died doing what he loved.' Could anybody love something that much...so much they'd die for it?

SUNDAY
APRIL 5, 1970
SOUTH VIETNAM

The chopper landed ten klicks away from where the F-4E had gone down. They were looking for only one man. The pilot's ejection seat had thrown him clear of the burning aircraft but his chute never opened. The Wizzo had radioed the flight leader that the area was swarming with enemy soldiers. The combined firepower of the circling F-4s, the responding RESCAP aircraft, and the Cobra gunships was not enough to get a slick in and out safely. The Wizzo had stayed on the air begging for help until the battery in his radio went dead. If he was still alive, it was up to Evans and his men to get him out.

It was late afternoon by the time they reached the area and the first thing they found were pieces of the wreckage. A large burnt-out section of trees was evidence of the huge fireball that resulted as the crewless aircraft slammed into the ground. Gianni had never seen a plane crash before and couldn't believe such a large plane could become so unrecognizable. They stayed hidden in the trees, well away from the wreckage, as Evans and Huebner studied the map.

"All right, the 'chute went down right about here, about two or three hundred yards from where we are now. Our guy was last heard from here, another two hundred yards past that. The bombing mission was to the northeast of where he went down, so we gotta' figure he won't head that way, and here's the wreckage over here. If he's still got his map, he's probably gonna' head southeast. See, we got a water supply right here and it still puts him in the right direction to eventually run into friendlies."

Huebner scratched the back of his neck and spit out a bug as he watched Evans point out the different map points.. "What if he's just stayin' put? They must'a told him we'd come looking."

"If you were stuck out here, would you stay put, especially with Charlie crawlin' around lookin' for ya'? Even if he knows we're comin', I think he'll still be scared enough to make a run for it." Evans looked over to where Gianni and Shadrack were resting. "We gotta' ask Gianni how this is gonna' work, but I'm thinkin' if we circle 'round the wreckage site and come up here, we'll either run into him or at least be able to find his 'chute. Gianni ought to be able to track him from there. What'da ya' think?"

"We stand a real good chance of runnin' into Charlie out here. This place was real hot."

"We gotta' try it. Go get Gianni."

Evans explained the plan to Gianni. "Looks good to me except for one thing."

Evans looked back down at the map to see where he'd gone wrong. "What's the problem?"

"The JP-4, the fuel from the wreckage. It'll fuck up Shadrack. We'll be walkin' right through the downwind scent. Dog's don't like that stuff, screws up their nose. We'd be better off if we circled 'round this way, upwind of it. He won't get messed up and he'll still be able to tell us if there are any Gooks close by."

Evans looked at Huebner, who just shrugged. "Okay."

Gianni knew this was nothing like the first mission. He couldn't help but see the bomb craters, the trees shattered by rocket strikes or blackened by napalm canisters, and the thousands upon thousands of shell casings littering the ground. This was beginning to look more like a war and the excitement he had felt was quickly being replaced by a feeling of dread.

Tuckett held up his hand. The entire squad was quiet, much quieter than they had been the other time, and Gianni sensed they were worried. Evans took time to check each man's position, then moved up next to Tuckett. "What'da ya' got?"

They were at the top of a small rise, just high enough to look out over the jungle for several hundred yards. "Movement, LT, over there, just to the right of that small clearing. Saw at least three of 'em."

"Which way?"

"Couldn't tell. They were on the edge of the clearing, then just disappeared into the trees."

"All right, hang loose, I'm gonna' go back and talk to Giancarlo, see if the dog can help us out."

Evans crawled back a few feet, motioned for Huebner to follow him, and made his way back to Gianni. "We've got Gooks, three of 'em, maybe more."

Huebner absentmindedly tightened the straps on his rucksack. "Gonna' be a real bitch trying to find our boy with them wanderin' around down there."

"Not if we can get them first." Evans shifted to his left. "Gianni, look, things could get real hairy for us. If we can get down off this rise without being seen, then circle 'round the Gooks, can Shadrack lead us back to where they are? I mean, can he pick up their scent like he did with that other pilot?"

"He'll take us to whoever is out there, but it could end up being our guy, the Gooks that Tuckett saw, or any other Gooks that might be out there. There's no way for him to pick out certain people. He'll find whoever is out there." Huebner was thinking over what Gianni said. "If the dog only finds those Gooks, chances are they're the only ones around. If he starts smellin' a bunch more, we'll still have time to back off and wait. And if we get lucky and he finds our boy right away, we can grab him and beat feet."

"Gianni, you've never done anything like this. If you don't think you're ready for it, just say so. We'll either find another way or back off for a while and see what happens." Evans looked up at Huebner who nodded his agreement.

"That guy's down there somewhere waitin' for help, LT, we gotta' give it a try. I'm just scared I'm gonna' fuck up."

"Just follow everyone else. If someone shoots at you, get down and shoot back."

It took half an hour to make their way down the small rise. Evans pulled the map out of his thigh pocket. "Here we are, right here. This is where Tuckett spotted the Gooks."

"Which way were they headed?"

"Don't know, only saw 'em for a second." Evans looked up from the map. "We gotta' know, Gianni, if they're still out there. We gotta' know."

Gianni studied the map for a few moments, then pointed to a spot. "Can we get down to here?"

"Yeah, I think so. What'da ya' got in mind?"

"I can quarter this whole area up through here where Tuckett saw the Gooks. If they're still there, I'll find 'em."

"Okay. Geoff, have Smith take the back and tell Robinson to stay behind Monie. If we run into trouble, we're gonna' need the gun up front. Gianni, if we do run into something, hit the ground and try to get back to the middle of the squad. Don't get hung out there all by yourself."

"Don't have to tell me twice, LT."

"Okay, let's move."

Gianni worked the dog slowly, staying as quiet as possible. As they reached the end of the first leg he signaled for the squad to stop, and dropped down to one knee. Monie moved up next to him, motioning the rest of the squad to remain where they were.

"What's up, Gianni?"

"We're gonna' turn here, head straight through and see if there's anybody back upwind."

"You all right?"

"I'm scared outta' my fuckin' mind! Aren't you?"

"Do squirrels live in timber? Of course I'm scared asshole...but bein' scared don't mean ya quit doin' ya job, now lets find this guy so we can get the hell out of here."

Gianni whispered the command "Find 'em" and the dog moved out, nose held high, testing the air. They had moved less than a hundred yards when the dog stopped, tested the air, turned right, and started up through the trees.

"Got 'em, LT."

"How far?"

"Can't tell yet, gonna' have to move in, see how strong the scent gets. This is real still air down here, we're gonna' get real close before we know where they are."

"All right, let's see who it is." Evans turned to move back and stopped to whisper in Monie's ear. "Don't let him fuck up." Monie nodded and moved out after Gianni.

The dog was now moving directly into the scent path. Gianni felt the eagerness running through the leash and tightened his grip on the rifle. He had already decided if he ran into anybody other than their lost pilot, he was going to hold down the trigger 'til the rifle was empty, then dig his way back to 'the World'.

As the scent got stronger, the dog strained at the leash, trying to pull Gianni faster and faster. He stopped suddenly, mid-stride, one front paw off the ground, dangling, like he had stepped on a thorn. His ears, as large as they were, stood straight up and pointed forward, absorbing every sound that mingled with the scent. Gianni dropped to the ground, the rest of the squad taking their cue from him.

Monie crawled forward, moving small twigs out of his way as he went. Gianni held a finger to his lips and pointed forward. They made their way back to Evans and Huebner. Monie quickly motioning them not to speak, picked up a small stick and wrote in the dirt, '3 men, 50 yds, coming'.

Evans nodded, reached up to his left shoulder and pulled the large K-bar knife out of its scabbard. Pointing at Monie and Huebner to do the same, he motioned everybody further back into the bush. The three men silently slipped out of their rucksacks. Spacing themselves four or five feet apart, they crouched in the tangle of trees and waited.

Shadrack was the first to hear the high pitched voices, his ears turning in the direction of the sound. What Gianni thought was only an expression became reality as the taste of fear filled his throat. He had to tighten the stock of his rifle to his shoulder to keep it from rattling as his entire body took on an almost uncontrollable shaking.

As the first enemy soldier passed within five feet of him, Gianni held his breath and stared at the AK-47 cradled in the man's arms. It took only moments, or an eternity, for the two remaining soldiers to pass him. As the third soldier walked abreast of Monie, the jungle seemed to explode as he sprang out of the trees and onto the man's back.

Startled by the noise, the first two soldiers started to turn but were caught in mid-stride by Evans and Huebner. Without a sound, Evans reached around the soldier's head, grabbed his chin and pulled it to the left. In one quick motion he drove the knife into the soft hollow behind the man's right ear and up into the brain. With nothing more than the sound of air escaping from his lungs, the dead soldier slid to the ground. Evans pulled out the knife, grabbed the front of the dead man's hair, tilted his head back and slit his throat.

Huebner reached his man at almost the same moment, but instead of taking the chance of missing the soft spot behind the ear, he had driven his knife through the side of the man's neck, pushing it forward and across, tearing through the carotid artery and the larynx. Frothy blood sprayed from the gaping wound as Huebner lowered him to the ground, the gurgling noise finally giving way to one last hiss.

Monie misjudged his reach around the soldier's head and as he tried to pull it back to expose the neck, the soldier's pith helmet slammed back into his face, bloodying his nose and lips. Knocked off balance, his knife missed its true mark and instead of slicing through to its vital depth, opened the throat with a bloody but non-fatal wound. Having dropped his rifle, the soldier pushed back at the pain of the knife and knocked Monie to the ground. Now free, the soldier, spraying blood as he moved, ran through the trees in the direction he had come.

Smith was already standing up and aiming his rifle at the running soldier when Gianni made it to his feet and pushed the barrel of Smith's rifle down. "No, wait."

"Motherfuck! Get outta' here, Cherry!"

Reaching down, he unhooked Shadrack's leash. "Get 'em, boy, get 'em!" The soldier had a several second head start but a running man is no match for a dog, especially one trained for such matters. Shadrack gave chase then leaped through the air, hitting the soldier in the back and knocking him to the ground. Unable to bite through the heavy rucksack, the dog went for the head, finding purchase on the back of the bleeding neck. With his vocal cords already torn by Monie's knife, the soldier hissed out his agony. Unable to pull the dog's jaws off the back of his neck, he rolled over and clawed at the knife attached to his ammo belt.

Running up behind the dog, Gianni saw the knife flash as it cleared the scabbard and the soldier try to raise it above his head. Without thinking, he pulled his own knife out of its sheath, grabbed Shadrack by the choke chain and pulled the dog back.

It wasn't until Evans gently grabbed him by the left shoulder that he realized what had happened. "Come on Gianni, come on, get up, it's all over."

Shaking uncontrollably, his hands and face splattered with blood, Gianni looked down and saw his knife embedded in the left eye of the enemy soldier. Shadrack sat quietly at the head of the man, blood dripping from his jaws.

"Gianni, Gianni, come on, we gotta' get movin', come on." Gianni looked up over his shoulder at Evans who was gently trying to pull him off the dead man. He looked back down, saw his knife again, then rolled off and emptied his stomach on the ground. The violent spew gave way to dry heaves and finally choking.

"Jesus Christ, the fuckin' cherry can't even stand the sight of blood. Motherfucker's worthless. Ought'a ship his ass back home to mamma 'fore he gets us all wasted."

Evans turned and grabbed Smith by the front of his shirt. "Shut the fuck up, Smith! You hear me? Just shut the fuck up. You're the asshole that was gonna' shoot the fuckin' Gook. What were you tryin' to do, let every Dink in the area know we're here? He probably saved all our asses, no thanks to you."

Evans put his boot on the dead soldier's chest and pulled out knife. "All right, let's get these guys stashed under the brush. Check 'em for papers, maps, anything. Come on, let's get squared away, we're pushin' our luck standin' 'round here."

Evans helped Gianni to his feet and slid the knife back in its scabbard. "Ya' gotta' forget about it, Gianni, it's over, done. You did what had to be done."

Gianni wiped the spittle off his lips with the back of his hand, then wiped the tears running down his face. His knees started to buckle and Evans helped steady him.

"Oh, Jesus, oh, Jesus Christ, I never killed anyone, I've never even seen a dead person before. Oh, God, LT, I killed him, I fuckin' killed him." Gianni started to shake again and Evans grabbed him by both shoulders.

"Snap out of it, troop. Goddamnit! Snap out of it. What'd you think this was, a fuckin' game? You think you were out here just to let your dog piss on the trees. Damnit, Gianni, this is the real fuckin' thing. People get killed, that dog was gonna' get killed."

Evans pointed down at Shadrack sitting next to Gianni. "You saved a member of this squad. That's your job, that's what you're supposed to do, and if it means having to kill someone, then Goddamnit, that's what you do. Now get your shit together and take us to that pilot, or do you think he'd rather die. If ya' can't handle this shit, we'll put you on a chopper to Tan Son Nhut as soon as we get back to the Palace, but right now we got a job to do and we need you to do it."

Gianni looked around, then walked over and picked up his rifle. "I guess I'm just not cut out for this shit, LT."

"None of us are. That's what makes us different from the fuckin' animals. None of us like it, ya' just do it and fuckin' forget it. Come on…let's go find us a lost Air Force puke."

They spent the next hour following Gianni and the dog as they quartered the downwind leg, searching for any more enemy soldiers, then followed the map reference to the area where the pilot had last transmitted. "It's gotta' be in that area right in front of us. If we can find it, maybe we can pick up his trail from there." Evans had the map on his knee and was pointing out the search area to Gianni. "How do you wanna' work it?"

"We're still a little west of where we wanna' be. We need to move over there, in that direction so we'll be downwind. Unless the Gooks have already fucked up the scent pad, we shouldn't have too much trouble."

Huebner crawled out of the stand of bushes carrying a flight helmet and a discarded survival radio. "He was here all right. Guess he figured this was useless weight." Huebner stuffed the small radio into one of his thigh pockets.

Tuckett looked around at the scarred trees and flattened bushes. "Jesus, they were droppin' shit right on top of him. Another few yards and they wouldn't have needed us. Must'a been a hell of a show."

"I'll try to get you tickets to the next performance." Huebner handed the helmet to Gianni.

"LT, why don't I try to pick up a track while everyone's takin' a break. Maybe we can get a jump on this before it gets dark."

Evans looked at his watch and nodded. "Geoff, let's spread 'em out, keep 'em well away from here. All right, Gianni, see what you can find."

After leading Shadrack into the stand of bushes, then letting him smell the inside of the helmet, it took less than two minutes for the dog to find the scent trail.

Reeling out the long leash, Gianni followed the dog into the bush with Monie close on his heels.

They followed the trail at an exhausting pace for two hours before Evans signaled a break. Gianni gave Shadrack a drink and rubbed his fur down with water before he took some for himself. Monie wiped the sweat off his face, then leaned back against his rucksack and pulled out a cigarette.

"I don't see how ya' can hump around out here all day and not want a smoke when ya' get a chance." He clicked his Zippo shut, took a long drag and blew the smoke at the bugs flying around his face. "If nothing else, it keeps these little fuckers off ya.'"

"When ya' grow up in Florida, ya' get used to bugs. Besides, the damn things smell like shit."

"Yeah, right. We piss on trees, shit in the bushes, eat cold food outta' cans, sleep in our clothes, go for days without a shower, you sleep next to a fuckin' dog, and you're worried about the smell of a cigarette! Good thing you're not in the Marines, they'd probably shoot ya' just to put ya' out of your misery."

"You're one disgusting motherfucker Monie, ya' know that?"

As darkness fell, Gianni slowed the pace, hoping to keep tangles in the leash to a minimum. Shadrack had lost the scent when they crossed a small stream but picked it up less than an hour later. The downed Wizzo, apparently hoping to confuse anybody that might be trying to follow him, had walked down the middle of the stream before crossing over. Once Shadrack had picked up the scent again, he glanced over his shoulder as if to say, 'This guy's gonna' have to do a lot better than this to fool me'.

It was a little after 2 a.m. and Evans was getting ready to call a halt when Gianni suddenly held up his hand.

"Why'd we stop, what'da ya' got?" Evans was crouching low to the ground and speaking in a whisper.

"Our guy changed direction, real sudden. He's headed this way now."

"So, he's lost, what's the big deal?"

"Shadrack's got something in the air, he's not paying attention to the track anymore. Look at 'im, see 'im testing the air. I think we got more than one guy out there."

Evans watched as Shadrack pranced around, sniffing the air, trying to get his head higher and higher. "Gooks?"

"You know more about this shit than I do. Who the hell else would it be?"

"You sure our guy's headed this way?"

Gianni nodded his head. "Yup."

"Damnit!" Evans looked back at the squad and motioned Huebner to move up. "We got company, Geoff. Gianni thinks we've got Gooks up ahead. Our guy changed direction, took off this way. Could be the Gooks are on his trail, too."

"Or they already got 'im."

"Fuck, either way we gotta' find out." Evans looked back to Gianni and Monie. "What about it, Gianni, can you get us up to 'em?"

"Yeah, I think so. I wanna' move toward our right, though, we can work the wind better that way."

"Let's do it. Geoff, brief everybody, keep 'em quiet."

Gianni and Dustin stayed well ahead of the squad, moving slowly, letting Shadrack test the wind. They had gone less than three hundred yards when Shadrack again turned to his left and strained at the leash. Evans and Huebner shuffled up next to them. "They're directly upwind from us now, LT. Shadrack's givin' a strong alert, they're probably pretty close."

"All right, Geoff, go with 'em, we gotta' know what's goin' on. I'll move the squad up here."

Gianni forced the dog to slow down. He watched as his ears twitched, rotated to the sides, then focused straight ahead. Whoever was out there, they were moving around making noise. Even though the sound escaped Gianni, Shadrack heard it and that's all that mattered.

Forty yards later Gianni heard it, too. A rustling sound, like something scraping against the ground. Huebner moved up next to him, motioned for him to stay where he was, then with Monie, disappeared into the darkness. Less than five minutes later they were back. Monie gave a worried look to Gianni as they headed back to the squad.

"We're in deep shit, LT, they got our boy." Huebner was breathing hard, both from the trek through the jungle and in anticipation of what was about to happen.

"How many?"

"Nine that we could see. Five of 'em are pretty close together, looks like they're asleep. Two more a little way away sittin' next to a radio shootin' the shit. Two more on the ground in front of our guy. One is asleep, the other is sittin' up with an AK on his lap."

"Shit. What about our boy?"

"Got him trussed up like a chicken waitin' for slaughter. Arms are tied over a pole behind his back. He's sittin' on the ground leanin' up against a tree. Looks like they got him tied to that, too."

"If he was dead, they wouldn't have him tied. At least we're not too late." Evans took off his bush hat and scratched his short cropped hair, trying to think of their next move. "Is there enough cover for someone to get around behind him?"

"Yeah, good cover. Gonna' have to be real quiet, though. The one guard that's still awake is only about five feet in front of him. All he's gotta' do is turn around. Our guy won't stand a chance."

Evans spit out a bug. "How far we gotta' go?"

"Hundred and twenty-five, hundred and fifty yards."

"Any heavy weapons?" Tuckett knew they couldn't survive a prolonged fight against anything other than light weapons.

"Not that we could see, just AKs."

Smith studied the diagram Huebner had drawn in the dirt, knowing instinctively how it would have to be handled. "They're spread out pretty good, LT. We're gonna' have to split up and hit 'em all at once. Someone's gonna' have to get behind our guy and cut 'em loose or they'll zap 'em for sure."

Evans looked up at Robinson. "Delmar, you think you can handle the gun by yourself?"

"No sweat, LT."

"Doc, I want you and Monie to work your way around behind our boy. When we open up, you cut him free and drag him behind the tree. Monie, you gotta' cover 'em. Watch out for the two guards, they're the closest. Don't shoot unless you absolutely have to; we're gonna' be across from you, we don't need to be blowin' each other away in a cross fire."

"All right, Delmar, I want you over here with Boardman and Tuckett. Take out the five sleeping Gooks, just concentrate on them. Smith, you and Huebner take the two by the radio. I'm gonna' take the radio itself, we don't need those fuckers callin' for help." Looking at each man, Evans was greeted with a nod of understanding.

"All right, let's rock and roll."

"Wait a minute, LT, what am I suppose to do?" Gianni was the only one who hadn't been mentioned.

"You can stay here and practice throwing up." Robinson nudged Smith in the ribs with his elbow. "Just cool it, man, leave the kid alone, he done his job."

"Motherfucker's worthless."

"All right, stow it. Gianni, you stay with Huebner and Smith. Robinson's right, you've done what you're here to do. Just keep your head down 'til this shit's over."

Gianni shook his head. Even though he knew Evans was trying to be diplomatic, he also knew Evans didn't trust him when it came to an actual firefight.

"Yeah, listen to the LT, Cherry, and make sure you stay in front of me. I don't want ya' trippin' over your own feet and puttin' a bullet in my back."

Evans reached over and grabbed Smith by the front of his ammo harness. "You just don't know when to shut the fuck up, do you, Laz?"

Schoonhoven and Monie dropped their packs and circled around the camp. Staying well in the bush, they stopped eight or ten feet behind the tied-up American. Staring through the darkness, Schoonhoven could see a rope running around the Wizzo's neck and tied off behind the tree. Another rope circled his body and was tied off below the first one. Schoonhoven pulled out his knife and flashed it at Monie to show he was ready.

One of the two men sitting by the radio lit a cigarette. His AK-47 was propped up next to him while his fellow soldier held his across his knees. The man looked up as two of the sleeping soldiers tossed and turned. He said something and they both let out a low laugh.

Trying to be as quiet as possible, Robinson picked each spot to place his size thirteen combat boots, leading the way for Tuckett and Boardman. Less than five yards from where they wanted to be, still too far inside the heavy brush for clear shots, Boardman swung his head around at the sound of something crawling through the brush. As he turned back, the tip of a branch hit him squarely on the bridge of the nose, bent slightly, then rebounded back to its original length, tearing a gash through the flesh and scraping across his exposed right eye. Blinded by the pain, his eyes involuntarily closed as he reached up with both hands.

It didn't matter what the two soldiers sitting by the radio heard, Boardman's rifle falling to the ground, or his muffled gasp of pain, they were instantly on their feet and firing long bursts into the trees. Tuckett rolled into Boardman's legs knocking him to the ground. Bullets tore through the trees over their heads, splintering wood and tearing leaves.

Hunkered down behind a thick trunked tree, Robinson fired a long burst from the heavy M-60. Still deeper in the bush than they had planned to be, most of the rounds impacted harmlessly into the trees, or dirt, between him and the firing Vietnamese. As effective as tracers can be when you need to know where your rounds are going, they also let your intended target know where they're coming from. As soon as Robinson pulled the trigger and the long red flashes left the barrel, the line of bullets flying over him dropped, searching out human form. Knowing that he was doing nothing more than announcing his position, Robinson pulled the gun back behind the tree, hoping the thick wood was up to the task of stopping hot metal. Unable to do any better than Robinson, Tuckett found his own tree and hung back to protect the still-blinded Boardman.

Gianni was lying between Huebner and Smith when the two Vietnamese soldiers started firing. Throwing his left arm over the dog, he peered up from under the brim of his bush hat just as hot spent brass from Huebner's M-16 hit him in the left cheek. He watched as Huebner's bullets struck the soldier who had been sitting on the log just below the throat, throwing him back and leaving him spread eagle on the ground.

Like a film being run in slow motion, Gianni simultaneously saw pieces of the radio fly off into the darkness. From somewhere off to his right, Evans continued to fire until the radio was only so much scrap.

Smith had already put one of the guards down and was now firing at the second one, his bullets ricocheting off the ground and flying over the now prone Schoonhoven and Monie. The second guard returned fire, bullets passing inches over Gianni's head, the crack of their supersonic flight forcing him deeper and deeper into the dirt. Paralyzed with fear, he pulled the dog closer and squeezed his eyes shut, trying to block out what couldn't be happening.

Flipping out the empty magazine, Smith was loading a fresh one when he looked over at the cowering airman. "Shoot, you motherfucker! Shoot your fuckin' gun!" Smith reached over and grabbed Gianni by the arm. "Goddamnit, you fucking coward, help us, motherfucker!"

He squeezed his eyes even tighter. He wasn't supposed to be there. He wasn't supposed to have to fight. He only had to find people. He wasn't trained for this shit. This wasn't supposed to happen. He was just some Air Force puke, he wasn't a soldier. Shit, he really wasn't anything more than a security guard with a four-legged partner to talk to when he got bored. He wasn't supposed to be there, but he was.

More spent brass hit him in the face, singing the tender flesh. He could still hear Smith screaming at him over the sound of instant death that was just inches above his head. Words from a lifetime ago came rushing back. *"It's not a game, Gianni, people die, and they die in horrible ways. You have to do things you never thought you would. Don't think about it, don't care about it, just do it. Do what it takes to stay alive. I've taught you all I can, you have the skill. If you need it, use it."* Gianni heard the words as plainly as if Hank was there lying next to him.

He wanted nothing more than to ask him what to do. 'Oh, Jesus, Hank, I'm so scared! God, I'm so scared! I don't want to die, not like this! Please, God, I don't want to die!'

The scream of Evan's voice pierced the clatter of gunfire. "Grenade, grenade! He's got a grenade!"

Gianni opened his eyes and followed as Huebner swung his rifle around to where the soldiers were still firing at Robinson and Tuckett. One of them had raised up and was preparing to throw a grenade. Huebner and Evans both fired at the same time. Bullets stitched up the soldier's chest and slammed into his left shoulder, throwing him backwards, the grenade rolling out of his hand and into the trees. Exploding with a loud "whhuummpp" and a blinding flash, it did nothing more than clear the jungle of already too many trees.

Smith was still firing at the second guard who was lying prone on the ground, his body protected behind a slight rise. Schoonhoven had already cut the Wizzo loose from the tree and he and Monie were trying to pull him back into the brush.

"Goddamn motherfucker, we never should'a brought your yellow ass out here! Fucking coward!" Smith kicked out another empty magazine and reloaded a fresh one as he glared at the cowering airman.

The words burned through his brain. 'Fucking coward'. Was that what he'd come here to find out? Was he nothing more than a coward, too scared to fight to stay alive? Too scared to fight to keep someone else alive? Had his father felt like this when he went into combat? Did anyone ever call him a coward? Did he freeze…or did he do what had to be done? No, his father wasn't a coward…even if his son was. Grabbing the end of the leash and shoving it under his chest, Gianni brought his arm around and pulled the rifle into his shoulder. As he sighted into the group of still firing soldiers, Hank's words once again filled his ears. "*Neutralize the nearest threat. Stay with the nearest threat 'til it's neutralized, then move on to the next one.*"

Gianni twisted around until he could see the soldier Smith was shooting at. Suddenly he wasn't thinking, he didn't hear the bullets crashing over his head or feel the hot brass that still bounced off his cheek. Sighting through the round peep sight, he saw the muzzle flash of the enemy rifle. Holding several inches above that he could make out the outline of the Vietnamese pith helmet. A target, not a man, not an enemy, not a living, breathing soul, just a target.

Gianni let his breath out. Hank had called it the 'moment of hesitation,' the period between breaths when your body is most stable. That's when you make an aimed shot. Gianni didn't think about it, it just happened. Good training, discipline, a born talent, it didn't matter, it just happened. He squeezed the trigger, once, twice. There was no need to look, no reason to want to see what had happened.

Even though he had never shot a man before, even though until moments before he had never even seen a man shot before, he knew that the first bullet had struck the target just above the tip of the nose. The hydrostatic shock of the fifty-five-grain bullet traveling at 3200 feet per second reduced the target's head to the equivalent of an exploding watermelon.

The second shot, already deprived of its own target, simply struck fragments of disintegrating skull and brain tissue. The slight disruption in the bullet's path caused it to veer slightly to the right and continue its flight off into the jungle. *"Neutralize nearest threat and move to the next. Stay with the threat until it's neutralized."* The words were coming faster now, the instructions clear, he knew what had to be done.

As calm as he had ever been, with less tension than shooting a practice round, he shifted his aim around to the four remaining soldiers. As he swung his sight past the two dead soldiers lying next to the destroyed radio, he saw one of the "dead" men inching toward a rifle lying on the ground, just out of reach. *"Stay on your target until it's neutralized. Don't leave the closest threat."*

Aiming at the crawling target, Gianni fired. The bullet struck on an angle at the beltline, passing through the soldier's leather ammunition carrier, traveling up through the stomach and impacting into the dying man's spine. The soldier was dead before the second bullet shattered the sternum and exploded the heart as it passed completely through the body and lodged in the ground.

"Neutralize the threat, then move to the next one." Gianni swung his rifle around to the four remaining men. One lifted himself slightly off the ground to pull a fresh magazine out of the ammunition carrier strapped to the front of his chest. Gianni pulled the trigger three times. Each bullet found its mark just below the arm pit.

"Keep track of your rounds. Always know how many rounds you have left." Gianni took a fraction of a second to count his shots. Seven fired, still have thirteen left in the magazine.

The three soldiers shifted around and directed their fire at Huebner, Smith and Gianni. Evans fired out of the darkness from their right and hit one of the soldiers in the hip. The bullet spun him around but he continued to fire. Monie moved up behind a tree, stray rounds no longer forcing him to stay down. Taking aim, he fired three times. Two rounds burrowed into the dirt in front of the wounded soldier's face. The third crashed through his neck, plowing its way into the rucksack lying beside him.

A hail of bullets kicked up dirt around the two surviving soldiers. Seemingly oblivious to the deadly threat, they continued to fire bursts from their AK-47s.

The firing had slackened, there were fewer of them left now. Bullets no longer whittled away at his wooden shield. Robinson crawled out from behind the tree and moved up far enough to see the two remaining soldiers. They were firing into the trees off to his right, he could see incoming rounds hitting the dirt all around. Shoving the big gun out in front of him, he aimed down the long barrel and squeezed the trigger. Disgusted with himself at having let the rest of his squad down, he watched as dozens of rounds tore into one of the soldiers. Chunks of flesh flew through the air as the right arm dropped to the ground, shot off just above the elbow. The scream of pain and terror was cut short as heavy bullets slammed into the side of the head, leaving nothing but the lower jaw and what used to be, only moments before, a human being.

The most primitive instinct in God's creatures is that of fight or flight. The lone remaining soldier had already tried fight, it hadn't worked. Seeing no other choice, he raised himself off the ground and started for the trees. *"Neutralize the threat. Don't leave it until you've neutralized it."* The threat now was not being shot or stabbed or watching a grenade fall at your feet. This threat was a man running to get help, to bring back a force big enough so Gianni and the rest of the squad would never see 'the World' again. Never drive The Car, never fight a bull, never sing happy birthday, or puke your guts out after an all night drunk. This threat was going to bring back people who would put an end to all that.

Everyone fired. The ground exploded at the running man's feet. The trees in front of him shook with the violent impact of hot metal, but still the man ran. He was nearing the trees, close to the safety of the darkness of the jungle, close to living long enough to see another blue sky. Gianni raised up to one knee, the running man's back filling his sights. *"It's not a man, he's not alive. It's a target, a piece of paper, a clay bird."* Gianni squeezed the trigger twice. Puffs of dust blew off back of the soldier's uniform. He staggered, dropped his rifle, and staggered toward the trees. The firing stopped.

One by one they turned to look at Gianni. He raised up off his knee, standing there, watching as the soldier, dying, but refusing to give up, stumbled toward freedom. The words came back. *"It's not a game, Gianni, it's for real. No one gets up after the director yells cut. People die, and they die in horrible ways."* Gianni raised the rifle. Three bullets, tearing through vital organs, blasting away chunks of ribs, snuffing out the life of a man who wanted nothing more than to live.

CHAPTER 8

TUESDAY
APRIL 7, 1970
CAMELOT PALACE

The chopper touched down on the small landing pad in front of the medical tent. A doctor and two medics were waiting with a gurney and quickly transferred the injured Wizzo to it. Schoonhoven briefed the doctor while the man was being moved.

"They worked him over pretty good. Knocked out four of his top teeth, probably butt stroked him with a rifle. Nose is broken, left cheekbone looks like it's been crushed, he was bleeding from both ears, and they broke all his fingers on his right hand. He may have some broken ribs, too, but I couldn't tell. We had to DI DI out of there soonest." He looked down to the gurney at the injured man who was groaning in pain. Crusted blood still clung to his neck below the ears and the awkward angle of his fingers sent a shiver through Schoonhoven. The grotesque swelling of his face, with blackened eyes and oozing flattened lips belied the fact that he would never again look like his Air Force Academy graduation picture. Schoonhoven looked back at the doctor.

"There wasn't mush I could do for him other than shoot him up with morphine so we could carry him."

Boardman jumped down from the helicopter and moved over beside Schoonhoven, a large, dull-green battlefield bandage covered his right eye. "Oh, Doc, would you mind taking a look at Boardman's eye. He took the end of a branch in it. I packed it with ointment and taped the eyelid closed, doesn't look too serious."

"Sure, no problem. Come on, troop, I'll have one of the other doctors check your eye while I take care of the flyer. And, Schoonhoven, good work."

Major Kancilla waited by the nose of the helicopter. As Evans pulled his rucksack off the chopper deck, Kancilla walked over and patted him on the back. "Congratulations, Will, you guys did a great job."

"Yeah, thanks, Major."

"Whoa, there, Lieutenant, what's the problem? I thought you'd be thrilled shitless with two successful missions in a row. What's the problem?"

Evans let the rucksack fall to the ground, took a deep breath, and turned to look straight at Kancilla. "Got real hairy out there, sir, we ended up in some deep shit." Evans briefed Kancilla, then looked over at the weapons carrier where the rest of the squad, along with Gianni and Shadrack, were sitting waiting to be taken back to the tent. "I'm worried about him, I think maybe we ought'a send him back to Tan Son Nhut."

"Wait a minute, I thought you said he came through in the end?"

"Shit, yeah, he came through. Never seen anything like it. I mean, he didn't just start shootin', not like some cherry out in the bush. It's like it wasn't even him out there, like someone else took over. One minute he's scared shitless, couldn't even move; the next minute, fuck, I don't know, it was like he'd been doing it all his life. After he wasted the last Gook, he just walked over to 'em, like he was walkin' down the beach or something, rolled 'em over with his boot and just stared at 'em. Didn't say shit, just kept starin' at 'em. Huebner had to pull 'em away so we could get outta' there. Hasn't said a word since, won't even talk to Monie, and they were gettin' pretty tight."

Kancilla pulled out a cigarette. "Shit, this dog thing was workin' pretty good. Hate to end it now."

"Yeah, I know. Works better than I thought it would. I guess we could try to get another team."

"You really think we should send 'em back?"

"I don't know, Major, I just don't know." Evans picked up his rucksack and walked over to the weapons carrier. Nodding to the driver, they headed for the tent.

They had awakened, one by one. Most had either headed for the showers or the mess tent. Smith sat on his bunk halfheartedly cleaning his rifle while he looked across the isle. Gianni had gone to sleep, not even bothering to strip off his dirty and sweat soaked fatigues. Shadrack, long ago bored with sleeping, was sitting up, his head resting on the cot next to Gianni's legs. Slowly Gianni started to move, turning one way, then another. Rolling from his back to his stomach, then over again. The dog lifted his head off the cot and stared at his master.

Suddenly Gianni started to shout, a pleading, sorrowful wail that scared both Shadrack and Smith. "NO, NO, Oh, God, NO. Dad! Dad! Help me, please, help me!!" Gianni rolled on the cot violently. The dog stood up and backed away, slowly. His master was in trouble, he needed to protect him. He looked around nervously, his jaws snapping shut in little silent barks. Gianni screamed again, "Daddy! Daddy! Help me! Please help me!!'" The dog paced back and forth, from the head of the cot to the foot and back again. He wanted to help, he wanted to attack the threat, but there was no threat. No enemy, no snake, no other dog, only his master in trouble. The dog looked over at Smith.

Smith was now standing in the aisle looking down at Gianni. Shadrack pranced over to him and looked up as if to say, 'You have to help him, help my master, I can't do it.' Smith looked down at the dog, at first worried that he might attack him. The fear quickly vanished when he saw the helpless look in his eyes. "Shit, dog, I don't know what to do. He be havin' a nightmare, ya' know, a bad dream."

Smith looked back at Gianni, still thrashing on the cot. "Must be one fucker of a dream, too." If they could have seen into Gianni's mind, they would have understood the terror. An enemy soldier, the last one Gianni had killed, was standing in front of him, gaping exit holes, blood pouring from the torn flesh where Gianni's bullets had insulted his thin chest. The soldier stood there, a leering smile stretching his lips taut, with his AK-47 aimed at Gianni, its bayonet turned out in front of the barrel. Gianni pulled the trigger on his rifle, again and again, each bullet missing its mark. The soldier walked closer, ten feet, eight feet, five feet. Gianni fired, and missed. He fired again, and again he missed. The soldier kept getting closer. Three feet, two feet, the bayonet was almost touching Gianni's chest. The rifle bucked in Gianni's hands, firing over and over and over, and missing over and over and over. "Daaaaad! Help meeeeee!! Help meeeeee!!"

Smith was as unnerved as the dog. He leaned over and shook Gianni's leg. "Hey, wake up, come on, wake up."

Gianni kicked his legs, still screaming for his father. "Come on, Cherry, you're dreamin'. Wake up, it's only a dream, you're all right, it's only a dream."

Gianni bolted upright, sweat running off his face.

"It's all right, man, you was only dreamin'." Smith took a step closer and put a reassuring hand on Gianni's leg. "You okay now, man. You awake?" Smith felt like he was staring into eyes that were somewhere else, somewhere he didn't want to go.

"Huh? Yeah, yeah, I'm awake, I'm all right." At the sound of his voice, Shadrack moved closer to the cot and laid his head on it next to Gianni's arm. Noticing the dog for the first time, he reached over and scratched behind his ears. "I guess I had a nightmare."

"No guessin' 'bout it, man, you was scary. You all right now?"

"Yeah, thanks." Gianni swung his legs over the side of the cot and rubbed his face with both hands, trying to bring himself back to the real world. He suddenly remembered the real world was the problem. People dying, people being tortured, and finding out, for the first time in your life, what real fear can do to you, or make you do. Smith walked back to his cot and picked up his rifle. Hesitating, he put it back down and turned around.

"Hey, Cherry, ah, Gianni. I'm sorry, man, I really am."

Gianni looked up at the black man standing over him. "Sorry about what?"

"What I said out there, callin' you a coward and all. I was wrong, man, I'm sorry."

Gianni dropped his head, staring at the wooden floor. "You weren't wrong, Lazirus, I am a coward. I was so fucking scared I couldn't move. I could'a gotten us all killed. I'm still scared. I'm so scared I can't even sleep without being scared."

Smith reached down and sat on Monie's cot. "Hey, we all be scared. Shit, man, you gotta' be fucking crazy not's ta be scared shitless when someone be tryin' to zap ya'. Damn, I 'member the first time I walked into the shit, hadn't been in-country more'n a few days. We was out on this daylight patrol, s'pose to be nothin' but a cake walk. Ya' know, go out a few klicks, turn 'round and come back in so's the old man could count it as another search and destroy mission. No big deal."

"Would'a been fine 'cept Charlie was waitin' for us. Let the point man walk by, then opened up on the whole patrol. Man, I couldn't get the fuck outta' the way quick enough. I shit my pants, I mean I really did, I shit my pants. I didn't know what the fuck to do. Everybody else was bustin' caps and throwin' grenades and all's I could do was try to find the biggest tree I could to hide behind."

"That's just it, Laz, you moved, you found a tree to hide behind, you did something. I froze, I just fuckin' froze. I was so scared I couldn't move."

"Yeah, ya' did, ya' froze. It happens. Some never get over it, can't handle the bush. Guys in a squad make sure those kind become REMFs."

"Become what?"

"REMFs, you know, Rear Echelon Mother Fuckers. Clerks, typists, paper pushers, that kinda' shit. Anything that'll keep 'em outta' the bush so's someone else don't get killed 'cause a' their fuck up. Man, those kinda' guys never get used to the bush, they just can't handle it."

"Then ya' got the guys that freeze and ya' never know how they would'a turned out 'cause they get zapped their first time out. It happens. Ain't nothin' ya' can do about it. Then ya' got guys like you."

"What'da ya' mean, guys like me?"

"Don't know, ain't never seen nothin' like it before. One minute you be tryin' to dig a hole, next minute you be a one-man army. Ya' got balls, man, I means it, ya' really got balls. That one motherfucker had me hugging' the ground so close I never got close to hittin' 'em. Shit, I came closer to zappin' Monie and Doc than I did him. You finally decided you been eatin' enough dirt and ya' take 'im out with yer first shot. Where'd you learn to shoot like that anyway?"

"I don't know, just got lucky I guess."

"Naw, man, luck is pickin' up a bitch in some bar and gettin' laid ten minutes later or havin' a hot run with the dice or not gettin' drafted. Uh-uh, you wasn't lucky, you knew 'xactly what you was doing. Well, anyway, man, like I say, I'm sorry 'bout what I called ya'. You paid your dues, man, ya' belong in the squad."

Gianni raised his head and looked Smith square in the eyes. "You mean that? You're not worried about goin' back in the bush with me?"

"Shit, yes, I'm worried, man, I's always worried 'bout the bush. I'm just not worried 'bout what you'll do."

"I appreciate that, Laz, I really do."

Smith put both hands on his knees and pushed himself up. "No sweat, man, no sweat." Smith walked back to his cot and sat down, then turned to look at Gianni over his shoulder. "Hey, Gianni."

"Yeah?"

"What made ya' do it? I mean how come ya' changed all's a sudden and jumped into the fight?"

"I remembered something someone said to me once."

"Well, whatever it was, keep 'memberin', it's gonna' keep ya' alive out there. Ah…there's one other thing, man. It's about the dog."

"Shadrack?" At the sound of his name, he walked around the cot and sat in front of Gianni.

"Yeah. It's not that I don't like 'im. I mean, I guess he's a pretty good dog and all. He sure as shit knows what he be doin' out there. What I's tryin' to tell ya' is…I's scared shitless of dogs. Any dog, not just him. Always have been."

"He won't bother ya', Laz, he's really pretty friendly."

"Don' matter, man. Friendly or not, I's scared of 'em. Don't know what it is, the teeth, gettin' bit, eaten alive, ya' know, that kinda' stuff. When he grabbed that Gook by the neck, it was all I could do to keep from takin' off through the bush. Can't stand it, man, just gives me the creeps."

"I'll keep 'em away from ya', Laz. I feel the same way about snakes."

"Thanks, man. Just wanted ya' to know, got nothin' personal 'gainst 'im." Smith picked up a rag soaked with gun oil when Monie walked into the tent.

"Hey, Gianni, I just ran into the LT and Huebner. They wanna' see you over at the mess tent."

"Think I got time to take a shower first?"

"Naw, they're waitin' for ya'. Besides, ya' don't smell any worse than the food."

Smith didn't even bother to look up from cleaning his rifle. "You white boys do have a God-awful stink 'bout ya' anyways."

Gianni pulled out a foot-long piece of cardboard with a pointed stick tacked to it and made his way over to the mess tent, ignoring the ever present comments about Shadrack's ears. As he reached the tent, he gave Shadrack the command to 'Stay' and pushed his hand-made sign into the ground. Troops entering or leaving the mess hall always stopped and chuckled at the lonely looking dog lying behind the sign that read: "I may look cute but I'll tear your balls off! Do Not Feed Me." For some reason, most of the troops thought that even if they couldn't stomach the slop they were fed, it would be great for the dog.

Evans and Huebner were sitting alone at the end of a long table near the rear of the mess tent. Two cups of steaming coffee sat in front of them. Gianni made his way around the other tables.

"Hey, LT, Sarge. You wanted to see me?"

"Yeah, Gianni, you eaten yet?"

"No, sir, just got up a little while ago."

"Grab some chow. The powdered eggs are great today. I think they used clean water to make 'em this time."

Evans took a pull on his cigarette and blew the smoke at the tent ceiling, away from Gianni. "How ya' feeling?"

"Okay, I guess. Didn't sleep real well." Gianni didn't want to discuss his nightmare. "Too hot."

"The dog okay?"

"Yes, sir, he's fine. He's outside waitin' for me." Gianni knew they hadn't wanted to see him just to shoot the shit. "Is there a problem, LT?"

"We're sending you back."

Gianni stopped the fork before it reached his mouth and set it down on the metal tray. "What? Why? I mean, aren't we doing what you wanted? Aren't we finding those pilots a lot faster than you could by yourself. Even the Major said we were doing a good job. I don't understand?"

"No, Gianni, you're doing a great job, really. Better than we had hoped."

"Then what's the problem? You afraid I'm gonna' fuck up again in a firefight? That's it, isn't it, the guys on the squad don't trust me."

"That's not it, Gianni. As a matter of fact, I don't think anyone on the squad even expected you to do what you did."

"Well, then why do you want to send me back?"

Evans and Huebner looked at each other. This wasn't going the way they expected it to. "Are you saying you don't want to go back?"

"No, sir. I mean, yes, sir. I mean, yes, I'm saying I don't want to go back." Gianni wasn't entirely sure that it had come out right. "I want to stay if everyone on the squad wants me here, me and Shadrack."

Huebner took a sip of coffee and lit his own cigarette. "I'll be damned. We figured after yesterday you'd want to be on the first chopper outta' here."

"Is that why you wanted to send me back, you thought I wanted to go?"

"Gianni, look, we made a deal with your Major. We got to keep you as long as you wanted to stay. We promised we'd look out for you and make sure you didn't get hurt. After what happened yesterday…there's no way we can make sure nothing will happen to you." Evans squirmed in his chair. "We figured it would be easier if we just sent you back rather than putting you in the position of having to ask."

"Look, LT, Sarge, if you want to get rid of me, then fine, I'll get my shit together and be gone. If you're leaving it up to me, then I'm staying." Gianni looked at both men and continued. "I know it's dangerous out there. I didn't before, not really, but I do now. And I know I can get killed out there, and I'm not thrilled with the idea. But why should I be able to walk away from it when the rest of the guys on the squad can't? Like I said, if the squad doesn't mind me being here, then I want to stay…and please pass me the Tobasco sauce."

Evans turned to Huebner who nodded his head. "All right, troop, that settles it. Have it your way. In for a penny, in for a pound. Same deal goes, though. You say the word and we'll get you back to Tan Son Nhut."

"I'll remember that, LT, believe me, I'll remember it."

It was a little after one in the morning. The rest of the squad was sound asleep. Shadrack knew his master was still awake and sat next to the cot with his head resting on the edge. Gianni tossed and turned, half afraid of falling asleep and reliving the nightmare, and half afraid of staying awake and wondering how he was going to tell his parents he wasn't at Tan Son Nhut. Giving up on the sleep, he pulled pen, paper, and a flashlight out of his footlocker and began to write:

Dear Dad,

Please don't be worried that I'm sending this letter to you at work, everything is all right. I wanted to let you know what's going on and maybe it's better if Mom doesn't know, at least not yet. Remember when I sent you a letter telling you about some Army guys that were coming out to the kennels to see a demonstration? Well, I put on the demo and they were real impressed. It turns out they were with a Search & Rescue team that goes out to find downed flyers. What I'm trying to say is, they needed a handler to help them out in the bush and I volunteered. Please don't be angry. I don't know why, but it was something I had to do. It's what our dogs are good at and it's how they should be used. I'm at an Army base called Camelot Palace about fifty miles from Saigon. It's not really much of a base, just a bunch of helicopters and tents. Looks kind of like what you'd see in an old war movie, except for the helicopters. We just kind of wait until there's a pilot they can't find, then we get dropped off a few miles away and we use Shadrack to track him. So far we've been out on two missions. The first one was pretty easy, we didn't see any Vietnamese and Shadrack found the guy hiding in a thick stand of trees. You should have seen the look on his face when we found him. I've never seen anything like it, Dad. I guess he thought he was really going to die out there and when we found him, I don't know, I guess it was like he was born all over again. You know, like he had a chance to make up for all the things he'd done wrong, do some of the things he'd never gotten around to doing before. It was really great Dad, really great. The second mission didn't go quite so well. We just got back from that one this morning. I couldn't sleep, I needed someone to talk to, and I guess maybe you'll understand. While we were out in the bush we ran into three Vietnamese soldiers. The LT decided they had to be taken out and it had to be done real quiet in case there were more Gooks around. The LT and Sgt. Huebner and Monie jumped the three Gooks with knives but Monie's guy ran off through the jungle. I turned Shadrack on the guy and he ran him down and grabbed him by the neck. Before I knew it, the guy had a knife in his hand and was going to kill Shadrack. This place is crazy, Dad, it doesn't make any sense. I killed a man to save a dog. I don't remember doing it, I don't even think I meant to do it. I threw up all over the jungle. The LT said I only did what had to be done. I guess he's right, Dad, but I can't get the picture out of my mind. We spent the rest of the day and most of the night tracking the pilot. We ended up finding him but the Gooks had him tied to a tree. We got into a big firefight, there were nine of them, and when the shooting started, I panicked. Dad, I was so scared, I didn't know what to do. The guys don't know it, but I was so scared I peed my pants. All I wanted to do was be home. All I wanted was to see you and Mom again and I didn't give a shit about anything else. I was a coward, Dad, as big a coward as there has ever been. Everyone else on the squad was firing and trying to save the pilot and I was laying on the ground frozen with fear. Maybe now I understand why you never talked about what happened when you were in the war. I guess you can't understand what goes on unless you're really there. It's not what I expected, not at all. I never thought about how much time you spend begging God to let you stay alive. Everyone was firing and then all of a sudden I heard Hank's voice, it was like he was standing right there telling me what to do. I know it sounds crazy, Dad, but it really did seem that way, and when I heard it, I all of a sudden knew exactly what to do. Dad, why is it that when we go to church, we're told not to kill, that it's wrong and it's a sin, but when two countries can't get along and they go to war, all of a sudden killing is right. I don't understand it. It was like what I'd been brought up to believe in didn't matter. All that counted was killing people that I'd never even seen before, people that until a couple minutes before I didn't even know were alive. Dad, in less than a couple of minutes I killed four more people. One of them was just trying to run away, not kill me or anyone else in the squad, just get away. I shot him in the back, Dad, I killed a guy by shooting him in the back. All I knew was I was sorry I had ever volunteered for the unit and I was going to tell the LT that I couldn't handle it. I felt that way right up until the time I saw the pilot we saved. They tortured him, Dad. They beat him almost to death. If we hadn't found him, they probably would have killed him, and at that moment, the moment I realized what they had done to him, I was glad I'd killed them. I don't understand it, he wasn't any threat to them, he couldn't fight, he didn't have a plane to bomb them with, he was done, he was a prisoner, he couldn't hurt them, but they still beat him and tortured him. It's crazy, the whole place is crazy. I know this letter probably takes you by surprise, Dad, and I know I'm not doing what I said I was going to do, but after seeing that pilot, I can't quit, not now. Please don't tell Mom what's going on. Keep sending my mail to Tan Son Nhut, they'll make sure I get it. I'll keep sending letters home just like always. I'm scared, Dad. I'm scared of what will happen if I quit and I'm scared of what will happen if I don't quit. I guess it all comes down to what you used to tell me: If you don't know what to do, do something. If you're right, you're right; if you're wrong, correct your mistake. I hope if I make a mistake I'll be able to correct it.

I love you Dad. I want to see you again.

Gianni.

FRIDAY
APRIL 10, 1970
BASE HOSPITAL
TAN SON NHUT AIR FORCE BASE

Major Guanella walked into the kennels just as Derr was pouring his third cup of coffee and poured himself half a cup. "Giancarlo is helping us win the war. At least he's trying to make sure that some of the people involved in it get to go home."

Derr walked across the room. "What's going on, is he all right?"

"I don't know, I'm not sure what's going on. They choppered in a downed Wizzo from Camelot Palace yesterday. A medic on board told one of the flight line SPs that a dog team found the guy and they'd gotten into a firefight. I guess he told a couple of his buddies in the Squadron and by the time it got to me this morning, it was blown all outta' proportion. Shit, to hear them tell it, Giancarlo stabbed some Gook, then blew a bunch more away. Anyway, thought maybe you'd like to drive over to the hospital with me and see if we can talk to the Wizzo."

"Why's he in the hospital, what's wrong with 'im?"

"Beats the shit outta' me. Let's go find out."

Guanella and Derr walked to the third floor nurses station and stood quietly in front of the counter as the WAF nurse completed her entries. "Oh, Major, I didn't see you."

"They choppered in a downed pilot from one of the Army bases yesterday. I wonder if you could tell us where we can find him."

"Oh, sure, that would be Lieutenant Garbus."

Guanella and Derr stood at the doorway and peered in. Lieutenant Ed Garbus, oblivious to their presence, was lost in his own thoughts. The injuries that Guanella had thought were exaggerated were every bit as numerous, and apparently as serious, as he had heard. Guanella knocked softly on the door jamb. Garbus turned his head slowly at the sound.

"Lieutenant Garbus, good morning. I'm Major Guanella, I'm the CO of the Security Police Squadron, and this is Sergeant Derr, he's in charge of the Patrol Dog Section here on the base. I wonder if we could talk to you for a few moments?"

"Come in, please, come in." The slurring of his words, and the low tone he was forced to use in made it difficult to understand him.

"Lieutenant, we know you're in pain and we're sorry to be bothering you like this, but there's someone we'd like to ask you about."

"The dog handler?"

Guanella and Derr looked at each other, then back at the injured man. "Yes, the dog handler."

THURSDAY
APRIL 16, 1970
FORT LAUDERDALE, FLORIDA

Vince Giancarlo parked the Post Office station wagon in the numbered space behind the building. Walking in, he placed the four empty mail trays on a stack of others and turned to sign out for the day. From his office, Frank Cipriani, the annex supervisor, called to him.

"Vince, hey, Vince, over here."

He looked around and saw Frank waving him over to the office. "Hi, Frank, what's up?"

"Got a letter for you, I think it's from Gianni."

"Why would he send it here?"

"Beats me, but if he wanted his mother to see what he wrote, don't you think he would have sent it to the house?"

Vince pulled over a chair and tore open the envelope. Frank watched as Vince slowly started to slip lower in the chair and heard the paper rattle as his hands began to shake. Frank knew Vince could have read the letter three times over, but still he sat there, staring. His eyes began to water and he rubbed his chin to hide his trembling lower lip.

"Vince, Vince, what is it? Is everything all right?"

Shaken back from his thoughts, he turned to look over at Cipriani. "It's Gianni, he went to war."

"I know that, Vince, we all know that."

"No, Frank, we all knew he went to Vietnam. This is different. Now he's in the war."

SATURDAY
APRIL 18, 1970
CAMELOT PALACE

Gianni lay on top of the sandbag wall surrounding the tent, his shirt and pants folded under his head, the metal dog tags around his neck unknowingly leaving a white tan line on his chest. His entire body, including the olive drab boxer shorts, was soaked with sweat.

"God, I can't believe how hot it gets around here."

"What?" Monie was sitting on the ground with his back against the sandbags throwing a tennis ball for Shadrack.

"I said I can't believe how fucking hot it gets around here."

"Can't hear ya', it's too fucking hot."

"Very funny. Hey, don't let him run around too much, it's even worse for him."

"Oh, okay. Come here, boy, Shadrack, come here." The dog slowly walked over with the dirty white ball in his mouth. "That's a good boy. Come on, lie down in the shade, here, lie down over here." The dog stood there and looked at him, then dropped the ball.

"Hey, Gianni, he won't do a fuckin' thing I say. Make 'im lie down, will ya.'"

Without bothering to look down at the dog, or even open his eyes against the blinding sun, Gianni said, "Shadrack, Down, Stay. There, happy?"

"Damn, I wish I could do that."

"It's not hard, just takes a little time, that's all."

"About the only thing I've been able to teach my horses to do is to come when I call 'em and to ground tie."

"What's ground tie?"

"Huh? Oh, that's when you don't have anything to tie the horse to, like a tree or a fence post. You just drop the reins on the ground and the horse stands there."

"They don't wander away?"

"Yeah, after a while they will, they get bored and start to look for something to eat. Gives ya' enough time to get 'em saddled or take a leak or maybe get a quick blow job."

"You teach your horse how to do that, too?"

"Asshole."

"Hey, Gianni."

"What?"

"What'da ya' gonna' do when your tour is up, when you get back to 'the World'?"

"Spend my leave time at home, I guess."

"How about comin' out to Colorado for a while. My mom and dad would really like to meet you. You could stay at the ranch, ya' know, just kick back for a while."

"Oh, I'm sure that's just what your folks would want, someone who thinks a cow only looks good on a plate next to a baked potato and an ear of corn."

"Naw, they know you're a Flatlander. I told 'em how fucked up you are. Shit, I even sent 'em some pictures of you and Shadrack."

"Oh, yeah?"

"Yeah. They wanted to know what was wrong with his ears. They like animals, even if they are stupid looking."

"You're gonna' be even stupider looking with his head stuck up your ass." Gianni raised up on one elbow and looked down at Dustin rubbing Shadrack's head. "Hey, give him a little water, will ya'."

Dustin unscrewed the top off the canteen and poured two fingers of water into the aluminum cup.

"You're learning."

"Don't worry, I won't give him too much."

Gianni lay back on the sandbags, swatting at a bug that was crawling across his chest. Dustin was just about to take a swig of beer when

Evans and Huebner, stripped to the waist, walked up. "Dustin, Gianni, how's it goin'?"

Gianni turned, shielding his eyes against the sun. "Hey, LT, Sergeant Huebner. Ya'll come down to slum around with the rest of these Army pukes?"

"Looks like we're gonna' be slummin' together for a while. We've got a mission."

Gianni pushed himself up and swung his legs over the sandbag wall hitting Dustin in the side of the head and knocking off his bush hat. Thinking Dustin wanted to play, Shadrack sprang forward and grabbed the hat off the ground. Holding the hat in his teeth and trying to pant at the same time, he sat there looking at Dustin with saliva soaking the green fabric. "Tell your dog to give me back my fuckin' hat."

"You're the big bad Army warrior, take it from 'im."

"Fuck you, sky cop."

"Lieutenant, see what I have to put up with. Open hostility toward the local Air Force contingent. I believe I'm offended to the quick."

Evans and Huebner both smiled at Monie's predicament. "Monie, as your Lieutenant and Commanding Officer, I feel it is your duty to uphold the honor of the entire U.S. Army and in true military fashion recover that piece of issued equipment. You understand, of course, that the dog is not considered a hostile opposing force, so any injuries you receive during the course of a combat engagement will not result in your receiving the Purple Heart. What it boils down to is you're about to get your ass chewed off for no good reason."

Gianni nudged Monie on the shoulder with the side of his boot. "Thank you, Lieutenant, for that clarification of the present situation. Monie, I believe the next move is up to you."

"Sergeant Huebner, I don't suppose you'd like to hand me my M-16?"

"Hey, I'm just an observer in this one. You got yourself into it, now I wanna' see you get yourself out. Besides, I've already seen what that dog can do. I ain't gonna' fuck with him."

"Come on, Gianni, tell him to give me back my hat."

"Oh, so you're admitting the Army can't handle the situation without Air Force help."

"Yeah, yeah, I need Air Force help. Now give me back the damn hat."

"I wonder if I should have you put that in writing? Naw, I guess it's good enough that we all heard it. Okay Shadrack, Drop It." The dog glanced up, then opened his mouth slightly. The hat started to fall out, caught on one of his lower canine teeth, then fell to the ground. Monie started to reach for the drool covered hat. "Look what he did to it, it's fuckin' disgusting. Goddamn Air Force pussies."

"Oh, oh, violation of the surrender treaty! Shadrack, Watch Him!"

Monie's hand shot back to his side as the dog bounced up to all four feet and started snapping and growling. "Goddamnit, Giancarlo, call him off, call him off!"

"What was that about Air Force pussies?"

"I take it back, I take it back! Make him stop it, come on, damnit, call him off!"

"Shadrack,. No, Out!" The dog immediately stopped his snapping and sat down with his tongue hanging out of the side of his mouth. "Good thing you didn't say anything about his ears. I might not have been able to control him."

"You're an asshole, Giancarlo."

"That's true, but I'm an asshole with a big dog."

Monie reached over slowly to pick the hat up and wiped the drool on his pants leg. "Cocksucker."

"Ooohhh, Shadrack, me thinks the enemy has not learned his lesson."

"Okay, guys, let's call a truce." Evans could barely force himself to stop the show.

Gianni brushed at the loose sand sticking to the back of his legs. "What's up, LT?"

"F-4 went down. Pilot and backseater are both okay last we heard, but the choppers couldn't make a pickup."

Monie pulled out a cigarette and lit it, the Zippo making an audible click as he pressed the cover closed against his leg. "Charlie?"

"Big time. Lots of SAMs, triple A and ground troops. Air Force sent a Jolly Green in with a jungle penetrator but it took boo coo hits. Made it about twenty klicks before it went down. Crew got picked up by another chopper"

"How do they expect us to get in there with that many Gooks running around? Even with the dog, we'll play hell tryin' to find 'em." Monie looked at Gianni for confirmation.

"They've got an emergency locator signal. A Bronco will be on station once we get in the area, should be able to lead us right to 'em." Evans reached over, took the cigarette out of Monie's hand and took a drag. "Gianni, we shouldn't need you to find these guys but you're gonna' have to tell us where the bad guys are, especially on the way out."

Gianni patted his left leg and Shadrack trotted over to sit next to him. "No problem, LT." He reached down to scratch between the big ears while the dog looked up at him.

All right, check your gear and get some sleep, we board the chopper at 0500." Evans couldn't resist one good-natured jab. "Oh, Gianni, for you Air Force types, that's five in the morning."

SUNDAY
APRIL 19, 1970
NORTHWEST OF BIEN HOA

Their chopper had been one of many ferrying ground troops out to an operation with some obscure name that would hopefully peak the interest of millions of viewers of the evening news. The pilot of their chopper dropped out of formation, landed quickly, and rejoined to the rear in what seemed like the blink of an eye.

Boardman kept the radio on until the choppers were out of range just in case they had been seen and needed a quick extraction. They had moved steadily through the jungle for most of the day, the last three hours spent avoiding enemy soldiers that Shadrack detected. By late afternoon, they were in the area of the crew's landing. Boardman spoke into the mouthpiece, then motioned for Evans. "Bronco driver needs a visual so he can direct us in."

Evans pulled out a small signal mirror, sighted through the hole in the middle and flashed it at the aircraft. "Roger that, wait one." Boardman tapped Evans on the arm. "He's got us, LT. Signal is to our northwest, probably not more than a klick or so."

"Okay, have him get away from here for now, we don't need him attracting attention."

Evans and Huebner shot a compass sighting, then gathered the rest of the squad around them. "All right, Gianni, I need you and Dustin up front, we need to know if we're headed into any Gooks. Tuckett, take the rear but stay close. The Bronco driver figures we've only got about a klick to go and you can bet we're not the only ones looking for these guys. Let's grab 'em and get the hell out."

Shadrack was checking the air constantly, walking from side to side at the end of the leash. Gianni held his hand up and waited for Evans. "I don't like this, LT."

"What's the matter?"

"It's Shadrack, he's gettin' scents from everywhere."

"What is it, what's he smell?"

"I don't know, it's real confusing, I've never seen him alert like this. It's almost like it's something he's never smelled before."

"That's great." Evans looked around the bush, then back at Huebner. "Come on, Gianni, take a guess, give us some help here."

Huebner moved up next to them. "What's the deal?" He knew something was wrong and the mustache bobbed up and down.

"Gianni says the dog's getting confused."

Huebner looked back at Evans. "Maybe he's smelling something off the pilot's flight suit."

"I don't think so, Sarge, he's used to flight line smells. This is different, real different."

"Well, whatever it is, we'll hold up here 'til we contact the Bronco and see if he can get a better fix on the beacon. At least that'll give us some idea of how close we are. No sense stumbling in there blind."

The Bronco radioed that the signal was coming from less than four hundred yards in front of them. Boardman moved closer to Evans. "He says the signal is strong and stationary, no sign of Charlie around the signal area."

"All right, make sure he's back here in forty-five minutes." Evans watched the dog as his head constantly moved back and forth and up and down. "This is fucked. If Charlie's not around, why didn't those guys try to signal the Bronco while he was flying over?" He looked at his watch, trying to figure out how long it was until dark. "We gotta' do something. I sure as shit don't want to spend the night around here. Gianni, can you lead us in any closer, try to find exactly where that scent is coming from?"

"Sure, I can take you right to it, I just don't know what it is."

"All right, let's get going." He turned and motioned for Monie. "You stay right behind him."

It took over an hour to cover another three hundred yards. Shadrack was frantic with the scents he smelled and constantly looked over his shoulder at his master. Gianni finally decided to stop the squad.

"What's he doing, Gianni?"

"Shit, Dustin, I don't know. Whatever he smells, it's gotta' be close. I just don't know why he keeps smelling along the ground like that. He usually only does that while he's tracking."

Evans and Huebner crouched down next to them. "You got something?"

"We gotta' be close, LT, the scent is real strong."

"This doesn't make sense. Look how the trees are starting to thin out. Shit, there's hardly any cover in front of us. Why wouldn't these guys stay in the thick brush to hide?"

"Wherever they are, LT, they gotta' be close. Maybe in that stand of trees up there. Look at Shadrack, he's starin' right at it." Evans looked at the dog, then moved his head behind his ears like Gianni had taught him. "Geoff, get Robinson set up right here, I want him to be able to sweep the whole area in front of us. Monie, you and I are gonna' check out those trees."

Dustin started to slip out of his rucksack and stopped at the sound of Gianni's voice. "LT, that doesn't make any sense if that's not where they're hiding. Shadrack can find them a lot quicker and a lot quieter."

"You sure you want to go out there?"

"No, I don't want to go out there, but it's the best way to do it."

"I suppose you want Monie to go with you." Gianni slid his rucksack off his shoulders. "No offense, LT."

"Yeah, right. Okay Geoff, let's get the squad set."

Gianni and Dustin crouched as low as possible and followed the dog. Gianni was still confused as the dog alternated sniffing the air and the ground. They covered the eighty or so yards to the stand of trees slowly, Gianni watching the dog and Monie watching everywhere else. The stand was no more than fifty feet long with the ground between filled with heavy brush. Rather than fight their way through it, they made their way around it. What they saw answered the question of what Shadrack had smelled.

Lying on the ground with their hands and legs staked out spread eagle were the two pilots. Both were completely naked and were split open from their necks to their crotches. Their genitals had been hacked off and stuffed in their mouths. Both had been shot just above the nose, pieces of their heads scattered on the ground around them. The swarms of crawling and flying insects made the bodies squirm, as if they were trying to shake off the repulsive flesh eaters. An emergency beacon sat on the ground between their heads.

"Oh, fuck, oh, fuck, oh, Jesus Christ Almighty! Oh, God, look what they've done to 'em!" The bile started to fill Gianni's throat and he knew he was going to be sick again. He turned around, starting to fall to his knees, when Shadrack jerked at the end of the leash almost pulling him off balance.

As he looked at the dog, he thought he saw part of the ground move. Shadrack kept his nose to the ground, looking first at the spot that had moved, then to his right, then to his left. All of a sudden Gianni knew. The dog had been telling them all along, he just hadn't listened hard enough. And now it was going to get him killed, him and Dustin.

Below ground! They had been below ground all along. That's why the dog had been bobbing his head up and down. He'd smelled the bodies and the Gooks hiding below ground. The dog had done his job, Gianni hadn't, and now they were all going to pay for his mistake. They had to warn the squad. They had to at least save them.

Gianni started to back up, keeping one eye on the patch of ground while trying to look around with the other. Dustin was leaning over the bodies pulling off the dog tags.

"Dustin."

"Yeah, man, hang on for a second."

"Dustin, we got Gooks in the ground, they're hidin' in the fuckin' ground!" Gianni tried to keep his voice to a whisper but the terror wasn't lost on Monie. He stood up and turned toward Gianni's back, his M-16 in both hands.

"Oh, shit, you sure?"

Gianni turned around slowly to face him. "I saw something like a trapdoor. That's what Shadrack has been alerting on. This is a fuckin' ambush, Dustin. We walked into a fuckin' ambush."

"All right, cool it. They want the whole squad or they'd have zapped us by now."

"We gotta' warn 'em, Dustin, we gotta' warn 'em. They'll come walkin' right into it."

"OKAY, OKAY, hang on! All right, I see it, just over your left shoulder. There's another one, further to the left of it." Dustin tried to quickly scan the ground behind Gianni. He spotted four more trapdoors, all covered with dried grass and branches, just slightly darker than the surrounding ground.

"All right, look, we gotta' make it into the stand of trees, it's the only way we're gonna' get outta' here." Dustin moved over half a step so he was completely blocked by Gianni. He reached up to his ammo harness and pulled off two grenades. "Here, take one of these. Hold on tight, I'm gonna' pull the pins. When I give the word, turn around and toss it at the hole. We ain't gonna' wait around to see what happens, we head for the trees, got it?"

Gianni heard another voice. *'Neutralize the closest threat, neutralize the closest threat'*. Monie wasn't sure what was going on but all of a sudden Gianni was calm, like he was just out on training.

Both men threw the grenades almost directly over each other's shoulder. Dustin did a quarter turn to the right and headed for the trees. Gianni yelled "Heel!" and with Shadrack at his side, took off after him. Moments later the air was shattered by two explosions followed by a piercing scream that lingered for several seconds. The fading sounds of the explosions were replaced by the chattering of AK-47s as the Vietnamese soldiers pushed open the trapdoors and started firing at the two fleeing men.

Monie dove head first into the trees and looked back just in time to see Gianni pitch forward onto his face.

"Gianni! Nnnnoooooooo! Oh, God, Gianni!" He was starting to push himself up when Gianni got back to his feet, ran the last five or six yards, and dove into the trees next to him. "Oh God, you all right, are you hit, are you hit?"

"No, no, I'm all right. I tripped on Shadrack's fuckin' leash!"

Monie fired two short bursts, then started yelling back through the trees. "Ambush! Ambush! They're in holes! They're in fighting holes!"

Gianni tried to keep his left elbow over Shadrack's back while he looked for a target. The hole he threw the grenade at was still the closest and he could just see the face peering out. Unless there had been more than one soldier in the hole, it hadn't been his grenade that caused the scream. Dustin was still firing short bursts on automatic, kicking up dirt in front of and behind the enemy soldiers.

'Neutralize the nearest threat, then go on to the next one'. Aiming through the peep sight, he squeezed the trigger and watched as the top of the soldier's head disintegrated, his body falling back into the fighting hole and the grass cover closing over him. Gianni and Monie both heard Evans moving the squad up. Monie started shouting again. "Watch the ground! They're in fighting holes!"

Bullets flew through the trees and into the ground around the squad. Evans and Huebner split the group and advanced from both ends of the tree stand.

Gianni looked for the next closest threat. Six, seven yards to the right of the first one and just behind. The soldier raised up higher, trying to get a clear field of fire. Gianni fired three quick rounds. The first hit the dirt just in front of the hole. The second two found their mark just below the breast bone and just above the soldier's ammo carrier. The reaction to the bullets impact was violent as the soldier jerked back, his body lying half in and half out of the hole.

Smith was the first to reach the tree line and fired off a whole magazine while he searched the ground for a target. Robinson and Schoonhoven slid down next to him and the air came alive with flaming red M-60 tracers. Schoonhoven broke off a belt of ammo and hooked the first round to the end of the belt that was quickly disappearing in the booming machine gun. Robinson walked the line of tracers to one of the holes and held the trigger as pieces of flesh and skull sprayed through the air.

Schoonhoven tapped him on the arm and pointed at another hole. Robinson shifted his aim, walked the line of bullets into it, and held it there until it was obvious no living soul would ever climb out.

Monie reached over and punched Gianni on the shoulder. "Cavalry made it!"

"Yeah, I just hope it's not Custer." *'Neutralize the closest threat before you move on to the next one.'* Gianni looked back out through the trees. Evans, Huebner, Tuckett and Boardman were on his right firing from the end of the tree line. Seventy yards in front of them the ground opened up and a long slender tube appeared. The Vietnamese soldier stood up with the B-40 rocket-propelled grenade launcher over his shoulder.

The four men shifted their fire in his direction. The fusillade of bullets tore into his chest and face throwing the soldier backward. A cloud of white smoke enveloped the now dead body as the rocket left the tube with a loud "wwwhhoosshh" and sailed off into the sky. Seconds later it exploded harmlessly in the jungle.

Monie was firing at one of two fighting holes dug side by side just to the right of the now silent rocket launcher. His bullets were kicking up dirt just in front of the soldier on the right. Gianni strained to see through the smoke and could just make out the American M-60 the soldier on the left was starting to fire. Tracers hit the ground and ricocheted off into the air as the soldier walked the line of fire toward the end of the tree line directly at Evans and his men.

Monie continued to fire at the man on the right, not realizing that he fed the belt of ammunition for the man with the gun. Gianni heard Tuckett yell, "Gun! Gun!," and watched as their bullets tore up the ground around the men. The long ago spoken words came back to him. *'Don't rush your shots, take your time and make them count. Always remember, fast is fine, but accuracy is final'.*

Monie shifted over on his side to pull out a fresh magazine. Beads of sweat flew off his face and landed on the hot gun barrel making a sharp sizzling sound. Shadrack tried to raise up and Gianni pressed down harder with his left elbow. "No! Down!" Monie looked over as he inserted the new magazine. "WHAT?"

"Wait! Aim for the M-60, shoot for the gun!"

Monie nodded his head and started firing short bursts, still doing nothing but kicking up dirt. Gianni peered through the peep sight. The big gun hid most of the soldier, only his two hands and the top of his pith helmet were visible. A soldier seventy yards away without a weapon is almost as harmless as no soldier at all. Gianni aimed for the side of the big gun. Three shots. The gun jerked to the left, a line of tracers digging a trench through the dirt in front of the surprised enemy.

A head, neck, and part of a right shoulder were visible. *'Identify your target and take your shot. Never give your target a chance.'* Gianni hadn't any idea who Hank was talking about when he told him about Machiavelli but he would never forget the words Hank had attributed to him. *'Never hurt your enemy just a little, don't give your target a chance.'* Gianni let out his breath. *'Shoot during the moment of hesitation'.*

He fired twice. The pith helmet went flying, filled with what used to be the top of the soldier's head. The cloud of fine red mist reminded Gianni of the famous film of President Kennedy's assassination. Monie stopped firing and just stared over the barrel of his rifle. Covered with pieces of the gunner's head, the soldier on the left dropped down in the hole and reappeared with his AK-47, only to be met with a hail of bullets from Robinson's own M-60. The bullets continued to tear at the body long after it was dead.

Two more trapdoors snapped open, the willingness to fight having fled its occupants. As the first soldier crawled out of the hole, his pith helmet fell off. Not even thinking about stopping to pick it up, he stumbled to his feet and ran, his back making an easy target. Monie fired twice, striking the soldier high between the shoulders. The soldier pitched forward, his body making a complete somersault in mid-air and landing on his back.

The last soldier, seeing the fate of his companion, never even tried to stand up or to carry his rifle with him. Instead, he crawled over the grass covered trap door and tried to snake his way toward the distant brush. Smith stood up yelling, "I've got 'im, I've got 'im", and started firing. The first three rounds hit the dirt several inches behind the soldier's feet. The forth shot went through the sole of the left boot and blew away part of the man's foot. His scream was enough to drown out the sound of the next two shots that entered the left hip and the lower left back. The soldier raised up slightly, then sagged to the ground.

Gianni searched the area looking for any unopened trapdoors and new targets. From his right he heard Evans yell "Keep your heads down", and a moment later, "Fire in the hole, fire in the hole!" Four grenades sailed through the air and exploded on the ground around the nearest holes. Dirt, grass, rocks, and pieces of bodies settled back to earth.

"All right, let's check 'em out!"

Monie pushed himself up and looked back at Gianni. "Watch yourself, don't take any chances."

Gianni ejected the magazine and inserted a fresh one. He nodded his head and patted his left leg.

Robinson and Schoonhoven covered the men as they checked the bodies for any sign of life. Gianni watched as they prodded the soldiers, or what was left of them, with the toes of their boots or rifle barrels. The mixture of smells was overpowering. Gunpowder, blood, urine involuntarily expelled either through fear or at the moment of death, and feces masked the normal smells of the jungle. Spent brass littered the ground lying under or next to body parts that bore no resemblance to their former shapes. Gianni walked through the carnage seeing, but not believing, the horrible destruction. *'We don't have weapons here Gianni, we have guns. Weapons are for killing people. We only shoot at clay birds.'*

Gianni looked down at the rifle in his right hand. *'Weapons are for killing people. Learn to use the weapon, it will keep you alive. It's not a game out there, Gianni, no one is going to yell 'missed bird' when you miss a shot. It's not a game, you could die.'*

He walked toward the last soldier Smith had shot. From behind him he heard Evans tell Schoonhoven to pull the two fliers' dog tags and heard Monie say that he already had them.

Gianni looked down at the back of the soldier. It moved, a jerky motion, like it was struggling to breathe. He told Shadrack to sit and dropped the leash. Holding the rifle in both hands, he rolled the body over with his boot. The soldier stared up at him, pain creased across his face. He tried to say something, something Gianni couldn't understand. His eyes pleaded for help, for mercy. Was he thinking about his family, a wife, children, or did he just want to live like everybody else in this Goddamn war? Gianni glanced behind him and started to call for Schoonhoven. Maybe the Doc could give him something for the pain, maybe he could patch him up good enough so one of the patrols they had seen could find him and take care of him. Gianni looked around for Schoonhoven, his eyes searching until they stopped at the two fliers staked out on the ground. The flies were still there gorging themselves on the rotting flesh. Hadn't they wanted to live? Had they thought about their wives or children while they were begging for their lives? What were their last thoughts while they were being slit open? Which one of these bastards had done it? Was it this one, or had he just stood and laughed? Gianni looked back down at the wounded man. He was still talking, his hands held over his chest, palms pressed together, either praying or pleading for his life. Gianni heard Evan's voice.

"Gianni, hey, Giancarlo, you all right? Let's get the hell outta' here."

"On my way, LT." Gianni moved his right thumb, switching the selector to auto. Letting go of the rifle with his left hand, he placed the barrel just above the soldiers upper lip. The man's eyes opened with terror and his words came faster.

"Now you know how it feels, asshole." The sound of gunfire shattered the silence.

The squad made its way back to the thick undergrowth of the jungle, the dead Vietnamese soldiers, along with the two mutilated American fliers, pushed back in their minds while they dealt with the new problem of getting safely out of the area. Evans pulled the magazine out of his rifle and checked the number of remaining rounds. Wanting to be ready for anything they might run into, he put the partially used magazine in the top pouch of his bandoleer and inserted a fresh one. He slapped the bottom of the magazine with the palm of his left hand to make sure it was seated properly.

"Goddamnit! All right, all right, we can't hang around here. Where's Huebner, where's Huebner?" Evans looked around the group of men and spotted the Sergeant. Picking up a small twig he threw it at Huebner to get his attention and motioned him over.

"We gotta' move, we can't hang around here. Which way ya' figure?"

"We sure as hell can't go back the way we came. Anybody heading this way will find our trail in a New York minute."

Evans nodded, then pulled out his map. "All right, look, this is where we saw those patrols, here, here, and here. See, they run right along this line. What if we try to skirt down here, try to stay well away from them, down to say here, then turn back to the southwest?"

"You figure on humpin' the whole way outta' here?"

"Fuck no, too many Gooks runnin' around out here, we'd never make it. I'm hopin' the Bronco can call in some air support, keep 'em busy so we can find a clearing for a pickup."

"How much longer 'til we make contact with the Bronco?"

Evans looked over at Boardman who held up five fingers. "We can't sit around here that long, we gotta' move now. Get the guys ready, tell Smith he's got the point."

"What about the dog? He can tell us if we're gonna' run into something."

Evans dragged his bush hat off his head and ran his hand through his hair. "You think Giancarlo can handle a fast point like that?"

Huebner cocked his head and looked Evans right in the eyes. "I think that kid is turnin' into a fuckin' machine."

"All right, Giancarlo and Monie up front. Show 'em which way to head and tell 'em we gotta' move quick. Have Smith take the tail end." Evans turned back to Boardman. "Try to raise the Bronco driver while we're on the move. Let 'im know what's happening. We're gonna' need some air cover and a pickup soonest."

Gianni took the aluminum cup away from Shadrack, put it on the bottom of the canteen, and moved out with Monie. The dog, moving with his head in the air, alerted several times but Gianni decided the scent was weak.

Boardman grabbed Evans by the back of the rucksack to get his attention and handed him the handset. Evans spoke into it, checking his map and nodding his head up and down as he listened. The drone of the airplane's engine could be heard as it came closer, then flew directly overhead. He nodded his head once more and handed the radio back to Boardman. "We got big-time trouble. The Bronco says the place is crawlin' with Gooks. Twenty-five or thirty of 'em back at the firefight, they're already trying to figure out which way we went. A bunch more roaming all over here lookin' for us, too."

"What about air cover?" Huebner knew they would be in deep shit without help.

"Four Cobras and two slicks from the Palace. They're gonna' be at least forty minutes, maybe longer."

"Any chance of some jet cover?"

"He's checkin' on that now, should be back to us any second..." Boardman moved up and handed him the radio.

Evans took the handset and spoke into it. He listened for a moment, checked the map and nodded his head. "Roger, out. Maybe things are looking up. We've got four F-4s scrambling from Tan Son Nhut, be here in fifteen to twenty."

Huebner grinned. "That was too fuckin' easy."

"The Bronco driver told 'em we had an Air Force guy on the ground with us." It was Evans' turn to grin. "I don't think he made it real clear that our boy isn't a pilot."

"All right, let's get going. The Bronco is gonna' make random passes, try to let us know where they are. Gianni, don't stop unless you think someone's real close, we gotta' put distance between us and the main patrol."

Lt. Col. David Runyon led the Pontiac flight of four F-4s off the runway at Tan Son Nhut and headed on the target vector. "All right gentlemen, let's go to burners, we've got some people on the ground in trouble." The four heavily-loaded planes jumped forward as each pilot pushed the throttles into afterburner.

"Hey, boss, what's an Air Force guy doing on the ground with a bunch of Army troops?"

"Not sure, I think he may be one of our guys that went down the other day. GCI says it's the Army Search & Rescue Team down there."

The pace was brutal, sweat poured off every man like they had been caught in a downpour. The air was thick with humidity and breathing was exhausting in itself. Robinson suffered the most, his already huge bulk with the heavy machine gun making him work doubly hard to maintain the pace.

Boardman heard the call sign and listened for several moments, then moved up to Evans. "We're in deep shit, LT."

Evans grabbed the handset and spoke to the pilot. Without stopping, he pulled out the map, checked the rest of the squad, then put the map back in his pocket and took out the signal mirror. Shining it through the trees, he continued to talk into the mouthpiece, nodding his head as he listened. Handing the radio back to Boardman, he moved up next to

Huebner. "We gotta' DI DI. That main force picked up our trail, they're only three or four hundred yards behind us, movin' fast."

"Shit, what about the patrols?"

"They're on our flanks, they already passed us, but they're gonna' run into the main force any minute now. This is gonna' be a big fuckin' party."

"Air cover?"

"F-4s should be here in a couple minutes. We got a clearing about 200 yards ahead, we gotta' make it to there and hold up for the slicks."

Huebner looked over to where Gianni was sitting on the ground pouring water on the dog and rubbing it on his chest. "I'm worried about the dog, I think the heat is getting to him."

Evans moved up next to them. Monie was holding Gianni's rifle and watching as he rubbed water into the dog's fur. "Problem, Gianni?"

"It's the heat, LT. We're moving so fast he hasn't had a chance to cool down."

"We've got another 200 yards to go, gotta' get to a clearing. Can he make it?"

"I don't know, LT, he's just way too fuckin' hot."

Evans rubbed the back of his neck, looked around at Huebner then back at Gianni. "Gianni, look, we've got boo coo Gooks on our tail and we gotta' get to that clearing. I can't risk the rest of the squad over a dog." Gianni started to say something. Evans held up his hand. "I know, I know, he's not just a dog, he's part of the squad." Evans felt like he was leaving a wounded GI to fend for himself. "Fuck, Giancarlo, I can't get people killed because a dog is holding us up. If he can't keep up, we leave him. I'm sorry, but that's the way it has to be."

Gianni poured the rest of the water on the dog and threw the empty canteen in the bushes. "He'll make it, LT, don't worry about it, he won't slow you up." Gianni looked up at Monie, then down at the dog, panting heavily, trying to cool himself off. "Don't worry, boy, I'm not going anywhere without you."

"Geoff, Smith, on point, straight ahead. Let's go, lets move it!"

Smith pushed past the men, then started out through the thick brush. Gianni gave a gentle tug at the leash and coaxed Shadrack to his feet. They had gone less than a hundred yards when the dog's back legs began to wobble. Seconds later all four legs gave out and he crashed to the ground. Gianni was on his knees pleading with the dog to get up.

Boardman listened to the handset, then moved over next to Evans. "They're right behind us, LT, couple hundred yards. The Bronco says we gotta' DI DI big time."

Evans shook his head, then stared at the ground. He crouched down next to Gianni. "I'm sorry, Gianni, we gotta' move, we can't wait for him."

Smith pushed through the men and moved next to Gianni. "Give me your ruck." Smith looked down at the panting dog. "If he was anybody else in this squad, we'd carry him, right, LT?"

"Yeah, yeah, we would. Go on, Gianni, give him your rucksack and pick 'im up. Come on, come on, what are you waiting for, a fuckin' invitation?" Monie helped Gianni out of his rucksack and took his rifle while Gianni picked the dog up in both arms.

"Tuckett, take the point, let's get moving, come on!"

Monie walked next to Gianni. They had only gone twenty-five yards when Gianni started to weaken from carrying the eighty-five-pound dog. Sweat poured off him and with both hands clutching fistfuls of fur, he was unable to wipe the stinging sweat out of his eyes. Monie put one hand under the dog, trying to ease the load as best he could. Gianni heard a voice and the big hand tugging on his shoulder made him turn.

"Hey, Cherry, hang on." Robinson pulled Gianni around to face him. "You checked out on an M-60?"

"Yeah, why?"

Robinson laid the big gun on the ground. "Here, you take the gun and give me the dog."

Gianni looked down at the machine gun lying on the ground, then back at the big black man. "Come on, Cherry, we ain't got all day!" Robinson reached forward and put his arms under the limp dog. "He ain't gonna' bite me, is he?"

The dog's breathing was shallow and labored. Gianni was worried that he might never bite anyone again. "Thanks Delmar, thanks a lot."

As they reached the clearing, they could hear men behind them crashing through the bush. Evans stopped at the tree line and grabbed Huebner by the arm. "We gotta' make it to the other side, it's the only way we can hold 'em off 'til the choppers get here."

Huebner nodded his head. "Come on, move it, move it, get across. Set up just inside the other tree line. Come on, let's go, let's go!" They were halfway across when the Bronco flew in low and fired two smoke rockets into the trees behind them. The sound of small arms fire was deafening as the Vietnamese soldiers tried to blow the slow-moving air-craft out of the sky. Clouds of white smoke rose through the branches into the sky as the small plane made a sharp right turn.

Just yards from the trees, two F-4's flew directly over their heads, no more than 500 feet off the ground, the sound of their massive jet engines not reaching them until the huge planes were well past. Evans turned just in time to see flaming rockets exploding in the trees they had been running through just seconds before. Screams of pain and horror could be heard over the loud explosions as branches, dirt, and pieces of bodies were thrown high in the air.

Each man found a large tree trunk to hide behind and settled down into the protective ground as low as he could get. Evans crawled next to Boardman. "Two more fast movers coming in, keep down, keep down!"

The two jets flew in low, the ground shaking from the ear splitting noise. Less than a hundred yards inside the far tree line, eight 250-pound bombs tore through the jungle. The impact raised each man off the ground several inches with the shock wave reaching them a second later. The sudden and drastic change in air pressure causing each man to stretch his jaw or rub his ears, trying to restore his hearing.

Soldiers appeared at the edge of the tree line and started across. Gianni looked around and saw Robinson and Monie lying next to each. Robinson had one arm over the dog as Monie handed him Gianni's CAR-15 and tossed several loaded magazines on the ground in front of him. Both men started firing at the advancing soldiers.

Gianni folded down the machine gun's bipod and took aim. Out of his left eye, he noticed only twenty or so rounds were left in the ammo belt. The squad's compassion at not having him carry extra belts of ammo was coming back to haunt him. "Ammo! Ammo! I need ammo!" He flipped up the tangent sight and began firing, tracers digging into the dirt as he walked the bullets into the two closest men. Both bodies fell backwards and lay still. Gianni sighted on a man to the right and pulled the trigger, sending a short burst into the exploding chest. "Ammo! Ammo!"

"Hold your fucking horses, Cherry!" Schoonhoven slid next to the big gun and connected his last belt of ammo to the four remaining rounds. "Can you handle this by yourself for a minute? I gotta' get some more belts!"

"Yeah, yeah! Go, go!" Gianni held the belt of ammo out away from the gun with his left hand hoping to avoid a jam from a kinked belt. "Go on, I've got it, I've got it!" He fired a burst at three men, the rounds hitting the dirt in front of them and ricocheting off into the trees. Raising his aim, one of the men spun violently as his right arm went sailing off into the air. Gianni cut off the man's scream of pain with a burst through the stomach and chest.

More men emerged from the trees, one of them carrying a B-40 rocket propelled grenade launcher. He knelt down and prepared to fire, aiming at the section of trees that spit out the tracers from Gianni's M-60. Gianni swung the gun over as the soldier's head exploded, his now lifeless body gently toppling over, hit by someone else in the squad. A soldier to his left reached over for the grenade launcher. His finger was just wrapping itself around the trigger when a combination of M-60 and M-16 bullets slammed into his body. As the finger involuntarily tightened, the large projectile left the tube and imbedded itself in the back of a soldier four yards away. Not having traveled far enough to arm itself, it failed to explode but achieved its desired result by severing the man's spine and bulging his stomach enough to tear the thick fabric of his ammo carrier.

Either oblivious to, or uncaring about the men being slaughtered in front of them, more and more soldiers ran from the tree line, firing from the hip. Evans picked up the handset and screamed into it. He looked up as the four jets formed into a single file and prepared to make a run on the clearing from the right.

Gianni kept firing, keeping an eye on the quickly disappearing belt of ammo. "Schoonhoven! Doc, Doc! Where's the ammo!?" Gianni squeezed off the last burst and heard the gun click down on an empty chamber as Schoonhoven flopped down on the ground beside him, his arms filled with glistening belts of ammo.

"Here, here. Open it up, come on, open it up!"

Gianni reached forward and flipped open the receiver cover as Schoonhoven placed the first round in place. Gianni snapped the cover closed and pulled back the charging handle.

"To your right, right, three of 'em!"

Gianni swung the gun around at Schoonhoven's direction and fired at the three soldiers. Both men saw the right knee of the first man get shot away as he crumpled to the ground. The other two men, seeing the fate of their comrade, threw themselves face down and fired long bursts at the M-60. The ground erupted in front of the big gun as Schoonhoven let out a loud grunt and grabbed his face with his left hand.

"Doc!"

"I'm all right! Keep firing, keep firing!"

'Neutralize the closest threat. Stay with it 'til it's neutralized, then move on to the next one.' Gianni let out his breath. Taking his time, he sighted on the first of the two men. Because of the long curved shape of the thirty-round AK-47 magazine, the men were unable to lie close to the ground. Both had their chests and heads exposed while they fired their rifles. Gianni aimed just above the first man's gun barrel. Gilded metal-covered rounds slammed into his chest just below the jaw, tearing through flesh, snapping and crushing bone as they tore out his back. Gianni shifted the gun slightly to the right as his bullets impacted the dirt just in front of the second man, then walked up into his chest and face.

The clearing in front of him started to tremble. The first of the F-4s had started its strafing run. Twenty-millimeter cannon shells slammed into the ground sending up geysers of dirt and rock. The already-dead bodies were thrown around as the huge rounds tore through them. Live soldiers were quickly transformed into smoldering piles of shredded flesh.

Gianni turned away from the carnage and reached over to Schoonhoven who was still holding his face. "Doc, let me see, move your hand, let me take a look!" Schoonhoven pulled his hand down, the fingers covered with sticky blood. Gianni reached up and grabbed his jaw so he could turn the head and get a better look. "It's just sliced open, bleeding like hell, but it doesn't look serious! Here, turn around, let me get to your ruck." Schoonhoven struggled to move around and still stay close to the ground at the same time. Gianni pulled out a green covered bandage and helped Schoonhoven wrap it around his cheek.

"Heads up, heads up! Here comes another fast mover."

Gianni looked up just as the second jet started firing its heavy cannon. The sound was constant, masking out the noise of each individual round. Gianni couldn't believe anything could live through the onslaught, but yet soldiers struggled to get up and make their way across the killing field. He caught a glimpse of Evans on the handset, yelling to be heard over the noise of the gunfire and jet engines.

"Over there, over there!" Schoonhoven pointed to a Vietnamese soldier, something clutched in his right hand, crawling across the ground.

Gianni moved the gun in his direction and pulled the trigger. A line of tracers passed over his back but still he continued to crawl. "Drop it down, Gianni, drop it down! You're too high, drop it down!"

Gianni lowered his aim and dirt flew up around the soldier. He raised up on both knees and cocked his arm back. Bullets tore through his waistline, shattering both hips, and the man crumpled forward. Moments later, the grenade lying on the ground at his finger tips detonated, tearing away most of his head and shoulders.

The third jet made its run, this time firing just inside the tree line, the heavy shells tearing apart men and trees alike. Shrieks of pain and the shouts of orders could be heard from across the clearing.

Evans' sudden voice could be heard above it all. "Cobras coming in! Cobras coming in! Popping smoke now!" Evans pulled a smoke grenade off his harness and threw the canister into the clearing. Yellow clouds of smoke billowed from it. He picked up the handset and spoke into it once again. The sound of chopper blades grew louder.

The first Cobra pilot made his run from directly behind them. Rockets streaked out from each side of the fierce looking machine. Thirty-eight 2.75-inch rockets tore into the trees followed by a stream of forty-millimeter grenades. Another gunship made a run at the trees just to the right of the first helicopter.

The Vietnamese soldiers caught out in the clearing made the mistake of looking up as the dark green machines swooped overhead. The burst of fire from the other side of the tree line was devastating. Gianni stopped firing as Schoonhoven connected another belt of ammo. By the time he looked back up, not a single live soldier could be seen.

Evans spoke to the Bronco pilot again and motioned Huebner to throw another smoke grenade. The canister landed several feet from the first as red smoke began to billow from it. Evans looked at the sky as he spoke into the handset. The sound of chopper blades could be heard coming in from behind them. Seconds later, the nose of a slick passed over and began to flare to a landing in the clearing.

Just as Evans shouted for everybody to move, a hail of gunfire erupted from the opposite tree line. With the helicopter blocking their field of fire, the squad was left helpless as pieces of metal were torn from the thin skin. The right side door gunner sprayed the trees and screamed for the pilot to lift off. Flying forward, he tried to gain speed before pulling up and out of the range of the trailing bullets.

Once the chopper was out of the way, the squad poured round after round at the opposite trees. Evans called the Bronco driver and had a short conversation. Handing the receiver back to Boardman, he yelled out a warning. "Napalm coming in! Heads up!"

Gianni looked over at Robinson lying over the dog's back, trying to cover it as best he could. Two of the F-4's roared in from the right, two tanks of napalm dropping from each plane. As the jungle erupted in a solid sheet of flame, two more planes dove down and made their drop. The air hung heavy with the smell of burning petroleum as the three Cobra gunships roared in. One Cobra fired its remaining rockets as the other two sprayed the trees with grenades and mini-gun fire. As they made pass after pass, the slick returned and dropped down into the clearing.

Evans jumped to his feet. "MOVE, MOVE, MOVE!!" Every man followed his lead with the right side door gunner urging them on as the left gunner continued to spray the trees. Bodies hurled through the open door, not worrying, or caring where they landed. Robinson made a mad dash, tossing the heavy dog out in front of him, and followed through the door. Two of the low flying F-4's passed by the left side of the helicopter, tearing up the jungle with cannon fire.

Gianni and Schoonhoven were the last to reach the door. Gianni pushed Schoonhoven through, then tossed the machine gun to Smith, and jumped in. The door gunner could be heard yelling through his microphone at the pilot, "GO GO GO!! Get us out of here!"

The helicopter struggled with the extra weight as it tried to move across the ground, slowly picking up speed as it rose higher and higher. Bullets smacked against the aluminum skin, two of them passing inches over Tuckett's head. Those who could see out the left door watched as the Cobras and F-4s expended the rest of their ammunition on the tree line.

Gianni crawled over the sprawled bodies, trying to get next to Robinson and Shadrack. As the dog saw him come closer, he raised his head off the deck and tried to lick his hand. "It's all right, boy, everything's gonna' be all right." Gianni looked up at Robinson. "Thank you, Delmar...I...ah..."

The big man flashed a white toothy grin then reached over and rubbed the dog's head. "Weren't nothin' Cherry...always did have a likin' for dogs."

CHAPTER 9

FRIDAY
APRIL 24, 1970
FORT LAUDERDALE, FLORIDA

Vince Giancarlo sat on the metal chair in front of Frank Cipriani's desk. A second letter had arrived, he stared at it in his hand, almost afraid to open it.

"Want me to leave you alone Vince?"

"NO! Ah, I'm sorry, Frank. No, please don't go. I mean, I'd feel better if you stayed around."

He stared at the envelope for several more seconds. What had he seen since the first letter…what had he done? Were things getting easier, had he gone back to Tan Son Nhut, back to being bored? No. If he had, he wouldn't have sent the letter to the post office. Vince glanced to his right as Cipriani put a can of Pepsi on the desk next to him. He muttered thanks, took a sip out of the can, and looked again at the envelope.

"I guess now we know what our parents used to go through, huh, Vince?"

"We were older when we went, Frank."

"We were still our parents' kids, I don't think age has anything to do with it." Cipriani took a sip of his own Pepsi and lit a cigarette.

"When he told me he was going in the Air Force, I figured everything would be all right. You know, no big deal, they didn't get near combat, just stayed on some base. I should have known he'd find a way to see what it's like."

"You raised him right, Vince, he's a good kid."

Vince's lower lip started to tremble. "I didn't think I'd raised him to get killed." Vince turned the envelope over and ran his finger under the flap, trying not to tear it any more than necessary.

Dear Dad,

I got your letter yesterday. It was sure great to hear from you. There was a letter here from Mom, too. She sounds fine, still worrying about me, though. Dustin's folks sent him a rope, you know, the kind cowboys use to rope horses and cows and stuff. I don't know why they sent it but you should have seen the smile on his face. He started running around roping everything and everyone in sight. He does something called heeling where you rope the back legs of a cow while it's running. Since there are no cows around here he waits until someone walks by, then he twirls this rope over his head, and when he throws it, the loop lands around the guy's feet. Then he yanks it real quick, the loop tightens and he goes flying right on his face. Dustin thinks it's the funniest thing in the world. I guess the humor is lost on the guy that gets roped. Anyway, I got your letter right after we got back from a mission. It was pretty much a cake walk. We went out after a Skyraider pilot. His engine took some rounds and he went down. The guy was pretty cool, he found a place to hunker down so the Gooks couldn't find him and decided to wait for us to come for him. Took us less than a day. You should have seen the look on his face when Shadrack found him hiding in the top of a tree. He must have been forty feet up, had branches built all around him, and had mud streaked all over his face. I guess he thought he was invisible. He pretty much was to everyone but Shadrack. We were all standing about twenty yards away from the tree, the guy never even saw us, and the LT threw a rock at him. This muddy face sticks out and starts yelling "don't shoot, don't shoot, I'm an American". Anyway, he came climbing down and the first thing he says is "What took you guys so long!" Can you believe that? He tells us that all the pilots know about us and if they get shot down and can't get picked up by a chopper, we'll come out and save their ass. He knew we were coming. I don't know, Dad, I can't describe it; it's weird when someone tells you they know you are going to come out and save their life. In one way it feels good, and in another way it's real scary. It's like they are leaving their fate up to us now, like we'll be able to get to all of them before the Gooks do, and it just doesn't happen that way. We don't get to all of them in time, and I don't know if I can handle it. Dad, I'm scared. Not about dying, that feeling goes away as soon the shit hits the fan. What I'm scared about is the killing. It's too easy. I don't understand. I enlisted because I thought it was my duty, something I owed to the country. Now I don't feel that way, it's like it doesn't even matter. I'm changing, Dad, and it scares me. I just feel like I'm going crazy and there's no way back. I didn't think it would be like this. I don't see how anyone could. You were right when you told me that there were things you saw that Mom didn't need to know about. I understand that now. I guess there are things in war that no one needs to know about. All I know is one minute I want to be home and the next minute I don't because I'm afraid nothing will ever be the same. Dad, I don't understand how life can change so fast, how can things go from being so great to so fucked up. I don't understand how I could go from wanting to be here to not knowing why the hell I am here. Why any of us are here. The worst thing, Dad, is how I could have taken you and Mom for granted, how I never really appreciated what I had, and how much you guys had given me. I guess that's the worst part, not knowing if I'm ever going to get to tell you that. I miss you, Dad, more than I ever thought I could. I love you both.

Gianni.

Cipriani heard the letter rattle before he saw his friend's hands trembling, holding the paper so tightly that the joints of his thumbs and fingers turned white. As he looked at the shaking paper, a small drop of moisture landed with a silent plop, smearing one of the ink written words near the bottom.

Cipriani got up, walked around the desk, and slid another metal chair in front of Vince. Slowly he sat down, stared at the floor for a moment, searching for a way to help his friend. "Vince, Vince, is everything all right, is Gianni okay?"

"Yeah, he's fine. I mean, he's not hurt or anything, physically anyway."

"He's having a tough time dealing with it, isn't he?"

"You went through it, Frank, we both did. You remember what it was like."

His eyes focused on his friend. "He'll work it out, Vince, he'll learn to hide it away like we all do."

"I don't know, Frank. I think this is different. We had a reason when we went, a real reason." Vince looked down at the letter, then back up at Cipriani. "He doesn't. None of them do. They don't even understand what they're doing over there."

"I don't either, Vince. It's a bullshit war and we all know it but you can't tell him that. You've got to give him a reason for being there, you've got to tell him he makes a difference. He's got to believe that, Vince, and so do you."

Cipriani looked over at the top of the desk. "There's a legal pad and envelopes in the top drawer. You take all the time you need, no one's going to bother you. When you're done, just seal it up and leave it on the desk. I'll make sure it goes out on time."

"Thanks, Frank, I appreciate it."

"Just tell him the way it is, Vince. Tell him the way it is."

SATURDAY
MAY 2, 1970
CAMELOT PALACE

Gianni and Dustin stood in front of the tent stripped down to their bush hats, green boxer shorts and combat boots. Even the constant dousing of water from a five-gallon bucket failed to keep the sweat from pouring off their bodies. Shadrack lay in the shade of the sandbag wall occasionally lifting his head to watch the uncoordinated antics of his master. Gianni threw the loop, somehow managing to rope his own head.

"Jesus Christ! How many times do I gotta' tell ya'? Swing your whole arm over your head, not just your wrist. Here, gimme the motherfucker." Dustin took the rope and started twirling a perfect loop around his head. "See, like this. Keep your whole arm moving and when you throw it, take a step forward with your right foot, and follow through with your arm. Like this." Dustin let the loop fly through the air. As it settled over the two entrenching tools stuck in the ground to simulate a pair of horns, he jerked back on the rope, pulling the loop closed and yanking the entrenching tools out of the ground at the same time.

"Yeah, real good. Ya' would'a broken the poor cow's neck."

"It's not a cow! It's a steer! And their horns are a shit load stronger than two shovels stuck in the fuckin' ground. Now stick 'em back in there and try it again, and remember to swing your whole arm." Dustin had been trying to teach Gianni to rope for over an hour and so far the closest he got was hitting a portion of the ground somewhere in the same hemisphere.

Dustin stepped back as he handed Gianni the rope. "That's it...no, wait, build the loop a little bigger, there, there, that's good. Okay. Keep your finger pointed straight, good, good, now swing your arm, faster, good, a little faster, good, good. Okay, keep your arm swinging, bigger circle around your head, good. Okay, now start to swing your wrist, just a little, not too much, you just want to rotate it a little so you get some zip in your throw. Good, good, that's more like it. Okay, now, get ready, keep your arm swinging, then step toward the steer and let 'er rip."

Gianni felt good. He was doing everything right, just like Dustin told him. This was going to be it. This was going to be the perfect throw, right over the steer's horns. He was going to do it, and if the shovels didn't say anything, so be it, he'd yell 'Mmmooo' for them.

He took a deep breath and held it. His right foot kicked up a little cloud of dust as he stepped toward his target. Beads of sweat flew off his face as he brought his right arm forward and let the rope fly. It left his hand just at the right instant. As the coils in his left hand began to unravel and follow the loop, Gianni watched it as if in slow motion. The perfectly formed circle of rope, defying all laws of nature, veered off in a ninety-degree turn to the left and landed with a loud "whack" right on top of the resting Shadrack. Startled from his half sleeping, half day-dreaming world, he let out a loud yelp and ran frantically around the corner of the wall.

"This is fuckin' hopeless! Now you're trying to scare your own dog to death. How the hell did you manage to do that! I saw it with my own fuckin' eyes and I still can't believe it. It's not possible! A rope can't do that, nothing can do that! How the hell do you make it go straight, then have it stop and turn left?"

Gianni was pulling in the rope, trying to re-coil it. "Hey, I'm in the Air Force, remember? We know all about aerodynamics and making things do weird stuff in the air and good shit like that. They taught it to us in basic. Classified though, very hush-hush. I'm sworn to secrecy; otherwise I'd be happy to explain how it's done." Gianni finished coiling the rope and handed it back to Dustin. "Here ya' go, I think I've demonstrated enough national secrets for one day."

He turned back toward the wall and saw Shadrack peeking around the corner, determined not to show himself until the rope was safely out of the hands of his master. "You! You chickenshit mutt! Ya' think I'd thrown a mountain lion on your back. A lot of moral support you are." Shadrack raised up off the ground and sat at the very corner of the sandbag wall, staying out of range just in case his master decided to try to throw the rope again.

"Don't look at me like that. You're lucky I didn't try to rope your ears. Even I couldn't miss that target!" Shadrack tilted his head as if to say, 'Try it, buster, and you'll carry your balls home in a box'.

"Now, now, don't get pissed off at your dog just 'cause you're more suited to being a cowpie than a cowboy." Dustin chuckled at his own joke.

Gianni walked over to the bucket and poured a canteen cup full of water over his head. "Stupid fuckin' sport! Who the hell would want to catch an animal by his horns anyway?"

The sound of Huebner's voice caused Dustin to turn around. "If you ladies are through, perhaps you'd like to have your mail."

"Hey, all right, mail call." Dustin draped the coils of rope over his shoulder and walked over to Huebner. Gianni filled the cup with water and put it on the ground for Shadrack.

"What'd your folks send you this time? A new saddle to go with the rope?"

"Pay no attention to the rantin' 'n' ravin' of AIR-MAN Giancarlo, Sergeant Huebner. He's just jealous because the Army has once again demonstrated the ability to perform difficult tasks that members of the Air Force have yet to understand, much less master."

"Monie, it seems to me the last time you two had a, shall we say, discussion about the merits of the Air Force and the Army, that dog almost had you for lunch."

"Never fear, Sergeant. The dog and I have come to an understanding. We both realize, and the dog will readily admit, that AIR-MAN Giancarlo is incapable of surviving on his own, and that is why, as fate would have it, he has had the good fortune of not only being teamed up with that above average specimen of man's best friend, but also being assigned to a vastly superior group of men, namely our squad, to look after him."

"May I also say, Sergeant Huebner, that much of the reason for the superior nature of our squad is a direct result of the courageous and dedicated leadership provided by yourself and Lt. Evans…"

"Blow smoke up someone else's ass, Monie. I got better things to do than listen to this horseshit."

"Ah ha. Well, in that case, Sergeant Huebner, give me my fuckin' mail, and if they sent me anything to eat, I'm not giving you any of it."

Huebner sorted through the stack of mail and held out a single letter to Monie. "Here ya' go, hot shot, doesn't look like any food this trip." Dustin took his letter and started toward the shade of the sandbag wall.

Huebner held out a single envelope for Gianni. Gianni took his letter and sat down next to Monie.

"So what's going on back in Colorado?"

"Awe, nothin' much. Dad says the pastures were just startin' to show some green and they got hit with a spring snow storm. Says they got almost four feet with seven-and eight-foot drifts."

"How the hell can you live in that shit? Four feet of snow, Jesus!"

"Naw, it's not as bad as it sounds. This time of year it's pretty warm. You don't need more than a heavy shirt or a real light jacket in the daytime and most of the snow will be melted off in two days. Besides, the moisture is good for the pasture. Few more weeks and that grass is gonna' be as green as goose shit."

"Gee, what a pleasant picture. Acres and acres of green goose shit."

"You have no appreciation for the finer things in life."

"Yeah, I guess I'm just a fuckin' barbarian. Damn, and I thought I had class just 'cause I piss behind the tree instead of in front." Gianni hung his head in mock shame and kicked the dirt with the heel of his boot. "How will I ever be able to look at myself in the mirror again?"

"I don't see how you could before. Hell, we've all known you were an uncouth bastard from the day you got here." Dustin edged an inch or two away to show his displeasure at being so close to an admitted member of a lower class.

Gianni was about to tear open the envelope when he noticed the return address. "It's not from my folks, it's from my dad." As he slid his finger under the flap to tear open the envelope, Dustin stood up and brushed of the back of his skivvies. "Hey, I'm gonna' go over and scrounge up a Coke. Can I take Shadrack with me? I won't fuck around, I promise."

"The last time you took him for a walk, you almost got us both court-martialed."

"Hey, it wasn't my fault! That guy started making fun of his ears so I tried to uphold his honor."

"Dustin', you don't uphold the dog's honor by telling him to tear the guy's nuts off and swallow them."

"You do it!"

"I know how to do it! Besides, he's my dog. I'm allowed."

"All right, I'll be good. Can I take him with me?"

Gianni looked over at the dog lying next to him. "Shadrack, you think you can swallow your pride for a little while and be seen walking around with an Army puke?"

Dustin paced back and forth in front of Gianni and the dog. "Well?"

"Give him a minute, will ya'! He's thinking about it."

"I don't fuckin' believe this. Now he actually asks the dog questions."

"All right, he says he'll go but he says you have to keep him on his leash so everyone will think you're forcing him to be with you."

"You're sick, Giancarlo, you're really fuckin' sick. I'm surprised they let you carry a gun. No, no, I'm even more surprised they give you bullets for it! Where's his leash, where's his...oh, there it is." Dustin picked up the leash from the top of the sandbag wall and attached it to Shadrack's choke chain. "Come on, Shadrack, let's get away from this whacko."

"Don't be gone long. And I better not hear any barking or people screaming!" Gianni tore open the letter as his dog and friend walked off.

Dear Gianni,

You're learning that in war you see things you didn't even know could exist. You're right when you say that no one can explain these things to you. You have to actually see them to believe them. I guess you're also finding out that when you're there, when you're doing the fighting, everything you ever learned seems to get pushed aside, and now that you are there you wonder what you, and your friends, are fighting for. You say you've forgotten the reason. Gianni, it doesn't matter. To the guys with the rifles, the men crawling through, and living in the dirt, the reason they went to war never mattered. When your uncles and I landed in Africa and Italy and Europe, it didn't matter why we were sent there. The Marines in the Pacific weren't there just to stop the Japanese. No one who has ever gone to war, and none of you who are there now, fights for the kind of reason you're trying to find. It's much simpler than that, Gianni. You fight to keep your friends alive. The guy on your right, the guy on your left, or men who are trapped, and want nothing more in God's world than to see their families again. Gianni, you're right, war is crazy, but you're not. The things you are feeling, the doubts you're having, it's all part of it. It's all part of the sickness of war. It goes away, son, please believe me, it goes away. You'll learn to put the memories in the back of your mind, but they'll come back when your son tells you it's time for him to fight. I love you, Gianni, more than life itself, and if I could trade places with you, if I could spare you what you're going through, I would. You're afraid that you'll never be the same. You're right, and there's nothing I or anybody else can do about that. But you'll go on. You'll learn to appreciate what you have, to be proud of what you achieve, and most of all, you'll have special memories, Gianni, memories that only a few people are fortunate enough to have. You'll have memories of the men you've helped save. The men who will always be thankful for what you did for them. Even though you might not see them again, never really know who they are, you'll know that their families will hold a special place in their hearts for you. Son, what you do is hard, I know that, but you do makes a difference, a great difference. The killing scares you because it gets to be easy. I asked my father the same things you are asking me. I can't think of a better answer than what he told me. It's not the killing that gets easy, it's trying to stay alive that keeps getting harder. There is no shame in being afraid Gianni, just as there is no shame in doing what has to be done. Do what you have to do, do it well, and when it's finished, come home to us. I love you, son.

Dad.

Gianni read the letter twice, his only movement to wipe away the moisture that rolled down his cheeks. He stared at the words just above where his dad had signed it, realizing how much he missed him, how much he still wanted to say.

Dustin and Shadrack returned as Gianni lowered the letter and wiped the tears away with his bush hat. Dustin crouched down next to him and sat a cold can of Coke in the dirt, pretending he hadn't seen what had happened. "Come on, Flatlander, let me teach you how to rope."

CHAPTER 10

They had been on three missions since Gianni received the letter from his father, and with each successful rescue their reputation grew. The last mission had been without incident. The two man F-4 crew had bailed out after losing both engines to ground fire. Having heard the stories of the Army Search & Rescue Team with the Air Force dog handler, they decided to hide until they came out to find them. After they'd been rescued, the Wizzo produced a small camera and he and the pilot had their pictures taken with Gianni and Shadrack, then with the other members of the squad.

On the chopper ride to the Palace, the F-4 pilot told Gianni that the squad, especially he and Shadrack, were becoming legends, and how it was an honor to be rescued by them. Gianni remarked that it would probably be better to forego the honor of meeting them again and try harder to keep their fighter from becoming part of the landscape. The

245

pilot had looked at Gianni, given him the thumbs up, and yelled, "Roger that, I'll try to keep it in mind."

Landing at Camelot Palace was even more of a circus with the two fliers demanding pictures of the squad while they were still in the helicopter, then as they were dragging their gear out of it. On the trip back to the tent, Evans commented that it didn't surprise him that Air Force pukes dumb enough to get shot down were equally dumb enough to go traipsing through the bush taking pictures for their vacation album.

Much as they relished in the feeling of rescuing helpless pilots, the constant pace was wearing on them. The periods of downtime at Camelot Palace were a welcome respite, but it wasn't going to last long.

Everyone was sitting or lying on their cots when Huebner walked in with a partially-filled, dirt-encrusted, green duffel bag. "I don't want to interrupt your beauty sleep, ladies, but I thought you might be interested in what I have in my grubby little hands."

Tuckett raised his head up off the cot and looked over. "Well, it's takin' two hands so we know it ain't your dick." Huebner casually walked over to Tuckett's cot, reached down, and with a violent yank turned it over on him. "My, my Tuckett, did we have a bad dream and roll out of bed?"

As Tuckett scrambled up, he muttered, a little louder than he intended, "needle dick bug fucker."

"Oh, Tuckett?" Huebner took a step forward which was enough to send the skivvy clad soldier racing to the far end of the tent. Huebner dropped the duffel bag on the cot and spread his arms like he was taking a bow. "Now, how 'bout we spend some time reading mail?"

Boardman jumped off his cot and slid next to Huebner. "Hey, we must be winning the war, two mail calls in seven days. Think this means something?"

Huebner dumped the mail on the cot and started sorting it. "Yeah, it means that the post office is the only part of the government that knows what the fuck it's doing." Huebner picked through the mail and handed

Tuckett a letter and a National Geographic. "Why don't you subscribe to Playboy like everybody else?"

"Hey, I get these for the articles, not the pictures."

"Yeah, right." Huebner continued to look through the stack of mail. "Doc, Doc, where ya' at, got one for ya'?"

Schoonhoven sat up and caught the flying letter before it hit the dirt-covered floor.

"Hey, hey, Robinson got two. Yo', Robinson, speak up, man, where are ya'?

"Did I hear my name mentioned by some white boy?" Robinson and Smith entered through the open tent flap loaded down with glistening belts of M-60 ammunition. Smith dumped his belts on one of the cots and scurried over next to Huebner.

"Let's me have my mail, Sarge, maybe one of my fine women sent new pictures. I's tired of lookin' at all that white pussy in you honkies' fuck magazines!"

"Stand easy, Smith, I'll get to yours." Huebner twisted around to Robinson and waited while he laid his ammo belts down. "Here ya' go, Del, got two for ya'."

Huebner went back to the diminishing stack. "Monie, three. One letter and two…what the fuck is this? Western Horseman? Wait a minute," Huebner turned the other magazine over so he could read the cover, "a catalog from J.M. Capriola, Custom Saddles and Tack, Elko, Nevada. Monie, where the hell do you think you are, Texas!?"

"Hey! Never say Texas to a Coloradan. Besides, we gotta' have some culture in this shithole." Monie reached across and snatched his mail out of Huebner's hand. "I've been saving up. As soon as I get home, the first thing I'm gonna' do is order me a new custom saddle." Monie thought for a moment and added. "Well, maybe not the first thing…"

Huebner picked up the last three letters and held them to his nose. The scent of the three different kinds of perfume was overpowering. He looked at the return addresses and noticed they were from three different women. He bent all three envelopes, checking for stiffness. "Sorry, Smith, no pictures this time."

Smith reached over Robinson's head and grabbed the letters. "Hey, no problem, they all probably go into fine detail 'bout what they gonna' do to me when I get home. I seen it enough to remember what it looks like. 'Sides, you horney white boys probably just try to steal my pictures when I's asleep."

Huebner looked down at the empty cot, then clapped his hands together and held them apart like a blackjack dealer showing he held no cards in his hand. "That's all, folks, ain't no more."

Gianni stared at the cot for a moment, then turned away, the disappointment showing on his face.

Huebner stood up and grabbed the green duffel bag. "Ow, wait a minute. What's this? Why I believe I forgot a package in here." Huebner reached in and pulled out a brown paper-wrapped box. "Hey, Gianni, Happy Birthday!" Huebner tossed the box through the air.

"What'da ya' mean, Happy Birthday? It's not my birthday."

"Oh, yeah? Then how come it's written all over the box in big red letters, I might add."

Gianni looked down at the package and saw the words, "Happy Birthday, We Love You" written on both sides of the package. He didn't have to look at the return address, he knew his mother's handwriting. "Hey! What's the date today?"

Schoonhoven came to the rescue. "It's the eighth, one day closer to going home."

"Son of a bitch! Tomorrow's my birthday! I forgot all about it." Gianni looked down at the package and for a moment forgot where he was, thinking back a year ago. How could things have changed so much in a year? How could he have gone from killing mosquitoes to killing people? "Damn, my birthday. I wonder what they sent me?"

Huebner folded up the duffel bag and sat down on the cot. "Well, young Airman, if you were the product of superior Army training, and if you had achieved the rank that Yours Truly has, the answer to your question would come to you as if second nature. But since you are neither, I will impart some of my wisdom on you. Open the fuckin' thing!!"

Gianni slid a knife under the twisted brown twine and sliced through the double thickness. He ripped open the taped end, trying not to tear the paper, his mother's speech from every Christmas and birthday party ingrained in his memory: 'Don't tear the paper, we can use it again next year.' The difference was that the paper was always some colorful foil wrap with a festive design. This plain brown paper was more famous for covering pornographic magazines than for wrapping birthday presents.

"Come on, boy, just tear the damn thing open!" Smith was enjoying the suspense as much as Gianni. "Damn you white boys, make a production outta' everything."

Gianni grinned as he grabbed the end of the folded paper and with a grand gesture tore it across the top. "There, happy?"

"No, open it up, let's see what they sent ya." Gianni slit the Scotch tape holding the box closed and looked inside. "Well, what it be? What'd they send ya?"

"Newspaper."

"What!"

"Newspaper. Crumpled newspaper. They sent me crumpled newspaper." Gianni, with a disappointed look on his face, reached in and pulled out balls and balls of crumpled newspaper. The pile of paper grew at his feet as he pulled out the last of it. Looking in the box, a huge grin spread over his face. "Alllll right!! 'S' cookies! They sent me 'S' cookies!"

Everyone looked at each other like he had gone crazy.

"'S' cookies? What the fuck are you talking about? What the hell is an 'S' cookie?" Huebner leaned over to look in the box.

Gianni reached in and pulled out two rectangular packages. "'S' cookies. That's what we call 'em. They're really Stella Doro Breakfast Treats, but they're shaped like an 'S,' see?" Gianni held up the two packages.

"They sent you cookies? Your people sent you fuckin' cookies for your birthday? Man, I been right all along, you white folk are strange." Smith took a good look at the packages and shook his head. "Cookies."

"Naw, man! They're not just any cookies. They're 'S' cookies. We used to have these all the time. My mom would get them for dessert or serve them when we had company. My dad says 'S' cookies are an Italian's second favorite thing."

"Yeah, what's the first?" Smith was still skeptical.

"I'm not sure, he never told me, said I'd figure it out."

Monie tried to look into the box. "What else you got in there?"

"I don't know, let me look."

Monie went to grab for one of the packages. "Here, I'll hold that for ya."

Gianni snatched it back. "Get your hands off my 'S' cookies!" Gianni looked over at Shadrack sitting on the floor watching the proceedings. "Shad, if he tries that again, kill 'em. No, better yet, shit on his bed and chew up his saddle magazine."

"You really know how to hurt a guy, Giancarlo."

"Yeah, well, just stay away from my cookies. Now, let's see. Oh boy, a new tooth brush. What a treat. Two tubes of Crest toothpaste, three paperbacks, a pair of Zories, pink ones at that."

"What the fuck are Zories?" Boardman leaned over to look.

"They're like slippers, only made of rubber." Gianni held them up for everyone to see.

"Zories? They're fuckin' shower clogs!" Boardman shook his head in bewilderment.

"Hey, you call 'em what you want, we'll call 'em what we want. Besides, shower clogs sounds too common. Let's see what else is in here. Hey, a new pair of Jams!" Gianni held up the multi-colored Jams for everyone to see.

"What the hell are those supposed to be?" Huebner stared in amazement.

"They're Jams. You know, a baggy bathing suit. The legs are supposed to go down almost to your knees. All the surfers wear 'em."

"You surf?"

"No, but I look real good in 'em."

"Yeah, I'll bet. Come on, open the cookies!"

"Wait a minute, let me see what else is in here." Gianni pawed through the crumpled newspaper on the bottom of the box and pulled out an envelope. "That's it. Just a letter."

Huebner sat down on the edge of the cot next to the duffel bag. "Good, read it later. Let's eat the cookies."

"No, Sarge, ya' can't eat 'em plain. Ya' gotta dunk 'em in coffee."

"Screw the coffee, give us a cookie."

"Uh-uh. We gotta' have coffee with 'em. That's the way Italians eat 'em and since it's my birthday, we're gonna' eat 'em right."

Huebner stood up shaking his head. "All right, all right. You heard the birthday boy." Huebner made a big show of holding his left arm up to check his watch. "The squad will reassemble in the mess tent in exactly…two minutes. There, happy?"

Everyone headed for the tent opening. Robinson and Smith walked out together with Smith grumbling as usual. "Delmar, I'll tell ya', Bro', it ain't bad enough we gotta' live with these white boys, now we gotta' eat like 'um."

"No problem, Laz. If you don't want no cookies, I'll eat 'em for ya'."

"Fuck you Delmar."

Gianni stuck his sign in the ground in front of the mess tent and Shadrack laid down behind it without being told. He walked up to the mess line, pulled an aluminum cup from the rack and turned to the men waiting behind him. "All right, now remember. Black coffee, it's gotta' be black coffee. No sugar, no cream, just black."

Four places back in line, Tuckett stuck his head around Schoonhoven. "You Wops sure make it hard to eat a fuckin' cookie."

Gianni filled his cup at the giant, silver-colored urn. "These are not just any cookies, Tuckett, these are 'S' cookies. They are worth any amount of trouble you have to go through." Gianni took his cup of steaming coffee and headed for one of the long empty tables. As the last man took his seat, Gianni stood up at the head of the table.

As keeper of the cookies, Gianni tapped the side of his cup with a spoon, making a dull thunking noise instead of the desired musical clinking. "Gentlemen, your attention, please." Gianni drew himself up straight and took a deep breath. "I am pleased and proud to present an Italian culinary delight." He glanced around at the faces and immediately forgot about the rest of the speech he had planned. "Actually, what I want to say is, I'm proud to share my birthday present with my good friends."

Schoonhoven, holding his cup in the air, speaking up over the hoots and catcalls, made a toast. "On behalf of myself and my esteemed colleagues, you can be part of our squad anytime. Happy Birthday!"

Each man raised his cup in salute with a chorus of Happy Birthday.

Smith suddenly stood up and pointed at Gianni. Robinson cringed, worrying that Smith might say something totally inappropriate. "Hey, Cherry!" The squad quieted down, waiting. "Your dog can be part of the squad, too, man. Happy Birthday. And tell yo' mamma, thanks for the cookies."

Gianni tore open the packages and walked around the table laying two giant "S" shaped cookies in front of each man, slapping at hands and telling them to wait until he had demonstrated the proper dunking procedure.

Picking up one of his own, he called for attention. "All right, listen up and look closely, I'm only going to demonstrate this once. Placing your left hand around your coffee cup, hold it firmly, but gently, using only enough pressure to keep the cup from tipping or sliding across the table."

"With the thumb and forefinger of the right hand, hold the cookie by one end of the big 'S.' Positioning the cookie over the steaming coffee, dunk approximately one inch in the coffee, two, I repeat, two times. An attempt to dunk more than two times will cause the cookie to become coffee logged and break off in your cup. This will result in masses of crumbs floating in your coffee, reducing the rich black liquid into something that resembles the top of a cesspool. The lumps of crumbs will then become lodged in your throat and you will choke to death right here at the table and fuck up my birthday party. Now, watch me."

Gianni grasped the cookie as he had instructed, dunked it twice and bit off the end. "Ooooohhhhhh, God, is that good. Oh, man!" Gianni pushed a crumb that was clinging to the corner of his lip into his mouth. "Gentlemen, bon appetit."

Smith looked over at Schoonhoven. "What'd he say?"

"Eat your fuckin' cookie."

"Oh." Smith dunked his cookie as instructed and took a bite. "Damn, he's right. This be bitchin'!"

Robinson was grinning from ear to ear. "Mama ain't gonna' like it but this beats her cornbread all ta' hell."

Gianni popped the last of his first cookie in his mouth and washed it down with a sip of coffee. While the others savored theirs, Gianni pulled out the letter and started to read.

Gianni,

Hi, son. Happy Birthday! Hope this package gets to you in time. If it gets there late, at least you'll know we were thinking about you. Your Dad says the stuff we're sending you is dumb but I don't. I know you can buy most of these things at the base exchange, except for the cookies. We'll celebrate your birthday for real when you get home. I miss you, honey. We both wish we could be with you on your birthday. I hope they give you the day off or something. Honey, I'm so glad you're on that base instead of being out in the jungle or someplace where the fighting is going on. We watch the news every night and it just breaks my heart to see those boys getting hurt and killed over there. I feel so bad for their mothers. Please be careful Gianni, I don't know what I'd do if something ever happened to you. I know it's foolish but I still worry. I hope Shadrack is doing good. When you get a chance, send us some more pictures of him. I think he's cute. Honey, please take care of yourself. We both love you and miss you very much.

Love, Mom.

Gianni stared at the letter, thinking to himself, 'Yeah, Mom, I'm sure lucky I don't have to live in the jungle and have people shoot at me'. As he looked at the letter, he heard Smith's voice over the noise. "Hey, LT, come over and have a cookie. This shit ain't half bad."

Evans walked to the chow line, filled a cup with coffee, then joined the rest of the squad. "Well, well, we got us a birthday boy. Happy Birthday, Gianni." Evans held out his hand to congratulate Gianni, then sat next to him. "All right, where're these famous cookies I've been hearing about?"

Gianni slid two cookies over to him. "Here ya' go, we've been savin' 'em for ya'."

Evans held one up and gazed at it. "Good size, ain't they?"

Boardman was just finishing up his last one. "Take a bite, you're gonna' wish they were bigger."

Gianni looked up at the commotion midway down the table. Smith was slapping at Huebner's hand as he tried to take a bite of his cookie.

"No, man, what you doin'? Ya' gotta dunk it 'fore ya' eat it. Damn! ya' gotta' tell these white boys everything. Don't you know how to eat a damn Italian cookie?" Smith shook his head and looked up at Evans.

"LT, how we supposed to run a strack squad when our second in command ain't got no class? The way he be tryin' to eat that cookie, ya'd think we was all in the Mo-rines or somethin'." Smith turned back to Huebner, who knew when he had been verbally thrashed, and watched as he tentatively dunked his cookie. "That's it, that's better. No, no, wait. Keep your pinkie out, keep it out. Hold out your damn little finger, man! There, now ya' got it. Okay, just dunk twice and let 'er rip."

After Huebner took his first bite, Smith looked down at the table and lowered his voice just slightly but so everybody could still hear. "Man, where'd you get those sergeant stripes, in a fuckin' crap game? And we're s'pose to win the war with this kind of leadership?" Huebner cowered like a little boy who had been scolded, then proceeded to eat the rest of the cookie.

Evans looked down the length of the table. "All right, guys, I hate to break up the birthday celebration, but we've got a mission."

Boardman blew a cloud of smoke at the tent ceiling and looked at his watch. "What's the rush, LT, it's only a little after fourteen hundred. We've got the rest of the day and all night."

"Nope, not this time. We leave just after dark."

"What! We never do an insertion at night. Shit, we won't even know where the fuck they're puttin' us down."

"Yeah, I know, but the weather guys say there's a big front movin' in. Everything will be socked in by morning and they're afraid the choppers won't be able to fly if we wait."

"Well, if the choppers can't fly, how the hell are they supposed to pick us up after we find this guy. What are we goin' after anyway?" Tuckett flicked the cigarette ash on the floor.

"One pilot, a Thud driver, went down northwest of here. Lot of ground troops, heavy small arms fire. Choppers took a lot of hits before they pulled out. A door gunner on one of the slicks got zapped, and the front seat guy in one of the Cobras got shot up pretty bad. Last they heard, our guy was holed up in some thick brush tryin' to stay outta' Charlie's way. We gotta' go find 'im."

Gianni looked around and saw the worry on each man's face. Even Huebner didn't like the idea, he was giving his mustache the chewing of its life. The missions were dangerous enough when they knew that if the shit hit the fan, they could get help within a few hours. If heavy weather moved in and stayed there, the choppers might not be able to fly for days. Even the jets couldn't fly through the low clouds.

Gianni nudged Evans' arm. "LT, if we get heavy rain and it keeps up, Shadrack isn't gonna' be much help. There's not gonna' be any scent in the air and the noise from the rain is gonna' fuck up his hearing. We're gonna' be blind out there as long as the rain keeps up."

"Can't be helped. We go out and do the best we can, and hope that we get a break. All right, let's get our gear ready and get a few hours sleep, we hit the flight line at nineteen hundred."

SATURDAY

MAY 9, 1970

NORTHWEST OF CAMELOT PALACE

The pilot dropped the chopper down into a clearing barely wide enough for the rotors to clear the standing trees. A sudden wind gust or a moment's inattention would have spelled disaster for them all. Not able to see the ground, the pilot decided to hover at three or four feet rather than take a chance of landing on an unseen tree stump or getting the skids tangled in hidden deadfall.

Gianni had been the third man out of the chopper. He slid out of his rucksack, then gave Shadrack the command to jump. Standing under him, Gianni took the weight of the dog full on his chest, trying to break the impact of the fall. A dog with a broken leg wouldn't have done any of them any good. If the weather permitted, they planned to have an OV-10 Bronco flying overhead most of the next day. It was easy enough to have several planes rotate throughout the day and if the clouds were heavy they would be invisible to prying eyes on the ground. If they ran into trouble, the Bronco wouldn't be much help other than to call for a chopper, but if the cloud cover was still solid, they wouldn't be able to find the squad, much less land.

Evans had them push through the thick bush for the better part of five hours, trying to put as much distance between them and the LZ as possible.

"All right, we rest 'til daylight. No smoking and let's keep the noise down. Smith, Doc, you've got first watch. We'll have a new watch every two hours. Robinson, keep your gun in the middle of the perimeter. If we get hit, we're gonna' need you to move fast." Evans looked around at the anxious faces staring at him. "Gianni, you and the dog stick close to Robinson. If something happens, you feed his gun."

The rains came a couple hours before daylight. Still asleep, Gianni swatted at the first few drops, subconsciously thinking they were more of the ever-present insects. It was the huge, heavy drops landing on his eyelids that woke him. Before he could even raise himself up on one elbow and shake the confusion out of his head, it really started to rain. Unlike the heavy rains he was used to in Florida where the wind blew the sheets of water sideways, this rain fell like it was shot out of the sky. It came down with a roar, blocking out the normal noises the jungle had to offer.

Rolling over on his knees, a puddle of water already forming under him, he pulled his rucksack closer and reached in to pull out his plastic poncho. Robinson looked over and smiled a wide, gleaming-white toothy grin, shook his head and pointed at the half in, half-out poncho, as if to say, 'Forget it, Bro', that ain't gonna' do you no good'. Gianni looked up at the clouds that enveloped the tops of the trees, then pushed the poncho back into his ruck. His bush hat was already waterlogged and streams of rain poured off it, running down the back of his shirt.

Those who had been sleeping no longer were, and everyone did his best to keep his equipment as dry as possible. Gianni thought about opening a can of fruit but that would have been like trying to eat a can of peaches under a waterfall. Instead, he pulled out a canteen cup, filled it with dog food and watched as Shadrack ate the soggy mess. Dogs didn't seem to be bothered much by life's little inconveniences.

As the clouds started to lighten from the unseen sun, Evans signaled the squad to move out. Three hours later, with the rain still as heavy, if not heavier than when it started, they stopped to rest. Evans made his way back to where Gianni and Dustin were sitting. Soaked to the bone, they didn't even notice the mud and pools of water that, in a different life back in 'the World', they wouldn't have considered walking through, much less sitting in. Evans crouched down next to Gianni and had to yell in his ear to be heard. "Would it do any good for the dog to be up on point?"

Gianni shook his head, then yelled back, "Shadrack won't be able to hear shit in this rain; can't pick up a scent either."

Evans shook his head up and down. "All right, 'til it lightens up, you stick with Dustin. Let me know when you think it's time for him to work."

Gianni made an 'O.K.' sign with his right hand and watched as Evans moved away to sit down next to Huebner.

Some of the men tried to light cigarettes, but after one or two puffs the wet paper refused to stay lit. The noise was incredible. The rain hit the trunks of trees and splattered off like a hose pointed at the side of a house. Leaves didn't quiver under the onslaught, they were just forced straight down toward the ground, the rain running off them and hitting the water-soaked earth like thousands of little gutter spouts.

Had the noise not been so deafening, the dog might have heard one of the three men step on a dead branch, its water soaked bark still dry enough to give off a muffled cracking sound. The men peered through the thick trees and bushes, trying for a better view as the downpour obscured their vision. Their once baggy, black pants and long sleeved shirts were now soaked and clinging to their skeletal-thin bodies. The leader of the three men carried an AK-47 rifle. Extra magazines filled pouches attached to a weathered ammo harness. Two American fragmentation grenades hung from one of the pouches, precious spoils of battle that would soon be used against their rightful owners. Vo Nguyen Giap grinned a rotted tooth smile. Killing American flyers held great honor, honor he had basked in many times, but killing those who came to rescue them would be the greatest of all. Unconsciously he reached inside the black shirt and fingered the five multi-colored Tactical Air Command patches sewn to the flimsy fabric. Ripped from the flight suits of American pilots he had executed, they represented only the men whose eyes he gazed into at the moment of death. Other patches still clung to the flight suits of invaders that rotted in the trees, screaming for mercy and swinging from their parachute harness as his bullets had ripped through their bodies. Then there were those who he let live just long enough to hear the sounds of rescue helicopters, to catch a glimpse of those who would take them home, only to die with life but an arms length away. There had been many, and there would be more.

The two men to his right were also armed with captured American weapons. One carried two claymore mines, still in their green canvas carrying bags. In his right hand he held a Smith and Wesson Model 15 .38 caliber revolver taken off a dead American flier.

The man next to him carried a .30 caliber M-1 carbine. U.S. forces hadn't carried them in Vietnam since the early '60s and his once-plentiful supply of ammunition had now dwindled down to a mere nine rounds that were loaded in his last remaining magazine. His short supply of ammunition and obsolete rifle no longer worried him. The American patrol carried the newest rifles and thousands of rounds of ammunition. The American M-60 machine gun was heavy and would be hard to carry through the thick jungle, but would shred American bodies as it had shred the bodies of so many of his comrades. No, he did not need to worry about his lack of ammunition anymore. By the end of the day, he would have all he could carry.

Boardman hung the telephone-like receiver back on his harness and duck walked over to Evans and Huebner. Cupping his right hand over the top of his eyes to keep out the heavy rain drops, he yelled into Evans' ear. "May be a wasted trip, LT. Bronco pilot says he picked up a signal from our guy's emergency transmitter."

"How far?"

"About fifteen klicks from here, maybe a little farther."

Evans looked at Huebner then back at Boardman. "What do they want us to do?"

"Keep heading for him in case they can't find him or if they can't make a pickup."

Evans shook his head in acknowledgment. "Get the rest of the guys over here."

Boardman scurried around to the rest of the squad, tapping each man on the shoulder or arm and pointing to Evans. As the men walked over, their tracks were quickly filled in by the torrents of falling rain. Evans had to yell to make himself heard. He briefed the squad on what the Bronco pilot had told them, then had Tuckett take the point. As they moved off, Monie moved up next to Gianni and flashed a big grin.

"How could you ask for more than this? You get to take a nice pleasant walk through the woods with your dog on your birthday."

Gianni thought about it for a second, then yelled back, "Yeah, I feel just like Dorothy and Toto in the Wizard of Oz. Lions and tigers and Gooks, OH, MY!" Dustin chuckled, then pulled the condom down tighter on the muzzle of his rifle.

Two hours later Evans motioned for the squad to hold up as he took the radio receiver from Boardman. He spoke into it, listened for several seconds then signed off and handed it back to Boardman. Looking around, he found Huebner and moved over next to him.

"The Bronco made voice contact with our guy. He's holed up in some thick cover. Says he hasn't heard or seen any Gooks since before dawn. Thinks they may have moved out."

"What's the plan? We still going in after him?"

"The Bronco called in an Air Force Jolly Green with a jungle penetrator. Two Cobras are going to try to make it through this shit, too."

"Lot of fuckin' good that's gonna' do. These clouds are damn near down on the deck. How they gonna' find 'im?"

"Our guy says the rain's stopped where he is. Clouds are breakin' up. They figure they'll be able to spot his smoke and pull 'im up through the trees."

Huebner looked down at the ground and pulled his right boot out of the mud with a sucking sound. A centipede clung to a mud ball stuck to the right side of his boot. "That'll work for me. I'd just as soon get the hell outta' this shit." He scrapped his boot on the side of a tree, knocking the centipede off. He tried to crush it by stepping on it but only succeeded in driving the bug into the soft ground. "Do we head back?"

"Not yet. They want us to keep moving toward him. Once he's up and outta' there, we head back the way we came then call for a chopper."

"Looks like we missed a good night's sleep for nothing."

"Let's hope so." Evans moved over to Smith and said something. The three men peering through the jungle watched as the black man started pushing his way through the trees and bushes.

The American patrol was still heading to the northwest, straight into the arms of their NVA comrades. The three VC would continue to shadow their movements and when the time was right, when the Americans were forced to turn and run for their lives, they would block their retreat and slaughter those who invaded their country. Inwardly each man beamed with the anticipation of the glorious fight that was yet to come.

The three men paralleled the movements of the Americans. They had seen the dog and it worried them. They had heard stories of this dog leading patrols to their hidden comrades when no human eyes could see them and no human ears could hear them. They would have to be careful. The noise of the rain masked their movements, but would the dog be able to smell them? So far he had showed no sign he knew they were there. Did the heavy rain make him no more than an extra mouth to feed? Was he just something else they would take pleasure in killing? The questions had no answers. They would have to wait and see. If the rain stopped, they would have to be careful. Very, very careful.

The squad heard the choppers fly overhead. The clouds were starting to thin out, not enough for it to stop raining but enough that if the choppers had flown directly overhead, they might have caught a glimpse of them. As it was, each man looked to his right and up as the machines thundered past.

The sounds did not go unnoticed by the men in black as they looked up with worried faces and scanned the sky. American helicopters! Why were they here? Were they bringing in reinforcements? Were they here to pick up the American patrol before they walked into oblivion? Things had gone well so far. The weather had kept them from being detected. The Americans were foolishly and unknowingly walking into their friends from the North. Could it be that fate would pluck them away unscathed? As the sounds of the helicopters passed, the three men smiled. No, they were not there to carry their prey to safety, they would not deliver these Americans from certain death.

Evans signaled for the squad to stop as Boardman handed him the radio. Gianni and Dustin sat down on the soaked ground while Shadrack lapped up water from one of the many puddles. Gianni stroked the back of his ears that drooped like broken rotors on a helicopter. He came away with a handful of wet, smelly hair.

Dustin was busy opening a can of 'Ham and Lima Beans' C-Rations. As he pried off the green metal lid a clump of congealed fat fell to the ground. He stuck his nose close to the pink and green mush and recoiled at it's pungent odor. "Jesus Christ! I don't know what smells worse, this shit or your reeking dog."

Gianni leaned over to peer at the Korean War vintage C-Rat. "Looks like someone already ate it then threw it back up." He made a face that would never have been mistaken as a compliment toward the Army's idea of nourishment. He leaned back and whispered into the dogs ear. "He's right though Shad, you are gettin' kinda rank. You're in for a big-time groomin' when we get back" The dog's ears perked up at the sound of his name and he moved even closer to his master's leg. "Yeah, you're a good boy. You don't like all this water, do ya'? Yeah, I know, you're a dog, not a fish, you want to be on dry land."

Dustin buried the can with its untouched slop then held both his hands under his bush hat and tried to light a cigarette. The Zippo worked fine, but even with the two-inch flame, he couldn't keep the cigarette going for more than two puffs. "Damn, I wish this fucking rain would let up. Can't even have a decent smoke." He threw the soggy remains of the cigarette in the bushes, wrung out his hat and put it back on. He looked over at Evans and Huebner crouching next to Boardman. "I wonder if those choppers got in to make the pickup?"

"Sure would be nice. I'm all for gettin' the fuck outta' here. Never seen rain like this."

"Shit, Gianni, this is nothin'. The platoon I was in, before they put this squad together, we'd go out on a Search & Destroy mission, stay out three, four nights at a time. It'd rain like this, and when we hunkered down for the night, we'd dig fox holes and by morning you were sittin' in a fuckin' foot of water. It'd pour over the sides of the hole like water over a dam. It was bullshit, pure bullshit. Guys were gettin' trench foot from always walkin' in water. Could never keep your smokes dry even if you kept 'em in a plastic bag. Had to strip out your ammo every night and clean it 'cause the mud got in the magazines. Shit, we were forever cleanin' weapons, almost every time we stopped for a rest break. Naw, this ain't nothin'. We'll get back to the Palace pretty soon, hit the show- ers, hope your mother sent some more cookies, and with any luck get a few days off before we have to come out here and find some other lost Air Force puke."

"Well, this is bad enough for me. "

Dustin tapped him on the arm and nodded toward Evans. "The LT wants us." They got up and moved over to Evans with the rest of the squad.

Evans waited until everyone was crouched down around him. "All right, looks like we took a walk in the park for nothing. Our guy got picked up a few minutes ago. The clouds are startin' to break up but they're still too heavy for a chopper to land here so we're gonna' hump back to our jump-off point. If they can't pick us up tonight, they'll come back in the morning."

Smith looked around at the rest of the squad, more than a little agi- tated that they'd have to spend another night in the bush. Monie wasn't the only one short enough on his tour to see 'the World' at the end of the tunnel. "Shit, LT! If'n the chopper can't land, how's they get that pilot outta' there?"

Evans let out a sigh and looked straight at Smith. "They used the penetrator on the Jolly Green, Lazirus. They only had to hover for a few seconds. How fuckin' long you think they'd have to sit up there trying to pull us out? They'd make one hell of a fuckin' target, don't ya' think!? Besides, we're not in any shit, we can wait."

Smith had been called down and knew it. "Yeah, LT, no problem."

"Okay, lets get outta' here. Tuckett, you've got the point."

The American patrol was moving again, but in the wrong direction. They were going back the way they had come, away from certain death, away from the deadly rewards that were waiting for the arrogant invaders. The three men knew what had to be done. There was no fear of death, no fear of failure. Uncle Ho had said it many times, proclaimed it to the imperialistic American nation and the world: 'We will win because we have to'. The three men would win, they would kill the Americans, reduce the number of invaders like so many stalks of rice harvested from the paddies. They would take their weapons and use them against more Americans, and when they were dead, they would use their weapons against yet more Americans, until their land was free of invaders. No, the three men had no fear of failure. They would succeed, they would win. Because they had to.

The squad pushed through the jungle for almost three hours before Evans called for a halt. The rain had lessened its assault by more than half but the water logged rucksacks, now heavier then when they started, drove them deeper and deeper into the sucking ooze. Each step was more laborious than the last as they struggled to pull mud encased boots out of the quagmire only to repeat the process over and over again. Even the dog began to tire as he sank three or four inches into the mud with each step. The steady rain, no longer repelled by the thick fur, plastered it against his skin like a wet sheet. Eighty-five pounds of bone, muscle and sinew began to take on the appearance of an emaciated stray mongrel. Like the men though, he knew they were headed home and despite the physical weariness, his canine spirit was high.

The men in black knew they must act soon, before the rain stopped and the dog was once again able hear things that made no noise and sniff wind where there was no wind.

The Americans acted as if the jungle had no surprises. Their soft bodies and minds made them anxious to return from where they came. Cautious and wary with their movements into the unknown, they now moved with assurance, like a lost child who sees its mother in the distance. The three men knew the time to strike was near.

They watched as some of the Americans tended to their weapons while others smoked cigarettes, trying to hold them under the protection of their hats. The dog, relishing in the caress of his master, sat at his side and tried to test the air for smells that were knocked to the ground by the falling rain. Giap motioned for the others to follow him. They moved slowly away from the patrol, already knowing where they would meet again.

Evans checked his watch. If they picked up their speed and shortened their breaks, they should be able to reach the LZ just before dark. They still might make it back to the Palace today. Picking up his rucksack, he moved over to where Gianni and Dustin were sitting. "Gianni, what'da ya' think? Can Shadrack work in this stuff now?"

"It's a shit load better than it was before, LT. He probably won't be able to pick up a scent while it's still raining but if it lets up a little more, he'll be able to hear if anything is moving around." Gianni glanced up at the patches of sky that poked through the tree tops. "Looks like it's gonna' break up pretty quick. We should be in good shape in a little while."

"Good. How about you take the point now, I wanna' give Smith and Tuckett a rest. Dustin, you stay right behind 'em." Evans glanced at his watch again. "Let's move out, maybe we can get back in time for some hot chow."

Gianni and Dustin pushed themselves to their feet and picked up their rucks. Gianni helped Dustin sling the two belts of M-60 ammo over his head.

"Shit, even powdered eggs sounds good right now." Dustin looked down and grinned as his stomach made a growling noise."

"Not me, I want a pizza. Everything on it, then topped off with mounds of anchovies."

"Anchovies! You eat that shit?"

"Nope, hate 'em with a passion. Everytime I see Huebner chewing on that stupid mustache it reminds me of 'em, ya know, like little mustaches lyin' there on top of the pepperoni. Aaauughh! Makes me wanna puke just to think about it."

Dustin picked up his rifle and checked to make sure the condom hadn't slipped off. "Well if ya hate 'em so much why the hell do you want 'em on your pizza?"

Gianni gathered up the dog's leash and started to move out. "That's just it, as much as I can't stand 'em, they're still better than the shit we have to eat over here."

Dustin shook his head as he followed Gianni through the bush. "You Air Force pukes sure got a strange way of lookin' at things."

The rain had slowed to what Gianni's mother called 'God's sprinkler system', a light steady drizzle the leaves could absorb, but the mud still made sucking noises as they struggled to pull their boots out with each step. With the lessening of the rain came the bugs, swarms of them, drawn to a free and easy meal. Gianni wiped at the side of his face, then looked at the coating of dead and dying bugs covering his palm when he felt a slight tug at the leash and noticed Shadrack starting to squat between two trees.

Dustin moved up. Almost as if he was embarrassed by being watched, the dog turned his head and stared off into the jungle. "Hey, Gianni. Does he do that on command?"

"Yeah, but only once a day." Gianni just stood there holding the leash, unable to do anything until the dog answered the call of nature.

"Damn, he stinks! What's he startin' to do, rot from all this water?"

"Hey, Monie, you don't eat roses, ya' know."

"Yeah, well, you can stand around here and gag, I'm movin' on. Catch up when you're done wipin' his ass." Monie made a big production of holding his nose with two fingers as he walked away.

The dog was still straining as Smith and Robinson walked by. "Hey, Cherry, why don't ya' put a diaper on that mutt, he's ruining the property values."

Dustin had looked over his shoulder for just a moment to see where Gianni was. As he turned back, his mind exploded in panic. In slow motion, as if someone had laid out a line of pictures in front of him, he saw his right boot set down in the mud just in front of the thin wire. The knot on his boot lace was pushing at the wire, drawing it tighter and tighter as his weight forced his boot deeper and deeper into the mud. His eyes raced along the wire to his right. It stopped at the dull green claymore mine, its two sharp pointed legs shoved into the ground.

In the slow-motion world his mind was racing through, Dustin didn't know if he was actually reading the raised words on the plastic front of the mine or if he just knew them from having set enough of his own: "FRONT TOWARD ENEMY". He knew what was going to happen. He couldn't stop it. His foot was going down, and forward, and nothing on earth would stop it from pulling the trip wire. Dustin was going to die and he knew it.

Whether to warn the friends he lived with, fought with, and killed with, or purely as an instinctive reaction by a mind that knew it was about to suffer a horrible death, Dustin opened his mouth in a human's most desperate wail of helplessness. "Noooooooooo!!!!"

The scream was cut off as the pound of C-4 plastic explosive detonated, sending six hundred steel ball bearings into, and through his body. To the men in the squad, it only took a split second to realize what was happening. Each man, except one, threw himself face down in the mud, Huebner's voice ringing in their ears. "AMBUSH! AMBUSH! AMBUSH!"

The thundering noise of Robinson's M-60 could be heard over the clattering of M-16s. Even though they may see no targets, no threats, men under attack, their very lives threatened with extinction, know they have to do something, and with the power they hold in their hands, the 'something' is to shoot. M-60 tracer rounds ricocheted off of trees and flew crazily in the air. Schoonhoven crawled through the mud and made his way up to Robinson. Twisting off one of the ammo belts around his chest, he broke open the links holding the belt together and attached it to the one disappearing through the side of Robinson's gun. The noise of the gunfire wasn't enough to drown out the screams.

"OOOHHH, GOD!! GOD!! GOD, HELP MEEEEE....! Aaaahhh...aaaahhh...Daaaad...Daaaad...make it stop!! Please...make it stop!! GOD...PLEASE HELP ME!!"

Another gun joined the fight but this time, instead of the bullets flying off into the trees, they slammed into the mud in front of Robinson and Schoonhoven. "To your right! To your right! It's coming from your right!" Schoonhoven lifted his left hand from the ammo belt and pointed to the trees. Robinson shifted the big gun around and held the trigger down, spewing out a long line of flesh-shredding bullets. During M-60 training, the instructors had continually yelled, 'short bursts, fire short bursts, you'll burn out the barrel with long bursts, keep them short, Goddamnit!' Short bursts were fine on the range, but a barrel in good condition didn't do shit if you took a bullet through the face because you didn't shoot the other guy first. Robinson sprayed the trees, searching for the target that was trying to kill him.

Schoonhoven tore the last ammo belt off his chest and attached it to the gun. Trying to watch the trees and the ammo at the same time, he kept four fingers under the ammo and his thumb on top as it made its way to the gun. He had to keep the mud that clung to the brass casings from jamming the gun. Smith lay in the mud to his left firing into the trees, hoping his rounds might find the unseen threat.

"Smith! Ammo! Ammo! Give me your ammo!" Schoonhoven held out his left arm toward Smith while he fed the gun with his right. With one hand, Smith tore off his two belts of ammo and tossed them to Schoonhoven.

The screams continued. Each man fired into the trees trying to drown out the pleas to the Almighty. Schoonhoven yelled in Robinson's ear. "I gotta' get to Monie! I gotta' help Monie!"

"Feed me! Feed me! Ya' gotta' stay and feed the gun!! The rounds tearing at the ground in front of the two men stopped as a new voice pierced the air.

"DUSTIN! DUSTIN…..!"

AK-47 rounds flew past Robinson and Schoonhoven as they tried to cut down the man foolish enough to try and make his way to a dying man. "Dustin!!" Gianni ran through the mud, bullets kicking up geysers of dirty water around his feet one moment, then, as the man in black shifted his aim, tearing at tree trunks and splintering wood around his face. Gianni staggered as two rounds slammed into his rucksack, tearing away chunks of fabric and spilling dog food as he ran. Something flew through the air, out of the trees. Boardman saw it arc in Gianni's direction.

"Grenade! Grenade!"

Robinson saw it land off to their left, less than ten feet behind Gianni. As hard as it was to move through the mud, as much as it sucked at boot-covered feet that wanted to move faster than they had ever moved, it also sucked at everything else. The grenade landed, its weight forcing it deep into the thick ooze. The explosion was muted, reminding Gianni more of a shotgun blast on a skeet range than a grenade in the middle of the jungle. Most of the shrapnel stayed in the ground, stopped by the heavy mud. Most, but not all.

Gianni was thrown forward as pieces of the grenade slammed into the back of his rucksack. He didn't feel the burning in his leg as the hot metal sliced through his flesh or see the rich red blood seeping out from the tear in his pants. Grabbing handfuls of soggy ground, he pulled himself forward, crawling the last few yards. Remembering the leash for the first time, he dropped it, turned to the dog and yelled, "DOWN! DOWN!"

Dustin's screams weren't as loud now. They came from a man who was losing the strength to plead for relief, from a man who knew there were worse things than death. Gianni raised himself up on one elbow, his eyes staring with horror as his jaw dropped, unable to utter the scream that stuck in his throat.

Parts of Dustin were gone. What had moments ago been his walking, talking, laughing friend was now a nightmare turned real. The legs that used to swing him up into a saddle ended just above the knees. The right leg was cut off clean, as if it had been run over by the wheels of a train. The left leg quivered uncontrollably with three inches of jagged bone sticking out from where his thigh was supposed to be. Blood pumped onto the ground turning the mud a pinkish brown with each beat of his heart. The inventors of the claymore mine had done their job well. The steel projectiles had not only shredded and blown away the green fatigue pants, they had taken away any chance of its' victim fathering a child.

Dustin raised his right arm, reaching for Gianni. It ended three inches below the elbow. Part of a hand, with only two fingers left, lay on the ground in front of Gianni's face. Pieces of the black plastic M-16 stock stuck out of Dustin's chest. Gianni screamed over the sound of the constant gunfire. "DUSTIN! OH, GOD, DUSTIN!"

The body was not that of his friend. It couldn't be. But the eyes! The eyes were. They pleaded for help. They cried for the help their friend could give. "GIANNI, OH, GOD, GIANNI! I CAN'T STAND IT, I CAN'T STAND IT! GOD, IT HURTS!" Blood poured out the corners of his mouth and rolled down to pool in the hollow of his neck. His voice was almost a whisper, but to Gianni, it was the loudest thing he had ever heard. "SHOOT ME! GIANNI, PLEASE...SHOOT ME!"

"NO! NO! OH, GOD! Dustin, please, please, hang on! We'll get you out of here! Please, OH, GOD, please, don't let him die!!!"

A new noise joined the fight. A rifle shot. The ground erupted next to Gianni's right arm, then another. Tuckett and Evans, lying in the mud behind him, shifted their aim and fired into the trees to Gianni's right. A voice shouted in his head: *'The threats, Gianni! Neutralize the threats!!'*

Gianni ignored the voice, ignored what he had to do. Another bullet tore by his head and dug into the dirt in front of his face, inches away from Dustin. The voice grew louder, almost pleading: *'Gianni! The threats, you have to neutralize the threats!!'*

In his mind, through his tears, he screamed back: 'Goddamnit! Fuck you, Hank! Fuck the threats! He's dying, my friend is dying!!'

'It's WAR, Gianni! People die, friends die! You will, too! Neutralize the threats!'

Gianni looked at Dustin. Trying to wipe away the tears with a muddy hand, he pulled himself closer, shielding what was left of his friend with his own body. Dustin shuddered with pain, his lips pulled back and a scream escaped. "Oh, God! Gianni! Gianni! Shoot me!! Please!! GOD!!! PLEASE!!!"

A bullet tore through the right shoulder strap of Gianni's rucksack, gouging out a path of torn and bloody flesh. Gianni might have felt it if, a fraction of a second later, the same bullet hadn't hit Dustin just below the corner of his mouth, tearing off his lower jaw. Dustin's head snapped to the left, blood pouring out from the missing bone and flesh. His head slowly turned back, the pleading eyes staring into Gianni's, begging a friend to do the unthinkable.

'It's not a game, Gianni! People die in horrible ways. They scream for their mamas, begging God to make the pain go away. People die, Gianni...people die...' Gianni nodded silently as he reached down and pulled the Smith and Wesson revolver out of its holster. As he brought it up in front of his face, he choked out a muffled good-bye.

The sound of Robinson's M-60 faded away as it found a target, silencing the sporadic fire of an M-1 carbine that had found its mark in Dustin's face. Evans screamed "GRENADE" as another small bomb sailed out of the trees. The muffled explosion went unnoticed by Gianni.

The voice came back just as loud as before: *'The threats, Gianni! Neutralize the threats!!'* Two bullets splattered in the mud as he dropped the revolver and reached for his rifle. Turning toward his right, he raised up, not to his knees, not in a crouch, not in a way to minimize the chance of being shot. He stood, as straight as he had ever stood, and walked into the bush.

The man in black had four bullets left in the revolver and quickly fired two of them from behind the tree. Seeing the mud kick up in front of the American soldier, he turned and ran. He was of more use to his country by running away than dying at the hands of this crazy American. Gianni raised the rifle to his shoulder and fired. The man in black flew forward, turned in midair, and landed on his back.

One by one the men in the squad rose to their feet. All but one, who would never rise again. Evans started to move over to Gianni when Boardman's shout stopped him. "GOOK! GOOK! There goes one!" Boardman raised his rifle and fired three times, the rounds hitting a tree next to the running man, causing him to stumble and drop his AK-47. The bolt on Smith's rifle locked back on an empty magazine and before the rest of the squad could turn and fire, Gianni screamed, "NO! Don't shoot! Don't shoot!"

Evans turned to look as Gianni reached down and unhooked the leash from the dog's choke chain. "GET 'EM, SHADRACK! GET 'EM!" The dog took off through the trees, gracefully jumping over dead branches and ducking under bushes and limbs. The running man could have had five times, even ten times the head start, and still lost. The dog hit him with all his weight as he leapt through the air, catching him in the middle of the back. Both dog and man tumbled to the ground...but the dog reacted much quicker.

Rolling back to his feet, the dog lunged for the exposed face as the man tried to push himself up from his knees. Biting down, the two lower canine teeth embedded themselves in the soft fleshy hollow between the left eyeball and eyebrow. The top teeth dug into the flesh of the man's forehead. With a violent jerk, more from instinct than any man-designed training, the skin covering the forehead peeled back allowing the force of the dog's attack to tear the rest of the scalp away from the skull.

The screams, combined with the taste of blood, sent the dog into a frenzy. Not hearing the usual "OUT" command, the dog parted his jaws, letting the scalp fall to the ground, then lunged and bit down on the exposed neck. One jerk of the head was all it took for the flesh to rip open, the screams dying off into a gurgling sound of blood and air escaping the man's body.

The men standing closest knew better than to move in while the dog was still standing over the body. As blood dripped from his jaws, the dog alternated his gaze between the man lying at his feet and his master standing thirty yards away. The dog saw the flicker of movement as Gianni patted his left leg. Without looking down, the dog leapt over the body and ran to Gianni's side.

It took only a moment for Tuckett and Boardman to look at the scalpless corpse, blood from its ripped open neck soaking the unseen Airmen's patches sewn inside the shirt, to realize it was no longer a threat. Boardman kicked at the pile of hair attached to the bloody flesh with the toe of his boot. "Jesus Christ, what a fuckin' way to die."

The muscles in Tuckett's chest flexed as he turned to look at Schoonhoven leaning over Monie's body. "Fuck 'im. It's too bad he didn't suffer longer." For Vo Nguyen Giap, the suffering had lasted an eternity.

Robinson and Smith stood over the dead VC with the M-1 carbine lying on the ground at his side. The heavy M-60 bullets had stitched up his chest blowing away chunks of flesh, exposing ribs and oozing piles of intestines, before hitting the man's head. All that was left was the lower jaw and part of the right cheek. Bits of skull, brain matter, and blood littered the soggy ground behind the body.

Smith picked up the Carbine. Without a word, both men turned and walked to where Gianni and Evans were standing. Gianni was bending down reattaching the dog's leash when Huebner's voice caused them all to turn.

"This one's still alive, LT." Huebner was crouched down, running his hands over the man's black pants and blood-soaked shirt. Gianni and Evans approached with Smith and Robinson a few steps behind. Huebner stood up holding an American revolver and a green web belt with a claymore mine pouch attached to either side. "This must be the motherfucker that set up the claymore. He's still got another one."

Gianni looked down at the wounded man, staring into the pain-ridden face. "He's a kid! He's a fuckin' kid!" The body on the ground flinched at the sudden shout. "Goddamn, motherfucker can't be more than twelve years old!!"

Huebner bent down and tore open the black shirt revealing a jagged and bleeding exit wound just above the boy's right nipple. His face was white with pain and fear. The steady light rain mixed with the blood on his chest and ran down his side to pool on the ground in a pinkish puddle.

Gianni put the palm of his hand directly in front of the dog's face, silently giving him the command to stay. Dropping his rifle on the ground, he pushed past Evans and grabbed the web belt.

"What the...what are you doing?"

Gianni ripped the remaining claymore out of its carrying case and started to unroll the wire. "What the fuck do you think I'm doing!?" He bent down and shoved the two pointed mounting legs into the muddy ground next to the wounded boy's head, far enough away so he could see the strange American words on the front of the mine. The boy's eyes grew wide with terror as he struggled to blurt out a foreign-voiced plea for mercy. His left hand dragged along the ground and weakly grabbed

Gianni's pant leg. Gianni looked down at the hand and followed it back
to the boy's face. "Yeah! Yeah, motherfucker! You're gonna' die, you're
gonna' die with your own fucking booby trap! You're gonna' die like
Dustin, only you're gonna' know it's coming!" Gianni pulled out of the
boy's grasp and pushed down on the mine, setting the spiked legs
deeply into the ground.

Huebner looked up as Evans leaned forward and put his hand on
Gianni's shoulder. "Come on, Gianni, not this way, don't do this."

Gianni swung at the Lieutenant's arm, knocking it off his shoulder
and stood up. "Stay outta' this, LT! This is between me and him. He's the
one that set that fuckin' claymore! He's the one that blew off Dustin's
legs! And now it's time for payback! Dustin's gonna' have his revenge.
Now get the fuck outta' my way!!"

Evans grabbed the young Airman by the collar of his shirt and
pulled him close to his face. Huebner tightened the grip on his rifle
as he saw the dog tense, ready to protect his master. "Dustin? Dustin's
revenge? Who the fuck do you think you are! Dustin is dead! He
doesn't give a FUCK about revenge. Dustin was a SOLDIER, troop. He
knew the risks out here. He doesn't need any fuckin' revenge. He
died out here tryin' to save one of your fuckin' Air Force buddies,
somebody who needed our help!"

Gianni reached up to break the lieutenant's hold but Evans held on
even tighter. "Ya' know, Giancarlo, up 'til now this has been nothin'
more than a little excitement for you. Yeah, sure, you got shot at, had to
kill some people, even seen some American pilots get butchered, but up
'til now they've all been strangers. No one you knew, no one you've
talked to, got to be friends with, no one you're gonna' remember the rest
of your life! Well, now it's personal, troop! Now you've had a friend get
killed! Well, let me tell you something, you little motherfucker! We were
all Dustin's friend! We knew him longer than you, we lived with him
longer than you, and we fought and killed with him longer than you!
And let me tell you something else! He's not the only friend we've lost

over here! We all knew other guys that have gotten killed, friends that we're gonna' cry about the rest of our lives!"

Evans released his grip and pushed Gianni back out of his face. "You wanna' kill this piece of shit? Fine! But kill him for the right reason! Kill him 'cause we can't drag a prisoner around with us! Kill him to put him out of his misery! Kill him 'cause he's the fuckin' enemy," Evans pointed at the boy lying on the ground, "but don't you think for one Goddamn minute you're different than any other man out here or that you're the only one who's gonna' cry over Dustin!"

Trying to keep one eye on the dog and one eye on the confrontation between Evans and Gianni, Huebner watched as Gianni looked down at the wounded VC, walked over to pick up his rifle, then grabbed the end of the leash and started heading to where Schoonhoven was pulling the dog tags from Dustin's neck.

He suddenly stopped, turned around, and walked back to where Evans and Huebner were still standing. He stopped at the feet of the wounded VC and stared at the frightened young boy. "He's only a kid, LT, a fucking kid!" The tears, mixed with the mud, made long dark streaks as they rolled down his face. His words came out in cut-off gasps, choked back from the lump in his throat. "What…what are we gonna' do with 'im?"

Evans nervously shifted his weight from one foot to the other and looked off into the trees. "I'll take care of it, Gianni. Go on, get back with the others." Gianni stared at him until he turned and looked back. "We can't take prisoners, Gianni, you know that."

The dog sat by his left leg, pushing against it, trying to get closer, sensing the mixture of hurt and rage. Gianni looked down at the dog then raised his rifle with one hand and fired a burst into the boy's chest. The bullets, passing through the body and hitting the ground underneath, raised the body with a violent jerk before it quietly settled back down, the last breath escaping with a low whistle.

"Not too long ago somebody told me this wasn't a game. He was right."

Gianni glanced down at the body one more time, then turned to walk back to where Dustin lay on the waterlogged ground. Huebner picked up the claymore mine, then followed Gianni. Schoonhoven stood over Dustin's body, his dog tags dangling from one hand and holding Gianni's revolver in the other.

Gianni sagged to the ground, kneeling over Dustin as the tears once again starting to flow freely. Within seconds his body was racked with throat-choking sobs. Without even knowing it, he dropped his rifle in the mud and hugged what remained of his once best friend. Evans and Huebner stood silently as the young airman grieved in the only way he knew how.

Schoonhoven moved closer to Evans and held out the revolver. Pointing to his right temple with one finger, he nodded down to Dustin's body. Evans peered around Gianni, staring at the side of Dustin's head. He looked down at the gun in Schoonhoven's hand, took it from him, and tugged at his shirt front to move him away from the rest of the squad. "What'da ya' think, did he have to do it?"

"He did him a favor, LT. No way Dustin would have made it even a couple more minutes. He could have been laying in a hospital and there still wouldn't have been anything they could do for him." Schoonhoven looked over to where the airman was lying over the broken and torn body. "The pain had to be unbearable. We all would have begged some-one to kill us."

"You saying you would have done it if you'd been able to get to him?"

Schoonhoven looked down at his feet and kicked at a clump of mud. "LT, I probably wouldn't have waited as long. The only difference is I wouldn't have had to shoot him. I'd have OD'd him on morphine, but, yes, I'd have done the same thing. So would you."

Evans tucked the revolver inside his ammo harness and lit a cigarette. He took a long pull and blew the smoke toward the sky. He watched as Robinson stood over Dustin, making the sign of the cross and saying a silent prayer. The rest of the squad stood around with their heads bowed, each saying good-bye in his own way.

"All right, it goes no farther than this. He was killed in action, got it, KIA. No one needs to know any different."

"No problem Lieutenant, but you're going to have to talk to Gianni." They both looked over at the sobbing airman. "He thinks he killed Dustin. You have to make him understand he was already dead. The only thing left for him was the pain."

Evans flipped the cigarette and watched as it fizzled out in a puddle. As he started walking back to the rest of the squad, he half muttered to himself. "The fucking kid should have stayed back in Miami. Goddamnit! He should have stayed in Miami!"

He stopped next to Boardman. "See if you can raise the Bronco. Tell 'im what happened, tell 'im we need a pickup ASAP."

Boardman nodded his head and pulled the radio handset off his harness. As he tried to raise the Bronco, he slowly walked away from the rest of the group.

The squad was huddled around Dustin's body with Gianni still kneeling next to it, quietly sobbing. Evans reached down and put a hand on Gianni's shoulder. "Gianni. Gianni, we gotta' go." Evans moved his hand under Gianni's arm and urged him to his feet. "Come on, Gianni, we gotta' go. Come on, come on." As Evans led Gianni to his feet, a glint of metal caused Gianni to pull away.

"Wait a minute." He bent down and reached into the poncho that Dustin's body was being wrapped in. Half fallen out of Dustin's fatigue pants pocket, conspicuously shiny among the torn flesh, blood and mud, was Dustin's Zippo lighter. Gianni gingerly picked it up and thought about Dustin's parents sitting at home in Colorado, planning on a Fourth of July celebration and Thanksgiving and Christmas and how they would enjoy all those things with their son. And Gianni thought about how they would enjoy none of those things, ever again.

Evans' voice brought him back to the jungle. When he looked up, Boardman was standing next to Evans and Huebner.

"All right, listen up. The Bronco found a small clearing about three klicks from here. He thinks it's big enough for a chopper. We're gonna' push right through to it, no stops. All this noise is gonna' have every Gook within ten miles headed this way. With any luck, we'll get to the clearing right about the same time as the chopper."

They walked for two hours, hacking at tree limbs and pushing through thick stands of bushes. Thorny branches, swarms of insects, and humidity that sapped the strength with each passing step went unnoticed by Gianni as he remembered the good times he and his friend had shared. He had only known Dustin for a short while, but was it time that built a friendship, or circumstance? They had stood side by side and killed those who had tried to kill them. Had they been merely trying to stay alive or had they been trying to keep each other from being killed? Was that what his father had talked about? The reason men went to war, to keep friends alive?

Gianni had done the same for the dog. Refusing to leave him when reason said he must. Was that what it was about? Was that what his father meant when, in his more serious moments, he told him, tried to ingrain in him, "Life is mostly magic, Gianni, with a little bit of tragic. Learn to live with the tragic and cherish the magic. It's hard, son, sometimes it's really hard, but the magic is always there, just find it, and cherish it. In the end, it's really all we have."

Dustin was gone. He would never ride through his father's pasture to check on the cattle; he would never put on the bright makeup and baggy clothes and step into a rodeo arena, risking his life to save a cowboy in trouble; he would never throw another loop or sit on the fence or smoke a cigarette or sip a glass of Jack Daniels and talk to his horse. And he would never, ever, be able to say to his parents the things he never quite got around to.

Magic? Where was the magic in that? It was only tragic. A tragic death that was a waste. A death that didn't have to happen. Shouldn't have happened. Except he died trying to do the same thing he did when he walked into that arena. It wasn't a bull this time, and the man he tried to help wasn't wearing a cowboy hat. It was a man, scared, alone, hurt, afraid of dying, wearing a pilot's flightsuit and waiting for Dustin. Waiting to be guided out of the arena, waiting to be saved by someone who knew the magic in what he did.

Dustin was gone, but the magic was there, and Gianni would never let it die. He would never forget his friend who gave his life doing what he had unselfishly done so many times: Trying to save someone else's. His memory, Dustin's memory, was part of the magic.

The words rang in his ears as he pushed through the bush. "Live with the tragic, Gianni, and cherish the magic."

CHAPTER 11

SATURDAY NIGHT
MAY 9, 1970
ON THE HELICOPTER

Gianni sat against the trembling bulkhead of the helicopter, the descending machine telling him they were approaching the safety of Camelot Palace. He rubbed the etched words on the lighter with his thumb. Too dark to see the inscription, the words were already engraved in his mind.

DUSTIN
MAY YOUR HAY NEVER MOLD
NOR YOUR HORSES EVER COLIC
COME HOME SAFE
LOVE MOM AND DAD
1969

He glanced down and looked at the shiny metal lighter as it glinted at him through the darkness. Is this what it all led up to? Is this what fate had in mind when he saw the story about the dead flier from a local high school? Was it his death that set the plan in motion that would eventually lead to a wet stinking jungle where Gianni would kill his best friend? It had been a year, it had been a lifetime. A lifetime that he would never know again.

As the helicopter landed, a waiting ammo carrier pulled up next to the open door. Dustin's body was loaded onto the stretcher laid across the back. Major Kancilla watched as it pulled away, headed for the morgue until it could be transported to Tan Son Nhut, and, ultimately, its last trip back to 'the World'.

Evans and Huebner jumped down from the chopper and walked over to Kancilla.

"Who is it?"

"Monie."

"Shit!" He slammed his closed fist against the nose of the aircraft. "Wasn't he gettin' short?"

Evans dropped his ruck and pulled out a cigarette. He thought about how close he was standing to the chopper, then lit it anyway. "Six weeks, couple days less." Taking a long drag, then blowing out a thick cloud of smoke, he kicked viciously at the rucksack at his feet. "GODDAMNIT!! GODDAMNIT!!…. GODDAMNIT!! A BULLSHIT MISSION! He died on a bullshit mission." Evans kicked at the rucksack again. "We didn't even need to be out there! We never even got to our guy!"

He took another drag on the cigarette and threw it in the dirt. Tugging his bush hat off, he rubbed his hand through his close-cropped hair. Turning away from Kancilla and Huebner, he wiped away the tears running down his face.

Kancilla looked at Huebner, then reached to Evans and put a hand on his shoulder. "It wasn't a bullshit mission, Will. You went out there to find a downed pilot. That's what you do, that's what's expected of you. No one knew the weather would break. No one knew the choppers would be able to get in there."

Evans spun on the Major. Spittle flew from his mouth as he spoke. "Yeah, but they DID get in there, DIDN'T THEY! And I lost a man, a good man, for nothing!" Evan's body shook with anger. The lump in his throat bobbed up and down as his bottom lip quivered.

Kancilla moved closer, his nose in Evan's face. "You listen up, Lieutenant! You think you're the only one who's lost a man? I sent him out there! I sent you all out there!" As the two men stood face to face, Evans seemed to shrink as Kancilla straightened to his full height. "I don't give a flyin' shit if the choppers did make the pickup before you got there! If they hadn't, you would have made it to that man, along with Monie, and you would have brought his sorry shot-down ass back here. And Monie might have lived, or he might not have. You don't know what would have happened if you'd kept going! Maybe you'd all be back here drinkin' beer right now, or maybe you'd have run into some deep shit and none of you would have made it back."

Kancilla backed off a couple of steps looking at the rest of the squad standing by the open door of the helicopter and at the doctor shining a flashlight on Gianni's shoulder. Kancilla turned back to Evans and lowered his voice. "It happens, Will. You don't like it, I don't like it, but it fuckin' happens. You've got a squad to take care of, Lieutenant, and you're Goddamn well going to do it."

Kancilla glanced back at the doctor with the flashlight. "Is Giancarlo your WIA?"

Evans slid the bush hat back on his head, then looked down at his rucksack. "Yeah. He took a round, or some shrapnel, I'm not sure which, when he was trying to help Monie. Schoonhoven patched it up as best he could."

"They were pretty tight, weren't they, Giancarlo and Monie?"

"Yeah, real tight."

"Well, Lieutenant, I think you've spent enough time feeling sorry for yourself." Kancilla nodded toward Gianni. "Maybe it's time to help that young troop deal with this."

Evans wiped his face with his fatigue sleeve and tried to pull himself together. "Yes sir."

Gianni had been taken to the medical tent. The doctor made him strip down to his skivvies and threw the blood-soaked and torn fatigue shirt away. He picked pieces of canvas thread from his rucksack shoulder strap out of the wound. Gianni winced but made no sound as the doctor poured antiseptic into the broad gash and told Gianni that he wouldn't be able to stitch it since most of the flesh had been shot away. Gianni gave a slight shrug at the news and continued to stare at the wall of the tent.

With the shoulder bandaged, Gianni swung his legs over the side of the gurney, anxious to get out of the tent and be alone. His right leg scraped against the white sheet, tearing open the crusted-over wound in his calf. The doctor saw the smear of fresh red blood on the sheet and leaned down to find its source.

"Jesus Christ, troop, you know your damn leg is sliced open? I've got to scrub out all the mud and shit that's in there and I'm afraid it's gonna' hurt like hell. This one we gotta' sew, troop. Good thing is it won't leave as big a scar as your shoulder is gonna' have."

Gianni muttered a simple "Yes, sir" and went back to his own thoughts.

The doctor finished and stepped back as he pulled off his surgical gloves. "Take it easy for a few days. No jumping out of helicopters or any of that shit."

Gianni eased his legs over the side of the gurney and slipped down to the floor. He gave an involuntary wince as his injured right leg made contact with the hard surface.

"Come back and see me in two days. I want to check the wounds and change the bandages, and don't get 'em wet."

Gianni walked out the front of the tent and was untying Shadrack from one of the tent stakes when Evans walked up behind him. "I figured they were gonna' keep you here 'til morning. I thought I'd come over and see how you were and maybe take the dog back to my tent for the night."

Gianni spun around at the sound of the voice, the tape covering his shoulder wound pulling at the hairs on the top of his back. "Huh, oh, that's all right, LT, I'll take him back to the squad tent. The doctor said there was no reason to keep me, I've just got a couple of scratches, they're really not much of anything."

"Huh, that's funny. When the medic came out a little while ago, he said you had two nasty looking wounds. Said you're lucky the shrapnel didn't slice right through the muscle of your calf."

Gianni gathered up Shadrack's leash and started walking toward the tent. "You know how these REMFs are, LT. They think a bee sting is reason enough for a dust off." Gianni looked over at his Lieutenant walking next to him. "I'm all right, really. It's no big deal."

Gianni stuck his right hand in his pant's pocket and rubbed the Zippo lighter. His thoughts raced back to what seemed an eternity ago in the jungle. He glanced up at the sky, at the stars shining through the breaks in the clouds. "What time is it, LT?"

"Couple minutes before twenty-two hundred."

"Funny, it seems like it should be a lot later." He took the lighter out of his pocket and held it up. "Ya' know, it's still my birthday. Two more hours." Gianni squeezed the lighter until the knuckles on his hand turned white. Tears started to run down his face and he wiped them off with the back of his hand. He let out a long sigh, trying to control the quivering in his lower lip.

As they walked along, slowly, Evans pulled out a cigarette and lit it. As he blew out a cloud of smoke, the breeze caught it and carried it high over his left shoulder. An American-made pleasure drifting high over a foreign land that was killing young American men.

Gianni stared at the lighter, his steps getting slower and slower until, unconsciously, he had stopped walking completely and just stood, stood and stared down at the rectangle of shiny metal. Without thinking, without really even meaning to, Gianni flicked open the cover of the lighter and pulled his thumb over the striking wheel. A burst of flame shot up and flickered three inches into the air.

"Goddamnit, Monie, ya' can't even adjust the flame on a fuckin' lighter!" The words came out in a rush of anger as he clicked the cover closed with a violent snap and clutched the lighter tightly in his hand.

"He kept it that way on purpose." Evans' voice seemed to boom in the silence.

"Huh? What'da ya' mean he did it on purpose? Did what on purpose?" Gianni half turned and stared at the Lieutenant.

"The flame, he kept it high on purpose. His parents gave it to him just before he left 'the World'. He had to pull the wick way out so it would light at the high altitude in Colorado but when he got over here, all the extra oxygen at sea level made it flame up. He used to say he wouldn't adjust it because it reminded him of home. As long as he could see a big flame, he knew he wasn't where he wanted to be."

Gianni flicked the lighter back open, lit it and watched the flame dance for a moment before snapping it shut. The flood of emotions came back as he tried to fight for control. "Why him, LT, why Dustin!?"

Evans flicked his cigarette off into the night. A shower of red embers fanned out as it hit the ground. "God, Gianni, I don't know. Why Dustin, why those two pilots that got staked out, why the fuck are we even here? I don't have the answers, I don't think anybody does. It's just the way it is, I guess."

"What the fuck are you saying, LT? Dustin died for nothing!?"

"NO! No I'm not saying he died for nothing." Evans backed away several feet, turned around and stared off at the distant perimeter wire. He tried to find the right words, the words that would make some sense of Dustin's death. As hard as he tried, the only thing he could think of was home.

He turned back to the young Airman, his arms outstretched, almost as if he was pleading. "Gianni, look, I don't know if this is gonna' make any sense but I don't know any way else to explain it." He rubbed his face with both hands as he searched for the words. "My father was a doctor, career Army. One of the places he was stationed was at the VA Hospital at Fort Meade, South Dakota. We lived there for almost six years."

As he spoke, Evans' eyes became distant, like he was reliving a time of his life instead of just telling about it. "It's a beautiful place…big open parade grounds, old stables from when they still used horses, the whole nine yards. It's in a beautiful part of the country, too. Lots of mountains and lakes, just a few miles from Mt. Rushmore. I mean, there's a lot to do there, a lot to see, and you'd think that's what I'd remember most about the place…but it's not."

"You know what I remember most, you know what sticks out in my mind? The sign at the entrance to the fort, 'The Price of Freedom is Visible Here'. A crummy Goddamn sign! Of all the years I lived there, of all the things I saw, that's what I remember most. 'The Price of Freedom is Visible Here'. That sign isn't sitting over some tank, Gianni, or a B-52. It's on a hospital, a Veterans Hospital. That's the price of freedom. People. Not money, not ideals, or any other bullshit. It's people. And that's what Dustin died for."

Gianni started to say something, when Evans held up his hand. "Wait a minute, don't give me that shit about how we shouldn't even be here and how we're not fighting for anybody's freedom. That's not what I'm talking about and you know it. This war is nothing but one big cluster fuck, and if the politicians ever get their heads outta' their asses, they'll either let us win this fuckin' thing or they'll send us home. Until they do that, Gianni, we're stuck. We do our job, whatever it takes. We do our job. Just like that sign, the price of freedom is visible here, too. Dustin's proof of that. He didn't die for country, Gianni, or Old Glory, or mom's apple pie, or any of that shit. He died for the freedom of one man, one pilot who needed his help to get home."

"That's what we do, Gianni. We try to give people their freedom, one lost pilot at a time." Evans was suddenly exhausted. He rubbed the back of his neck with both hands, craning his head to look at the sky. "Don't ever think he died for nothing, Gianni, because he didn't. Dustin's death wasn't a waste, Gianni, it was the price of freedom. One man at a time"

Gianni's leg was starting to throb as he eased himself down to the ground. Shadrack laid down next to his master, nudging up as close as he could. Gianni reached over and rubbed him behind the ears.

"LT, there's something I've got to tell you about Dustin, about how he died." Gianni was staring at the dirt between his legs, watching a beetle carry what remained of another insect.

"I know about it, Gianni. Doc told me out in the bush."

The sobs came, violent and uncontrolled. Tears ran off his face, dropping with silent plops in the dirt. "I killed him, LT. I killed Dustin! OH GOD! GOD! I killed him!!"

Evans dropped down to one knee and shook the young Airman until he looked up. "Gianni, you didn't kill him! You didn't! He was dying, he was already dead." Evans grabbed him by both shoulders and shook him again. "Gianni, listen to me! There was nothing any of us could have done for Dustin. He was hurt too bad, Gianni, he was dying." Gianni's body continued to be racked by sobs. He struggled to catch his breath, choking on the lump in his throat.

"Gianni, don't do this, don't do this to yourself! There was nothing else that could be done! If you hadn't done it, one of us would have. You think we could have watched him suffer like that? You think any of us wouldn't have asked someone to do the same thing if we'd been in his place? Gianni, listen up, listen to me, damnit! Dustin was dying and there was nothing we could do to change that. Nothing! The only thing left for him was to die screaming in pain! Do you hear me!? You let him out of that, Gianni, you gave him freedom from the pain!"

Evans was shaking now, too. The rage was building up in him at the memory of the past day. "Gianni, you didn't kill him. You set him free, you set him free of the pain. You let him die like a man, Gianni."

The sobs racking Gianni's body slowly subsided. As he caught his breath, he wiped his nose and the tears off his cheeks with his hand. Evans pulled a pack of Marlboros out of his shirt pocket and tapped one out into his hand. Gianni, still clutching the lighter, looked at the cigarette, then up at Evans.

"Let me have one of those, will ya', LT."

Evans tapped out another cigarette and handed it over. "I've never seen you smoke before, Gianni."

"I never have, LT. There's a lot of things I never did 'til I came over here." He looked at the lighter, flicked it open, lit it and held it to the end of the cigarette. Evans smiled as Gianni's body convulsed with the hacking, choking cough of a first-time smoker.

"Smooth, huh."

Gianni sucked in a breath of fresh air, fighting off the dizziness from his first taste of nicotine. "Yeah, this is great."

"You'll get used to it."

"I guess so. I got used to this place."

"You never get used to this place, Gianni. You just put up with it." Evans stood up, then reached down and helped Gianni. "Come on, I'll walk you back. You need to get some sleep."

"Thanks, LT, but I think I'm gonna' stay up a while. I need to write a letter."

Evans thought about the letter he was going to have to write to Dustin's parents. "Gianni, be careful what you write…there are a lot of people that don't understand what goes on over here."

"Yeah, LT, but there are some that do…they've never forgotten."

MONDAY
MAY 18,1970
FT. LAUDERDALE, FLORIDA

Frank insisted he use the more comfortable chair behind his desk, then closed the glass office door as he left the room. Vince had read the letter twice now, not quite believing what he had read. Two lines shouted over and over in his mind: 'A booby trap Shadrack might have found if I had been where I was suppose to be', and 'a booby trap that would have hit me if he hadn't'.

How does a father feel grateful that the hand of fate pushes his son aside so that another may fall in his place? Was it right that one father's son had to die so that another's might live?

Vince had been there. He had been to war, lived through it, had seen fate take the lives of so many. He had seen men standing next to him, friends, fiercely bonded together by the horrors of battle, die in a hail of gunfire while he lived to see it happen time and time again. Fate had its own ideas, its own order of life. It was free to pick and choose those who would live and those who would die. Some would be spared for just a short time, just long enough to see the next battle and experience the overwhelming grief that comes with seeing a friend die.

For those who were lucky enough to have fate count them as the living, there was a price to pay, a price they would continue to pay for as long as they were able to draw a breath. A price not unique just to men who have survived combat but to all who have stood up to death while those around them fell.

Vince Giancarlo stared at the letter and cried uncontrollably, relieved that his son was alive but knowing that for the rest of his life, no matter how long or how short, his son would pay that price. He would forever be tortured with the unanswerable question: "Why me?"

CHAPTER 12

One week to the day after Dustin had died, they went out on their first mission with the new man, Dwight Machael, a twenty-one year old from Redmond, Washington, who, on his second tour in Vietnam, thought he had seen it all. That is, until he watched Gianni and Shadrack track a downed Thud pilot throughout the day, finding him hiding in a half-submerged cave on the bank of a river in total darkness. Back at the Palace, Machael had spent twenty minutes telling the pilot that he had to be the luckiest flier on the face of the earth. The pilot, still shaken from what he thought was going to be certain death, pumped each squad member's hand and thanked them profusely. All except Gianni. As the chopper landed, he had guided Shadrack to the tent, never even looking back at the grateful pilot.

That had been their one and only mission, and the days had dragged by since then. Gianni spent most of the daylight hours twirling and throwing the rope, trying to remember the instructions his friend had given him. On the days that it was too hot to stand in the sun and throw the rope he groomed the constantly shedding dog. Finding a piece of broken thorn in one of his paws he had walked him over to the medical tent, hoping one of the doctors could remove it and avoid a flight to the Vet at Tan Son Nhut. While the doctor probed the paw with a pair of tweezers, leery of a patient the could rip his face off, Gianni remembered one of Dustin's favorite rodeo jokes. 'Hey, Gianni, what's the difference between a Vet and a taxidermist? Nothing, either way you get your dog back!' The jokes, always the jokes. Even though he was ten thousand miles away, Dustin was never really out of the arena.

After dark Gianni could always be seen wandering around the base, looking at the stars, lighting a now ever-present cigarette, and listening to the different music that blared from the tents. He lived on three or four hours of sleep, falling into his cot only when his body screamed for rest. As much as he needed the sleep, his mind was cursed with nightmares and memories of a friend he would never see again.

He dropped the rope, slid to the ground and rested his back against the sandbag wall. Unscrewing the top of the canteen, he took a long swallow, then half filled the canteen cup and set it in front of Shadrack. As the dog's tongue snaked in and out of the aluminum cup, a large black beetle crawled across the ground in front of him. Ignoring the water, the dog tilted his head, waiting for the beetle to come into range, pinned it with one big, heavy paw, then watched as the beetle burrowed into the dirt and reappeared several inches away. Not to be outdone by such a primitive evasive maneuver, the dog inched himself forward and once again pinned the hard shelled insect. Gianni watched the scene repeat itself until he was distracted by Huebner's voice. "What are you gonna' do, become an entomologist?"

Gianni looked up at the sound of the voice. "Huh?"

"Bugs. You gonna' study bugs?"

"No, Sarge, just killin' some time." The dog, tiring of the game, lunged forward and crushed the beetle between his teeth. "I guess

Shadrack likes to play with his food."

"If I was a dog, I'd spend more time licking my balls and less time eatin' bugs." Huebner dropped the green duffel bag on the ground and reached inside. "Mail call. Got one for ya."

Gianni reached up and took the letter. "Thanks, Sarge, appreciate it."

Huebner dropped down to one knee, steadying himself with one hand on the bag. "Hey, Gianni, you all right?"

"Yeah, Sarge, I'm all right, just miss Dustin is all."

"We all do, Gianni. We all miss him, but there's nothin' we can do about it. Ya gotta' put it behind you, kid, put it in the back of your mind." Huebner wiped the sweat off his face with his right hand. "You gotta' keep your head on straight out there, Gianni. You can't be distracted, none of us can. The last thing Dustin would want is for one of us to get zapped because we weren't paying attention."

"I hear ya', Sarge. Don't worry, I'll handle it."

Huebner pushed himself up and swung the duffel bag over his shoulder like a young, dark haired Santa Claus in fatigues. "I believe you will, Gianni, I believe you will."

It was just after ten at night. Some of the squad was already asleep while the rest lay in their cots reading or smoking. Gianni swung his legs over the side of his cot, attached Shadrack's leash, and with a slight pat on his left leg, walked out of the tent. The stars twinkled in the cloudless sky, the darkness doing little to diminish the sweltering heat. Swarms of mosquitoes flew around his head and Gianni wished he had doused himself with insect repellent before leaving the tent. Rather than go back, he lit a cigarette, blowing clouds of smoke in an attempt to discourage the blood-sucking onslaught. He looked out toward the invisible horizon. It was hard to believe that somewhere out there people were waiting to kill him. Him and everyone else on the base. Less than six hundred yards away in any direction, troops stood guard along the fence line. Manning machine-gun nests with claymore mine detonators lying within easy reach, stacks of M-16 magazines placed next to rows of grenades, and starlight scopes pointed out toward the killing zone, the men waited.

The night air was filled with the different sounds of men preparing for war, and men trying to forget the war. Music from radios mingled with helicopter engines coughing to life as mechanics tested the big machines before the next day's missions. The night air carried the low revving, throaty growl of the ammo carriers delivering rockets and mini-gun ammo to the loaders who cleaned, oiled, and caressed the guns and launchers like proud owners who had saved for years and bought them with their own money. Men sitting outside their tents reading letters from home, updating their tent mates on the latest news, or passing around pictures of sweethearts, brothers, sisters, parents, and newborns that some would never live long enough to hold.

Gianni walked up and down the rows of tents, filling his lungs with the ever-present smells of aviation gas, hydraulic fluid, and diesel fumes. As much as the smells reminded him of the war, the music made him forget. Music came from everywhere. It seemed the sounds from each tent defined its occupants, branding a lifestyle or an area of the country they called home. As Gianni walked, he took it in, relishing the memories the different songs brought streaming back. From a tent off to the right the Beach Boys sang about their real fine "409". For a second, Gianni remembered driving The Car through the parking lot next to the Yankee Clipper on a Friday night with Chuck slapping the dashboard in time to the music on the radio. Farther off, SteppenWolf belted out "Goddamn The Pusherman" while the whole tent tried to drown out the line by changing it to "Godbless The Pusherman".

As he walked along, songs faded out, only to be replaced by different music. Mitch Rider screaming at the top of his lungs reminded him of the time he and Chuck had gone to Code 1 on Federal Boulevard to see the band in person. They had spent as much time cruising the parking lot as they had inside listening to the band. One tent was playing Country Western, or goat ropin' music as Chuck called it. Gianni thought of Dustin and how, if he was there, he would probably have known the name of the song and what group was playing it.

Through it all, through the mixture of different music and voices and sounds preparing for war, a familiar sound rose above it all, sounds he hadn't heard in what seemed a lifetime. He was drawn to it. Using his ears like Shadrack, he tilted his head, trying to get a bearing and moved in on the sweet sounds of home. At first he wasn't quite sure what it was. He had heard it before, many times, but the sounds weren't quite clear enough to name it. Suddenly he had it! Of course, what a dummy! How many times had he opened the front door to those sounds from the family room hi-fi? He could almost see his father sitting in his big oyster-white recliner, moving his foot in time to the big band sound of the Glenn Miller Orchestra playing "In The Mood".

He stopped and cocked his ear to the chorus of saxophones suddenly replaced by the saxophone solo. He smiled to himself at the thought of his father jumping up from his chair, pulling the watering can out of his wife's hand, and the two of them jitterbugging in the middle of the room. Right now he couldn't think of anything he'd rather see than his parents dancing. The upbeat trumpet solo kicked in and Gianni followed the sound. Past the rock and roll, past the Motown, past the goat ropin' music. He quickened his pace and headed toward the sound of home.

The music built to a screeching crescendo, then, it stopped. Gianni's heart sank. For a moment he had forgotten the war, forgotten about Dustin, and forgotten that he wasn't home. His pace slowed. He almost stopped, almost turned around, when his ears were greeted by yet another familiar sound. This time there was no mistake, there was no doubt, he knew it instantly. Glenn Miller again, only this time the song was "Little Brown Jug".

He remembered sitting in front of the TV with his mother and father watching the "Glenn Miller Story" with Jimmy Stewart and how he had played this same song for June Allison. Gianni quickened his pace, almost running, afraid that the music might end and he'd never find it again. He got closer and closer, pushed forward, almost in a trance by the memories of home and his parents.

The music ended but was quickly replaced by another Glenn Miller tune, this one accompanied by the vocals to "Don't Sit Under The Apple Tree". The scene flashed in his mind as he saw his father take a candle out of the holder on the coffee table and dance around like he was holding a microphone, lip-syncing the song to his mother. Gianni had thought it was stupid at the time, but maybe it wasn't. Maybe it was all part of living, part of enjoying life, acting the fool in front of someone you love just to see them laugh, just a little inane way of saying "I Love You". Maybe it was part of the magic.

He made his way between two tents, walked across the dirt pathway, and stood in front of the home of the music. He had seen the tent before, but never really noticed it. It was just like the dozens and dozens of other tents on the base, green canvas turned light brown from the blowing dust and burning sun with rows of sandbags stacked all the way around. It was just like the rest of the tents except for one thing: The two-foot-tall white cross wedged in the top of the sandbags at the front of the tent.

The Army might be part of the government, and the government might believe in the separation of church and state, but for men who otherwise might not be religious, combat had a tendency to change those feelings, and the Army made sure those men had access to a place of worship. It may not be a real church, or synagogue, or place that resembled anything back in 'the World' but it didn't matter. God wasn't that particular. He would listen to the prayers, questions, and fears of frightened men no matter where they were.

Gianni stopped in front of the tent and listened. The music didn't seem as loud as it should have been. How had he heard it so clearly from so far away and now it didn't seem any louder? Certainly not as loud as the rock and roll or goat ropin' music. It was loud enough to reach

Gianni, pleasantly strong enough for the heavy, big band rhythm to be exciting, enough to carry his thoughts all the way back home, but yet not loud enough to disturb anyone who didn't care for that type of old-fogey music.

He stood there long enough to hear the song end, only to be followed by what sounded like a piano starting to play scales, then by the strong, heavy sound of a trombone. Gianni thought for a moment then smiled a big broad grin. "Damn, I'm better at this than I thought. I know all of these".

His foot began to tap at the quick upbeat sounds of Count Basie playing "Jumpin' at The Woodside". He remembered his mother telling him how she and his father used to go out to the ballrooms and dance all night to the sounds of the big bands. Guy Lombardo, The Woody Herman Band, Jimmy Dorsey, Tommy Dorsey, anyone who played the "good sounds", as she called it. It was funny how the simple things in life became so important after you thought you might never see them again. What was it Chuck's father used to say? 'You never miss the water until the well runs dry.' It hadn't made any sense, until now.

Gianni walked over to the sandbagged wall, told Shadrack to lie down, then jumped up to sit on the deteriorating bags. He lit a cigarette and listened, listened to the "good sounds." He just sat. Sat, listened, smoked and remembered. The sandbag to his right was stained with black ash from rubbing out the butts and a small pile of filters was growing on the ground below his feet. Shadrack raised his head and stretched to sniff every time Gianni dropped one. You couldn't be too careful, someone might drop something that was edible. The record, or tape, or whatever it was had been changed and the Mills Brothers were singing "Up A Lazy River" when someone walked out of the tent. "Good evening."

Gianni noticed the insignia of a major on the man's right collar and a small cross pinned to the left one. "Oh, excuse me, sir, ah, I mean

Father. I didn't mean to be hanging out around your tent." He started to push himself off from the sandbags.

"No, no, stay where you are." The man glanced down at the dog, then quickly back at Gianni as if he had suddenly recognized him. "You're the Air Force troop, aren't you? "

"Yes, sir." Gianni held out his right hand. I'm Gianni Giancarlo."

"I'm Father Szuch, the base priest."

"A pleasure to meet you, Father."

"No, it's not. You're as uncomfortable as hell by me surprising you like that, but thanks for saying it anyway."

He was right, Gianni had been uncomfortable by being caught sitting in front of someone's tent, a priest's tent no less, but now the uncomfortable feeling slipped away at the man's understanding.

"What's your dog's name?"

"Shadrack." The dog raised his head at the sound of his name. The priest bent down and scratched him behind the ears, noticing for the first time their huge size. "Looks like God was extremely generous in the ear department."

"Either that or He was having an off day and wasn't paying much attention."

The priest chuckled as the dog turned his head, trying to direct the scratching fingers to a better spot. "Yes, I guess He does work in mysterious ways." Gianni watched as the older man took a pipe out of his fatigue pants pocket, charged it with Borkum Riff, and blew a huge cloud of smoke at the sky. "It's a beautiful sky tonight."

Gianni looked up and saw nothing but the same old sky he saw every night. "Yes, sir, I guess it is." As they looked at the sky, the Mills Brothers started singing their rendition of "You Always Hurt The One You Love."

"You know, Gianni, except for a couple of the older officers on the base, you're the only one around here that likes big band music."

"To tell you the truth, Father, I didn't know I liked it until just a little while ago." He listened to a few bars of the music. "My dad and mom listen to this kind of music all the time," a mischievous grin snaked across his face, " unless I get to the hi-fi first. I, ah, I guess I absorbed more of it than I thought. Back home I wouldn't have been able to name any of these songs and now…I don't know why, but I know all of them." The soft, melodic voices of the Mills Brothers surrounded him with a feeling of safety. More than he had ever felt being inside the wire. "I guess I just miss my folks…and this reminds me of them."

"Memories are a good thing Gianni, sometimes they keep us going when we'd rather give up, when it would be easier just to quit." Gianni thought about it for just a moment and was nodding his head in agreement when the song ended and was replaced with "Paper Doll". Dustin had been right, it wasn't the girls he missed, fooling around in the backseat of The Car at the drive-in or in the life-guard stands at the beach. What he missed were all the things he had taken for granted. The simple things. His mother watering the plants or her singing her little Italian songs while she made dinner. His father coming home from work and sneaking over to the hi-fi to change the station or put on a stack of his 78's. Complaining about Chuck's smoking or even getting angry with himself when he missed an easy shot at a clay bird. Back in 'the World', in his other life, he had never thought that missing a shot might get him killed. Dustin had been right, and now Dustin was dead.

The priest licked the tip of his forefinger, then used it to tamp down the burning tobacco. Holding the pipe away from him, he looked into the bowl. Satisfied, he wiped his finger on top of one of the sand bags, then took a long pull, letting the smoke escape out the sides of his mouth.

"You miss your friend Dustin, too, don't you."

Gianni was surprised by the statement and turned his head with a jerk. "How'd you know about Dustin? How'd you know we were friends?"

"Gianni, I'm the base priest, remember? I don't just hear confessions and conduct Mass on Sunday mornings. Major Kancilla sees to it that I know about everyone seriously wounded or killed. In this case the

Major didn't have to tell me. Dustin's dog tags showed he was Catholic. I administered the last rites."

For a brief few minutes he had forgotten the pain of Dustin's memory. Now it all came rushing back. "Does it help, Father? I mean, if someone is already dead, if they've been dead for a while, do the last rites help?"

"Who's to say, Gianni. All I can tell you is that if you believe, if you have faith in God, then yes, I think it helps." The priest saw a tear fall from Gianni's cheek and land on the sandbag between his legs.

"It's not fair, Father. Goddamnit! It's not fair!" Gianni made no apology for the use of God's name nor was the priest surprised or offended. The hardest thing to understand, the hardest question to answer, was why God would let bad things happen to good people. The priest didn't have the answer. No one did.

"He was getting ready to go home. He only had another six weeks!" The tears started to flow faster, falling off his cheeks and making soft plopping sounds on the sandbags.

The priest stood silent for a moment, gently sucking on the pipe stem. "I understand you and Dustin worked pretty much as a team, out in the bush."

"Yeah, ah, yes sir, we did, right from the start. When I came into the squad, he kinda' watched over me, taught me what to do. I think he just wanted to be near the dog; he liked animals, he was real comfortable with them." Gianni was lost in his memories, lost in what might have been. "I guess we both came from two different worlds and we wanted to see what each other's was like." Reality suddenly rushed back. "I don't think either one of us ever thought we wouldn't get to go home."

The priest knew what the young Airman was going through. "Gianni, I know you're looking for an answer, a cold hard reason for your friend's death...but I'm afraid it's not always as simple as that. There is no answer for why these things happen, not one you're going to accept. At least not now."

His life's calling was gratifying to him, it brought a sense of peace and fulfillment, even an answer to the age-old question of why we were here. For him, and others like him, the answer was easy. To serve Him. To spread the Word, to console those who believed. The hard part, the almost impossible part, was to console those who had never believed, or those who had lost their belief. The priest had stood before many others who had lost friends in combat, or parents who would never see their sons again. It never got easier, and each time it tested his faith.

"Gianni, I can stand here and quote from the Bible, tell you that it's God's will and that we shouldn't question that will. You've heard it before. I can tell you all that, Gianni, and if I thought it would help, I would, but it's not what you want to hear, it's not what you need to hear." The priest looked around, at the row of tents in front of him, at the dog at his feet, and at the sky above him, searching for the right words. "Why are you here?"

Gianni looked up at the priest. "What?"

Father Szuch pointed at the ground violently. "Here, here, in Vietnam. Why are you here?"

"I don't know! Everyone keeps asking me that. My parents, the guys in the squad, the guys back at Tan Son Nhut. I don't know why I volunteered, I don't know why I just didn't go to college. I wish I'd never seen this place or any of the shit that goes on over here!"

Now the priest's words were coming faster. The hurting Airman had to answer his own questions, had to find his own reasons for experiencing hell on earth. "No, Gianni, no, that's not good enough! You could have found a million reasons for staying away from here. A million of them, but you decided to be here. Why!?"

He jumped off the sandbag wall, Shadrack leaping to his feet at the sudden movement. "Because it was the right thing to do! All right? Are you happy? I don't have a good reason. It was just the right thing to do. My father went to war, he didn't question it, he just went. It was something he had to do and this was something I had to do!" Gianni was shouting at a priest. "What the hell do you want me to say? That I came over here to be a hero, or I thought I could win the war all be myself, or I wanted to fight for God and country? Well, it's not that glamorous, Father! It was just the right thing to do!"

"Yes, yes, Gianni, it was the right thing to do. In a world that is filled with wrong things, it was a right thing to do. Just like when you go out after those lost pilots. Gianni, it's the right thing to do. When your friend died trying to save someone else, he was doing the right thing. Gianni, you want answers to all the things that are wrong in life but you forget to see all the right things. All the beautiful things, all the life, all the happiness instead of the misery, all the good things instead of the bad things. You want proof that God cares, that God helps those who can't help themselves. What about you, Gianni? What about Dustin, and the rest of the men in your squad? Maybe he sent you to help those pilots. Maybe you're His tool to bring families back together? Maybe you're the answer to someone's prayers. God works in mysterious ways, Gianni, and maybe this time he's working through you."

For the first time in many minutes, Gianni noticed that the music was still playing. He listened to the "good sounds" for a moment, remembering the words of his own father, then turned back to the priest.

"Kinda' like magic, huh, Father? Kinda' like magic?"

"I guess so, Gianni. I guess it is kind of like magic."

As he walked farther and farther from the tent, the music seemed to stay just as loud, and for a fleeting second he could almost see the smile on his father's face as Louis Armstrong's gravel voice sang "What a Wonderful World".

WEDNESDAY
JUNE 17, 1970
SKIES OVER CAMBODIA
THIRTY MILES SOUTHEAST OF PHNOM PEHN

Lieutenant Colonel David Runyon pressed the microphone button and gave the order for the other three F-4s to drop their external fuel tanks. This had been their farthest incursion yet into Cambodia and they had flown with the extra tanks to ensure they would still have plenty of fuel to get back to Tan Son Nhut. It almost seemed like President Nixon meant business this time. He had ordered the bombing of Cambodia to help stem the constant flow of Communist troops and equipment into South Vietnam.

At first everyone thought a few days of bombing and strafing, some well placed rockets and sticks of napalm, would convince the North Vietnamese that trying to push through Cambodia wasn't such a good idea. It hadn't turned out that way. American pilots and ground troops had a much higher opinion of their military might than the enemy. Soldiers, weapons, ammunition, and SAMs continued to flow in ever-increasing numbers. Rather than being able to fly in, drop their ordinance, and fly back for a cold beer and a steak, pilots had to use every tactic they had learned, and some they made up, to survive the skies over Cambodia.

Being shot down was something to avoid at all costs, even to the point of not completing the mission. A parachute landing in the middle of the heavily-occupied jungle almost certainly meant spending the rest of the war as a POW, or never seeing the next sunrise.

Runyon craned his neck and looked at the other three aircraft. "All right, everybody, heads up, three minutes to target. Check 'em and drop 'em. Keep your eyes open, we don't need any surprises now."

Tepley chuckled and said, "What's the matter, getting cautious in your old age?"

"I just want to get older, that's all."

Tepley had been watching his threat indicator screen. "We're clean and green, no threats or warnings. Coming up on target in one minute. Now's when it's gonna' get hairy."

Runyon hit the microphone. "All right, dropping down to angles two, let's do it."

The three pilots followed their leader down toward the deck, eyes searching for the telltale puffs of Triple A's or the bright white flash of a SAM leaving its launcher. The Wizzo of three was the first to shout a warning. "Gun radar to the right! They're painting us, they're painting us! Locked on, they've got a lock, to the right, two o'clock!"

Runyon pressed his microphone. "Three, Four, break to the gun, take the gun! Two, stay on target, follow me to target!"

The pilots of three and four turned slightly to the right, hoping to place their rockets on top of the antiaircraft gun before the gunners could blow them out of the sky. Three's Wizzo saw the gun before his pilot did. "A little more to the right, more to the right, there, there! Just behind that clearing, there, there, take it, take it!!"

The pilot fired four rockets, two from under each wing, white smoke trails snaking down, leaving a twisting residue in the sky. The rockets disappeared through the tops of the jungle canopy and exploded with a tremendous burst of orange flame and a huge visible shock wave as they found their mark, destroying the radar controlled gun and detonating its store of ammunition.

"Scratch one gun!"

"One to Three and Four, Two and I will make a run from south to north. Hang back, then come in east to west." Runyon pushed his throttles forward, trying to gain every ounce of speed without having his heavy bomb load tear his wings off. He watched the target pipper, waiting for the instrument to tell him the precise moment to pickle the load.

Tepley's shout broke his concentration. "Missile warning, missile warning! Radar's everywhere! Jesus Christ, they suckered us in, there're fuckin' everywhere!!" Tepley's eyes went from his threat warning indicator to the jungle below him and back to the instrument. "Locked on, locked on, they've got us locked!! Launching, launching, they're launching!!" Streaks of flame and clouds of white smoke broke through the trees as the massive missiles started their journey skyward. "Get us outta' here, get us the fuck outta' here!" Tepley's voice was riddled with panic.

Runyon twisted his head from side to side. "One to Two! Pickle now, now, now!!" As the two pilots dropped all their bombs, the planes shot forward, relieved of the extra weight and wind resistance. Not landing exactly where they had planned, missing most of the stores of replacement SAMs and trucks loaded with munitions waiting to be transported across the border, the bombs had a devastating effect nonetheless. Pieces of bodies flew into the air, some unrecognizable as such. Machine guns, rifles, and B-40 rocket launchers were twisted into useless pieces of junk. Stores of rice were destroyed, individual grains propelled through the air at speeds great enough to shred flesh and tear out eyes.

"Four SAMs, three o'clock!! Break left, left, left!!"

Runyon kicked hard rudder, pushed the stick to the left and forward, diving for the tree tops. The four telephone pole-size missiles, unable to follow the frantic maneuvers of the big jet, screamed past it sailing off into the blue Cambodian sky, exploding harmlessly out of range.

Tepley was quickly distracted by the sensation of small thumps on the aircraft and the sound of tearing metal. Looking down at the jungle, he saw the flashes of small arms fire directed at them from between the trees. "We're takin' hits! Get us up, get us outta' here!!"

Runyon pushed the throttles into afterburner and pulled the nose up. Tracers followed them, passing by the canopy on both sides, then falling behind as the aircraft gained altitude.

He nosed the aircraft over, reducing the rate of climb and picking up speed. His mind raced. He pressed the intercom button. "Tep, how we doin'?"

"We've got some holes, leading edge, right wing. Part of our left flap is shredded. Everything else is green."

"One to Mustang flight. All right, time for some payback. Three, do you have target in sight?"

"Roger, to the west at my nine o'clock."

"All right, listen up. We're gonna' have one chance at this so let's make it good. Leader and Two will make a pass from west to east. We'll salvo remaining rockets and keep their heads down. Three and Four, when we make the pass, you come in from the north. Rockets on the approach, then pickle everything else on target. Tep, you all set back there?"

"I don't like this shit, Boss. We're way too close to going home to be fuckin' around like this."

"Relax and enjoy the view. Threats?"

"Radar's hot all around us. Guns and SAMs. No lock, we're okay, for now."

"Let's do it." Runyon nosed the aircraft over and started his dive, the wings of his plane just slightly ahead of his wingman. Trails of black smoke, the ever present curse of the big General Electric engines, streamed into the cloudless sky, announcing to all those with an interest that company was coming.

Runyon stared through the target sight, trying to ignore, but involuntarily flinching at the tracers that began to fill the sky. Tepley shouted a warning. "Gun radar locked on. They've got us. Jink, Jink!"

Runyon twisted the stick to the right, away from his wingman only yards to the left, then nosed the plane over in an even steeper dive. The tracers were thicker now. Men trying to save their lives the only way they could, by shooting down those who would kill them first.

Tepley's helmeted head hit the left side of the canopy as the plane lurched suddenly to the right. "Jesus Christ, what the fuck was that!?" Runyon grabbed the stick with both hands and kicked in left rudder, struggling to keep the plane from spinning out of control. Scanning his instruments, he shouted, "Tep, check us, check us."

Tepley looked out the right side of the canopy. "Boy, is the crew chief gonna' be pissed! The right wing is gone!"

Runyon was still struggling to keep control. "What'da ya' mean gone? It can't be gone!" He reached over and decreased power slightly on the left engine, letting the higher power setting of the right engine work against the tendency of the plane to turn to the right.

"Hey! I've seen gone, and it's gone. Two, maybe three feet from the tip."

"Goddamnit!" Runyon pulled his eyes away from the instruments just long enough to glance out the canopy. Tepley hadn't been exaggerating. At least three feet of the wing was gone and pieces of the aluminum skin were still peeling back. If the low bidder could build a plane that would stay in the air in this condition, imagine what they could do if they really wanted to spend some money.

Runyon spun back to the cockpit, reduced throttle on the left engine even more and pressed the microphone button. "Leader, Mustang flight. We're out of it. Jettisoning rockets and heading south. Make your run, then form up on me."

The gunners on the ground, watching as the rockets left the underside of the wings and crash harmlessly into the jungle, intensified their fire at the floundering fighter. Tracers arched up at the aircraft, crisscrossing the sky in front of it, behind it, and into it. Pieces of metal flew off as bullets and shrapnel tore at the thin skin. Runyon felt the heavy thud as something hit the nose of the aircraft just below and in front of the cockpit. His instruments blinked on and off, then came back on as the circuit breakers reset. A small wisp of smoke started to rise from the cockpit floor, the acid stench of burning electrical wires noticeable through the heavy rubber mask. Fire in the cockpit is an aircrew's worst nightmare. If it doesn't cause an explosion from being fed by the pure oxygen in the life support system, it leaves little choice but to eject. Runyon reached forward and hit the oxygen emergency shutoff. "Tep, Tep, kill your air, kill your air!!"

Tepley had seen the smoke rising and didn't need to be told twice. He took a last huge gulp of the cool oxygen and hit the cutoff switch. "Can you hold it!?"

"Yeah, yeah, I think so! I think I got it." The smoke continued to rise, getting thicker by the second. Runyon started to cough in his mask and his eyes began to burn from the smoke seeping in under his visor. "Gotta' get rid of the smoke! Blow the canopies, blow 'em!!"

Tepley reached forward and pulled the canopy release handle. The forward canopy raised up off its latches and blew back in the slipstream, just missing the aircraft's tail. The rear canopy followed a fraction of a second later. With a tremendous rush of air, the smoke was sucked out.

"Right engine's hot, climbing fast!!"

Runyon hit the microphone button. "Mayday Mayday Mayday! Mustang flight, One has a Mayday!! Fire in the cockpit! Had to blow canopies! Cannot make it back! Repeat, cannot make it back!"

"Roger One, Two copies. How long can you stay with it? Advise."

Runyon looked at his instruments. He turned his head and watched as more of the aluminum skin peeled back from the damaged wing. The temperature gauge was buried in the red and thick black smoke billowed out the back of the right engine. "Right engine's gonna' go any second!"

Two's pilot reached forward and with a gloved finger punched button six on his radio. The preset emergency frequency squawked to life in his headset. "Lion, Mustang Two, we have a Mayday. Mustang One is hit, cannot continue, repeat, Mustang One is hit, cannot continue."

"Roger Mustang Two, Lion copies. RESCAP will be notified. Time on station?"

"Fifteen mikes to bingo, over."

"Roger Mustang Two, copy. Mustang One will be without cover for thirty to forty mikes from your bingo."

Two was about to raise his flight leader when flame shot out of Runyon's right tail pipe followed by a huge ball of black smoke. As the engine quit, the aircraft spun violently to the right, throwing itself into a flat spin. Runyon jerked the stick all the way to the left, kicked full left rudder and chopped the throttle to the left engine in an attempt to straighten out the stricken aircraft. It took only a moment for him to realize if they didn't bail out now, they never would. Still fighting for control, Runyon screamed over the intercom. "Get us out, NOW, NOW, NOW!!"

"Oh, GOD, not again!" Tepley's words were almost lost by the roar of the ejection seat as he reached down and pulled the yellow and black handles.

THURSDAY
JUNE 18,1970
CAMELOT PALACE

It was just after two in the morning when Evans and Huebner walked down the aisle between the cots, pulling the metal chains to turn on the four hanging light bulbs. "All right, guys, let's wake up." Evans kept his voice low. This wasn't basic training and there was no reason to scare sleeping men. Slowly, one by one, the men opened their eyes and began to sit up or swing their legs over their cots.

"Listen up, listen up. Air Force has a problem and they want to know if we can help." Evans looked around the tent to make sure everyone was paying attention. "They've got two guys down, an F-4 crew. They went down yesterday. Rescue spent most of the day trying to make a pickup, lost two Skyraiders to ground fire. The Air Force wants to know if we'll go in and try to get their guys out."

Schoonhoven was the first to speak. "What's the big deal, Lieutenant?" He looked around at the rest of the men as if asking permission to continue. "Since when do they ASK us to get some of their guys?"

Evans knew what was coming, and even though he thought he knew what the reaction would be, he wasn't sure. "This isn't a normal mission, Johnathan. It involves a little more than a simple pickup. This is a volunteer mission only."

Schoonhoven pushed himself to his feet. "Well, like I said, LT, what's the big deal?"

Evans looked over at Huebner again who worked at the mustache and shrugged his shoulders. "They're in Cambodia."

Runyon and Tepley lay at the bottom of a thick stand of trees that were almost choked off from life by the even thicker stand of bushes that grew around them. They had tried to sleep, taking turns while the other stood guard. Afraid to do anything more than lie in an unmoving position for fear of rustling leaves and branches, the two men only pretended to sleep. Their bodies were covered with crawling creatures, drawn to a feast of dried and oozing blood from the dozens of scratches and scrapes. Hardly a square inch of exposed skin had escaped the ravages of running, walking, lunging, plunging, and finally, crawling through the natural traps and barriers of the jungle.

The sun was just starting to rise, just starting to show faint streaks of light through the thick canopy. It would make it easier to see those who wanted to kill them. It would also make it easier for the killers to see them.

They had been awake now for almost twenty-four hours. Physically they were tired, almost worn to the point of exhaustion. Mentally they would soon reach the point where their minds would begin to fail them. They had to make a choice: Try to make it away from the men searching for them and risk being killed or captured, or stay in the area, avoid detection, and hope to be rescued.

Over beers or dinner they had asked several of the pilots at Tan Son Nhut what they would do if they were shot down. They had all said the same thing. "If you gotta' punch out, find a place to hide and stay put, they'll come and find ya'. Dig a hole, climb a tree, anything, just make yourself invisible and wait for that damned dog to walk up and piss on your leg."

Tepley was lying with his left cheek on top of his left hand, every once in a while raising his head an inch or two and trying to gently shake some of the insects off. His right hand lay on the ground next to his face, tightly clenching a blue steel .38. Runyon lay on the ground behind him, trying to stay on his side and avoid putting any weight on the ribs he had broken during his landing. He kept his gun in his left hand, using his right to apply pressure to his ribs, trying to relieve some of the pain.

Runyon tapped Tepley on the shoulder and pointed out through the branches. Less than twenty yards away was the start of a clearing, two hundred yards past that were four NVA soldiers making their way just inside the opposite tree line. The men walked slowly, looking for any sign of the two American flyers that had avoided them. They had watched dozens of their comrades die as the American war planes and helicopters swooped down, dropping their deadly cargo and firing their hellish mini-guns in an attempt to rescue them. They had driven off the American jets with their SAMs and damaged some of their helicopters, but it had been costly. Rockets from one of the jets had landed in the trees, just above a group of hiding men. The metal shrapnel had killed every man in the area. Some took all night to die, their screams and moans reminding the survivors that the American fliers must be found, and made to pay.

One of the soldiers looked to his left out across the clearing. The sun was getting higher now, strong enough to reflect off the thousands of shell casings that littered the ground. He remembered the day before, the day the planes dove in low, dropping bombs and napalm and firing rockets.

He remembered the propeller-driven Skyraiders. Slower, much slower, than the American jets, slower, and with a distinctive sound. You could hear them coming, you could hear them before they appeared over the tree tops. Unlike the jets that dropped their bombs and flew past before you ever heard them, the Skyraiders announced their arrival.

The soldier could see yesterday in his mind. He could see the slow plane approaching, flashes from the machine gun barrels mounted in the wings as it spit death. He could see the bombs drop slowly from under its wings as they fell to earth, tearing apart the men he had lived with and fought with for years. He could see the barrel of his AK-47 pointed at the sky spitting its own death. He fired and fired and his comrades fired and they hit the big slow plane again and again and again, and still the plane continued to fly, swallowing the bullets like a bird swallows insects.

The soldier remembered. Remembered how the big plane had turned around, coming back directly at them, and almost, as if in a dream, had dropped the last two bombs from under its wings. He remembered how the men to his right, running for the cover of trees, ran right under the falling bombs, pieces of their bodies thrown into the air.

The man remembered how he was thrown through the air by the blast, his clothes shredded, his body pelted and pierced by flying rocks. He remembered how he lay there unable to breathe, unable to draw air into lungs that felt as if they were on fire, and unable to move, to do anything to save his own life. He lay there watching as the big slow plane turned around again, coming back to kill those who were still alive. He watched as the wings began to spit fire, the ground exploding as each bullet searched for a human target. The ground began to erupt closer and closer to him, searching him out. Death was approaching. He closed his eyes, ready to accept it with the picture of his wife and child in his mind.

He opened his eyes, not at the sudden stinging of a quick death or the numbing, then burning, of a lingering torture, but at the sound of cheering. He opened his eyes and focused on the big plane as it flew over, smoke and flames billowing and streaking out of its engine. Had

not the bomb blast dulled his hearing, he would have heard the different sound of the engine as well, the dying gasps as it tried to take its
pilot to safety.

The soldier remembered yesterday well. Remembered the solemn
vow he had taken to find the American fliers. To find them and to make
them pay.

Runyon whispered into Tepley's ear. "We gotta' decide. We either try
to make it outta' here, or we stay and wait for help."

Tepley was terrified. The first time they had bailed out, when they
were running through the jungle, he thought he couldn't have been
more scared. He was wrong. Now men were actually looking for him,
wanting to kill him. He was starting to shake. The soft, almost sound-
less rustling the leaves and branches made as his body shook almost
unnerved him. Certainly the men looking for them could hear it. They
would turn, directly at the sound, then move in closer, until they could
see the two cowering men pleading for their lives. Tepley could see the
smiles, the terrifying grins, as they prepared to take out their revenge.
His body shook harder, heaving now as he tried to suck in air that had
seemingly disappeared.

Runyon shook his shoulder and whispered at him again. "Come on,
Tep, snap out of it! Snap out of it, damnit!"

Tepley blinked his eyes hard, trying to focus on the reality in front of
him, not the nightmares in his mind. He released the grip on his gun
and wiped the sweat, and bugs off his face. Runyon was asking him
what they should do. Wanting him to make the decision that might
mean whether they lived or died. Why the hell should he have to decide?
This was the military, the U.S. Air Force, for God's sake. Runyon was the
goddamn Lieutenant Colonel, not him. He was supposed to make the
decisions, give the orders, take charge, and all that Rah Rah bullshit. He
rolled back toward Runyon so that his mouth was next to his ear. Fuck
the rank, screw the military protocol. If he was going to die, he was sure
as hell going to have some say in how it happened.

"Let's give it 'til tomorrow night. If no one comes lookin', we go."

Runyon moved his head so Tepley could see him, then nodded in agreement. It was a relief that Tepley wanted to wait instead of make a run for it. Runyon had already made up his mind. Had Tepley suggested otherwise, he would have nixed the idea.

The two men watched as the four soldiers walked along the tree line. The one soldier who had been looking out across the clearing had turned back to the other three, said something, then followed them until they were out of sight.

Runyon and Tepley both gave a short-lived sigh of relief.

They tensed up at voices coming from behind their hiding spot. Runyon slowly turned his head. They had chosen their hiding place well, even if it had been pure luck. Although the voices were clear, Runyon couldn't see anything through the heavy branches and leaves. It sounded like another three or four men. He placed his hand on Tepley's shoulder and gave a gentle squeeze. Tepley looked up as Runyon moved his hand back to his mouth and put a single finger across his lips. Tepley nodded. Both men unconsciously held their breath as the group of men began to move, the voices first getting louder, then changing direction and fading away.

The chopper flight had been a long one and they hadn't been inserted until well after daylight. The OV-10 Bronco flew high enough not to be heard and could only be seen as a tiny speck against the blue sky. With any luck, anyone seeing the aircraft from the ground would only suspect it was looking for SAM sites or truck parks that were waiting to transport their cargo after dark. Anything would be preferable to figuring out its real mission, directing a team trying to sneak into the area and rescue two American fliers.

The Cambodian jungle was identical to South Vietnam, and totally different. The trees, the bushes, the bugs, the heat, everything was the same, but yet they all felt as if they were seeing it for the first time. There was an unfamiliarity to it that didn't exist on the other side of the border. Gianni felt like the first man through the giant wooden gate in the movie King Kong. The jungle was the same on both sides of the gate yet one side had a sinister feel to it. This jungle had the same feeling. All the men were on edge. Their sixth sense was working overtime and they didn't know why.

Evans dropped to one knee, then motioned for the rest of the squad to gather around. "All right, listen up. The locator beacon hasn't moved in several hours. That means one of three things. They're holed up and waiting for us to come get 'em, they're dead, or Charlie has the beacon and is setting a trap. The Bronco hasn't been able to get real close but he's seen boo coo movement down there. Lots of ground troops, and you can bet what they're looking for."

He pulled out a cigarette and lit it. "According to the Bronco driver, we've still got four, maybe five hours to go before we're in the area. That's if we don't run into any trouble." He pulled the map out of his thigh pocket, unfolded it and spread it on the ground. "All right, we're here and this is where we're going." He took a drag off the cigarette, then pointed at the map again. "Trails here, here, and here. Charlie is moving stuff down them now. We stay well away from 'em. Got clearings big enough for choppers here and here."

He waited while each man leaned forward to get a good look at the map. "Gianni, I want you and the dog on point from now on. We need to stay away from Charlie." Evans took another drag and looked up at the rest of the men. "We'll be in deep shit if we make contact before we reach our guys. We need to do this clean. Understood?" Each man in the squad nodded silently.

"Okay, when we get to this point, I'll contact the Bronco. They've set up a little diversion that might give us a chance of pulling this thing off. We're gonna' have F-4's, Cobras, and Skyraiders on station for support. They're gonna' bomb and strafe this area here. We're hopin' Charlie will be busy enough not to notice us. When they start making their runs, we move in to here."

Evans looked up before continuing. "Gianni, you're gonna' have to find these guys as soon as we get there. We ain't gonna' have time to fuck around." The young Airman nodded his head. "All right, let's move."

It wasn't a question of if they were going to be found, it was a question of when. The NVA soldiers had searched all around them, several times peering into the tree line where they hid but never pushing their way through the heavy cover. As enemy soldiers passed by, Runyon and Tepley were repeatedly thrown from the heights of elation to the depths of despair.

The two men silently watched as three soldiers stopped at the edge of the trees directly in front of them. Two of the men propped their rifles up against their legs and lit cigarettes. They stood there, several times looking over at the stand of trees Runyon and Tepley were hiding in, before finishing their cigarettes and moving on. Runyon and Tepley both let out collective sighs and relaxed their white knuckled grips on the revolvers.

Runyon pulled out his plastic water bottle, studied its contents, then took a small sip and handed it to Tepley. Talking directly into his ear, he tried to keep his voice as low as possible. "Well, you're supposed to be the fuckin' navigator. Know of a quick way outta' here?"

"I haven't got the faintest fuckin' idea."

They continued to lie under the branches while the sweltering heat became more and more unbearable. As they lay there, both men wondered if anyone was really going to try and rescue them. Punching out over South Vietnam was one thing. Cambodia was another matter entirely.

The dog started to alert. When Gianni first noticed it, he motioned Evans up to him, pointed down at the dog, then tapped himself on the chest and pointed at Smith. Evans nodded his head and watched as Smith dropped back several paces behind Gianni and the dog. They stopped every few minutes as the dog tested the air.

It took over three hours to cover less than three klicks. Several times the squad had to melt into the trees, covering their presence as much as possible in the thick undergrowth as NVA soldiers crossed their path or paralleled their movements, searching for the downed flyers. Each man knew that without the dog on point, they would almost certainly have run into one or more of the patrols.

They had been moving for twenty minutes after their last close encounter when Evans signaled a halt. As the men tried to make themselves invisible behind trees or bushes, Evans took the handset from Boardman and raised the Bronco.

"All right, he's calling in the fast movers now. Should be here within thirty to forty. We'll move up as close as we can before they get here. He says the signal is coming from right here and hasn't moved." He held the map so every man could see. "They're either holed up waiting for us or we're gonna' have some big time trouble. If we're lucky, we'll be able to narrow down where they're at while the Air Force is making their runs, call for the choppers, move in, grab 'em, and get the hell out." He looked up and searched the face of each man, not knowing what he was looking for. "All right, ten minutes, then we move.

Evans crawled over to where Gianni and Smith were sitting. "When we movin' out, LT?"

"In just a minute." He pointed at the map. "This is where the signal is coming from, right here. It hasn't moved all day. I need you to move us along here, in this direction.

Gianni studied the map. There was no way to get where the beacon was coming from without crossing part of a clearing. "If we can get up to here, LT, and if the wind is right, Shadrack will be able to tell if there's actually someone hiding in there or if the Gooks just set up the beacon."

"How's he gonna' do that, how can he tell?"

"If there's someone in there, the scent is gonna' be real strong. If it's just the beacon, it'll be real weak."

"How we gonna' know who's in there?"

"LT, I'm a dog handler, not a fuckin' mind reader. I guess we could yell at 'em and see if they know who won the '39 World Series."

"Great plan, Gianni. How long did it take ya' to come up with that one?"

"I pride myself on being quick in clutch situations."

"Yeah, quick and dead." Evans folded the map and put it back in his pocket. "We'll figure out what to do when we get there."

Gianni looked over at Smith who was listening to the conversation. "See, don't you feel better bein' in such capable hands, Laz?"

"Shee-it, looks like we's got nothin' to worry 'bout long as the LT is thinkin' this far ahead."

In less than thirty minutes Gianni raised his hand and crouched down in the bushes while he waited for Evans and Huebner to make their way up.

"What'da ya' got?" Sweat was pouring off Evans as he wiped an arm across his face.

"Lots of scents, real strong." All three men looked down at the dog sitting next to his master but with his nose stuck high, sniffing the air.

"Can you tell what it is?"

"Yeah, sure. It's people. Ours or theirs, I don't know, but it's people. I'd say they're pretty close, too. Not enough breeze to carry a scent very far and still have it be this strong. Looks like it's comin' off from our right a little," he raised his arm and pointed off through the trees.

"Okay, Geoff, hold the squad here. Smith and I will move up and see if we can spot anything." He and Smith started to slip out of their ruck-sacks when Gianni put his hand on his arm.

"LT, Laz and I can do this a lot better. You're gonna' have to go stum-bling around out there trying to find something. Shadrack will work the scent right up to where it comes from. He'll lead us right in. We can find what's out there a lot quicker than you can."

Evans glanced over at Huebner who gave a slight nod with his head. "Okay, leave your rucks here. Just find out where the scent is coming from and get back here." Gianni nodded at Evans and Huebner, then stood up.

Smith pushed himself up and stood next to him. "Okay, white boy, you ready?"

"Shit, I'm Italian remember. I was born ready. Just lead me to the woman."

With a sweeping gesture of his left arm, Smith invited Gianni and the dog to lead the way.

They made their way back through the trees. Both men pulled out their canteens, Gianni pouring some in the aluminum cup for Shadrack before he sipped any for himself.

"What'd ya' find." Evans was growing impatient, the fastmovers were due any minute now.

"You tell 'im, Gianni. I ain't lookin' to be the bearer of bad news." Smith leaned back on one elbow and took another sip from his canteen.

"We got a Gook convention, LT. They're wanderin' around everywhere. Looks like they're lookin' for our guys but they're doin' a half ass job of it." Gianni took another swallow of water. "Most of 'em are stayin' in the clearing or just inside the tree lines. They're looking around but mostly wastin' time."

"How far up?"

"Ninety, hundred yards maybe, off to the right like we thought." Smith nodded his head in agreement. "Comes right out at the end of the clearing like we hoped. Let me see the map, I'll show ya'."

Evans pulled out the map and spread it on the ground.

"Here, right here, see. Wait a minute...this map is fucked. This clearing, right here, it's three, four times the size the map shows. It's damn near as big as the Palace except it's a rectangle instead of a circle." He looked at Smith who nodded. "Here, this end right here, along the north tree line, this is where we are now, this is the north end of it and it runs south…gotta be at least six hundred yards." As Huebner listened half the mustache disappeared into his mouth. Things got worse as Gianni continued. " The west side, here, will be on our right when we're facin' the clearing. The beacon is comin' from over here, in the trees on the east side. They're at least two, two hundred and fifty yards apart. It could be real trouble, no way we can defend it. Shit, it'd take half the Palace to hold it."

Evans threw a disgusted look at Huebner then muttered a well deserved, 'fuck', to himself. "What about our guys, can you get to 'em?"

"That's another problem LT. Our tree line, the north end, it doesn't run all the way to the east side of the clearing…where the beacon is. There's about twenty, twenty-five yards of clearing. No way to get to it without crossing open ground."

"This is great, just fucking great! What about Charlie, how many?"

"There looked to be five or six of 'em sitting around smokin' right over here next to the west tree line. We spotted another group here, about fifty or sixty yards further up, to the south. They were all movin' away from us. Over here, next to where the signal is coming from, there were four more.

Evans shook his head, dragged the bush hat off and ran his right hand through his hair. "Shit! Just what we need, a fuckin' Gook on every doorstep. Anything motorized? Trucks, weapons carriers, self-propelled guns, anything like that? Maybe what you saw might be all the company we'll run into?"

"No, not a chance. Down at this end of the clearing, the south end, we saw boo coo movement. Couldn't get a clear view but we could see the tops of some heads way down here and we spotted some dust about here, in the southeast corner. Probably troops moving around. Right down here where the tree line starts, it looks like there's some thinning. Looked like a trail leading into the bush." Gianni looked back over his shoulder at Smith. "What'da ya' think, Laz?"

Smith pushed himself off his elbow and looked over at the map. "Yeah, right there, same side where our guys might be, only down at the end, in the southeast corner. We could have a problem, LT." He leaned forward and rotated the map so Evans and Huebner could get a better look at what he was talking about. "This, right here, is where the fast-movers is gonna' hit, the south end of the clearing?"

"Yeah, right in there. Why?"

Smith rubbed the side of his face, wishing he had a cigarette. "See's how that trail, starts here, at the end of the clearing, and runs off up through here? When them fastmovers hit, we be figurin' that Charlie down here, around our guys, heads up to where the shit is hittin' the fan to see's if they can help out, right? Shee-it, what happens if Charlie up here 'cides to beats feet down that trail to gets to the clearing?"

"Why would they do that? "

"'Cause theys knows our guys still be in the area, least'n they thinks they is. No ways they be havin' that many guys 'round that clearing looking for them 'ceptin' for that. When them fastmovers hit, they just might be figurin' we gonna' make a grab for 'em."

"Laz, we're here, everything's in motion, and it's too late to change the plan now. We gotta' go with what we got."

"We can change one thing. There be four fastmovers comin' in, right? What's if we call the Bronco, have 'm hold two fastmovers off station, let the other two make their runs while's we call for the chop-pers ands try to make the grab. If Charlie do try to get to the clearing, the last two fastmovers can hit 'em in here, 'long the trail. That's keeps 'em tied up in the trees. We's got Skyraiders comin' too, they keep the dudes in the clearing busy 'til the choppers set down. We load up, and back to the Palace."

Evans rubbed his chin. He stared at the map, trying to find some fault with Smith's plan that would lead to disaster. It looked good. It actually gave them better protection and a better chance of getting out.

"Geoff, what'da ya' think?"

"I think he's got a point. It's not a bad idea to keep two in reserve, especially if a shitload of 'em try to make it to the clearing. Even if they don't, that still gives us two birds plus the Skyraiders for cover. I say we do it."

Evans picked up a short piece of branch and tossed it at Boardman, motioning him to raise the Bronco.

"All right, it's no problem to hold two off station. The other two will drop on the original position and save their guns in case we need extra help. They'll be here in about ten. Choppers are waitin' about twenty klicks from here, they'll come into the area with the Skyraiders." Evans checked his watch. "All right, let's move on up to the edge of the clearing, see if we can get a better idea where our guys are before the shit hits the fan. Gianni, you and Laz lead us in. Okay, let's move it."

To the American troops in Southeast Asia, the snake was known as "The Two Step" in the mistaken belief that if you were bitten, you would only live long enough to take two steps. Unknown to most troops, the name was actually attributed to several different snakes found crawling along the ground or hanging from trees throughout the region. The snake that hung motionless in the branches just inches above Tepley was from the family of snakes known as the "Trimeresurus", commonly known as "The Pope Pit Viper", or, as American troops referred to it, "The Two Step."

The snake, normally a tree dweller, had been drawn to the area by the abundance of small frogs and lizards that feasted on the crawling and flying insects who were, in turn, feasting on Runyon and Tepley. The snake had made its way through the branches, silently dropping down closer and closer to the ground. Without so much as bending a branch or disturbing a leaf, it lay in wait, perfectly camouflaged with its green and brown striped body. Two and a half feet long and as thick as a broom stick, it was almost totally indistinguishable from the surrounding trees.

With its thin, black, fork-shaped tongue darting in and out of its mouth, the snake was perfectly willing to wait for one of the hapless frogs or lizards to wander into striking range. What the frogs and lizards instinctively knew was that the snake's venom would mean almost instant death. What the American troops didn't know was that not only was the venom not toxic enough to cause death in two steps, if given proper medical aid within a reasonable amount of time, the snake's bite was never fatal.

Gianni and Smith stopped four yards inside the tree line. Shadrack stared at the right boundary of the tree line some seventy yards away. Gianni followed his alert and watched as five NVA appeared from just inside the trees. He tapped Smith on the shoulder and pointed. Smith nodded his head and crawled back to where Evans and Huebner waited.

"We got five Gooks to our right, LT, just came outta the trees."

"What about our guys?"

Smith shook his head. "Still tryin' to spot 'em."

Evans tried to peer through the heavy cover but could see nothing more than the soles of Gianni's boots. "All right, Geoff, spread the guys out," Evans pointed out a line inside the trees. "Put Tuckett down on the end, on the right, then Robinson and Doc next to him. If most of the Gooks are on that side of the clearing, I want the gun over there."

Gianni looked over his shoulder as Evans moved up beside him. He saw the NVA troops slowly walking down the tree line, then another group farther down the clearing. The dog held his nose high in the air and tried to peer through the trees. "There's still more of 'em in there, LT." Gianni pointed to the right side of the clearing. "He's got a strong alert."

"Can you tell how many?"

"Naw, not really. Scent must be real strong 'cause he's not paying much attention to the guys in the open, looks at 'em every couple seconds but goes right back to the scent."

Evans looked out over the whole clearing. He could barely see movement down at the end near where the trees thinned out to form the trail. He turned back to the trees on the right side of the clearing, hoping that whoever was in there would come out so they'd know what they might be up against. He knew they wouldn't be able to snatch their guys and slip back into the trees. They had to find 'em while the choppers were still in the air, get 'em to the clearing and be ready for a pickup as soon as a chopper touched down. He wiped the bugs off the back of his neck before turning back to Gianni. "How we gonna' find out if they're in there?" He pointed to the trees on the left side of the clearing.

Gianni already knew what the answer was. "There's only one way, LT. I gotta' take Shad in there and look for 'em."

"We gotta' figure out another way, Gianni. You'd never be able to make it with those Gooks in the clearing. They'd cut ya' down before you got ten yards. We gotta' find another way in."

"LT, we don't have time. The F-4's are gonna' be here in a few and we gotta' be ready to move."

Evans thought about what the young Airman was saying. The F-4s didn't carry enough fuel to back off and wait. He rolled over slightly and pulled out a rock that had been digging into his hip. "Gianni, this could get real hairy and it goes way beyond what you volunteered for."

"LT, I volunteered to help find downed flyers. We haven't found these guys yet so the way I figure it, the job's not over." He looked to his left, past Evans' head and down through the trees running alongside the clearing. "When the F-4's make their run, these guys in the clearing should be distracted long enough for me to move down there to the end of the cover. That shortens the time I'll be in the clearing. Once I hit the other tree line, the wind will be in Shadrack's face, it'll only take a couple minutes to find 'em. Then we'll move up near the edge of the trees. When the choppers are overhead, I'll toss smoke out in the clearing. That'll be the signal for you to call 'em down. Then we beat feet, load up, and it's adios, motherfuckers."

"What if you can't find 'em?"

"I'll work my way back the way I went over, then wait for you to come up with another brilliant plan."

"This is gonna' be a one shot deal, Gianni. If they're not over there, we're outta' here. With 'em or without 'em, we're on the chopper."

Evans looked at his watch, then tried to scan the sky through the small breaks in the trees. "They should be on station any minute. Stay here and keep an eye out, I'm gonna' check the rest of the guys."

Gianni nodded his head and turned back to the clearing while Evans pushed himself back through the bush.

As it got hotter and muggier, the bugs got worse. With nothing to do but lie there and try to keep from moving, their minds had nothing to concentrate on but the overwhelming craving for water. Each minute of waiting was worse than the last, with no end in sight. Both men had been thinking the same thing. They had outsmarted themselves by hiding in the bush and not making a run for it the night before when they might have stood a chance of escaping in the darkness. No one was coming for them, no one was going to rescue them.

Runyon moved slightly, trying to relieve the pressure on his ribs. Tepley raised his head to look at him. The branch above him shuddered as if blown by a breeze, except there was no breeze. The branch bent back, abruptly stopped, and once again became invisible among the rest of the similar looking but motionless branches.

"You all right?"

"Yeah, just trying to get a little more comfortable, that's all. What about you?"

"Oh shit, I'm doin' great. Can't think of any place I'd rather be. Christ, we've got beautiful weather, gorgeous tropical gardens, exotic drinks, and wonderful neighbors who are dying to invite us to a party. What more could a guy ask for?"

"Gee, and to think I was worried you'd be upset with me for bringing you here. We'll have to come back on our next vacation." It wasn't much, but for a split second both men forgot about their life and death struggle.

"You slick talkin' devil, you. You always know just what to say. Next year I'll wear that little shorty flightsuit you like so much." Tepley chuckled to himself and was about to add something when the air erupted with the sound of two F-4's screaming overhead at less than 500 feet.

As the planes passed, both men heard shouts of warning coming from all around them. Branches cracked, their leaves making a whooshing sound as they snapped back to their original position as soldiers hurried through the tangled growth. Runyon and Tepley suddenly realized that it had been a trap all along. The soldiers that had spent the day carelessly searching the clearing, walking, talking, and smoking, had been nothing more than a diversion. The real searchers had been holed up in the thick jungle just like they had.

It wasn't just the two pilots they were interested in. It was whoever was coming to rescue them. They had known, known without a doubt, that unless the Americans were convinced their two pilots were dead or taken prisoner, they would make a rescue attempt. The Americans were predictable, and because they were, more of them would die. Countless times they sacrificed many to save one or two. For a country that was so powerful, a country that could so dominate the world, their people were soft with compassion. Instead of annihilation, they settled for mere punishment, and instead of military might, they hungered for words at a peace table.

Soldiers yelled at each other, giving and obeying commands. From six hundred yards away Runyon and Tepley could hear the screaming of rockets leaving their rails under the wings of the F-4's. Fireballs rose into the sky as they found their marks, slamming into trucks and ammunition carriers hidden under the jungle canopy. They could hear men crashing through the trees making for the clearing, trying to decide whether the jets were there to give the downed pilots time to run, or if they were there as a small part of something else.

Runyon raised his arm off the ground and gave Tepley a tight squeeze on the shoulder. "Looks like they didn't forget us!"

Tepley was overcome with emotion at the thought of rescue. "Please, God, please, let 'em get us out of here."

Runyon picked up the emergency radio and switched it on. Cupping his hand over the built-in microphone, he whispered into it. "Mustang One, this is Mustang One, does anybody copy, over!?"

"Mustang One, this is Corvette leader, I read you five by five. Hang in there, Mustang. Papa Rooster has come to take the little chicks home!"

Tears dropped from Runyon's cheeks and softly plopped on the ground as he stared at the radio. "Wild Bill, is that you!?" Major William "Wild Bill" Dixon grunted into his oxygen mask microphone as he pulled his aircraft up in a five G climb.

"Who'd...aaarrrgh...you expect...aaarrrgh...the Wizard...aaar-rrgh...of Oz?"

"Bill, we're in deep shit down here, there's Gooks all around us."

Dixon leveled the wings and pulled the throttles out of afterburner. "We got boo coo help for ya'. Two more F-4s waiting just off station with choppers and Spads a couple minutes out."

Runyon could still hear voices all around him, even over the noise of the explosions. "Corvette One, be advised that the choppers can't land, I repeat, the choppers can't land! This whole area is crawling with Gooks! Do you copy?"

"Roger Mustang, I copy. Be advised there is a rescue team on the ground at your location. Bronco's call sign is Daisy Mae, needs confirm on your location. Can you advise?"

The two F-4's jinked through the air, avoiding the lines of tracers that climbed up through the trees. Debris from exploding vehicles and tons of weapons and ammunition littered the sky as the pieces reached their highest altitude, then slowly fell back into the jungle. Dixon led his wingman out of range, then lined up for another pass.

"Roger, Corvette. We're in the bush, east side of a large clearing. We can't see you but it sounds like you're hitting to the south, of us. Copy?"

"Roger, Mustang. Daisy Mae has a good signal. Hang in a little while longer, the guys on the ground are gonna' come get ya'. I'll monitor, out."

Tepley had been watching Runyon as he spoke to their fellow pilot. There was no question about it now. They hadn't been forgotten. Runyon gently set the radio on the ground, then pinched the bridge of his nose with his right hand, trying to stem the flood of emotion. "Few more minutes, Tep. Few more minutes and we're outta' here." He smiled at his friend and backseater.

Tepley's entire body sagged as he sighed in relief. He was about to tell Runyon something when a small greenish frog that had been perched near his shoulder jumped at a large flying insect that had landed on the back of his neck. As the frog swallowed the black bug, its sticky feet found purchase on the sweaty grimy skin. Not concerned with being totally quiet anymore, Tepley raised his right arm and swatted at the unwelcome visitor.

The snake sensed that the frog was within range as it landed on Tepley's bare neck. Its long patient wait was about to be rewarded. The strike was quick, silent, and off its mark. Tepley's finger's brushed against the frog, causing it to jump off his neck just as the snake expected to sink his fangs into the small greenish body. The snake missed his intended prey and buried his needle like fangs into the fleshy hollow of Tepley's neck. The snake recoiled just as Tepley's hand slid down and grabbed at the stinging bite.

"OH, FUCK!! What the hell…." Before Tepley could finish getting the rest of the words out of his mouth, the snake struck again with a viciousness that was lacking in the first attack. He felt the thump just above his wrist and thought it was nothing more than a branch. Even when he brought his arm around to the front of his face, he still thought it was a green branch stuck in the fabric of his flightsuit. The thought stayed with him until the end of the branch began to shake itself trying to draw its fangs out of the material. The rest of the branch lost its wood-like appearance and wrapped its full two and a half feet around his arm. The scream of terror was unlike anything Runyon had ever heard.

Gianni watched as the jets made their first bombing run before starting down the tree line to the point where he had planned to make his dash into the clearing. He was crouched in the trees when the scream seemed to drown out the deep rumbling of the bombs. He froze, not comprehending what he had heard. He turned his head and noticed the dog staring at the thick tree line only twenty yards from where he crouched. The dog's ears stood straight up, his head tilted in puzzlement as anguished pleas of help poured from the jungle.

"OOOOOOOHHHH, GOD!! GET IT OFFFFFF!! GET IT OFF MEEEEE!!" Tepley shook his arm violently, the snake wrapped tighter and tighter around his arm. Its head jerked back in an attempt to free its fangs from the tight weave of the flightsuit fabric. Runyon grabbed at his friend, reaching for the knife attached to his survival vest. As Runyon pulled at his body, Tepley sank even deeper into panic. Runyon grabbed for his vest harness as Tepley jumped to his feet, shaking his arm out to his side and pleading for help. He thrashed around, slamming his arm against branches and trees, trying to rid himself of his greatest nightmare. "OH, GOD!! GODDDDDD!!! DAVID, HELP MEEEEE!!! PLEASE HELP MEEEEE!!"

As Runyon pushed himself to his feet, grabbing at his chest to stem the sudden stab of pain from his broken ribs, Tepley blindly started to run through the thick cover. Crashing into trees, tripping over creeping vines, and slashing his skin on thorns and branches, he ran directly for the clearing.

Four of the NVA soldiers, crouched on the other side of the clearing, watching the jets make their bombing runs, fell to the ground and trained their rifles on the sounds of Tepley's screams. As the voice pleading for help echoed through the air, more and more soldiers headed back toward the end of the clearing.

Gianni flattened himself on the ground behind the trunk of a tree, silently commanding Shadrack to do the same. He watched as one of the four soldiers pointed at the tree line across the clearing and shouted something. Over the screams of the thrashing man, another voice could be heard pleading with him to stop and get down. Gianni looked down through the trees hoping to spot Evans or one of the other squad members coming to tell him what to do.

As he turned back to the tree line, a man dressed in the flightsuit of an American pilot burst out of the bush. His sudden acceleration of speed after breaking through the tangled brush caused him to stumble and fall forward. As he tried to push himself up from the ground, Gianni could see that his right arm was three or four times bigger than it should have been. The man got to his knees, shaking his arm violently. As he rose to one foot, Gianni noticed that the arm of his flightsuit was a brighter green than the rest of it.

In an explosion of horror, he realized it wasn't the fabric that was a different color, but a snake coiled around the man's arm, all the way up to his elbow. An overwhelming feeling of revulsion surged through his body as the man got up to both feet, screaming for help, and unknowingly running to his death.

The man's path was that of a broken field runner, two or three steps to the right or left for every two or three steps forward. The further he ran, the more uncertain his path became, degenerating to the point where he resembled a stumbling drunk. His screams, not lessening in urgency and panic was suddenly drowned out by a barrage of gunfire. The ground around his feet erupted as bullets dug into the dry earth, sending up geysers of dirt, rock and grass.

Oblivious to the shower of death falling all around him, the panicked man continued to stumble forward, still shaking his right arm and slashing at the bleeding and dying snake with the knife that he now held in his left hand. As his hand rose into the air and started back down with the sharpened blade glistening in the sun, a volley of AK-47 bullets slammed into him, piercing flesh and shattering bone. His body had barely hit the ground when Evans, enraged at the sight, fired a long burst at the four closest soldiers.

Runyon had been chasing Tepley when he stopped suddenly, realizing that the clearing lay only feet ahead of him. He heard the sound of a single M-16 being fired from the trees to his right, instantly joined by the sound of a machine gun. As he pushed himself to his feet, his eyes followed a line of tracers coming from the hidden machine gun, tearing up the ground as the bullets made their way to the face of one of the enemy soldiers lying less than two hundred yards away. His mind wasn't prepared for what he saw as the heavy bullets tore into the man's face, exploding the head as if it were nothing more than a raw egg. Runyon froze in his half upright stance as the air around the man filled with pulverized pieces of skull and brain, turned red by vaporized blood. As the soldier's headless body was thrown back it rolled over and settled against the soldier next to him.

Smith sighted along his rifle barrel and fired three quick rounds at a soldier who had flung himself to the ground. The first round dug into the dirt just in front of his knee, with the second shot hitting several inches away. The third shot, however, slammed into the man's ankle, blowing away the top of the boot and most of the foot. Driven by pain and the horror of seeing the mangled foot, the soldier reached for it

with his left hand. The thought of mercy never entered Smith's mind as
he fired three more rounds, sending the bullets through the back of the
man's neck.

Not knowing what to do, Gianni had started to make his way
through the trees toward the squad when a movement to his left caught
his eye. He threw himself down, spun his rifle to the left and tightened
his finger on the trigger. As his sight picture became clear, he jerked the
rifle barrel up into the air, unable to stop the trigger squeeze quick
enough. The bullet sailed over and behind the running figure. Instantly
the ground around the second American exploded with impacting
bullets. Gianni pushed himself to his feet, switched his selector to
automatic, and fired a long burst at the source of the fire.

"GET DOWN!! DOWN, DOWN, GET DOWN!!!", Gianni
screamed at the pilot. A grenade flew from inside the tree line. Dirt,
grass, and rocks filled the air but the enemy soldiers' fire continued.
More soldiers from the far end of the clearing had arrived. Reluctant
to get too close to the squad's deadly fire, they threw themselves to the
ground, splitting their attention between the running American and
those hiding in the trees.

Gianni took careful aim at a soldier who was foolish enough to raise
up on both his knees for a better shot. Three bullets tore into the man's
chest just below the neck. With his finger still pulling the trigger, a
stream of AK-47 bullets ripped through the sky as the man toppled over
on to his back.

Gianni turned back to the pilot who had stumbled and was trying
to regain his footing. Gianni heard him screaming a man's name and
tried to out-shout him. "STAY DOWN! GODDAMNIT, STAY DOWN,
WE'LL GET YOU OUT OF THERE!!" The man paid no attention,
pushed himself back to his feet, and without even trying to avoid the
flying bullets, ran for his friend. Ten yards away from where Tepley lay,
the man grabbed for his left leg while doing a complete somersault in
mid-air, then landed on his chest. Blood seeped from the hole in his

left thigh, a dark red circle steadily growing larger against the green of the flightsuit.

The pilot pressed the palm of his hand over the wound, then started to drag himself toward his friend, pulling at clumps of brown weeds or half-buried rocks. Dirt erupting into the air marked the spots where bullets had missed their mark. Gianni stared as the man pulled himself forward, crying his friend's name.

What force drives a man that he would hurl himself into almost certain death? What is it that makes him ignore his own safety, his own survival, and crawl forward until his last breath escapes his lungs and his last drop of blood falls to the ground? 'There is no greater love than that of a man who will lay down his life for another'. Gianni had heard it, or read it, or perhaps both, in school. At the time he had shrugged it off as so much drivel. Now he knew that the man crawling across the dry earth in front of him was proof of the overwhelming truth in those words.

He jerked to the right as two more grenades sailed out of the trees and exploded short of their mark. Robinson's big gun kept up a constant stream of fire, its tracers ricocheting off the ground in front of the enemy soldiers and flying into the jungle behind them. Two soldiers were close to the crawling pilot and were, at the moment, his greatest threat.

As the dirt settled from the grenade explosions, both soldiers returned fire into the tree line. One of the soldiers turned and waved his right arm at the men to his right. He watched them push themselves up into a crouch and run forward as the line of fire shifted in their direction. Now was his chance. Without bullets flying over his head or crashing into the ground around him, he could kill the pilot in the clearing. He switched the selector on his AK-47 to semiautomatic and raised up slightly on his elbows. The crawling man made a small target but one careful shot would be all that was needed.

The single shot dug into the ground just in front of Runyon's face, kicking up dirt, grass, and razor sharp pieces of rock. Runyon thought he had been shot again as his head was thrown back, the pain piercing to the center of his brain, forcing the scream from his mouth. The soldier raised himself slightly higher at the sound of the scream and looked out at the man clutching his head and rolling in agony. He smiled slightly to himself. It was better that the arrogant American suffer before he died. He settled back down on his elbows, took a deep breath, and sighted down the barrel of his rifle.

Gianni turned at the sound of the scream and saw Runyon rolling on the ground, his face and head wrapped with bloody arms. As the anger built at seeing the wounded American, the voice once again filled his head. *The closest threat, Gianni! Neutralize the nearest threat!!*' The shot had come from one of the two soldiers a hundred yards in front of the pilot.

Gianni saw one of the men raise up on his elbows and stare at the pilot. He pulled the rifle snug into his shoulder, let out a breath, and squeezed the trigger. He had aimed for the center of the man's face, knowing that if he was off two or three inches in either direction it wouldn't matter. The shot struck high, just below the brim of the man's helmet. The bullet's impact sent the helmet flying, with the top of the man's head still inside. His body, already leaning over the rifle, merely fell forward and lay still.

Giving a command to the dog, he started to work his way down to the squad, then glanced one more time at Runyon still, holding his head and face, rolling in agony. He looked back down through the trees at the sounds of his friends yelling out warnings of new targets. Without thinking, he pushed through the heavy brush and ran toward the American in the clearing.

Boardman was trying to talk to the Bronco and fire his rifle at the same time. Clouds of blue smoke from the constant barrage hung heavy in the air as men fired volley after volley, each rifle silenced for a split second as a fresh magazine was slammed home. Robinson's M-60 spit lines of tracers, stopping only to shift to new targets. Boardman crawled to Evans, screaming to get his attention over the din of the firing. He thrust the handset at the Lieutenant and pulled a new magazine out of his bandoleer. The conversation took only seconds. Evans nodded his head several times, looked up at the sky, shook his head violently back and forth, screamed a string of obscenities into the handset, then tossed it on the ground. He moved closer to Huebner. "We're gettin' out!!"

"What!!?"

Evans threw his arm over his head as bullets tore at the tree trunk above him sending splinters of wood down on both men. "They're pullin' us out! Gooks are headin' here from every direction! They're all around us!!" He held his arm out and pointed down to the end of the clearing. "Down at the corner, on the trail, there's more than a hundred of 'em headed this way."

Huebner craned his neck trying to see if any of them had made it to the clearing when a movement to his left caught his eye. "OH, FUCK! GIANNI! NO! NO! GET BACK, GET BACK! Huebner was screaming at the top of his lungs. He started to push himself up when Evans grabbed the back of his rucksack and pulled him down.

"Stay down, Goddamnit! Just fuckin' stay put!!"

"WE GOTTA' GET 'IM, WE GOTTA' GET 'IM OUTTA' THERE!!" Huebner tried to slip out of the rucksack but Evans grabbed hold of the ammo carrier harness and kept him pinned to the ground.

"Geoff, listen, listen!! We can't help him out there! We gotta' wait for the choppers!" Evans tried to yell over the thunderous noise of the firing. "BOARDMAN! BOARDMAN! RADIO!!" AK-47 bullets tore through the branches above them, peppering their hands with wood splinters and shredded leaves. Evans pulled the handset up to his face and shouted into the receiver. Huebner kept up his fire as Evans talked to the Bronco pilot. Dozens of NVA soldiers were making their way from the far end of the clearing and Huebner knew that without air support, Gianni wouldn't be the only one that would take his last breath in the Cambodian jungle.

Evans shook his head violently up and down and screamed into the handset, than tossed it back to Boardman. He pushed a fresh magazine into his rifle, then looked down through the trees at the rest of the squad. "Aircraft comin' in now. Keep your head down!"

Huebner watched Gianni as he stumbled, falling hard on his chest as the ground around him was torn up with bullets. The dog, trailing his leash behind him, stayed within three feet of his master. Gianni was twenty yards from the pilot.

Huebner started to get up again, only to be pulled back down by Evans. Two F-4's passed over their heads, the noise from the big engines drowning out the sound of the firing. The dirt in the clearing exploded into hundreds of geysers as twenty-millimeter rounds tore at the hapless soldiers. Men threw themselves sideways or simply covered their heads with their arms in an attempt to avoid the huge rounds. The firing from the jets stopped suddenly as rockets slashed from beneath their wings, white smoke and flames trailing as they exploded into the ground at the far end of the clearing.

As the jets flew over the end of the clearing, Huebner looked back to where Gianni had fallen. Gianni was up to one knee, looking at the turning jets, then back to his right as a new sound took their place. Two Cobra gunships dropped in low over the trees, their turret mounted mini-guns pouring rounds at the soldiers in the clearing. AK-47's fired toward the sky, creating a deadly gauntlet. Pieces of thin aluminum skin flew off as bullets tore at the lead helicopter.

Gianni started to get to both feet, then looked up again as the air was filled with the WHUMP WHUMP WHUMP of forty millimeter grenades leaving the launcher tubes and exploding along the length of the clearing. Soldiers poured from the tree lines. Jumping over dead and dying comrades, running forward, trying to get to the Americans in the trees. Wounded men, covered in blood, or dazed from grenade and rocket explosions, dragged themselves forward, stopping long enough to awkwardly change magazines or take ammunition from a shattered body that had no further use of it.

Gianni spun back at the wounded pilot, no longer rolling on the ground but still clutching his face and crying his friend's name. A dozen or more soldiers, taking advantage of the lull in the firing as the Cobras reached the end of the clearing, rose up and charged toward Gianni and Runyon. Staying on one knee, he aimed and fired twice. The soldier closest to him fell in a heap, his rifle chattering across the dry ground. Gianni shifted his aim to the next closest threat and was about to pull the trigger when his target's chest suddenly exploded in a mass of blood and torn flesh. M-60 tracers filled the air as two more soldiers, caught in Robinson's murderous fire, writhed in pain as the life quickly seeped out of their bodies. Fire from the squad made quick work of the rest of the men.

Gianni jumped to his feet and ran to where Runyon lay bleeding. "EASY, SIR! TAKE IT EASY, I'M GONNA' TRY AND GET YOU OUTTA' HERE!!" Gianni picked a threat and fired at it. Pieces of skull flying in the air told him the threat was neutralized. He put his left hand on the pilot's arm and gripped it slightly, trying to figure out what he was going to do next. "Hang in there, sir, just hang in there! Where are you hit, how bad is it!?"

"OH, GOD! I can't see, I can't see anything, I think I'm blind!! OH, GOD!! My leg, I'm hit in the leg too! The left leg!! God, it hurts!!"

Gianni's mind was racing. Their only chance was to stay where they were and hope the chopper could land close enough to drag the pilot to it. "It's all right, sir! You're gonna' be all right! We've got choppers comin' for us. One of 'em will land right here, we'll get you on, don't worry, don't worry."

Gianni fired off the remaining rounds in his magazine and snapped in a fresh one. He looked across the barren ground at what seemed like hundreds of enemy soldiers trying to get closer. He didn't see how in the hell they were going to live through the hail of fire. Either a chopper had to land now or they had to make it to the trees before they were shot to pieces. He was still trying to figure out what to do when a loud WHOOSH passed over his head and exploded less then forty yards behind them. Shadrack yelped in pain as rocks and dirt rained down.

"OH, GOD!! What was that!? What was that!?" Runyon was starting to panic. Out of his element, and unable to see, his mind could only imagine the worst.

"It was a grenade launcher. It came from the tree line in front of us!" Gianni aimed at where he thought the rocket had come from and fired a full magazine, hoping to keep it from firing again. His hopes were short lived as the smoking trail of another rocket sailed through the air, passing well over their heads and exploding in the trees behind them.

"Goddamnit! We gotta' let the air cover know where that motherfucker is!" Gianni was thinking that he'd give anything he had if he had some way to talk to them when he remembered the rescue beacon. "The beacon, your emergency beacon, doesn't that have a radio built into it!?"

"Yeah, yeah it does." Runyon grunted out the words through his pain.

"Can I talk to the Bronco or the jets!?"

"Yeah, sure," He groaned as another wave of pain racked his body. Even though his bleeding had slowed, he had already lost a lot of blood and was on the verge of going into shock.

"Stay with me, stay with me, I need your help!" Bullets crashed into the ground next to Gianni and a piece of rock tore into the top of his shoulder. He let out a quick cry of pain as he grabbed for the stinging wound.

"Oh, God, are you hit, are you all right!?" Runyon started to panic at the thought of being out there all alone again.

"I'm all right! I just got nicked, that's all." Gianni leaned over the pilot, running his hands over his survival vest looking for the emergency radio. "The beacon! Where's the beacon, I can't find it! Where's the fuckin' beacon!?"

Runyon' voice was weak with hopelessness. "It's in the trees. I forgot it back in the trees."

"Shit!!"

"I'm sorry, God, I'm sorry." Runyon sounded like a small child apologizing for dropping ink on a priceless carpet.

"It's all right, it's all right, I probably couldn't figure out how to use it anyway." Gianni knew it wasn't all right and it wouldn't be long until the gunner found the range and put a rocket right on them. He looked at the dog lying near his feet, then reached down and unhooked the leash. "You're gonna' have to take care of yourself, Shad. It looks like the shit is gonna' get real deep."

"What!? What'd you say? Who's Shad? Is there somebody else here? Who else is here? Runyon's body slumped, exhausted from asking the questions.

"No...no, no one else is here...it's just my dog."

Runyon turned his head toward the voice. "Your dog...you're...you're the Air Force dog handler we heard about." Tears flowed down his cheeks, not entirely from the pain. " Oh Jesus, you really did come for us!"

Gianni looked up as the ground around them shattered under the onslaught of bullets. More and more soldiers broke through the tree line. The Cobras were completing another pass, firing rockets and spraying troops with mini-gun fire. Bodies, both wounded and dead, littered the open ground, but more and more rushed in to take their place.

The two F-4's came in low, firing the last of their rockets into the clearing, then dropping four tanks of napalm at the edge of the trail. The smell of burning gasoline filled the air and a thin smile spread over Runyon's lips. "We may not live through this but they're sure as hell gonna' know we were here."

Another rocket grenade exploded in front of them. Gianni threw himself over the wounded pilot's body, covering him from the falling debris. "Fuck! This guy is gonna' have us pegged pretty soon." He looked over his shoulder at the trees Runyon had been hiding in. Even if he made it, he'd never be able to find the radio.

"Frank."

"What?" Gianni leaned closer to hear what he was saying.

"Frank, Frank Tepley, my Wizzo, out there," Runyon lifted a hand off his bloody face and pointed behind his head, "Frank still has his radio." Gianni looked at the body laying twenty yards away. The dead, sightless eyes stared back at him.

Schoonhoven was attaching another belt to the quickly disappearing one that was being eaten up by Robinson's gun. He saw Gianni out of the corner of his eye and shouted a warning. "Gianni's moving, Gianni's moving!!"

Each man saw the him start to run forward, lose his balance, then get up and run again. The ground exploded around his feet. Robinson held back on the trigger as empty brass kicked out the right side of the gun. Halfway down the clearing, two of the F-4's opened up with their nose guns, tearing apart soldiers that were still too far away to be any real threat.

As Gianni threw himself to the ground behind Tepley's body, he slid into the arm with the snake. A sudden shiver of revulsion swept through him. Bullets slammed into the ground around him and tore at the air over his head. A new sound hit his ears as rounds started to impact into the Wizzo's body. Pieces of flesh tore off as the bullets wasted their energy on an already dead man. Wiping away the gore, Gianni reached over the body and groped for the radio. Two bullets tore into it causing the chest to heave as if taking a deep breath. Gianni grabbed the radio and pulled it out of the pouch, hoping that it was still in one piece. The fire intensified, pieces of flesh shredded from the body as bullets searched for a live target.

Shadrack started to stand as he saw his master running toward him but dropped back to the ground at the shout of "DOWN, DOWN!". Gianni threw himself headfirst to the ground, then crawled the last few feet.

His heart was pounding as he gasped, trying to suck in a breath. The sudden WHOOSHING sound caught him by surprise and he barely had time to cover Runyon before the rocket exploded less than twenty yards away. Shrapnel screamed over their heads as dirt and pieces of rock half-buried them. Gianni felt the sudden sting as a piece of hot metal sliced through the flesh above his ear. As he dragged himself off the pilot, spitting out dirt and grime, blood ran down the right side of his face, mixing with the dust and sweat.

"How the fuck you use this thing!?" He flipped one of the switches and heard a sudden screech of static. Runyon perked up at the sound.

"Here, let me have it. Give it to me."

Gianni, glad to get rid of the radio so he could have both hands free, handed it over. "Raise somebody so we can give 'em some fire direction! Make it quick, we're runnin' outta' time." Gianni squeezed the trigger repeatedly at the trees where the rockets had been fired. He had to keep the gunner from firing again.

"Corvette Leader, this is Mustang One. Corvette Leader this is Mustang One, do you copy?"

Gianni couldn't help but look over at the wounded pilot. Seconds ago he could barely talk. Now, as he tried to raise his fellow pilot, back in his own element, his voice was strong and confident. He sounded more like an executive ordering lunch than a man who was almost certainly about to die. He saw a slight smile form on the pain ridden face as the pilot in the F-4 acknowledge the call.

"Hey, Wild Bill, we got a problem down here. Some Gook is takin' pot shots at us with a...wait a minute," Runyon turned his head towards Gianni, "what'd ya' call it?"

"A B-40!! A fuckin' B-40 rocket launcher!!" Gianni dropped his head in exasperation and shouted into the dirt. "Forget its Goddamn name!! Just get him to kill the fuckin' thing!!"

"Yeah, right. Ah, Bill, we got a Gook down here shootin' a B-40 rocket launcher at us. Nasty piece of ordnance, don't you know, blows the shit outta' everything. You think maybe you could contact Daisy Mae and have one of those Cobras do a tap dance on his head?"

"Roger that, Mustang, wait one."

Gianni sighted at a soldier running forward. He missed with the first shot and hit him with two more shots through the pelvis. He fell screaming in pain. The words rang through his mind. *'Never hurt an enemy just a little. Stay with your target 'til it's neutralized.'* He sighted down the barrel, started to pull the trigger, then stopped. He was going through ammunition at an alarming rate and the last thing the wounded soldier was thinking about was finding his rifle and getting back into the fight. Rather than shooting the man again, he shot the man who was bending down to check on his friend.

As he looked over the clearing, he saw two slicks flying over the jungle a a mile away. Several hundred yards behind the slicks was a larger, slower, Jolly Green Giant. Gianni's hope of rescue was distracted as a lone Cobra came in low and fast, firing rockets at the clearing and strafing the ground with its mini-gun. As enemy guns raised up to track the helicopter, a second Cobra dove in behind it, pumping out forty-millimeter grenades and spraying hundreds of rounds of machine-gun fire. Gianni watched as bodies and pieces of bodies were thrown into the air or driven flat against the ground. The fire from the squad in the trees to his right slackened for a moment, then resumed with all its fury.

"Mustang One, this is Corvette Leader. Got a little surprise for you but we're gonna' need the target marked."

"Roger Corvette, wait one." Runyon laid the radio on his chest and used his hand to wipe off some of the blood running down his cheeks.

He rolled his head to the left so Gianni could hear him better. "They need the target marked."

"WHAAAT!?"

"The target, the target, they need it marked for a run!"

"Jesus Christ, you Air Force guys really are a pain in the ass! What do they want me to do, ask the Gook to wave a red flag!?" Gianni sighted at a wounded man who was trying to get a machine gun in action. He squeezed the trigger just as a line of Robinson's tracers slammed into the man's side, throwing him away from the gun. Gianni let out a deep sigh and mumbled to himself. "Shit, that was a wasted fuckin' round."

He looked up to where the rocket grenades had been coming from and saw movement. He fired four rounds at the trees when the bolt locked back on an empty magazine. "SHIT!" He fumbled for a fresh magazine in the bandoleer slung over his chest.

"What's goin' on, we need to mark the target!"

"All right, all right! Listen, tell 'em I'm gonna' throw smoke in the direction of the launcher. Have 'em hit the tree line west of the smoke. You got that?"

"Yeah, no problem."

"Okay, popping red smoke now!" Gianni pulled a smoke grenade off his ammo harness and threw it in the direction of the trees. The grenade hit the dirt, made a popping sound then started to billow out thick red smoke.

"Corvette leader, this is Mustang. Red smoke on the ground. Target is west of smoke in the tree line. Copy?"

"Roger, Mustang. West of smoke, in the trees. Keep your heads down!"

Gianni tried to see through the cloud of smoke that spread out low over the ground. A new sound caught his attention and he quickly looked up and to his right. A Skyraider dove in low, fifty caliber machine gun rounds tearing into the trees, blowing branches and leaves into the air. Rockets leapt out from under each wing, streaking down and exploding inside the tree line. Small, secondary explosions erupted just inside the trees. Gianni watched, recoiling in horror, as a soldier stumbled from the thick brush totally engulfed in flames. Pieces of flaming uniform dropped to the ground as it burnt off the man, setting the dried grass on fire. Nerve shattering screams were suddenly choked off as the soldier crumpled to the ground, the grateful recipient of dozens of AK-47 rounds administered by horrified, and well-meaning comrades.

The Skyraider completed its turn, then lined up for a second run. Flying fifty yards inside the tree line, the plane released its canisters of napalm. Thick black smoke highlighted by a huge sheet of yellow flame rose above the trees. Agonizing screams penetrated the noise of gunfire and roaring aircraft engines as burned and wounded soldiers dragged themselves out of the trees.

The ground beside Runyon suddenly exploded into dozens of small geysers. Gianni jerked his head to the left and dropped down close to the ground. "What the fuck!!? Jesus Christ!! Call your guys! Call your guys! They're movin' on us, they're comin' in!!" Dozens of soldiers were up and running across the clearing, using the bombing run to get closer to the two Americans. The crack of bullets was deafening as they flew inches over the two men and the dog. Shadrack barked his rage as clumps of dirt jumped and jerked as rounds dug into it, leaving gouges and torn trails in the ground.

"Corvette Leader, Mustang One, Mayday! Mayday! Mayday!! We got Gooks headin' for us! Can't hold 'em, they're comin' across the clearing. We need cover!!"

"Stand by, Mustang!"

Within seconds, two Cobras dove for the clearing, coming over the trees that were still on fire. The choppers flew side by side, mini-guns spitting bullets, tearing up dirt and bodies alike. Rallied by the courage of their comrades facing death, dozens of other soldiers pushed themselves up and followed the charge. Tripping over dead and dying friends, men pushed themselves back to their feet and fired their rifles from the hip. The Cobras flew the width of the clearing, stood on their tail rotors, turned quickly and made another pass. Both choppers spewed out grenades, the lead aircraft firing his last one less than a second before his wingman.

Gianni fired short bursts, trying to force the still advancing soldiers back to the ground. When he saw the last of the Cobra's grenades hit the ground and explode, he realized they either had to try to make it to the trees or die where they were. "We're going back to the trees!! We gotta' try to make it to the trees!!"

Runyon shook his head back and forth, the sudden burst of pain taking him by surprise. "I can't make it, I can't walk!" He pulled his right hand away from his face, reached across his chest and pulled his revolver out of its shoulder holster. For the first, time Gianni saw the jagged gash on the pilot's forehead. Dirt, pebbles and blood filled both his eye sockets and was starting to dry into a hard mess. "You go! Take the dog and go!!"

Gianni fired off three more quick shots. "No way, I didn't come all the way out here 'cause I was bored! We're both gettin' the fuck outta' here!"

Runyon dropped the radio and grabbed Gianni's shirt sleeve. "Listen to me! I can't walk…I can't see! I wouldn't make it two feet. Now, take your dog and get the hell out of here!!"

Gianni picked the radio up out of the dirt and yelled into the microphone. "Corvette Leader, Corvette Leader, Mayday! Mayday!, come in, come in!!"

"This is Corvette Leader, identify yourself."

"Corvette Leader, this is Mustang One!"

"Go, Mustang. Where's Colonel Runyon!? What happened to Colonel Runyon?"

"He's here, he's all right, but not for long! We need cover! We gotta' head for the trees, we got Gooks comin' up on us! We're gonna' head for the trees, east, east of where the smoke was!"

"Roger, Mustang! Get out of there now or they'll be too close for us to help you!!"

Gianni stuck the radio into his shirt and pushed himself up to his knees, trying to stay as low as possible. He grabbed the front of the wounded man's flightsuit, pulled him up to a sitting position, then drove his shoulder into the man's stomach. Runyon gasped in pain as Gianni heaved him farther over his shoulder and struggled to push himself to his feet. The roar of jet engines was deafening as the two standby jets joined the fight and dove in, one after the other, strafing the clearing with their twenty millimeter cannons. Screams and cries of agony filled the air as once again living, breathing, human beings were instantly turned into heaps of mangled flesh and bones.

Behind the F-4's came the Skyraiders. Hundreds of fifty caliber bullets streaked through the North Vietnamese soldiers as they ran, crawled, and shot at the two Americans. Gianni pushed himself to his feet, holding his rifle in his right hand as he tried to balance the heavy pilot over his left shoulder. He looked down at the dog, shouted "HEEL", then shakily started to run.

Smith had just kicked out an empty magazine and was reaching for another when he spotted the movement. "Gianni's up! Gianni's up! Cover 'em!!" He pushed in the full magazine and shifted his fire with the rest of the squad at the mass of men making their way across the clearing. Dirt kicked up around Gianni and the dog. He lost his balance, started to fall forward, then threw himself to the right. Runyon landed hard on him, tearing open the wound on his shoulder even further. Gianni felt the warm torrent of blood running down his arm.

"Please, leave me here, get to the trees! The both of us can't make it!"

Gianni pushed himself up to both knees, then straightened his legs with a grunt. "I thought you fighter jocks were supposed to be small wiry guys? You ought'a' drive a tank instead of a fuckin' jet!" He hefted the wounded man, wincing at the strain while trying to keep his balance, and headed for the trees.

Boardman grabbed Evans by the arm and shook it violently. He jabbed the handset at him and yelled over the noise of the gun fire. "Deep shit, LT, really deep shit!"

Evans snatched the receiver and shouted into it. While he was listening to the Bronco, he turned over his shoulder and tried to peer through the trees behind him. Shaking his head, he looked down the tree line at the rest of the squad, then back out to the clearing. More and more soldiers poured out of the trees, screaming as they ran across the open ground.

What had been total chaos now seemed to take on a definite plan. Most of the men raced for positions that would concentrate their fire on Evans and the squad. The rest of them continued their pursuit of Gianni and the wounded pilot, trying to stop them before they reached the trees. Smaller groups of men entered the trees farther down the clearing in an attempt to cut off the two Americans and the dog in case they did make it out of the clearing.

Evans shook his head up and down as he shouted into the handset one last time, then tossed it back to Boardman. He pulled a smoke grenade off his harness, then leaned closer to Huebner. "We gotta' DI DI now!!?"

Huebner pulled the trigger twice more even though he had turned to look at Evans in amazement. "What!? What'da ya' mean DI DI? Gianni's still out there! We gotta' get him!"

"I know it, Goddamnit! I know he's out there! We got Gooks movin' up behind us. Daisy Mae spotted 'em through the trees. We won't be able to hold 'em off, Geoff, and the air cover is runnin' out of fuel and ammo. We gotta' go now or we never go! If we're not outta' here in the next three minutes, we're all gonna' die! Every fuckin' one of us! Now you get your ass down the line and tell the men that air cover is gonna' make one last pass and when the chopper hits the ground, every swingin' dick better be gettin' on it! You got me, Sergeant!!?"

For a moment Huebner glared at Evans, then his gaze softened. He knew if he were in charge, he'd have to give the same order. They couldn't get everyone killed in a hopeless display of loyalty. Evans' responsibility was to get his men out alive, as many as he could. His voice was almost a whisper and Evans could barely hear it.

"They'll be ready to go. Just give the word." He pushed his rucksack aside and headed down the trees to the rest of the men. Ignoring his rifle that lay on the ground just in front of his face, Evans rested his forehead on top of his hand and squeezed his eyes tight. As his body trembled, tears seeped out and fell softly to the dirt. Moments passed until he raised his head and turned to look at the rest of the men. Faces stared back at him, faces that showed anger, disbelief, and understanding, all at the same time. Still clutching the smoke grenade, he wiped his face with the back of his hand, pulled the pin, then picked up his rifle and waited.

The noise was deafening, and caught off guard, Gianni fell forward just yards from the trees as the jets came in again. They dropped down from over the tree line where the squad lay in wait. Flying four abreast, their wing tips almost overlapping, they let loose with a devastating barrage of cannon fire. The Skyraiders pulled in behind them in an attempt to clear an area for the helicopter to land.

Gianni glanced over his shoulder at the carnage, then grabbed Runyon by the collar of the flight suit and dragged him the rest of the way into the trees. Falling down, exhausted, and amazed they were still alive, Gianni struggled to catch his breath as he peered out through the branches at the clearing. Three soldiers were still running at the spot where Gianni had entered the trees, somehow avoiding the hail of bullets that fell around them. Gianni threw his rifle up to his shoulder and fired a long burst. All three men went down in a tangle of twisted arms and legs. Movement caught Gianni's attention and he watched an object sail through the air out of the trees. A moment later thick yellow smoke lifted into the air.

"They're callin' in a chopper. They just popped smoke in the clearing."

"Oh, God! How the hell are we supposed to get back out there?"

"We're not. There's no way we'd make it through that again."

"That's it, then, huh? I'm sorry I got you into this. God I'm sorry."

Gianni turned to Runyon. "Game ain't over yet. We've still got a chance."

"How? You just said we'd never make it out there."

"Not out there…back farther in the bush."

"Back in the bush! Are you crazy!? They can't land a chopper in the bush!"

Gianni pushed himself to his feet. "Come on, let me help you up so we can get the hell out of here." He reached down and grabbed Runyon by his vest harness and gave a tug. He started to lean over to carry the man when Runyon pushed away from him.

"No, wait. There's no way you can carry me through these trees. Let me see if I can walk."

"All right, lean on me, I'll guide you."

Gianni moved around to Runyon's right side, letting the pilot put most of his weight on him. He shifted his rifle to his right hand and took a couple of slow steps. "You gonna' be able to make it?"

"Yeah, yeah, I think so. Let's keep going."

The Skyraiders dove on the clearing, crisscrossing the open ground and providing a deadly curtain of protection with their machine guns. The slick raced in and flared to a landing inside their protective perimeter. Before the skids had even settled in the dirt, Evans and the squad had broken through the trees and were racing for their salvation. Schoonhoven had clipped another full belt of ammo to the M-60 and Robinson ran with the belt hanging over his outstretched left arm while he fired the big gun from the hip. Tracers streaked out across the clearing, tearing at bodies, both alive and dead.

As they got closer to the waiting chopper, Tuckett and Smith threw grenades to the sides, then followed them with long bursts of automatic fire. Neither man noticed as pieces of shrapnel flew back at them, slicing open flesh and turning their green fatigue fabric red with blood. The door gunners screamed encouragement as they swept their own M-60's back and forth. Hundreds of spent machine gun casings clattered to the deck of the helicopter and spilled out onto the ground. The pilot and co-pilot, staring at the running men through the Plexiglas windshield, waved frantically, urging them on in hopes of lifting off before the aircraft was shot to pieces. The men ran hard, knowing their lives depended on it. Evans and Huebner were the last. The rest of the squad, crouching on the deck of the helicopter or standing out on the skids, joined the two door gunners firing into the clearing and surrounding trees. The white smoky trail of a B-40 rocket flew across the ground, exploding just behind the tail rotor. Shrapnel, dirt and rocks peppered the aluminum skin and rocked the aircraft back and forth. Spotting the rocket launcher team less than two hundred yards from the slick, a Skyraider pilot dove hard and shredded the men with his wing guns. Three separate explosions bore proof that the bullets had tore into more than flesh and bone.

As Evans and Huebner ran for the helicopter, the door gunner screamed into his helmet microphone at the pilot.

"Get ready, they're almost here!!"

"Goddamnit, get 'em on!! We gotta' go, we gotta' go!!" The windshield shattered as bullets passed through it and tore at the padded bulkhead behind the co-pilot's head. Blood ran down his face and neck as pieces of Plexiglas sliced into him. The pilot turned in horror as his partner threw both hands up to his face, blood seeping through the fingers of his gloved hands. He pressed the intercom button connected to his gunners. "We're outta' here now!! We're going!!"

The right side door gunner continued to fire his pole mounted machine gun. "No, wait, wait! They're almost here! Couple seconds, couple seconds!" The pilot increased power and RPMs, ready to lift off as soon as the two men hit the skids.

Less than ten yards from the side of the helicopter Evans screamed and tumbled forward to the ground. What remained of his rifle clattered off to his right as razor sharp pieces of the plastic stock sliced into his forearm. Huebner, managing to keep his feet, reached over to help his Lieutenant. "No, no, I'm all right." Evans pushed himself back up and tried to regain his balance. "I'm all right. Let's go!" Holding his injured right arm, he dove through the open door of the helicopter.

Gianni headed deeper into the jungle, bending back branches, snapping off sharp dead limbs and warning Runyon when he had to step over logs or around bushes. Shadrack stayed out in front and tested the air for scents. Gianni kept his eyes glued to the dog, stopping and helping the wounded pilot down to the ground when the dog indicated that threats were near. Shouts of commands and directions echoed through the trees. Bursts of automatic fire clattered around them as overanxious soldiers fired at what they thought, or hoped, were trapped Americans.

The mission had not gone as planned, but each man knew that it might end this way when they volunteered. Gianni had one chance left to get the pilot out and he was going to do his best. He half led, half dragged the wounded man as far as he could before he had to stop to catch his breath.

He poured a little water into the pilot's mouth. "I'm gonna get a bandage on these wounds, get the bleeding stopped." He poured some of the water on Runyon's forehead and let it run into his eyes. Dried blood and dirt washed away as Runyon started to blink, breaking up the hard and caked mess that had been holding his eyelids shut. As the water flowed, he reached up and started to rub both eyes with a thumb and forefinger. At first he saw streaks of light, then shadows, then a dirt covered, sweat streaked, blood caked face looking back at him. He shook his head slightly, rubbed his eyes again and smiled at the young Airman. "Christ almighty, I've got scars older than you!"

"You can see? You can see me!?"

Runyon blinked his eyes hard, cringing at the stinging from the dirt still in his eyes. "Yeah. They hurt like hell, but I can see. I think I had a shitload of dirt and blood in 'em." He blinked hard again, tears dripping down his cheeks, flushing away more of the dirt. "They're gettin' better. I think I'll be all right."

"Good, good, that's gonna' help." Gianni looked down at the man's survival vest and pulled a field dressing out of its pouch. "You got a nasty fuckin' gash on your forehead." He wrapped the long gauze ends around the head several times, then tied it off in the back. Without saying a word, he pulled the knife out of his ammo harness, slit the leg of the pilot's flightsuit and inspected the wound. "Boy, I'll bet that hurts like a motherfucker!" Pulling another field dressing out of the pouch he tied the bandage over the gaping hole in the leg.

Runyon looked down at the blood-soaked flightsuit and the dull-green bandage. "Looks like my flying days are over." Gianni gave a little grunt as he tightened the gauze and tied it off. He screwed the top back on the canteen and slipped it back in its pouch. Pushing himself to his feet, he looked around at the thick jungle. Both men could still hear the sounds of aircraft crisscrossing the tree tops. They had to do something fast before they ran so low on fuel they had to leave station.

"How the hell do you think we're gonna' get outta' here?"

Gianni reached into his shirt and pulled out the emergency radio, then jerked his head up toward the sky. "There's a Jolly Green up there somewhere."

Runyon looked at him for a moment, then a big grin spread across his face. "Jungle penetrator!"

"See, now you know why they pay you the big bucks. Can't get anything by you." Gianni looked down at Shadrack, decided that the scents he was picking up weren't that strong, then handed the radio to Runyon. "Here, call your buddies. We'll stand a better chance of getting the chopper here if they recognize your voice.

Runyon took the radio and switched it on. "Corvette Leader, this is Mustang one! Corvette Leader, this is Mustang One, do you copy?"

"David!? David!? Is that you!? This is Corvette Leader!"

"Yeah, Bill, it's me. We still got a little problem down here."

"Jesus Christ, we figured they got you for sure." Runyon smiled and shook his head slightly. "Ah, Mustang, Daisy Mae would like to know if you've got any kind of plan for getting out of there or are we suppose to fly cover for you 'til the end of the war?"

"We have a plan, Corvette Leader, I just don't know what it is yet. Wait one."

Runyon pushed himself back so he could sit with his back braced against a tree, then held out both his arms and shrugged. "I assume you do have a plan?"

"Tell your guy we're gonna' try to get deeper in the bush, then we'll call in the Jolly Green and pop smoke for the penetrator. With any luck, the Cobras and Skyraiders still have enough machine gun ammo to cover us while they're pullin' our asses outta' here."

The door gunner pressed his hand against the side of his helmet so he could hear the pilot better. He shook his head and shouted into his microphone trying to make himself heard over the noise of the rotor blades and the wind rushing through the open door. He leaned over and shook Evans on the shoulder, motioning him to move closer.

"Your two guys made contact with the F-4's. They're all right!"

Evans shook his head in acknowledgment. "What about a pickup? Are they gonna' be picked up!?

"There's a new flight of F-4's headin' in, should be on station any minute. They're gonna' fly cover while your guys try for the Jolly Green."

Evans turned his head and shouted back into the side of the gunners helmet. "Tell the pilot to turn around. We're going back to help 'em."

The gunner shook his head back and forth violently. "Can't do it, Lieutenant! Co-pilot's hurt and we're running low on fuel."

Evans grabbed the front of the man's shirt and pulled him close. Huebner pushed himself closer to Evans trying to hear what was going on. "You tell the pilot to turn this fuckin' helicopter around now! That's my man down there and we're going back to help him, you got it!?"

The gunner spoke into his microphone, then looked up at Evans and shook his head. "Pilot says no fuckin' way! We're low on fuel and we're not going back!"

Evans' body started to shake with anger as he fought for control. He turned to Huebner and shouted into his ear. Without saying a word, Huebner turned and crawled into the cockpit. Less than half a minute later, every man was reaching for something to grab on to as the helicopter made a quick 180-degree turn.

Gianni and Runyon had pushed on, trying to put distance between themselves and the NVA. Runyon's leg wound continued to bleed and he lost strength with every step. As quick as the choppers were running out of fuel, Runyon was running out of blood, and if they didn't get him help in a hurry, the entire mission would be for nothing. Gianni eased the wounded pilot to the ground and looked up at the sky. Sunlight streaked down through what should have been a heavy green canopy. The blueness of the sky was a sharp contrast to the widely spaced limbs covered with leaves. Not quite a clearing, and certainly not wide enough for a chopper to try a landing, it was wide enough for the chopper crew to see where they were to lower the jungle penetrator.

Gianni leaned Runyon up against the trunk of a tree, then took the radio from him. He looked down at the dog, checking for any strong alerts before he called the F-4's. Shadrack held his nose high in the air testing the breeze for a scent, then tilted his head to listen for anything he might have missed. A quick glance told Gianni there were scents all around them and it was only a matter of time before they were found. He keyed the radio while he kept watching the dog.

"This is Mustang One, do you copy?"

Four new F-4's had replaced the ones that were running out of fuel. "Mustang One, this is Edsel Leader, go."

"Edsel Leader, we've found a small clearing, the Jolly Green should be able to see us. We're ready for pickup soonest. Advise Jolly Green that LZ will probably be hot. Expect contact when smoke is popped. Over."

"Roger Mustang. Wait one."

Gianni looked around, trying to peer through the trees. Shadrack paced back and forth sniffing the air. Runyon pushed himself up against the tree, wincing as the broken ribs sent a stab of pain through his chest. "There's something we haven't talked about."

Gianni held the radio in his left hand and looked up through the trees waiting for the F-4 to call him back. "What's that, Colonel?"

"How we're all gonna' get out of here." Runyon tried to push himself up even farther. "That jungle penetrator can lift two people, not two people and a dog. There's no way that dog can get up at the same time."

"Yeah, so? What's your point?" Gianni kept his back to Runyon but his eyes were looking down at the dog.

"When you pop that smoke, every Gook in the country is gonna' be headin' to this spot. If we're lucky, the chopper might have time to pull the penetrator up one time. That's if we're lucky."

Gianni spun around, cutting Runyon off before he could say anything else. "Don't worry about…" He never bothered to finish the sentence as the voice from the radio interrupted him. "Mustang One, this is Edsel Leader."

"Go, Edsel Leader."

"Mustang One, the Jolly Green needs a marker for your position. Over."

"Edsel, this is Mustang. Advise the Jolly Green we're firing a flare. When they're overhead, we'll pop smoke."

"Roger Mustang. Pop flare now! Repeat, pop flare now!"

Gianni hit the flare he had pulled out of Runyon's survival harness and flinched as the inside of it shot up out of his hand. Like a Roman candle, the flare shot upwards, bursting through the trees, then exploded into a white hot ball. The Jolly Green Giant spotted the flare almost immediately and turned the big lumbering aircraft in its direction.

"Mustang One, Jolly Green has a visual on the flare. Pop smoke on their rotor noise! Copy?"

"Roger, Edsel, stand by." Gianni started to pull off one of his last two smoke grenades, then hesitated. "Colonel, do you still have a smoke canister in that vest?"

Runyon flipped open the cover on the canister pouch and handed it to Gianni. "Yeah, here you go."

"Good. Let's get you up and ready." Both men looked up as they heard the helicopter getting closer. "When I pop this smoke, we're gonna' start havin' company so we ain't gonna' have time to fuck around. I'll help you on the penetrator and give them the signal to haul away." Gianni reached under Runyon's left shoulder and pulled the shoulder holster to the front of his chest. "If you see anything moving down here, pull this thing out and shoot 'til it's empty. Don't worry about hitting anything, just try to keep their heads down. Got it?"

"I'm not going up there alone. It'll hold the both of us. We can both make it in one trip!"

"Yeah, Colonel I know. The only problem is there's three of us." Gianni looked down at the dog who was still prancing back and forth, alerting in almost every direction. The scents were getting closer and Gianni knew that as soon as the smoke started to drift through the trees, the NVA would see it and the shit would definitely hit the fan. He looked up through the trees as he talked. "Don't worry about it, we'll be right behind you. Just do me a favor. Don't screw around gettin' off the thing, have 'em get it back down here ASAP."

Runyon shook his head slowly. "It's not worth it, it's just not worth it. He's just a dog!"

"No, Colonel, he not just a dog, he's part of the squad...he's my friend...and I'm not going to lose another one." The sound of the rotors suddenly got louder as the big helicopter flew directly over their heads, then disappeared beyond the tree tops. Gianni pulled the pin on the smoke grenade, shook it in the air to help the smoke disperse, then threw it several yards away.

"Look, Airman, I'm ordering you to leave that…"

"With all due respect, sir, fuck you! Now, get ready, and remember, tell 'em to get that damn thing back down here."

Runyon leaned against Gianni as a voice squawked over the radio.

"Mustang One, this is Edsel Leader. Jolly Green verifies yellow smoke. Copy?"

"Edsel Leader, this is Mustang, yellow smoke is a roger. Have 'em step on it, will ya', we're gonna' have company any minute."

"Roger, Mustang, they're turning now, When company arrives, advise on position, we'll try to give 'em the door prize."

"Roger, Edsel, keep your eyes open. Out."

Gianni stuck the radio in his shirt and flipped the selector on his rifle to automatic. The helicopter suddenly appeared, a white helmeted crew member leaning out, trying to look through the trees. His right hand held the microphone attached to the helmet close to his mouth as he gave the pilot hovering instructions. As the helicopter settled over the tree tops, the heavy yellow penetrator started down on its cable.

Runyon looked up at the helicopter, then back at Gianni, knowing what was going to happen but hoping it wouldn't. He yelled, trying to make himself heard over the noise of the rotors. Gianni was holding his rifle in his right hand while trying to support Runyon and watch the trees at the same time.

"Ya', Colonel, what's the problem?"

"Your name, I don't know your name!?"

"What!?"

"Your name!"

"Gianni. Why?"

"My wife's pregnant, little surprise from my R & R in Hawaii. If we have a baby boy, I'm gonna' name him after you!"

Gianni turned away from the trees and looked directly at the Colonel. A broad smile spread across his face. "Thanks, Colonel, I appreciate that but I'd rather you named him Vincent!

Runyon looked at him with a puzzled expression. "Vincent? Who's Vincent?"

"Someone special, Colonel. Someone real special."

The penetrator dropped down within two feet of the ground as Gianni made a grab for it. He flipped down the metal seat and helped Runyon throw his legs over it, then wrapped his arms around the metal support. Gianni slipped the safety rope around his waist and clipped the end to the support. With any luck it would keep him attached to the penetrator if he got wounded again on the way up.

"Good luck, Colonel! See ya' in a couple minutes!"

Gianni looked back up to the helicopter and jerked his thumb in the air. The cable tightened as Runyon started to rise. He was halfway up through the trees when the door gunner swung his M-60 around and started firing as the crew member operating the winch yelled into his microphone at the pilot. Tracers from the machine gun tore down into the trees, the sounds of bullets ricocheting off of limbs, causing Gianni to turn around. Two figures were just pushing their way through the brush when the rounds from the helicopter tumbled them to the ground. Yelling "HEEL," he ran for the cover of a large tree.

Looking down, Runyon saw figures running below him and jerked his gun out of its holster. As a soldier stopped and raised his AK-47 toward him, Runyon pulled the trigger six times. Although not hit, the soldier ducked and hesitated long enough for the door gunner to shift his fire and walk a line of bullets through the man's chest. Gianni looked up and saw Runyon hanging at the end of the cable less than ten feet from the open door. The big green helicopter shuddered as it took hit after hit, an easy target as the pilot held it steady, refusing to pull out and risk snapping the cable with its swinging human cargo.

The sounds of more helicopters caught Gianni's attention. Two Cobras flew past the Jolly Green, firing their mini-guns into the trees. The screams told Gianni that at least some of the bullets had found their mark. Figures moved behind bushes to Gianni's left. Without aiming he fired a long burst. Two of the figures fell, one of them draped over the bush, the body bouncing up and down on the springy branches. The third figure tried to back away and was cut down as Gianni emptied his magazine. Leaves, twigs, and pieces of branches were tossed in the air along with flesh and blood. As he punched out the empty magazine and inserted a fresh one, the voice on the radio called him.

"Mustang, this is Edsel, the Jolly Green is going to pull away, then turn back to reposition for your pickup."

"Negative, Edsel, negative! LZ is too hot, repeat, too hot!" Gianni didn't know it was possible to feel so alone or so helpless, but he couldn't watch an entire helicopter crew plus the man he had tried so hard to save die trying to help him. He looked up at the chopper just as Runyon was being pulled in through the open door. The chopper lowered its nose, trying to gain speed as it pulled away, bullets leaping up from the trees as it struggled to get out of range.

Bullets slammed into the tree trunk and tore at the ground around his feet. He dropped to the ground, using his body to cover the dog. A grenade sailed over a stand of bushes, hit the tree and bounced back several yards. The explosion tore into the living wood, pieces of hot metal tearing out chunks. Debris was still settling to earth as three men, firing their AK-47's from the hip, rushed out of the bushes. Gianni lifted his head just in time to pull the CAR-15 to his shoulder and fire five rounds, all three men died instantly.

Shadrack strained to get up, fighting at the weight of his master. Threats were all around and it was his job to protect the one that protected him. Gianni yelled "DOWN" and shifted his weight so the dog couldn't move. He fired at what he thought was the dim outline of a pith helmet peering over the roots of a tree. The radio lay on the ground next to his right elbow and seemed to reach out as the voice yelled for him.

"Mustang! Goddamnit, Mustang! Are you there!? Come on, kid, answer me, dammit!"

Gianni picked up the radio in his left hand leaving the rifle in his right, ready to fire. "Edsel, this is Mustang!"

"Dammit, kid, don't scare us like that! Hang on another couple of minutes, kid, the chopper is comin' back for ya.'"

He turned to look behind him, trying to see any movement through the trees and bushes. It wouldn't be long before they started moving in around him and then he wouldn't have a chance in hell.

"Mustang, listen up, we're gonna' try to give you a little breathing room. Do you have any smoke to mark your position for the fastmovers?"

Gianni reached down to his ammo harness and felt the remaining smoke grenades. "Roger, Edsel, two smokes left."

"Okay, Mustang. On my command, pop smoke and keep your head down. A flight of four is comin' in with shake and bake. It's gonna' be close, kid, so hunker down real good."

Gianni scooted Shadrack's back end farther under his chest and tried to cover the dog completely without crushing him. He pulled three magazines out of his bandoleer and laid them at the base of the tree. Bullets slammed into the ground next to his hand sending pieces of rock tearing into the flesh. He jerked his hand back, sucking in air at the stinging pain. The soldier who had fired raised up and fired again, hitting the tree twice, inches from Gianni's face. More angry than scared, Gianni's thumb flipped the selector to auto as he swung the rifle and pulled the trigger. Rounds slammed into the soldier's AK-47 knocking it out of his hands as the rest of the burst ripped his chest apart, covering the front of his uniform with red, frothy blood. The soldier hiding behind the trees next to the dead soldier panicked and turned to run. The thin fabric of his uniform shirt did little to slow the bullets that shattered his spine.

"Mustang One, this is Edsel. Flight of four in position, pop smoke NOW NOW NOW!!"

Gianni pulled the pin on the grenade and tossed the canister around the tree. Purple smoke sputtered out the bottom, then billowed with a whooshing sound. Gianni never heard the sounds of the jets. The concussions of the bombs exploding lifted him off the ground. As he landed, the dog let out a cry of pain. The noise of the explosions blocked out the sounds of splintering trees and the screams of men being torn to shreds.

Not knowing that only one of the jets had dropped its bombs, Gianni started to relax when he was thrown into the air again as four explosions, even closer than the first, erupted. They were followed by two more explosions, then two more, to his right. The thought that no one could live through such explosive power was suddenly more terrifying when he remembered that he was in the middle of it.

The jungle in front of him came alive with movement. Soldiers, unscathed, along with those only slightly wounded, started to push through the thick growth. Their only hope of survival was to get close to the American. The pilots wouldn't risk killing one of their own.

Gianni fired before the first soldier had even untangled himself from the thorny bush. As each man dropped, or spun from the sudden impact of the bullets, Gianni shifted his fire to a new target. He fired instinctively. He tried to keep track of his rounds but twice was surprised when the bolt locked back on an empty magazine. Bodies littered the jungle floor, some screaming from gaping wounds while others quietly moaned as they slowly bled to death.

The ground leapt up to greet him again. Two jets had come back for another pass. The Bronco had warned them of soldiers moving closer to Gianni's position. The bombs landed closer, violating every rule of close-in support. Shock waves rolled over him, sucking the breath out of his lungs. He heard a voice far off. It seemed like hours before he realized it was coming from the radio.

"Come on, kid, answer me!! Mustang, are you there, can you hear me!?"

He picked up the radio and tried to get his mouth to work. "Yeah, yeah, I'm here! Go ahead."

"Are you all right, Mustang, can you move!?"

"Yeah, I think so!"

"All right. The chopper is comin' in now! Cobras will give cover fire while the fastmovers lay in napalm! You gotta' make it quick, kid, everyone is low on gas up here and that place is gettin' real crowded down there!"

For the first time Gianni noticed his right arm was covered in blood. He didn't know where the wound was and didn't take time to look. "Yeah, tell me about it!"

"All right, just hang on, we're gonna' get you out! Stand by and be ready to move! Good luck, kid! Out."

The rumble of the Jolly Green's engine almost drowned out the sound of the Cobras. As Gianni looked up, he saw the huge camouflaged underbelly of the chopper slowly gliding into position. The white-helmeted crew member leaned out, one hand on the penetrator's cable, the other pushing the microphone to his face. The Cobras swept by, spraying the jungle with machine-gun fire.

As the cable started to lower the bright yellow rescue chair, bullets flew up to meet it. The Cobras shifted their fire, tearing at the patch of jungle that gave little protection to the guns hiding there.

Another helicopter slipped in behind one of the Cobras and fired down into the trees. Grenades rained down as the door gunners raked their pole mounted guns back and forth. A huge black man supported an M-60 between his legs, holding his left arm out with a belt of ammunition draped over it. It only took a moment for Gianni to recognize the faces of the men looking down at him.

The penetrator was halfway down when Gianni stood up, emptied a magazine at the figures in the bush, and made a dash to where the penetrator would land. He shouted at Shadrack to "HEEL" and inserted a fresh magazine. He made it to the pickup spot while the penetrator was still fifteen feet above his head.

As he looked up, he saw Runyon's head poke out of the helicopter doorway next to the white helmet. A small smile of recognition spread over Gianni's face just before he heard the loud WHOOSH and felt the sheet of heat envelop him. As the roar of the jet engines trailed off, they were replaced by screams of burning men. Thick black smoke rolled through the trees, the jungle shook and turned into a blast furnace as more napalm canisters exploded, spreading their flaming deadly cargo. The helicopter rocked from side to side as the pilot tried to fight the shock wave.

The white-helmeted crew member jerked his thumb up, urging Gianni to hurry. Men pushed through the bushes firing at the escaping American. A round tore into Gianni's side, tearing at the flesh and burning like the napalm itself. As he spun and fell to the ground, he held the trigger down, spraying the trees and brush, hitting the man that had shot him without ever knowing he was there. He pulled himself to his feet, using the penetrator as support.

Not knowing what to do, Shadrack pranced in circles, barking and growling, wanting to help his master. The men in the slick fired into the trees in front of Gianni while the Cobras used what little ammunition they had left to tear at the bush to his sides. Twenty-millimeter cannon shells missed the helicopters by scant yards as the jets added their own firepower to the carnage on the ground. Gianni had only seconds left to get on the penetrator before the helicopter was blown out of the sky.

He shouted at the dog, trying to make himself heard over the noise. Shadrack turned at his voice and started back to his master. Two feet in front of him, he veered off and broke into a dead run. Gianni turned and saw the NVA soldier standing next to the tree, the AK-47 pulled into his shoulder. He could almost see the man's finger tighten on the trigger. Bullets slammed into the ground, then abruptly stopped. The sound of his rifle had been replaced by desperate screams.

As Gianni looked, he saw what had been a human face crushed between two powerful jaws. Above the noise of the helicopters and the gunfire, he was sure he could hear the crunching of bones as they broke and collapsed on one another. The body jerked as Shadrack shook his head and bit down harder, killing the one that would have killed his master.

The penetrator was swinging now as the pilot fought for control. The helmeted crew member waved frantically, screaming for Gianni to get on. There would be no time for Gianni to call the dog, get on the penetrator, lift the dog on his lap and be pulled up. The helicopter had to leave now or it never would.

He looked up, knowing that what he was about to do meant his death. Too many men would die for what was already a hopeless cause. Gianni dropped his rifle to the ground, reached up, and with blood-covered fingers, pulled out the clovis pin holding the penetrator to the cable. The helmeted crew member watched in horror as the bright yellow metal chair fell to the ground.

He looked up long enough to see the helicopter disappear, then turned and fired a full magazine into the bush. He screamed at Shadrack to "HEEL", then ran for the heavy growth behind the now grounded penetrator. Bullets followed him as he slid to the ground and crawled behind the cover of a tree trunk. The intensity of the fire had slackened and as far as he could tell, most of the NVA were hunkering down or dying from their wounds. He had to put distance between him and them, and he couldn't do that with some of the soldiers still firing at him.

He reached for a fresh magazine and noticed there were only two left. He jerked one out and slammed it home. Two magazines left, forty rounds, plus two grenades and his thirty-eight with eighteen rounds and a smoke grenade. He dropped his head and sighed, flinching as rounds tore at the dirt beside him. His thumb flipped the selector switch back to semi-automatic.

A burst hit high in the tree above him and a shattered branch fell across his legs. As he turned his head, he saw movement off to his left. A single soldier crawled along the ground, trying to make for the cover of a large tree. Shadrack, hunched low, stared at the man and growled low in his throat. Gianni would have to expose himself to get a shot at the man. He had only seconds before the soldier reached the tree, then it would be too late. The words came back to him. *'Neutralize the closest threat.'* He had to neutralize the threat, but how?

The dog shifted his weight. Gianni looked down and knew what had to be done. He slipped the metal choke chain off the dog's neck. He pointed at the crawling man and shouted "GET "EM." As the soldier, seeing the dog running for him, tried to push himself to his knees and raise his rifle, the dog left his feet and hit him full force in the chest. An involuntary scream of terror turned into a sickening gurgling sound.

He peered around the tree and spotted two more forms rising up on their knees trying to see what had happened. Taking a breath and letting it out like Hank had taught him, he fired four quick shots, killing both men. The smoke from the rounds still floated around the end of the barrel when he shouted "HEEL" and fired at another man raising up. The dog slid in next to his master as another dying soldier tumbled to the ground.

Gianni reached over and rubbed the top of the dog's head. "We gotta' get the fuck outta' here, Shadrack." He turned and surveyed the jungle. There was no wind, not even a breeze, but there was the overpowering smell of napalm and burning bodies. He jumped to his feet, tapped his left leg, whispered "HEEL", and disappeared into the trees.

CHAPTER 13

SUNDAY
JUNE 21, 1970
FORT LAUDERDALE, FLORIDA

The first day of summer was starting out to be a beautiful day as Vince and Bernadette sat in the screened-in patio enjoying a leisurely breakfast. The sweet smell of the orange and mango trees in the back yard floated over the mosaic tile table that held a pot of coffee and a plate of bagels. Yet to be read sections of the Fort Lauderdale News lay scattered at the foot of their chairs as Vince lingered over the front page story of North Vietnamese troops gaining control of the main highway linking Phnom Penh with Saigon. President Nixon kept saying the war was winding down but it seemed every day American troops were getting more and more involved in a hopeless struggle. It wasn't the kind of war Vince was used to, and it was getting harder to understand. He gave a small sigh before picking up the sports page. Football he understood.

Air Force Major Ronald Vermillion pulled the blue Rambler staff car into the driveway and turned off the ignition. As he pulled the keys out, he turned to his passenger. "You ready, Father?"

Major Anthony Russo ran his hands around the collar of his Air Force jacket, making sure the wind from the rolled down window hadn't disrupted his appearance. He pulled a small loose thread off the clergy insignia pinned to his left lapel and gave a low sigh. "Not a very pleasant way for these folks to start off their day."

"There's never a pleasant time for news like this, Father, but if we didn't get here early in the morning, we probably wouldn't catch them at home."

Father Russo nodded his head toward the well kept house, then to the quiet surrounding neighborhood. "What a shame. From growing up here to dying in some jungle." He let out another sigh and tugged again at his jacket. "God does work in mysterious ways...mysterious ways indeed."

"He may not be dead yet, Father."

Vince was just taking a sip of coffee when the doorbell rang. His wife put her hand on his arm. "I'll get it. Finish reading your paper, and while you're at it, see if Burdines is having any sales."

Vince looked over his shoulder. "Can't we have just one day when we don't have to buy anything? I only work for the Post Office, I don't own it."

Bernadette's response trailed off as she walked through the living room. "It's your job to make the money and it's my job to spend it. It seems like I'm better at my job than you are at yours."

She still had a smile on her face when she opened the door. The two men filled the doorway, their Air Force dress blues out of place in the quiet family neighborhood. Neither man smiled. Major Vermillion softly cleared his throat, already knowing what he wanted to say but trying to avoid it any way he could.

"Mrs. Giancarlo? Mrs. Vincent Giancarlo?"

Bernadette's mind flashed back to a time long ago. During World War II, the sight of a Western Union messenger at the door meant a loved one wasn't coming home. Neighbors would stare out their windows at the unlucky house where the devastating news was being delivered. She had been one of those neighbors, selfishly hoping that the Western Union car would stop in front of somebody else's door and not hers.

Bernadette Giancarlo stood there staring at the two men, almost feeling the eyes in the surrounding houses peering out of windows at the blue staff car with the bright yellow lettering parked in the driveway. Vermillion cleared his throat again and repeated his question. "Are you Mrs. Giancarlo, Mrs. Vincent Giancarlo?"

Bernadette's hand flew to her opening mouth as she stumbled back two steps. "OH, NO! GOD, NO!! JIMMY! JIMMY!!"

Vince Giancarlo dropped his coffee cup at the sound of his wife's screams. He raced through the living room determined to protect his wife from the unknown danger. He saw the two Air Force officers standing in the open doorway and his heart sank as he realized why they were there. Bernadette rushed to him, clinging desperately as her body was racked with sobs.

Major Vermillion stepped into the living room followed by Father Russo, who quietly shut the door. "Mr. Giancarlo?"

Vincent wrapped his arms around his wife and urged her to calm down. He already knew what the men had to say. "Yes, I'm Vincent Giancarlo. Is it our son? Is it Gianni? Is he all right?"

Vermillion glanced at Father Russo, then back at the distraught parents. "Mr. Giancarlo, Mrs. Giancarlo, I'm afraid I have to inform you that your son, Airman Gianni Giancarlo, has been officially declared as missing in action."

"OH, GOD! NO, NOT GIANNI! PLEASE, GOD, NOT GIANNI!!"

Vince Giancarlo hugged his wife tighter, pressing his cheek against her head as his tears fell and mingled with her hair. "Honey, listen, listen to what he's saying. Gianni's not dead, he's missing. He's lost, that's all, he's not hurt, he'll be all right, they'll find him." Vince Giancarlo wanted desperately to believe what he was saying. His son was in the middle of a war and when the government declared someone missing in action, it usually meant they couldn't recover the body.

Bernadette tried to control her sobs and wiped some of the tears away with one hand while clinging to her husband with the other. "Missing? How can you be missing from an air base? How can my son be missing? All he did was walk along a fence! How can he be missing!?

Vincent looked down at the floor. Vermillion glanced at Father Russo, then back at Vince and Bernadette. "There must be some misunderstanding, Mrs. Giancarlo. Your son wasn't guarding any fence line. He worked with a special Army unit...out in the jungle." The expression on his face didn't go unnoticed by Vince. "Ma'am, your son...ah...your son volunteered to help an Army Search and Rescue team find shot down pilots. Ah, he and his dog found men that probably would have died, or been captured if it hadn't been for them. I...I don't understand how..." Vermillion was confused and looked to Father Russo for help. The priest's eyes welled with moisture as he slowly shook his head in helplessness. Vermillion cleared his throat, stumbling for a way to console the grieving mother. "I can't say this officially, I mean on behalf of the Air Force, but from what his file says, your son is a hero."

"No, this can't be right! I have his letters from Tan Son Nhut! We even have pictures, pictures of him and his dog and of the base and his friends! There must be a mistake!"

Bernadette looked up at her husband. Vince's eyes glistened from the tears as he struggled unsuccessfully to speak without his voice breaking. "Major, can you tell us what happened? How was our son declared missing?"

Vermillion looked down at the floor, started to say something, then thought better of it and looked Vincent directly in the eyes. "Yes, sir, I can. He and his team volunteered to be inserted into Cambodia to rescue an F-4 crew that had been shot down. It was strictly voluntary, they weren't ordered to go. They found the crew, but your son and the pilot were separated from the rest of the team and weren't able to get to the helicopter for extraction out of the area. Even though the pilot had been wounded several times your son managed to move him to safety then call in another helicopter and strap him on to what they call a jungle penetrator. The pilot was pulled aboard…but, ah, the helicopter was taking numerous hits from ground fire. They, ah, ah, they were able to drop the penetrator back down for your son, but…he refused to leave his dog behind…when he realized the helicopter was in danger of being shot down…he released the rescue penetrator. Mr. Giancarlo…your son probably saved the lives of every man on that helicopter."

Vincent's attempt to keep his voice from cracking was in vain. "Gianni, what about Gianni? What happened to our son?"

"He was last seen trying to evade ground forces in the area. Sir, let me emphasize, when your son was last seen, he was alive and evading hostile forces. There has been no report of his capture and there is reason to believe he was able to get away from the enemy troops pursuing him. He is experienced at operating in the jungle and I'm told that with the use of his dog he may be able to avoid capture for a long period of time."

Bernadette continued to clutch her husband, not quite believing what was being said about her son. Experienced at operating in the jungle? How could they be talking about her son? She pushed herself away from her husband's chest and looked up into his face.

"You knew! You knew he wasn't at that air base anymore, didn't you? You son of a bitch!! You bastard!! You knew my son was out there risking his life!! Goddamn you!! You knew and you didn't tell me!!"

Major Vermillion and Father Russo watched as the man standing in front of them seemed to shrink before their eyes. The pride that had shown in his eyes moments before was replaced with the look of sorrow and pain for his wife, the mother of his son. His voice trembled as he spoke, tears flowing freely as he reached for his wife's hand.

"I couldn't tell you, I couldn't." The trembling man looked at the two officers for understanding, then back at his wife.

Bernadette pulled her hand away, not wanting to touch the man she thought had betrayed her. "He's my son, Goddamn you! I'm his mother, I had the right!!" Her body was racked once again with sobs as her husband blankly stared at her.

Without another word, she turned and ran to the bedroom. All three men could plainly hear her cries of anguish. All three men also knew that there was nothing that could be done, nothing that could be said to ease the pain of a mother losing her child.

SATURDAY
JUNE 27, 1979
THE GIANCARLO HOME

The week had lingered, each day longer than the last. Vince had called Frank Cipriani at home on Sunday night, telling him the news about Gianni. Before he could mention that he wouldn't be in to work for awhile Frank had told him to stay home, take care of both himself and Bernadette, and not to worry about how long he was out. His job would always be waiting. The next day had been a constant stream of Post Office employees stopping by the with baskets of fruit, floral arrangements and sincere words of encouragement and hope. Chuck had almost lived at the house, hoping for word that Gianni had been found safe…and dreading that they would hear otherwise. Hank called or stopped by at least once a day, always holding out hope that no news was good news. Vince had called Major Vermillion twice during the week to see if there had been any word. The Major assured him that if he heard anything, they would be the first to know. Father Russo made it a point of staying in contact, sending a short note in the mail and a quick but thoughtful phone call every couple of days. The outpouring of warmth and concern helped to soften what otherwise would have been an unbearable situation.

Bernadette had already convinced her husband to go back to work on the following Monday, knowing that sitting around waiting for word that might never come was killing him. Although she didn't say it, she knew that going back to work would give him a sense that everything was going to be all right and that life had to go on while they were waiting for that time to come.

They were sitting in the family room, listening to the ever present big band music and trying to make small talk about nothing in particular when the doorbell rang. Vince jumped out of the oyster white chair and ran through the living room, not quite sure why he was racing. His heart skipped a beat as he opened the door to the light blue uniform shirt, regaining his composure when he recognized his long time friend from the Post Office.

"Hi Vince...how, ah, how are ya doing?"

"Good Joe, you know, good as can be expected I guess."

Joe Sheppa stood in the doorway, the heavy leather postal bag slung over his shoulder as he fidgeted with the stack of mail in his hands. "Vince, I, ah, I didn't want to bother you, you know, but...I would have put your mail in the box but I figured you'd want to see this right away." Along with the rest of the mail he held up a brown manila envelope. "Its got a return address from Vietnam," he was nervous and uneasy, not knowing what to say to a friend whose son was missing in combat, "maybe its from one of Gianni's friends or...well I figured you'd...I wanted to give it to you in person."

Vince reached out and took the mail with shaking hands. He looked down at the large envelope and ran a dry tongue over his lips. "Would, ah, would you like to come in for a while Joe? Have a cup of coffee, a Coke, ah...I, I could make..."

"No, no Vince, I better get back to the route, I ah…I hope its good news Vince…I really do."

"I know Joe, I know. Thank you, from Ann too, thank you."

Bernadette was still sitting in her chair in the family room, head back, eyes closed, listening to the music but not really hearing it. When she heard the front door close she opened her eyes and watched as her husband slowly made his way through the living room.

"Who was at the door?"

"Huh? Oh, that was Joe, mail's in." He stopped at the edge of the living room and stared at the envelope in his hand.

"Jimmy, what is it, what's the matter?" She pushed herself up in the chair, a sudden shiver shooting through her body.

"Joe delivered this…it's from Vietnam."

Bernadette walked over and took the envelope from her husband's shaking hands. "The return address is from a Father Szuch at that Army base, Camelot Palace." She looked up at her husband, her eyes showing the excitement that they were about to hear from someone that may have known their son. She handed it back as she spoke, her voice barely above a whisper. "Jimmy, Jimmy open it, please, open it. He must have known Gianni, he must be writing to tell us about him."

Vince took the envelope and led her to the family room table. "Ann, don't get your hopes up. This is from a priest, they have to write to the families when someone is missing or…well, they have to write. Besides, how would Gianni know a priest, we couldn't get him to go to church anymore, even when we bribed him?" Vince stared at the envelope for a moment then pulled a chair out and sat down. "Do you want to read it?"

"No, no, you go ahead." Bernadette wrung her hands together, hard enough for her fingers to turn white from lack of circulation.

Vince tore open the envelope and peered inside. He shook out a hand written letter and another sealed white envelope. Across the front were the words:

TO MY PARENTS
VINCENT AND BERNADETTE GIANCARLO
TO BE OPENED AND READ ONLY IF I AM DECLARED DEAD
OR MISSING
GIANNI GIANCARLO

He held the envelope so his wife could read the front of it then laid it gently on the table while one of Bernadette's white-knuckled hands shot to her mouth. After checking the inside of the manila envelope one more time, he began to read the handwritten letter.

Dear Mr. and Mrs. Giancarlo:

By now you have been notified that Gianni failed to return from his last mission and has been declared as missing in action. As the Priest here at Camelot Palace please let me extend both my prayers and deepest condolences during this heartbreaking time of uncertainty. It is never easy for me to write a letter of this nature, especially when the young man in question is usually one of the hundreds of nameless faces that goes about his duties in hopes of time quickly passing until the day he rotates home. It is rare that I come to personally know, in more than a spiritual sense, any of the men. Gianni has been the exception. Over the last few weeks, Gianni and I have spent a great deal of time together, both talking and listening to music. I hope you will be pleased to know that Gianni has become quite the big band aficionado. His knowledge of the bands and song titles came as a surprise to him at first but soon he realized that growing up and listening to, what he sheepishly called, the good sounds, had indeed made a great impact. When we sat and listened to the music, he was at peace with what he saw over here and what he was asked to do. He used to tell me that if the Chattanooga Choo-Choo couldn't get him back to 'the World', then he'd settle for being there in his mind. We used to talk for hours on end about how you and he, Mr. Giancarlo, would race for the hi-fi and fight over the music that would be played. As I write this, it brings a smile to my face as I remember the time he told me that when he was in the squad tent he would listen to rock and roll to, as he put it, keep up the image, but that he couldn't wait to sit outside my tent and look up at the stars with his dog's head in his lap and think of home, and of you. We talked about his car, or, The Car, and of the riding lawn mower that he never gets to ride and of his friends Chuck and Hank, but most of all, we talked about you, his parents. Like many of us who have seen combat, or the aftermath of it, he realized that there were many things he never told you, didn't know how to tell you. Much of it can be explained away to the feeling of youthful immortality, the thought that there will always be a tomorrow. War changes that and Gianni came to know that for some, there is no tomorrow. It is important for me to tell you, and I pray, with all my being, that some day soon, Gianni will be able to tell you himself that he holds a love for you that few people ever experience. Although Gianni never attended one of my church services I sometimes feel that he has a better understanding of what religion is all about than I do. His actions, his willingness to possibly sacrifice himself to help others, his feelings of right and wrong, speak volumes to the kind of boy, man, he is. He once half-jokingly told me that he was practicing his own religion, the 'do right' religion. He said you taught him to always do right, even if it wasn't in his best interest. Do right by people, then stand to be judged. In a sacrilegious way, I agree with him, and I admire him. I admire him for his views, and for the parents who raised him. You have reason to be proud of your son as he is of you.

As you can see, I have enclosed an envelope addressed to you. Gianni brought it to my tent as he was leaving for the mission to Cambodia. He asked me to make sure you received it if he didn't come back. I have put off writing this letter for several days in the selfish hope that one of the search missions would find him. I have prayed that I see him sitting in front of my tent, tapping his foot to the music and scratching the head of that big eared dog, but, some prayers take longer to be answered than others. I will not give up hope, as I know you will not. I do not say this lightly but somehow I believe that Gianni will make it through this and once again you will be together. May God bless the both of you and hold you close to his heart.

Sincerely,
Father Edward Francis Szuch
Major U.S. Army

Vincent stared at the letter as Bernadette slowly inched a hand across to him and laid it on his arm. She bit her lower lip, hoping the pain would keep her from breaking down. Several seconds passed until he was able to refocus his eyes, wipe away the moisture and choke down the lump building in his throat.

"God, I always thought he hated our music." Bernadette's voice was barely more than a whisper.

Vince turned to his wife as he set the letter on the table. "He did, when he was here. Things have a way of changing when you're away from home…when you're…you know." He picked up the sealed letter and ran it through his hands, comforted by touching that which his son had held between his own hands. He turned the envelope over, gently running his fingers over the sealed flap. His body shuddered as he wondered if the moisture that had sealed the envelope was the closest he would ever get to a kiss from his son again.

"It was a hell of a nice thing for that priest to take his time and write a letter like that." His voice cracked as he spoke. "It means a lot…more than he could possibly know." He wiped at his eyes again as the tears slowly made their way down his cheeks.

Bernadette stood up, reached behind her chair and pulled a tissue out of the box sitting on the counter of the kitchen pass-through. She blew her nose gently, dabbed at her eyes and sat back down. "That boy Dustin, the one you told me about, I wonder if he wrote a letter like that to his parents?"

"I don't know. I don't know if he even had met him, but, ah, I'd like to think he did. After…after it happened, after Dustin died, Gianni sent me a letter…he mentioned that he had written to Dustin's parents, he didn't say anything about this Father Szuch."

They were making small talk. On one hand they wanted to tear open the letter from their son and read the words he felt so compelled to write and on the other hand they wanted to delay what they knew might be the last they ever heard from him.

Bernadette pulled small pieces off the tissue in her hand as she tried to control her anxiety. "Open it Jimmy, please. I have to hear what he has to say." She worked at the tissue furiously as she asked herself how life could have changed so drastically in less than a week.

Vince tried to peel back the sealed flap without tearing the envelope, knowing that no matter what the letter said, whether his son came home or not, it was something that he would keep and cherish 'til his dying day. He set the envelope aside, smoothing it with the palm of his hand. Unfolding the letter and clearing his throat, he began to read.

Dear Mom and Dad

The fact that you are reading this means I didn't make it back from our mission, alive anyway. I'm going to give this to Father Szuch to hold, I expect he'll know how to get it to you. By now the Air Force has told you what happened to me, or at least whatever it is they know. Obviously I can't tell you. I can tell you though, whatever it was, it was worth it. The one thing I've learned over here, the thing you've always told me, it's better to help someone else then worry only about yourself. You were right, I know that now. I guess that for the first time, I actually feel like I've done something really important, something good. Because of Shadrack and the guys on the squad, there are men who are still alive who would have died. I don't really know much about any of the pilots that we rescued but I figure they all had parents, or wives and kids that won't be burying their son, or husband, or father, because of what we did. That makes me feel good, better than I have ever felt. I can imagine the pain you must be going through, I know what I went through when Dustin died but please, please, know that I died doing something good, something that was really worthwhile. Mom, please don't be mad at Dad for not telling you what I was doing. I made him promise not to tell. I didn't want you to worry, and I'm not sure I could have done what I needed to do if you had known. If you haven't read the letters I sent Dad, I guess you can read them now. I can't even remember what I said in most of them but I guess it was what I was feeling at the time. I do remember that in one of them I felt like the biggest coward in the world. I never wanted to feel like that again. Maybe that's why I knew I had to go on this mission, I couldn't live with myself knowing that men might die because I was scared.

It's early in the morning and the rest of the guys are getting ready for the mission, taking showers and such. We're going into Cambodia, we've never been there before and for some reason, I needed to write you this letter. We're going in to rescue an F-4 crew that got shot down on a bombing mission. I wonder if either of them wrote a letter home before they left or if it's only done in the movies and I'm the first one to ever do it. I guess it doesn't matter.

I have so much to say to you but I don't know how to say it. I hope you know that I love you both and that I couldn't have asked for better parents, or friends. The sad thing is, I didn't really know you were my friends until I got over here. Father Szuch says I shouldn't worry about it. He says a lot of people never realize that their parents are some of the best friends they'll ever have and that I'm lucky I realized it so young. I wish I could have told you.

I don't have time to write letters to Chuck and Hank so would you tell them that I have thought about them every day and that I miss them. Tell Chuck that I couldn't have loved him more if he was my own brother. Hank needs to know that the hours he spent coaching me on the range, the things he taught me, they kept me alive when things got bad. It was almost like he was standing next to me, telling me what to do, pointing out the danger. Whatever happened to me on this mission, tell Hank that there was nothing he could have taught me different. It was just my time.

Dad, all the things you wrote about, the things you told me in your letters, they all helped this place make sense. I know that I was here to help other guys make it home, I know that I did that. We all did that.

I'm sitting on my footlocker writing this and Shadrack is lying on the floor looking up at me. I really hope he makes it through this. What ever happens, I hope he makes it back and gets a new handler. He's earned it.

Lieutenant Evans just came in and told us we have to get moving. I don't really want to end this, there's still so much I want to tell you, so much I want you to know, but there's two guys out there who need me more than you do right now. Mom, you're probably crying, but please, try to understand, I did what I had to do and I'm not sorry about it. Dad, if anyone ever asks, I hope you can say you had a son you were proud of. Please remember what you've always told me, it's a little tragic but mostly magic. What we did here, the men that got to go home, we kept the magic alive. I have no regrets.

I love you both with all my heart!

Goodbye
Your loving son,
Gianni

The sounds of whispered sobs shook Vincent Giancarlo out of his near trance. His wife had her head buried in her hands. The table shook with each tortured cry of anguish. He laid the letter on the table, careful not to wrinkle or tear the pages. He stared at his son's letter until the tears in his eyes blurred his vision and the lump in his throat made it hard to breath. He tried to control the rage by clinching his fists until his fingernails dug blood-red semi-circles in the palms of his hands. His mind raced with thoughts of his son, and the words he had just read. With swiftness and violence that had laid dormant for twenty-five years, he scooped up the crystal sugar bowl and flung it against the wall over the TV.

"NNNOOOOO!! NNNOOOOO!! HE'S NOT DEAD!! HE'S NOT DEAD!! GOD DON'T LET MY SON BE DEAD!! Vincent Giancarlo, a man of pride, wisdom, and compassion, fell to the floor, covered his head with his arms, and rocking back and forth in primordial defense, wept like a baby.

FRIDAY
JUNE 26, 1970
CAMBODIA

The rain started before dawn. At first it had been just hard enough to allow Gianni and Shadrack to quench their thirst, but what started as a refreshing shower quickly turned into an eye stinging, skin burning downpour. Gianni sat hunched forward with the dog's head in his lap, trying to protect him as best he could. The rain broke open the scab that had formed on his shoulder. Blood, mixed with rain ran down his chest under the torn and shredded fatigue shirt. Back in 'the World' the injury would have been serious enough for his parents to rush him to the hospital. In the middle of the jungle it was nothing more than an inconvenience compared to his other wounds.

They had spent most of the first day hiding. Several times the dog had alerted him to approaching patrols and they had been able blend into the deep bush, watching as their pursuers walked within feet of them. At one point Gianni had crawled under a thick stand of growth, pulling the dog in after him as voices seemed to be circling them. They lay there for over three hours while soldiers, some obviously wounded, searched the area. It wasn't until growing weakness and a growling stomach reminded Gianni that he had to eat something that he realized his rucksack was still lying on the ground where the rest of the squad had made their stand. As the day grew later the patrols became fewer and fewer but they had traveled less than a long rifle shot from where they had started. They were close enough to still smell the oily remnants of burned out napalm, the sweet sickly odor of burned bodies, and the occasional scream of a soldier begging for escape as fate dealt him a slow, and lingering death.

Three separate times helicopters, Spads, and a Bronco flew over the area, drawing fire from the troops on the ground. None of the aircraft ever returned the fire, fearful of hitting the one man, invisible under the jungle growth, that they were looking for. All radios were tuned to the rescue frequency, their listeners praying to hear that lone voice. The dog looked up each time an aircraft passed overhead but Gianni only dropped his head in bitter disappointment, knowing that if they moved, attracted any kind of attention, they would end up like the Wizzo still laying in the clearing.

Just before nightfall on the first day, when the aircraft were no where to be found and they enemy patrols had grown frustrated with their fruitless search, they employed a new tactic. Reconnaissance by fire. Gianni had just lapsed into that abyss between alertness and sleep when the sound of a shrill whistle jerked him back to the moment. Before the sound had even died away the jungle exploded with the staccato bursts of automatic weapons. Far off, close, and very close, the gunfire rang with the urgency of desperation. They were trying to get him to move, to run for safety. The bullets were not intended to kill, an unknown dead body meant nothing to the gunners. Rather, they were meant to flush out their prey, as a mongoose would flush out a snake to be killed. The onslaught lasted for over ten minutes. Gianni would never know if it had been training, instinct, or paralyzing fright that kept him hugging the ground as bullets tore at the trees and bushes around him. He clamped a hand around the dog's snout, choking off the risk a whimper, a growl, or a fatally ending bark. The longer the firing continued the darker it grew. Tracers that had minutes before streaked through the trees now cast an iridescent glow as they ricocheted off trees and danced crazily through the air. Unable to do anything else, Gianni thought for just a moment that the green tracers used by the North Vietnamese were prettier than the red tracers used by Americans. He wondered who made the decision what color to use...and if it made a difference when they hit you?

It was totally dark when he heard the whistle again, either farther away or just not as loud over the sounds of the gunfire. The firing stopped, as abruptly as it had begun. He heard orders being shouted, voices acknowledging and men pushing their way through the bush. The sounds all headed in the direction Gianni and the dog had come. Back to where friends in a helicopter watched as he cut away his survival…back to where a dead American flier lay…back to where it had all started.

They had stayed hidden for another four hours after the voices and sounds of movement had faded away. His only chance…their only chance, was to rely on the dog's keen senses and move at night. As the sun broke through the trees on the second day they had found an almost impenetrable stand of trees and bushes to hide in. He had given the dog some water then taken a shallow sip himself. He tried to settle into a comfortable position and almost screamed as a wave of pain engulfed him. It wasn't until that moment that he noticed how seriously wounded he was. His right hand had swollen to grotesque proportions. With pieces of rock and splintered wood imbedded in it, it had quickly become infected. Trying to make a fist was an exercise in agony. His side burned with the ferocity of a hot iron laid against the flesh. Peeling the blood encrusted shirt away, he saw for the first time, that a bullet had passed through him. He couldn't remember if it had entered from front to back, or back to front, but there were two seeping, oozing holes, just below his ribs. It was when he reached for the canteen to wash out the wounds that he discovered the cause of his blood soaked arm. A bullet, a piece of shrapnel from a grenade or one of the bombs, it didn't really matter which, had sliced through his upper arm, the flesh opened almost to the bone. The stark white meat quivered under the blood and dirt that filled the wound. It hadn't taken long for the insects to swarm to the gory meal. The wound over his ear, forgotten since the firefight, throbbed with each heartbeat. Gentle probing with his left hand satisfied him that it had crusted over although the bugs were busy at work, trying to uncover yet another meal.

Properly cleaned and dressed, none of the wounds would have been fatal, but untreated, in the middle of a green-leafed cesspool, unchecked infection held the promise of a slow and agonizing death. As he tried to clean the wounds he was suddenly overcome with emotion more than pain. Growing up with palm trees, warm ocean water, fast cars, and protective parents hadn't prepared him for this. Nothing could have. The last sounds he heard before he passed out was his own sobbing.

The days of pushing through the jungle had taken their toll, not only on flesh but on fabric as well. His fatigue pants looked more like part of a child's hobo Halloween costume, ripped to the point where more flesh was exposed than covered. The loss of the thin protection left his legs vulnerable to every thorn, branch and insect. Long scratches were caked over with dried blood while other areas were red and swollen from pieces of thorns imbedded too deeply to dig out. Ugly reddish splotches covered what little uninjured flesh was left, lasting reminders that insects were more than buzzing little creatures that made it difficult to sleep.

The sweat, the mud, the constant movement, the lack of water to bathe in, resulted in the inevitable. Crotch rot. Back in 'the World' it had been a bitch, itching like hell with constant burning and pus oozing onto your underwear. It was a bitch, but curable with liberal doses of ointment. In the bush, the crotch rot quickly got worse and worse until it was almost unbearable. He had already ripped the legs off his skivvies, trying to keep them from bunching up and cutting into the raw bleeding flesh. Every time he scratched, pieces of skin rubbed away, causing the area to ooze and bleed even more. The smell of what he feared was rotting flesh was almost overpowering.

Could it kill him? If he managed to make it out, would he be the only one in the whole goddamn war to make it through all this shit and still end up dying of crotch rot?

Shadrack moved his head as Gianni reached down and frantically scratched. The rain pounded down with no sign of letting up. His back was stiff and ached from bending over so long. When he tried to raise up, a shot of pain raced through him like he'd been hit with a baseball bat. It took more than a minute before he could sit upright and turn his body to the right and left. The dog looked up, then nuzzled his nose against the side of Gianni's leg.

"Ya', I know, boy, you're hungry. So am I. Real fucking hungry." During their days on the run, Shadrack had managed to catch and kill what Gianni figured were two large rats. He had no idea if rats actually lived in the jungle but whatever they were, the dog ate 'em. The hunger in Gianni had been so overpowering that he had torn off a piece of the flesh and gingerly put the bloody raw meat in his mouth. He managed to chew it and force it down but within seconds his stomach rumbled and forced it back up, along with a stream of throat burning bile. It had taken half of what he had left in his canteen to quiet the choking and retching and cool the fire in his throat. He hadn't eaten, or tried to eat, since then, but at least the rain had solved the problem of water…for now.

"Shad, you're gonna' have to find your own food again. I'm not gonna' be much help unless we run into a McDonalds or an Arbys." Gianni smiled slightly at the thought of the Arbys. He looked back down at the dog. "Don't worry, buddy, one of the beef and cheddar's is for you."

He reached over and scratched the dog behind the ears, then looked around their hiding place. "We can't sit here forever, Shad, we gotta' keep movin'." He grabbed his rifle and used it to push himself up. "I'm not sure where the fuck we're goin' but if we keep heading south, we're either gonna' run into some friendlies or eventually go all the way around the world and end up where we started." He looked back down at the dog. "Why do I think, with our luck, that's just what's gonna' happen."

He shifted the rifle to his left hand, dug at his crotch with his right, wiping the blood and greenish pus on what was left of his pants, and pushed out through the bushes.

FRIDAY
JULY 10, 1970
CAMBODIA/SOUTH VIETNAM BORDER

He was close to being dead and knew it. Infected and putrefied flesh hung in strips from his arms and legs. He was covered with scabs of dried blood constantly being chewed open by the swarms of insects the stench attracted. His hair was so matted with dirt, blood, bits of twigs and dead insects that it took on a shell-like quality, forming a sort of helmet around the head.

He couldn't remember how many days ago he had unhooked the ammo harness and let it fall to the ground. The padded strap had rubbed against the open wound on his shoulder causing enough pain for him to lose the use of his right arm. He had tucked the hand into his shirt front to try and relieve some of the weight on it. The buttons of the shirt were the first to go, then, within a day, the rotting fabric simply disintegrated. Unable to keep the arm from moving, the open wound refused to scab over. The sticky feeling of blood and puss dripping down his chest was a constant reminder that if he didn't find help soon, he never would.

Several times he had heard helicopters and what he thought might be a Bronco pass over. When his mind had still been working, he had cursed the fact he had left the emergency radio at the base of the tree. Now that his mind really wasn't working, he knew that if he heard another helicopter, he'd pop a smoke grenade to attract their attention. He'd pop the grenade...if only he hadn't left it attached to the ammo harness.

During the rains he had filled the canteen, but it lasted only two or three days, he couldn't remember. The dry, thirsty ground swallowed up any puddles the rains had left and they had gone more than two days before finding a small, mud-choked, animal waste-infected stream. Without his water purification tablets, he knew he risked coming down with malaria but that was better than dying of thirst. Besides, he had already fallen face first into the stream and filled his parched throat and shrinking belly before giving any thought that it might kill him.

The dog had shakily stood next to him, lapping at the dark, dirty water while his eyes searched the trees and his ears twitched. Not knowing about malaria and not susceptible to its deadly symptoms, the dog drank, then rolled in the water trying to cool off and soothe his torn and bloody paws. They both drank their fill and after Gianni had filled the canteen, they headed south again.

Trying to figure the right direction by watching the sun during the day, they stumbled on. The malaria finally took hold, alternating in brain-frying fever and bone-numbing chills. With the infections racking his body and the open wounds refusing to heal, He fought to lead the dog in any direction his legs would take him. Pushing through the thick cover, constantly falling as the creeping vines and exposed roots grabbed at his boots and slashed at his legs, he cried with relief as they stumbled onto a narrow trail.

With massive amounts of sleep, food, and medical attention, he might have noticed the sandal and boot prints along with the bicycle tire tracks and he might have remembered to stay off of trails. Having long ago been reduced to nothing more than an animal trying to survive on instinct, he noticed nothing. All his pain-racked, disease-ridden body knew was that it was easier to move when there were no trees or bushes trying to hold you back.

For the rest of the day and part of the night, he half led, half followed, the dog down the trail, not knowing and not caring what direction they were headed. When he got to the point where he couldn't keep his eyes open any longer and spent more time tripping over his own feet and falling down than standing up, he pushed through the bush on the side of the trail. Even an animal's instincts tells it to hide when it sleeps.

He managed to hold the canteen in the crook of his right arm while he unscrewed the top with his bleeding left fingers. The chain holding the top of the canteen rattled against the plastic side as he struggled to hold it over his mouth. How many times had he done that over the last half day, forgetting that he had long ago sucked out the last drop? The anger built up and exploded in weakened fury. With all his strength he tossed the canteen to the side, startled when it bounced off the tree next to him and rolled back to settle against his leg.

With his swollen right fist he beat the ground, begging God, his parents, the Devil, anybody, for help. Should he have tried so hard to avoid the Gook patrols that had looked for him? Was this better than a POW camp? Or a bullet? Would they have let him surrender? Maybe. What about the dog? No, they would have killed him. Did it make sense to give up being rescued to save the dog only to let him be killed later? No...it didn't make sense...none of it. Why hadn't he left the dog and gone up the penetrator with the pilot...what was his name...he couldn't remember...he wasn't sure he ever knew it. Why didn't he leave the Goddamn dog!

An insect settled on his open eye and he blinked hard to get rid of it. What had he been thinking about? The dog. He was going to die because of a dog. There were better reasons to die than that. You could die for a friend. Yes, a friend was a good reason to die. You could die for a debt. To repay the debt of someone who risked their life to save you. Yes, yes, that was a good reason to die. You could die because someone counted on you to help them. Was it so bad to die that way? No, no, it wasn't. That's what it was all about. He remembered the words from somewhere. 'You fight for your friends. For the man on your left, the man on your right, for the man that can't help himself'. Your friends...yes, you fight for your friends.

Wasn't the dog his friend? Wasn't he as good a friend as Chuck or Dustin or Smith or anybody on the squad? Hadn't the dog saved his life, all their lives? Didn't he owe him a debt? Hadn't the dog counted on him...didn't he count on him now? What were the words...what had Dustin called it? Cowboy up...there comes a time when you have to cowboy up. Had he done it, had he cowboy'd up to save a friend? Would his mother ever understand…could she? His father, and Hank, and Chuck's father, they had all been there, they would understand. The last thoughts he had before he passed out was that it was good to die for a friend…and the dog was his friend.

The sun rose, set, and rose again before he ever opened his eyes. His flesh was burning with fever and it took a long while before he could figure out where he was. He managed to turn his head slightly and was greeted by the warm breath of the dog as he weakly licked his master's face, praying in his own canine way that his master would get up and lead them home. A small smile spread across Gianni's face. He squinted his eyes until the dog's face came into focus and slowly moved his arm until he could feel the matted fur.

"I'm sorry, boy, I'm sorry." The sound that tried to pass for a voice was more of a croak. The dog's ears perked up at the sound and his head tilted to the side as if he wasn't sure it was his master talking. He inched his weakened body closer and nuzzled his master's face with his dried and cracked nose.

Gianni tried to smile again but his face contorted with pain as he was gripped in a bone-racking coughing spasm. Black phlegm spotted with bright red blood dribbled out of his mouth and slowly made its way down the side of his face, matting his growing beard and offering yet another table of fare to the swarming insects.

"I'm…I'm not gonna' make it, Shad, I'm not gonna' get us outta here." The dog tilted his head even further as he tried to understand the sounds. "God, I wish you knew what I was saying. I wish you knew enough to get out of here and find your way back." A swarm of insects lifted off his body as he was racked with another fit of coughing. Too weak to wipe the blood coated phlegm from his chin, he turned his head away from the dog and stared straight up. The leaves on the trees hung down without any breeze to stir them. The beating wings of the hovering insects gave a fuzzy, out-of-focus view of the blue sky and white clouds that tried to push their way through the jungle canopy. In a moment of clear and lucid thought, Gianni knew he would never again see a cloud-specked Fort Lauderdale sky, or his parents. He knew he was about to die, but he didn't know where. Did it matter where you died if you didn't die at home?

He knew he couldn't save himself but he could still do something to help the dog. With all the strength he could muster, he reached up and dragged the chain holding his dog tags over his head. He rolled his head back to the dog.

"Here, here boy, bring your head here." The dog slowly pushed himself up and stood over his master. "Here, take these and go find someone to help you. You've done enough for me, boy, it's time to look after yourself."

The dog tried to stand still, weaving back and forth on weakened lags. Gianni eased the chain over his head, rubbed behind his ears, then slipped into the gray darkness that awaited the blackness of death.

The point man had stopped the squad some hours earlier and motioned the Lieutenant forward to show him the boot prints. The squad leader decided it was probably some Gook who had stripped them off a dead GI and was now the envy of his comrades. They had started down the trail again following what they thought were VCs shuttling supplies into Vietnam. The point man figured the Lieutenant was right but he couldn't figure out why the VC was dragging his feet and falling down so much. Maybe he was wounded. With any luck, the bastard would die screaming in pain.

He moved slowly, checking the bush on each side of the trail, looking for any sign of an ambush. He saw what appeared to be another spot where the VC had fallen down. Mixed in with the scuffed dirt were several dark spots. He raised his hand to stop the squad, then knelt down to run his fingers over what he already knew was dried blood. As he did so, one of the grenades hanging on his ammo harness banged against the plastic stock of his rifle. The noise was not loud, barely enough for the men several yards behind to hear, but loud enough for a dog with abnormally big ears and an overwhelming desire to help his master.

The dog's ears twitched. They rotated on top of his head like a radar antenna searching for a signal, then stopped in the direction of the sound. He slowly and painfully raised his head off his master's chest and turned to sniff the air. What air that was moving was coming from the wrong direction and he detected no scent. He started to lower his head again.

The point man rubbed his fingers over the dried blood and smiled to himself. From the looks of the wandering tracks and the blood he was leaving, this was one Gook who would soon be donating his American boots to one of his comrades. The soldier wiped his fingers on his pants, put the butt of his rifle on the ground, and pushed himself up. Turning back to the rest of the squad, he waved his arm, motioning them forward.

The loose sling of the machine gun swinging against the ammo on the machine gunner's chest made no more noise than the grenade but it convinced the dog that a threat was near. The dying Airman made no sound or movement as the dog pushed himself up and padded off through the trees.

The point man didn't see the movement through the bush but the man five yards behind him did. The sounds of the soldier throwing himself to the ground and the rest of the squad following was enough for the point man to drop and look back for direction. He followed the aim of the soldier's rifle and squinted to see through the heavy cover. A slight movement caught his eye and he tightened the grip on his rifle as he sighted down the barrel. The wounded VC was going to die a lot sooner than he expected.

He watched as the limbs and leaves moved, slowly at first, then faster. The wounded soldier was trying to get to the trail. Maybe he wanted to surrender. The point man followed the movement with his rifle, holding up his left hand as a signal not to fire. He would give the man a chance, a very small chance, but a chance nonetheless. If he made one wrong move, a move the point man even thought was wrong, it would be the last thing he ever did.

Beads of sweat dripped off his forehead, stinging his eyes and blurring his vision. He pulled his left hand back to his face and wiped it. He was blinking hard, trying to regain his sight, when the VC broke through the brush and crawled onto the trail. The man was small, much smaller than the point man expected. He sighted carefully, then lowered the rifle in shock and stared.

"What is it, Walden, what'da ya' got?"

"It's a fuckin' dog!"

Lieutenant Rob Saunders had seen a lot of different things since he'd been in Vietnam. Water buffalo, snakes, monkeys, lizards, live and dead Gooks, he had even talked to troops that swore they had seen elephants and tigers, but the one thing he had never seen was a dog out in the bush. Oh, there were plenty of dogs in Vietnam. They were always running around the villages, scavenging whatever they could find and finally being eaten themselves by the villagers. Sure, he had seen dogs…but never in the bush.

"What the fuck is that doing out here?"

"Looks like somebody's dinner decided it didn't want to be the entree."

"Yeah, maybe, but I don't think so." Saunders turned to look directly at his point man. "You ever see a German Shepherd running around over here?"

"Naw."

They turned back to the dog and watched as it pushed itself to its feet and started to slowly walk toward them. Its head hung low, the dry and swollen tongue limply flopping out of its mouth, it stumbled, weaved from side to side, fell down, then struggled back to its feet. All of its ribs stuck out against the paper-thin flesh, moving in and out as the dog panted in the sweltering heat.

Walden raised his rifle and sighted at the thin chest. "I don't care if he's Rin Tin Tin, I'm not lettin' that mangy piece of shit get near me. Be just my luck to die of rabies."

Saunders was trying to figure out what to do when he saw the sun reflect off something under the neck. His hand shot out and grabbed Walden's rifle.

"Hold it! Did you see that? There's something hanging under his neck."

Walden lowered his rifle and tried to see what the Lieutenant was talking about when the dog fell to the ground, a small metal tag sticking out from under its fur.

"Whoa, he does have something around his neck. What the fuck?" He turned to look at his Lieutenant.

Saunders turned back to the squad and motioned for them to move off the trail. "Come on, we're gonna' see what the hell's goin' on." They duck-walked closer to the dog, checking both sides of the trail as they went. Three feet away, the men stopped and stared.

"Jesus Christ, are those dog tags!?" Walden pushed the bush hat on his head farther back and wiped his forehead with the back of his arm.

"Sure as shit looks like it." Saunders glanced back over his shoulder at the rest of the squad, then at the dog again. "I'm gonna' see if I can get closer."

He pulled his knife out of its scabbard and handed his rifle to Walden. "Man, I hope this fucker doesn't try to bite me." Saunders wiped his lips on his sleeve and slowly moved forward. "That's a good dog. Nice doggy. Don't bite me, doggy, I just want to see what you got around your neck. Good dog, good dog."

The dog tilted his head at the sound of the voice and raised up slightly. The dog tags hung at the end of the chain giving Saunders a better view.

"They are dog tags." He slowly reached out, letting the dog smell his hand. "That's a good dog. Don't bite me, just smell. Yeah, good boy." Feeling a little braver, Saunders moved up and knelt next to the pitiful animal. He reached down and carefully pulled the chain over the dog's head.

"Holy shit!! I don't fuckin' believe this!!"

"What it is, LT, what'da ya' got?"

Saunders looked up at his point man, holding the dog tags out in front of him. "You remember hearin' about the Air Force guy that was lost on a rescue mission up in Cambodia? These are his tags!"

"What!?" Walden moved closer and took the dog tags. "They are his tags! Shit, I'll bet this is his dog! The Air Force dog!"

"No way. How the hell would he have lasted out here this long?"

"I don't know but it has to be him. Shit, a German Shepherd out here, it has to be him."

Saunders looked down at the dog and gently stroked the top of his head. "Poor guy, you're really fucked up, aren't you? I'll go get the Doc and see if he can do anything for him. Shit, I don't fuckin' believe this." He moved back down the trail.

The medic knelt over the dog and ran his hand over where he thought the heart should be. "I don't really know anything about animals, LT, but I can tell you this dog is fucked up! Look at 'im. His paws are torn to shreds, he's dehydrated to the point where he's actually dying of thirst, and he's so thin you can almost see through 'im." The medic rubbed his hand over the dog's belly and shook his head. "I think the best thing we can do for him is put him down." He looked up at his Lieutenant and reached for his bag of medical supplies. "I can give him an overdose of morphine, he'll never feel a thing. Just basically go to sleep."

"No, hold on for a while. Isn't there anything else we can do? Get him to drink, maybe eat something?"

"Not that simple, LT. He needs fluids in his system, not just his stomach. We'd have to put him on an IV, get some nutrients in him along with the fluid."

"You carry that kind of stuff?"

"Yeah, but I don't know how to give it to a dog. I mean, I don't know how much is too much or what will help 'im or what will hurt 'im." The medic looked around at the men standing over him, then back at Saunders. "Shit, LT, he's a fuckin' dog. Even if I could keep him alive, there's no fuckin' way he's gonna' walk outta' here."

Saunders pulled out a pack of cigarettes and lit one. As he snapped the cover of the zippo closed, the dog flinched and raised his head off the ground. Struggling, he pushed himself up on all fours and turned to the bush behind him.

Walden lit his own cigarette and chuckled. "Hey, I think he knows you're talking about zappin' him! Looks like he's trying to DI DI outta' here." The dog shakily started to walk down the trail.

"I'll be a motherfucker! What the hell is he doing?" Saunders took a long drag and shook his head. "You really think he understood what we were saying?"

"LT, he's a dog, not Mr. Ed. How the fuck is he gonna' know what we're talking about?" Walden was starting to wonder himself.

As they watched, the dog slowly walked down the trail and gave a low, mournful bark, pausing every few feet to look back over his shoulder.

Saunders dropped the cigarette and crushed it with the toe of his boot. He looked back at the squad, then at the medic. "Keep everybody in the trees. Walden and I are gonna' see what he's up to. Come on, let's go."

When the dog found where he had come out, he disappeared into the thick underbrush. "What's he doin'? Where the hell he goin'?"

Walden didn't like the idea of leaving the squad and pushing off into the trees. "Shit, I don't know. Maybe he's gonna' show us where elephants go to die or he knows a short cut to the nearest whorehouse."

"Just keep your eyes open." Saunders used his thumb to flick his selector switch to full auto and stepped into the trees.

They followed the dog for less than ten minutes. He crawled through a thick stand of bushes and disappeared. Walden was trying to see through the bushes when they both heard the dog give a weak bark.

Saunders pointed to the end of the bushes. "You stay here and cover me. I'm gonna' make my way around there and see if I can find him."

"LT, maybe I better go with you."

"No, stay here. If I run into trouble, you're gonna' have to make it back to the squad and show 'em where I'm at." He duck-walked to the end of the bushes and disappeared.

It took a minute to find the dog, and when he did, he couldn't believe his eyes. He knelt down next to the body, dropping his rifle on the ground. The slow, uneven rise and fall of the chest told him that the body was barely alive.

"HOLY FUCK!! Walden, Walden, get over here! Walden, come on, move it!!"

Hearing his Lieutenant's excited voice, Walden jumped up and ran around the end of the bushes. "Jesus Christ, is he alive?"

"Yeah, but not by much." Saunders had his canteen out and was slowly pouring water over Gianni's face, trying to wet his lips without the water draining down his throat and choking him.

"Motherfuck, is he the Air Force guy, the guy missing up in Cambodia?"

"I think so." Saunders put the canteen down and dug the dog tags out of his top pocket. He held them up so he could read the name better. "Yeah, look, Gianni Giancarlo. See, Giancarlo, that's what his name tag on his shirt reads. Jesus Christ, I can't believe it. How the hell did he do this?"

Walden was kneeling down next to the young Airman checking for wounds and calling his name at the same time. "He's really fucked up, LT."

Saunders picked up the canteen again and carefully started to wash away some of the blood and dirt from Gianni's face. "Go get Doc! GO! GO!"

Four men held a stretched out poncho over the medic as he put an IV in both of Gianni's arms. The radioman knelt under a tree frantically trying to raise anybody to arrange for a dustoff. Two soldiers sat with Shadrack, slowly feeding him small pieces of boned chicken from their C-rations. One of the soldiers held an IV bag over his head while the life saving liquid dripped through a needle in the dogs left front leg. Driven by hunger and thirst, the dog nonetheless kept his gaze on his master as he painfully tried to swallow the food. The medic injected Gianni with antibiotics and collected canteens to pour over his body in an effort to reduce the fever.

"What'da ya' think, Doc?" Saunders was smoking another cigarette and pacing back and forth, not knowing what else to do.

"It'll be a fuckin' miracle if he makes it. I don't know how he hung on this long."

"Keep 'im alive, Doc, ya' gotta' keep 'im alive."

"LT, I'm a medic...not God."

One of the soldiers holding the poncho shouted at the medic. "Hey, Doc, Doc, he's trying to say something! He's coming around!"

Saunders and the medic moved under the poncho. Saunders bent over, laying his ear next to Gianni's lips.

"What is it, what'd he say?"

Saunders looked up, wiping away what obviously wasn't sweat. "He's asking for his father. He wants his father."

TUESDAY
JULY 14,1970
FORT LAUDERDALE, FLORIDA

It was just after ten in the morning. The doorbell rang and Bernadette, watering the potted plants in the family room, hoped it wasn't another reporter. There had been a constant stream, all wanting to get a story of the local boy missing in action. When he was home, Vincent had handled it, answered all of their questions about school, his friends, how he had volunteered to be a dog handler, and how he turned down the assignment to help guard President Nixon and asked for an assignment in Vietnam.

He answered all their questions until they asked how it felt to have a son killed in such an unpopular war. It was then that Vincent Giancarlo told them his son was not dead, that he was missing in action, and that popular or unpopular, no man had ever been prouder of a son. A reporter from one local television station chose to question how a father could really believe his son was still alive when all the reports said he was being chased by enemy soldiers and all rescue attempts had failed. The television station actually aired the film footage of the reporter being physically thrown out the front door.

Chuck had been a permanent fixture at the Giancarlo house for the first two weeks, refusing to venture farther away from the house than the rear bumper of The Car parked in front of the garage door. Obsessed with the fear that he might miss a phone call or news report about Gianni, who he adamantly referred to as his brother rather than mere friend to reporters, fell asleep night after night in the oyster white recliner after the National Anthem had signaled the end of the broadcast day and the grainy black and white snow of the television screen cast pebbled shadows across the family room. The morning sun would have found Chuck slumped in the chair each day, if, in his own nightmare of sleepless nights, Vincent hadn't slipped quietly into the room, gently awakened his surrogate son and guided him to Gianni's waiting bed. The nightly ritual was not without tears, on both parts, or a father's vain attempts to explain to his son's best friend that there were no answers to the questions he asked.

Chuck's full time stay ended on a Tuesday night, when, leaning against the passenger door of The Car, playing a mournful blues tune, one of many that seemed to dominate the guitar in his hands, Vincent appeared at his side. Sliding down to the ground, he rested his back on the car door and turned to look at Chuck's tear streaked face.

"It's time son." The expression on Chuck's face was of confusion and desperation. That of a young man trapped in a ring of fire, frantically searching for the one slim path to safety. "I don't know how long it's going to take for us to hear that Gianni is all right…that he's coming home. It's going to happen…I know it's going to happen…but, until then, it's time for you, for all of us, to move on…to get back to life…back to living."

That had been the last night of falling asleep in the recliner, of racing to the kitchen every time Vincent or Bernadette answered a phone call or being guided, zombie like to his brother's room. Life had to go on, tragic or magic, life had to go on.

As Bernadette opened the door, the sight of the two blue uniforms caused her to step back, her mouth opening in a silent scream. Major Vermillion reached for her, grabbing her arm, and stepped quickly inside the house. Father Russo held up both hands, a smile spreading over his face.

"It's all right, Mrs. Giancarlo, it's all right! He's alive, they found him! Gianni's alive." Vermillion was shaking his head up and down as he spoke, trying to make his words understood. "Listen to me, Mrs. Giancarlo, Gianni is alive, they found him!"

She turned to Father Russo who was standing there with what even he would call a shit eating grin. "It's true, Mrs. Giancarlo. They found your son. He is alive."

Her knees buckled as sobs of joy came unabashed. Both men stepped forward to catch her under the arms before she collapsed to the floor and led her to the couch. She looked back and forth at each man, hoping this wasn't some type of cruel joke.

"Please, oh God, please, is it true, is it true!"

Vermillion shook his head again and smiled. "It's true, Ma'am. He's alive. An Army patrol found him last Friday. Actually, his dog found the patrol and he led them to Gianni."

Bernadette looked at Vermillion in disbelief. "His dog?! Shadrack, the dog with the big ears?"

Both men laughed and shook their heads. "I don't know about the big ears, Ma'am, but his dog led the patrol to him." Vermillion glanced at Russo out of the corner of his eye. "I'm not sure, but I'd say we had a little divine intervention there."

"Oh, God, I can't believe it, I can't believe it. Oh, God, Gianni, you're alive, you're alive!" She snapped her head up and looked directly at both men. "His father never believed he was dead. He said all along Gianni would come back to us. He never believed he was dead." Bernadette dropped her head to her hands and said a silent thank-you that her prayers had been answered. "Is he all right? Is Gianni all right?"

Vermillion shuffled uncomfortably for just a moment, then answered. "Mrs. Giancarlo, you have to understand, your son has been through a great deal. When they found him, he had numerous wounds, he was dehydrated, suffering from malnutrition, malaria, and very severe infections. He was airlifted to a hospital in Japan. He's there now and he's receiving the best possible care." He stared at her for a moment. "He's going to make it, Mrs. Giancarlo. It'll take a while…but he's going to make it."

Bernadette's hands where shaking even though she was squeezing them tightly. She was basking in the glow of the good news when suddenly she realized what was missing. "Oh, my God! Jimmy! Jimmy has to know! We have to tell him!" She jumped up off the couch and reached for the priest's hands. "Oh, please, we have to find my husband! He has to know about Gianni, he has to know!"

Father Russo smiled even broader. This task was something they were going to enjoy. "All right, Mrs. Giancarlo, all right, we'll find him." He looked at Vermillion.

Vermillion already had his file folder open and was turning to the family notification section. "Mrs. Giancarlo, it says here Mr. Giancarlo works for the Post Office, the Seminole Annex on Broward Boulevard. Can we call him?"

"He probably won't be there. He handles Special Deliveries, he doesn't have a set route. Oh, God, how are we going to find him?"

Father Russo held her hands, patting them with his own. "Don't worry, we'll find him." He smiled widely and looked directly into her eyes. "This news is too good to let go undelivered."

Vermillion glanced around the living room, searching for a telephone. "Is there a 'phone I can use?"

Bernadette looked over at him, almost laughing at the absurdity of the innocent question. Funny the things one thought of at a time like this. "In the kitchen." She pointed around the corner.

"Good, thank you. Oh, what's your husband's supervisor's name?"

"Cipriani, Frank Cipriani."

"Frank Cipriani speaking, can I help you."

"Yes, Mr. Cipriani, my name is Major Vermillion, United States Air Force. It is imperative that I contact Vincent Giancarlo as soon as possible and I was wondering if he happened to be in the building at this time?"

Cipriani suddenly lost the smile on his face. He dropped the pen he had been holding and stiffened in his chair. A singular thought flashed through his mind. He stood up, then dropped his right hand to the top of the desk to steady himself. "Ah, no, Major he's not here right now. I, ah, I don't expect him back here 'til later this afternoon, probably somewhere around four-thirty or five."

"I see. Do you have any way to get in touch with him?"

"No, no, I'm afraid not. He could be almost anywhere. Is this about Gianni? Did something happen to Gianni?!"

Vermillion hesitated for just a moment and smiled to himself. "May I ask, sir, do you know the young man?"

"Yes…yes, I do. Very well!"

"Then it is my pleasure to inform you that Airman Giancarlo has been found alive and is recuperating in an Air Force hospital."

Vermillion picked up the telephone again and dialed his office at Homestead Air Force Base. "Public Information Office, Captain Askinazy speaking."

"Paul, this is Major Vermillion. I'm having a small problem, can't seem to find the Airman's father."

"Anything I can do?"

"Yes, grab the emergency notification list and contact every radio and TV station in the Fort Lauderdale area. Tell them we're trying to find Mr. Giancarlo…and why."

Tana Hetrick was dusting the furniture with a can of Pledge and a pair of her husband's old 'Fruit Of The Looms'. She pranced around the living room trying to keep time to the Crew Cuts singing "Sha Boom, Sha Boom" on the radio. She didn't hear the repeated chimes of the door bell and probably never would have known someone was at the door if she hadn't happened to notice the Post Office station wagon parked in front of the house. She peered out the window and saw the mailman standing on the porch waiting for someone to answer the door.

"Oh, I'm sorry. I had the stereo on and I didn't hear you."

Vincent Giancarlo managed a weak grin. "That's all right, Ma'am, I know how it is. I have a Special Delivery for you."

She reached out and took the package, scanning the return address. "Ooooh, it's from my mother. I wonder what she could be sending?"

"I do need you to sign for it." Vince Giancarlo held up his clipboard and noticed the pen was missing.

"Oh, I've got a pen in the kitchen." She turned and trotted off to the rear of the house. She was almost back to the middle of the room when the radio suddenly fell quiet. She stopped in mid-stride and turned toward it.

"Well, that's strange. I wonder if the power went off." She looked up at the clock and noticed that the minute hand was still moving. "Huh, I wonder what happened to the station?" She was just about to turn back to the waiting mailman when the DJ's voice distracted her.

"Ladies and gentlemen, this is Rick Shaw. We have an urgent request from Homestead Air Force Base. Many of you know about the local Air Force man who was reported missing while on a rescue mission in Cambodia several weeks ago. Since that time, his parents have waited for news of their son's safety. Today we can all be part of that news and help locate Vincent Giancarlo, the young Airman's father. Mr. Giancarlo is a postal employee and is in the Fort Lauderdale area currently delivering Special Delivery mail. If you see Mr. Giancarlo, tell him to call his home immediately."

The only time Tana Hetrick could remember a newscaster's voice breaking up was during the report of the Kennedy assassination. This was the second time. "If you see Mr. Giancarlo, tell him his son is alive! His son Gianni has been found and is alive!"

Tana Hetrick stared at the radio for just a second more, then turned back to the door. "Isn't that GREAT! They…" Her words were cut off as she saw the mailman gripping the side of the door frame trying to hold himself up while tears rolled down his face and his body heaved with sobs of joy.

MONDAY
AUGUST 17, 1970
FORT LAUDERDALE

The previous four weeks had turned out to be something the Giancarlo's could never have imagined. On the six o'clock news they had seen a high school picture of Gianni, then the picture of him after graduation from Security Police school, as Walter Cronkite reported to the nation what Gianni had done, the story of his survival, and how he had been found. Vince sat bolt upright and beamed with pride as the newscaster referred to his son as a hero. Just as proud, Bernadette Giancarlo wanted nothing more than to have her son home again. Waiting to hear from him while he recuperated was getting harder and harder.

The living room was crowded with thousands of letters from well-wishers, and a few from parents who were not as fortunate and needed to share their grief with people they felt would understand. Among the stacks of letters was a pile they would always keep, the letters that meant the most, the ones not from public officials, dignitaries, or celebrities, although there were dozens of those. No, the ones they would ultimately cherish as part of the magic were the letters that came from the people who knew Gianni.

A letter from Father Szuch explaining how his faith had been re-enforced and his commitment to always be where young men put their lives on the line to answer the call of their country. Letters from Gianni's Squadron Commander, Kennel Master, and Base Commander at Camelot Palace. Letters from every man on the Search and Rescue team, with an especially poignant letter from Lieutenant Will Evans trying to personally apologize for leaving Gianni in that godforsaken Cambodian jungle.

The one letter that meant the most, however, the one containing words of grief, of happiness, of pride, was the letter from the Monie's. They spoke of the friendship between Dustin and Gianni and how they thought of Gianni as their own son, and when word of Gianni's rescue reached them, how they felt the same emotional elation as Gianni's own parents. They spoke as only parents who lost a son in war could speak, with that unashamed and straightforward honesty of how pleased they were that their son's friend would soon be home where he belonged.

They received two other letters, one from Lieutenant Colonel David Runyon, explaining how their son had saved his life; the second, written in a feminine hand, from his wife. In words choked with emotion, she thanked the parents of the young man who had saved her husband, the father of their unborn child and thanked them for raising their son with the belief that honor, and integrity were things worth fighting for.

It was rare that Vincent could knock on a door or ring a bell without the occupant either recognizing his face or recognizing the name pinned over his uniform pocket. On the few occasions, when he started to get annoyed by all the attention, he would stop for a moment, think about how things easily could have turned out much differently, smile broadly, and remind himself that this was definitely part of the magic.

They had gone to bed right after the eleven o'clock news. The euphoria of knowing Gianni was alive was starting to diminish with the ache of wanting him back home. The luminous hands on the Baby Ben showed just after three o'clock when the telephone rang. It was just starting its fourth ring by the time Vincent was awake enough to reach for the receiver. As he tried to speak, he could only manage a hoarse croak. "Hullo?"

"Yes, hello. Is this the Giancarlo residence?"

Vincent pushed himself up slightly on one elbow and rubbed the sleep out of his eyes. It couldn't be a reporter calling at this hour. "Yes, yes, it is. Who's calling?"

"Sir, this is Staff Sergeant Mattingly at Homestead Air Force Base. I have an overseas Autovon call for you from Japan. Go ahead, Japan, your party is on the line."

"Hello, Dad? Dad, it's me."

There had been a time, a fear he kept buried deep inside himself, when he thought he might never hear his son's voice again. Now, as that fear was finally laid to rest, the emotion poured out, uncontrollably. He threw his legs over the side of the bed, hunched over, a man not beaten, rather, a man victorious, but without the strength to hold himself erect. "Oh, God, Gianni! Oh, son! It's so good to hear your voice!"

The thousands of miles that separated them were not enough to hide what his father was going through. "Dad, Dad, please, don't cry. Dad, please...I'm all right, Dad, I'm gonna' be all right."

Vince wiped his eyes with the back of his hand, then turned suddenly at the touch of his wife's hand on his shoulder. "I've missed you, son, we both have. We've missed you terribly."

"I've missed both of you, Dad. I guess I never realized how much you could miss someone."

"Gianni, when are we going to see you? When are you coming home?"

"I'm not sure, Dad. I hope not much longer. I guess I've still got some infected wounds and the malaria pretty much took everything outta' me. I'll be fine, though, Dad. Don't worry, everything will heal. Everything physical."

Vincent Giancarlo knew what his son was saying, knew that he was scared. "It'll all get better, Gianni, I promise. It all gets better."

As much as the distance couldn't hide the emotion coming from Fort Lauderdale, it was no more successful in hiding the emotion that came from Japan. "I can't get it out of my mind, Dad. I can't forget about Dustin. I see him all the time. I remember all the good times we had, then I see him lying there in the mud. I see his blood all over me and I know it was my fault."

There was a moment of quiet and Vincent started to say something when his son began to speak again. "Dad, you know what you used to tell me about the magic? How to always cherish the magic? It scares me, Dad. It scares me. It's like there is no magic, it disappeared, and I don't think it'll ever be back. God, Dad, I'm so scared!!?"

"Gianni, son, listen to me. Listen!" Vincent rubbed his hand through his hair, searching for the right words. "Gianni, please, it doesn't go away, it's always there. This phone call, the fact you're coming home to us, the men you saved who went home to their families, that's all part of it. Gianni, that's what it's all about. It's the simple things, the things we take for granted. It's family, friends, helping someone when they can't help themselves, it's doing the right thing. That's what its all about, Gianni."

"What happened to Dustin can't be undone, son. It's what happens in war…don't let it take over. Remember the good times you had, the times when you helped each other and the people you brought back home. You'll deal with it, Gianni, I'll help you. So help me God, I'll help you. You'll be all right, son, you'll find the magic again. It's not gone…it's not."

The base operator broke in before either one of them could say anything else. "I'm sorry but you only have three minutes left."

"All right, operator, thank you." Vince turned back over his shoulder and looked at his wife. "Gianni, our time is almost up, I'm going to give the phone to your mother so she can talk to you. I love you, son…I miss you."

"I love you, too, Dad. And, Dad…thanks."

Vincent Giancarlo handed the telephone to his wife and disappeared into the darkness of the house.

Bernadette threw on a robe and walked barefoot to the dinning room window. After staring out for just a moment, she went to the kitchen and made a pot of coffee. Returning to the window, she sat down at the dinning room table and watched as her husband, in the soft glow of the garage floodlights, lovingly rubbed coat after coat of wax on The Car until well after sunrise.

EPILOGUE
NOVEMBER 9, 1970
WASHINGTON, D.C.

A black Cadillac limousine picked them up at Andrews Air Force Base shortly after ten in the morning. Gianni, his mother, father, and Shadrack rode in silence as the car slowly made its way through traffic, purposely taking a route that would pass by some of the nation's most beautiful monuments. Gianni cracked open the side window and blew cigarette smoke through the small opening. He absentmindedly snapped the cover of the Zippo open and closed over and over again. The dog sat between his legs staring up at him, unsure of what was going on.

"Nervous?"

Gianni turned to his father sitting in the jump seat across from him. "Huh? Oh, yeah, I guess so. You know, meeting the President and all. I guess I'm afraid I'll screw up or say something I'm not supposed to."

"You'll be fine, son, don't worry. Besides, what can he do, send you to Vietnam?" The familiar saying had become a little inside joke between them over the last few weeks and Gianni broke a slight grin.

"Yeah, right, what can he do?" He turned back to look out the window, still snapping the cover of the Zippo. He thought about what was yet to come. They would be back in Fort Lauderdale the day after tomorrow and the day after that he was going to fly to Colorado. He had talked to Dustin's parents twice since he had gotten home and the last time they had asked if he could spend a few days with them. As he stared out the window, he wondered what he would say to them, how he would tell them he killed their son.

Vincent looked at his son, sensing what was going through his mind. "They'll understand, Gianni. Their son is gone and now you're the closest thing they have to him. They're just as proud of him as I am of you and they want to hear what he did. You tell them about the good times, the things he did to save those pilots, the things he did to help you. Tell them that he died for a reason. It's what they need to hear, son. Believe me, it's what they need to hear."

What they needed to hear? No, what they needed to hear was the sound of their son's voice. What they needed to hear was something Gianni couldn't give them, something he had taken away forever.

The limousine pulled up the long drive, stopping at the top of the South Lawn. An Air Force Chief Master Sergeant opened the rear door while Gianni led Shadrack out. The Air Force band stood at attention just left of a podium set up at the top of the lawn less than a hundred feet from the White House. Standing around talking were all the Chiefs of Staff, the Commanding General of the 7th Air Force, members of Congress and assorted Cabinet officials. Spread out in front of the podium were at least another two hundred people, most in uniform, others in civilian dress.

Gianni was guided to a spot several yards in front of the podium when the band struck up the Air Force hymn. As the French doors to the White House opened, the band played "Hail to the Chief." The President walked to the podium and waited, the thunderous applause and standing ovation ending only after he held up both arms.

The speech lasted a little over six minutes, with the President looking over at Gianni's parents several times and thanking them on behalf of a grateful nation for raising a son who 'unselfishly placed the lives of others before his own'.

As the President moved away, the Air Force Commanding General slid behind the podium. "Airman First Class Gianni Giancarlo, upon recommendation of the Commander in Chief and by Act of Congress, for gallantry in the face of fire…" and read the official Order of Commendation.

The President lifted the Medal Of Honor out of a velvet-lined case, stepped down from the podium, and trying to keep a watchful eye on the dog, stopped directly in front of Gianni. He placed the royal blue ribbon attached to the medal around Gianni's neck, smiled and waited while the crowd erupted into applause. The band played "Stars and Stripes Forever".

Gianni and the President stood side by side as he accepted the congratulations of the General.

"You better hope Gianni decides to re-up when his enlistment is over, General. You wouldn't want to lose a good man and a good dog." The President smiled and put his hand on Gianni's shoulder.

"We know we can't lose the dog, Mr. President. Once they're in, they're in for life."

The President may be the Commander in Chief of the armed forces but he can't know all the rules. "What do you mean, he's in for life?" He looked down at the dog sitting next to Gianni. "After all they've been through, they'll be separated if Gianni leaves the service?"

"I'm afraid so, Mr. President. Once a dog is accepted into training, it stays in the service until it can no longer perform its duties. After that, it's destroyed."

Gianni gave a slight flinch at the word and reached down to touch the dog.

"Wait a minute, General, hold on. You mean to tell me that after what this dog has done, the lives he's helped save, he hasn't earned the right to stay with Gianni."

The General was uncomfortable being put on the spot. He hadn't made up the damn rule. He wasn't even sure how he knew about it. "I'm afraid that's the policy, Mr. President."

"Well, it's damn foolish if you ask me." The President's voice was getting a little higher and his words were coming faster. "How can we change it, who has the authority to make an exception?"

The General quickly saw his way out. "Well, Mr. President, I would have to say you do. You could authorize an exception in this case."

The President turned toward Gianni. "Well, what do you think, Gianni? If you decide not to re-enlist, would you like to keep the dog?"

"Mr. President, I'd like nothing better. Thank you, sir."

"Good, that's settled."

The President had stood quietly as Gianni shook hand after hand from the horde of politicians and ranking military officials. After an appropriate amount of time, and when the President figured Gianni had suffered more than his share of embarrassment, he slowly held his hand up.

"Ladies and Gentlemen, on behalf of Airman Giancarlo and his family, thank you all for attending. After what this young man has been through, I think it's only fair we give him a break. Besides, even if he's not hungry, I am, and we have a lunch reception waiting for us. Again, thank you all for attending."

The President extended his arm and directed Gianni, his parents, and Shadrack up the lawn toward the White House. They had covered almost half the distance when the President stopped, rubbed his chin, and sheepishly turned to Gianni.

"Gianni, I wonder if I could ask you a question about your dog?"

"Yes, sir."

"His ears, Gianni? What's wrong with his ears?"

A smile spread across his face as he turned, staring directly into his father's eyes. "They're part of the magic, Mr. President, they're just part of the magic."

About the Author

Gioacchino (Jack) Giampapa served as an Air Force Patrol Dog Handler assigned to the Presidential Protection Detail in support of President Nixon. After discharge he joined the Dade County Public Safety Department, (Miami, Florida) where he was a member of its original Hostage Rescue Team. He now resides in Colorado and Florida.